Such Fine Boys

Les Brookes

First edition published by York Mansell 2013.

Cover design by Pro Book Covers (probookcovers.com).

For Phil,
and to the memory
of my mother and father

PART ONE

June-August 1984

Where to begin? I guess with Neil, an old flame of mine. Our paths rarely cross now, but I ran into him one evening at Quentin's. To be honest, clubs are not really my scene, but I was feeling a bit lonely that Friday night, having just broken up with someone. Not a rare occurrence back then: at that time I was always breaking up with someone, but we'll put that to one side for the moment. Neil asked me what I was doing, and I said, 'Oh, you know, the same old thing.' 'And what's that?' he said. So clearly not the closest of relationships. Anyway, I reminded him, and then, to brighten the conversation, I mentioned that I was going to Yorkshire the following week, to attend a conference in connection with my work. A conference? He looked mildly interested. Where exactly? Norfield? Oh yes, he knew the place well and could recommend the Black Horse, a big friendly pub not a stone's throw from the centre. 'The Black Horse,' I mused, nodding and committing the name to memory.

Neil came back and stayed the night. Well, it met a mutual need. He was keen, I was lonely. We had a quick but lively bash, and then fell asleep. In the morning he was off before sunrise. He drives a truck for a haulage firm in Tooting. He let himself out quietly while I was sleeping and I've not clapped eyes on him since. But when I got up a couple of hours later, there was a sketch map of Norfield lying on the desk. It was roughed out on the back of an envelope and the Black Horse was located by a cross. What sticks in my mind now, though, is the command that was scrawled at the foot of the page and heavily underlined. It read simply *Don't forget*. I mean, how could I have known then just how binding those words would turn out to be?

The map was surprisingly accurate, by the way. Neil has

a phenomenal memory for places. He's an off-the-cuff guide to Britain.

I enjoy conferences up to a point, that being the moment when a powerful voice starts to dominate the discussion. In Yorkshire this moment arrived on the first day, a development that did not bode well for the coming week. The voice belonged to Jerry Klein, a tall rangy figure from Cardiff with an unruly mop of white hair. Now I had met Jerry on several previous occasions – he hardly ever misses a conference – and actually I rather like him. He's an amiable busybody, energetic and well-meaning. Unfortunately he suffers from a failure to see that the world loves him rather less than he loves himself. So when he started to speak that first morning, there was an audible shuffling of papers. The pompous opening, the slow delivery, the declaration that he had a number of points to make, all suggested that we were in for the long haul, and the buzz of interest in the room quickly slumped. Indeed, it was soon clear that most of the delegates had escaped to some other place. Some were doodling, some were staring at their feet, and one or two seemed to have nodded off. At one point during his lengthy address I caught the eye of my old friend Alice, who was sitting beside me. She met my look with a shrug of despair.

She and I and some others went for a meal at Ghandi's that evening, followed by a drink at the hotel bar. And this, with variations, is how I spent nearly every night that week. For keen though I was to follow up Neil's suggestion, there's an obligation to be sociable at these events, a code of conviviality that's difficult to dodge. In my experience conferences are all-consuming events, offering few opportunities to slip away. So, as the week wore on, I abandoned any notion of visiting the Black Horse. In fact I was all set to drive back to London on the Friday, straight after the final session. But when the moment came, I changed my mind. As I sat in the car, my hand on the ignition, I felt a spasm of revolt. After all, there was no necessity to tear home. It had been an exhausting week and the thought of the long drive was not enticing. It would be much pleasanter to leave the next morning. Besides, now that the thing was over and the delegates had departed, I needed to offset a sense of anti-climax, as well as satisfy my sense of frustrated curiosity. Above all, I needed to unwind.

So I returned to the hotel and checked in for a further night.

I was given the key to the very room on the first floor that I had vacated that morning. I let myself in and glanced around, noting the welcome aroma of fresh linen. Clean and functional, with minimal furnishings and some prints of local landmarks, the little box felt comfortable and familiar, and I nodded with satisfaction. But I didn't hang about. I simply flung my suitcase onto the bed, checked my appearance in the mirror and brushed some hairs from my jacket. I then made straight for the hotel lounge. The aloof young barman who had worked there all week was reading a newspaper. He looked up. I ordered a Scotch and he served me in stony silence while trying to stifle a yawn. But finding a seat was no problem; apart from a sad elderly couple, sipping cocktails and looking thoroughly disappointed with each other, the place was empty. So I carried my drink across the room and sank into one of the deep leather armchairs. The Scotch was smooth and relaxing, and very soon I felt my lids begin to droop. In fact I must have drifted off completely, for when I next glanced at my watch it was well after seven.

After a shower and a word with the receptionist, I dined at an obscure little bistro not far from the hotel and then took a stroll into town. Neil's map was tucked in my back pocket, and I checked it against the town plan on display in front of the public library. This was reassuring – the two corresponded, at least in broad outline – and I set out in search of Bagot Lane, a narrow street off George Square. The map and my instinctive sense of direction were both helpful here, and after one brief detour, I found it with no trouble at all. The Black Horse, however, was up at the top end, on a curve to the left, so I didn't come across it until I was almost alongside. I then sauntered past, surveying it from the narrow pavement opposite. It was just as Neil had described it: solid, spacious, slightly down-at-heel. It was also crowded, as I could see, for the windows and doors were open to the warm June night. A few guys were drinking in the street, others were perched on sills, some of them sitting sideways, their arms clasping their knees. By this time I was feeling nervous, of course, just as I always do before entering an unknown bar. I caught my reflection in the glass of a ground-floor window and ruffled my hair, sweeping through the forelock with spread fingers. It's a habit of mine, actually; I'm *always* ruffling my hair.

I crossed the street and steered a path through the crowd blocking the entrance, all the while acutely conscious of turning heads, appraising eyes. This negotiation was only part of the ordeal, however, for on the other side of the door I had to push through a heaving crush of bodies to the bar. But here, to my amazement, I found myself standing next to a vacant stool. I glanced round furtively, convinced that one of the regulars sat here every night like a fixture, and that to occupy this space would be a breach of etiquette. But there were no stern faces warning me off. Indeed, no-one seemed in the least interested. So I hauled myself onto it and settled into place with an immense feeling of relief and gratitude. I was trying to look cool, but my face felt hot and I was desperate for a drink. I reached for my wallet, drew out a fiver and waved it high above my head in an attempt to attract attention. And again I was in luck: an eager young barman appeared before me in an instant, like a genie from a bottle.

'Hi, Matt. Long way from home?'

I stared. 'Excuse me?'

He grinned and pointed at my chest. I glanced down. The name badge that I had picked up at the conference, proclaiming *Matt Hopper, South London*, was still pinned to my shirt. I had worn it all week and forgotten it.

I looked up and grinned back. 'Well now, there's my cover blown. No more the Mystery Man.'

The barman chuckled. Sandy-haired and freckled, he had warm eyes and a sparkly green stud in his right ear.

'So what's your poison?'

'Ah, something long and cool. A pint of whatever this is.'

'Si, señor. Coming up.'

He drew the pint expertly, scooping the head with a stick to remove the excess and carefully mopping up the spillage. I was impressed. Competent under pressure, genial and obviously popular – he drew smiles from every customer – this was a guy who knew his work and seemed to enjoy it enormously. Yes, an absolute delight, in fact. And as I lifted the foam to my lips and handed over my fiver, I decided not to let the opportunity slip.

'Er, pardon my boldness,' I said, flashing my special smile, 'but one-sided introductions are not allowed.'

'It's Billy,' he said, returning the smile. 'Nice to meet ya. Welcome t' Norrie.'

We reached out and shook hands. But as I was seeking for some way to extend the conversation, he threw me a look of rueful apology and slid off to serve a customer who was clamouring for attention further down the bar. This was disappointing, and as I swigged my beer and eavesdropped on the conversations around me I again felt conspicuously alone.

But then, glancing over my right shoulder, I came face to face with the guy on the stool next to me, an elderly man whose mop of rusty hair was obviously a wig and whose slumped posture suggested that he had been in the bar since opening time. His shabby, bohemian look – he was wearing open-toed sandals, a grubby white shirt and old canvas trousers rolled to the ankles – was topped by a red bandanna knotted at the neck, though somehow the whole effect was sad rather than jaunty. His bloodshot eyes were set in a face as saggy and wrinkled as an elephant's bottom.

'Hullo,' he intoned in a dark smoky voice. 'Isn't it *hot* in here tonight?'

He was rolling his eyes in emphasis and flapping himself with a skinny white hand.

'It certainly is,' I said, neutrally.

'You're not from round these parts, I see.'

The man gestured towards my shirt and then stared into my face with a look of intense curiosity.

'Up on business,' I replied, hastily removing the name badge and slipping it into my side pocket. His face was now so close to mine that I could smell the booze on his breath.

'Well, you've certainly come to the right place, dear,' he chortled. 'This is the place for business.' He grinned weirdly and, clapping a hand to my knee, broke into a loud braying that made me want to run for cover.

I forced a smile, turned away and stared into my beer. I was relying on coolness to dampen his ardour. But after a brief period of silence I felt a tap on my shoulder and the old boy came nosing back.

'Hope you don't mind my asking, but where exactly are you staying?'

'Oh … it's some little place I stumbled on,' I said, indicating direction with the vaguest of gestures. 'I forget the name.'

'Because,' said the man, coughing politely from behind a hand, 'if you don't mind sharing, I've a charming little studio over the Venn Gallery in Bridge Street, which is scarcely a stone's throw . . .'

I smiled, shrugged, and raised my palm in a kind of appreciative salute. The man gave another cough and began to scratch the back of his neck very vigorously, as if bitten by an insect. I again turned away and began studying a blank spot on the wall behind the bar with keen concentration as I awaited his next move. In the following tense moments, however, his interest presumably passed its peak and moved on, for when I next glanced over my shoulder he was nowhere to be seen and the stool was now jointly occupied by two teenage boys who were fused together in a French kiss of Rodin-like abandonment.

I supped my beer and surveyed the scene for a while. But then a glance at my watch gave me quite a jolt. It was already almost closing time, and clearly my only chance of speaking to Billy again was to buy another drink. But there was now a crowd besieging the bar for last orders and catching any barman's eye was not easy. It was not until well after eleven – at a moment when I had lost all interest in being served and was doodling on a beer-mat – that I heard myself being addressed by name and looked up from my handiwork as if shaken from a dream. And here was Billy again, greeting me with another smile and setting before me another pint of my chosen brew.

'Thirsty?'

'Mmm, I think I could manage another.'

'In that case, have this one on me.'

'Is this what they call northern hospitality?'

'Call it what you like.'

'Well, cheers.' I returned his wink. 'You're a lovely fella.'

'Ah, go on, I bet you say that to all the boys.'

'No, I mean it. I've had my eye on you.'

'Oh yeah.'

But it was true. I was bewitched. His smile was heart-stopping, and I gazed at him transfixed. At the same time I was keenly aware of the passing moment, of the need to act if I were not to miss my chance.

'So, Billy …'

'So, Matt …'

'You close in ten minutes.'

'We do.'

'And what's your advice? Where should I go then?'

'Don't ask me, I never go anywhere.'

'Perhaps I could walk you home.'

'How quaint. I knew you were a gentleman.'

A colleague from behind the bar was calling to him and signalling that he could do with some help. Billy nodded over his shoulder and then turned again to me, raising his eyebrows and sighing theatrically.

'Don't go away,' he grinned. 'I'll be back.'

'I'll be waiting,' I said.

*

Billy locked up at just after midnight, and then fell back against the door as if punch-drunk. Clearing the bar at closing time had required great firmness and patience, and I could see that it was a great relief to slide the bolts behind the final customers. He turned to face me.

'Giles and Big Ron,' he groaned. 'Always the first in, always the last to leave.'

'Always?'

'Well, Tuesday to Saturday. On Sundays they stay at home, and on Mondays they play darts for the team at the Osborne.'

'So who have you scooped up tonight?' quipped Patrick, Billy's fellow barman.

I was introduced.

'Well, watch your step, young Matt.' Patrick tapped his nose. 'Don't be deceived. Many have been lured onto the rocks by this bold trollop.'

Billy thrust out his lips in mock petulance. 'Thank *you*, dearest.'

He and Patrick had already sprung into action, for there was a heap of clearing up to do. Billy was collecting glasses, Patrick was shifting crates, though clearly that was just the start of their nightly routine. Somewhat awkwardly I stood and watched for a while, and then, feeling a need to make myself useful, volunteered to help. Not a problem; they readily accepted me as part of the team. A cloth was thrust into my hand and I was set to work. And though I admit that I don't normally leap at the chance to wipe down tables in the early hours of the morning, it was such a delight to be sharing this backstage intimacy with Billy that I viewed the task with pleasure. In fact my tiredness entirely evaporated and I worked as in a dream. It was a great wonder, this turn of events. After all, it was scarcely more than a couple of hours since I'd entered the pub.

Between us we made good progress, so that in twenty minutes the task was almost done. And it was at this point, as I was returning from a far corner of the room with a couple of stray empties, that Billy, who had paused for a moment to lean on his broom, drew my attention to a large framed photograph in a recess behind the bar.

'Stan and Betty,' he explained. 'The landlord and missis.'

The picture showed a large, florid couple, beaming fulsomely at camera. Stan's handlebar moustache suggested an RAF background; Betty had a pendulous chin and was obviously shorter, her gold-rinsed hair offset by the glint of her jade earrings.

'Mm, they look a jolly pair.'

'What? Don't you believe it. Miserable, conniving skinflints!'

'Too true,' called Patrick over his shoulder as he vanished into the cellar.

Later, Billy opened the door of what appeared to be a cupboard. I peered in and gazed upward, bemused and slightly out of breath.

'Yet more stairs?' I sighed. 'Heaven's my destiny.'

'This is the final flight,' he said.

Final it might be, but it was steeper than any so far and led to a garret with walls so low that a visitor was obliged to duck on entering – indeed, enter almost on hands and knees. Yet the room itself, though sparsely furnished, was delightful. The ceiling, which started close to the floor and sloped upward to a central high point, was painted dazzling white, and the lightly varnished beams and boards, the tall dormer window and glass panels in the roof gave an exhilarating sense of airy spaciousness, of closeness to the starry sky. In the centre of the room, a sofa and two easy chairs were arranged around a red shaggy rug. There was a desk with a reading lamp and a double bed against the far wall.

I stood looking around for a while, and then turned to face Billy. He moved forward, took my hands and kissed me gently on the mouth.

'So … here we are … and thanks for seeing me home.'

I gave an amused snort. 'Don't mention it. Stairway to paradise.'

He giggled, and then indicated the room with a sweep of his hand. 'So what d'ya think? Neat, eh? And all my own work.'

'Yeah, nice place … and handy… up here, over the pub.'

We were gazing at each other now with a mixture of ardour and shy hesitancy. Trembling on the brink, in fact. Clearly someone should take the lead, and it felt like my turn. So I raised my arms, took a step towards him – and quite seamlessly we embraced. Then, leaning forward, I pressed my lips firmly to his with an eagerness that was tinged with slight anxiety. Was all this too sudden? Apparently not. He was clearly as keen as I was. His mouth fell open with all the dewy freshness of a flower – I shall never forget the taste. It was a moment of pure bliss, in fact. Of pleasure so intense that my head began to reel. And though nothing quite matched that first moment, there was more to come. For soon he was hugging me close, nibbling my neck and pushing his crotch into mine. And as my limbs soaked up the pervading warmth, I felt an eager excitement spreading upward from my loins.

Saturday broke blue and gold, flooding the room with light. I came to consciousness slowly and lay for some moments in a state of vague puzzlement, listening to the unfamiliar silence and trying to connect with my surroundings. I lifted my head and glanced around. Billy, still asleep, lay sprawled face-down on the bed beside me, his slim naked body brazenly displayed, save for his ankles, which were still entangled in the sheet that he'd attempted to kick away. I gazed on his sleeping form for a while, feasting on every feature – the long neck touched with fine hairs, the knobbly spine, the chiselled calves and buttocks – as if admiring a sculpture. I gazed, in fact, with a desiring infatuation that I could never have shown if he'd been awake. I then rose quietly, pulled on my undershorts and reached for my cigarettes, which were still lying on the floor beside the bed. And when he awoke five minutes later, I must have looked very relaxed, lolling on the sofa, drawing deep on a filter tip.

'Make yourself at home, why don't ya?'

'Sorry, this is the way the day begins. Not with a bang but a gasper.'

'Ah, no problem. You look cool – like in the old movies.'

'Don't encourage me, I'm trying to give up.'

'Anyway, fabulous morning.'

'It certainly is.' I patted the sofa. 'Come over here.'

'I'll put t' kettle on first.'

He rose and stretched, rubbing his eyes and screwing up his face as if slightly hung over. I watched him intently, not quite able to hide the deep fascination behind my look of casual appraisal.

'You okay?' I asked.

He groaned. 'Not at my best. How do I look?'

'Bloody gorgeous, but too distracting. Cover yourself up.'

'I don't like covering up, I like to hang loose.'

I grinned and shook my head. 'In a word, you're a slut.'

He nodded vigorously and pulled on a white bathrobe. Filling the kettle meant a trip to the floor below. On his return, he apologised. He was out of milk and teabags. Black instant coffee was now all that he could offer. However, it was not quite Hobson's choice: it could be taken strong or weak.

'I'll take it strong,' I said, cheerily decisive.

When it was made, he brought the steaming mugs to the coffee table and joined me on the sofa.

'The problem is, I'm not really a breakfast person.' He snuggled up and rested his head on my shoulder. 'There's not a crust or bean in the place. Are you hungry? We could go out.'

'I'm fine,' I said.

But later we went to Dylan's on the Square. Billy ordered a large mug of milky coffee, I went for a double espresso, and together we tucked into a couple of fat croissants and a plate of French fries. He wanted to know what I did. I told him I worked for a charity, a day centre for the homeless. And the conference? What was that about? I pulled out the now crumpled programme from my jacket pocket and handed it to him. He scanned it and then attempted to read the rather overblown blurb. After a while he looked up and shrugged.

'Impressive, eh?' I grinned. 'I'm now an expert on questions of mental health and the living conditions of people on the streets.'

He shook his head dazedly. 'And you like it, do you? What you do?'

'Like it?' I said. 'Well, I dunno. I love the weekends, I know that.'

'Me too.'

'You do?' I looked at him in surprise. 'But that's your busiest time, isn't it?'

'Oh sure, when I'm on. But this weekend I'm off. My brother's getting married.'

I stared at him. 'Getting married? . . . What, today?'

He nodded.

'And you're going to the wedding?'

'Yup, this afternoon.' He glanced at his watch. 'In just a few hours, to be precise.'

I was thunderstruck. This was a great blow. I'd been looking forward with keen desire to our spending the rest of the weekend together. For a few moments I was too overcome to speak. Then, when I did find my tongue, I had to struggle to hide my disappointment.

'Well, I can't allow that,' I joshed. 'You might elope with the best man.'

'I *am* the best man.'

I smiled. It was a struggle, though, and the smile quickly faded. Behind the light banter I was feeling suddenly desolate.

'Anyway,' he said, 'I can't miss the Big Bozo's wedding, can I?'

I drank some more coffee, looked away, fell silent.

'Nah, spose not.' I was painfully aware that I sounded like a sulky child.

'Hey look, I'm sorry.' He turned with a regretful shrug,

reached out and squeezed my arm.

'Yeah, so am I.' I shook my head ruefully. 'I thought this was *our* weekend.'

He looked at me curiously, studying my face for some moments as if he sensed the way I felt. As if struggling with his own disappointment, in fact.

'So is that it?' I said, almost pleadingly. 'What do I do now? Go home?'

He scratched his chin and nibbled away at his lower lip. He seemed to be trying to make up his mind about me. To be wondering whether, on so short an acquaintance, he could trust his judgement. Then suddenly he slapped the table.

'No,' he said abruptly, lifting my hand and kissing it. 'Look, I want you to come too. As my guest.'

'As your guest?' I stared at him for a moment in disbelief, then threw back my head and laughed. 'I mean, are you quite sure about this?'

He grinned and nodded. 'Yeah, absolutely. After all, I'm entitled, damn it. I'm the best bleedin' man, for fuck sake.'

'But I don't have an invitation.'

He gave a loud snort. 'Tcha, don't let that bother ya. Anyway, they'll all be too pissed to notice.'

I laughed again – this time with helpless mirth – and spread my hands wide in a resigned shrug. 'Well, in that case, haul me on board.'

So in a trice it was decided. I felt like a man reprieved. Threat of sudden rupture had become promise of new intimacy. I inspected myself. Was there a problem of dress? Not really. My shirt and jeans needed sprucing up, but my jacket was quite respectable. And from the inside pocket I drew forth a red silk tie – the one that I always take to conferences, even though there's rarely any call for it. I rolled it out with a grand flourish and held it to my neck. Billy was moved to gentle applause.

The service was a small, informal affair at the local registry office, with perhaps fewer than thirty guests present. We were expected to make our own way there, so we went on foot. But it started promptly at three, and due to a mistimed detour to the supermarket we arrived with just a few minutes to spare. The groom, Billy's older brother Paul – thickset and broad-shouldered, with bristly blond hair – was sitting gazing at his feet with the look of a condemned man, though he managed to raise an anxious smile as Billy slipped in beside him. Concerned not to appear too intrusive, I took a seat in an empty row just behind the main party. At three o'clock sharp, the steady tread of Bach's 'Air on the G String' was abruptly replaced by the soulful strains of Dionne Warwick's 'This Girl's In Love With You'. And at the same moment, as if stirred by this call to attention, the resplendent lady in the front row – whose showy pink hat was the most striking feature in the landscape – turned and smiled graciously at me with a look of distant curiosity. In cheekbones, jaw-line and curl of the mouth she was unmistakably Billy's mum.

A dark-suited official, who had been conferring with a colleague at the side of the room, now took centre stage and indicated that the guests should rise. He stood with a calm priest-like air, a large book resting on his widespread hands. The music faded and the guests turned to view the approaching bride, who was now moving up the centre aisle, escorted by a ruddy-faced man with a stubbly grey beard. Slim and pretty, her tight-fitting blue-grey dress reaching to her ankles, her hair piled high and falling in ringlets round her face, she looked composed and radiant. I tried to recall her name. Billy had mentioned it. Was it Gail? Anyway, her entrance certainly added sparkle to the otherwise routine ordinariness of the proceedings, for the following stages of the ceremony passed with run-of-the-mill efficiency, the couple declaring their vows without stumbling and Billy performing his duties with quiet capability. A minor interruption occurred during the signing of the register, however, when a young woman was seized by a fit of coughing and obliged to leave the room.

At the end of the service, I tagged along behind the other guests as they drifted out into the afternoon sunshine and gathered in clusters on the steps of the building. It seemed there was no official photographer, but several people were taking snaps and an extrovert man was wielding an expensive camera with the air of a professional and trying to arrange people into well-balanced groups. I hung about on the fringes, but soon felt a tap on the shoulder. It was Billy. And standing next to him was the lady in pink.

'Mum,' he said, 'meet Matt.'

He flicked a finger between us like a metronome.

'Hullo, Matt. I'm Irene.'

She had a firm handshake, though up close she looked different. Her mouth was hard, I noticed, and her face lined and weathered.

'Nice day for it,' I said.

She nodded and smiled.

'So.' She fiddled with her pearl necklace. 'Have you known our William long?'

'Not long,' I said, opting for tactful reticence.

'He's got such a lot of friends. I meet a new one every week. They come, they go.' She passed a sly glance between us. 'Ee, that's a busy old place, intit? What's it called again?'

'The Black Horse,' said Billy, firm and prompt. 'As if you didn't know.'

'Well, funny if I didn't.' She gave a fat chuckle. 'Everyone knows. Anyway, perhaps I'll drop in sometime. Could do with a bit o' company missen, now that Pete's on nights.'

Her laughter rose edgily and then suddenly broke, sputtering down into the dark rattle of a smoker's cough.

The buffet at the Crown was laid out on a long linen-covered table. It was a plain but tempting spread, and more than adequate for the small number of guests. The six varieties of sandwiches were identifiable by pennant, and there were also plates of sausage rolls and vol-au-vents. In the centre a single-tier cake in white icing bore the inscription *Good Luck* in silver-foil lettering, and at the side were a couple of smiling waitresses offering glasses of champagne from a drinks table. Most of the men in the party, however, soon returned from the bar with pints of 'the real stuff', and within half an hour of the party's arrival the small room had become a riot of conversation and unrestrained laughter.

'This is my friend Matt,' Billy would say whenever someone approached, though I was sometimes left to introduce myself, he having slipped away to have a word with an aunt or cousin. It was at a moment like this that I found myself talking to Cheryl, an engaging chatterbox with a beguiling accent who worked at the shoe shop in the Brigham Arcade.

'I think I know you, don't I?' she said. 'Haven't I seen you at the George?'

'Unlikely,' I grinned. 'I've never been this way before.'

'So how do you know the happy couple?'

I held up my hands in mock-surrender. 'I don't. Not at all.'

'Oh really?'

'Look, keep it under your hat, I'm just a gatecrasher.'

She giggled. 'I think maybe you're a friend of Billy's?'

'That's a shrewd guess.'

'Billy's got some lovely friends.'

'Thank you. You're very nice yourself.'

Cheryl introduced me to her blank-faced boyfriend, who was known to everyone as Judd. Judd had a bone-crushing handshake and seemed to be already into his sixth pint. Speaking slowly with a slight slur, he gave me a laboured explanation of how he had come by his nickname. Apparently, it derived from his initials: JD for Joe Dodd. I nodded politely, but conversation was clearly not his natural medium – even, or perhaps especially, after ample lubrication – so I was glad when my efforts to look interested were interrupted by the bride's father, who had risen to his feet and was calling for everyone's attention.

'Ladies 'n gents,' he boomed, though most of the guests were far too absorbed to notice, and minutes passed before the rowdy gathering could be quelled into silence. At which point he too fell silent, apparently overcome with stage fright, and we waited expectantly while he coughed nervously, loosened his collar and fiddled with the cutlery. He then glanced quickly round the room as if looking for someone to feed him the next line.

'Gerr on wi' it, Perce,' some bloke shouted, and the room erupted into coarse laughter.

'Ah, shut it, gobshite,' Perce flung back.

He then cleared his throat again.

'Ladies 'n gents, what d'ya think? Am ah up ta dis?' A chorus of rude responses. 'As theurr norrz, ah can knock up a dodgy set o' shelves.' Hoots of laughter. 'Ah can drive in excess o' t' speed limit.' More hoots. 'Ah can pick a fight wi' a landlut.' Hoots and shrieks, plus cheering and whistling. 'But Ah'm not wha' you'd call a born natural a' speech-making.' All the foregoing, plus a round of applause. 'So dis part o' t' proceedings will be shoart – li' wee beeam Ted.' More applause as little Ted rises and takes a bow. 'Anyway, welcome ta ye orl for comin dis afternoon ta share dis 'appy event, 'n celebrate t' marriage o' wee daughta Gail to young Paul 'eear.' Wild applause, grins from Gail and Paul. 'Some o' theur av cum some distance, ah know, and ah should mention in particular uz wife's sista Molly, whoa 'as travelled orl t' way fra St 'Elens in spite of 'a back trouble 'n gammy leg.' Yet more applause as a bosomy lady in a flowery frock stands up and takes a bow.

Unfortunately, after the huge success of these opening remarks, Perce appeared to warm to his role, even wallow in it, and we were now treated to some sentimental stories about Gail, interspersed with fulsome tributes to her beauty, sweet nature and loving kindness. The guests listened politely at first, but then grew restless. In fact, some could scarcely conceal their embarrassment and impatience. Perce, fine as a clown, was rather unpalatable when it came to sincerity. And what had happened to that promise to be brief? By way of compensation, the speeches by Paul and Billy that followed were snappy to the point of slickness and amounted to little more than a series of toasts peppered with a few tired old jokes.

Shortly after this, partly to avoid further interaction with Judd, I excused myself and made off to the bar, where I ordered a lemon spritzer with a large helping of ice. The peacefulness of the place at this hour was a welcome relief from the noise of the reception room, and it was a pleasure to perch on a stool here, free from the need to exchange civilities. Someone had left a copy of the Norfield Gazette lying on the stool beside me, and I spent some minutes flicking through it, though the only thing that aroused my interest was the group of footballers pictured on the back page, at whom I gazed with lingering admiration. But then, glancing round, I saw Billy, who was sitting at a table in the company of a nervous, weasel-faced man. The man was a guest at the wedding who had previously attracted my attention, for there was something about his demeanour and body language that was intriguing, even mildly disquieting, though it was difficult to say exactly what. I studied him closely until, with a sudden rush of self-consciousness, I realised that my glance had become a stare. I was just about to turn away when Billy caught my eye.

'Hey, Matt. Come and meet Arthur.'

Arthur threw me a quick glance as I approached. He looked strained, and the hand he held out was limp and clammy. The unsettling mannerisms – the twisted smile, the eyes that constantly moved – were even more noticeable now, seen at arm's length, so to speak, and I was struck again by the pallor of his skin, so totally at odds with his light pink jacket and matching bow tie. After the handshake, I pulled up a chair and looked at Billy in expectation of some further introduction. But Billy's eyes were on Arthur, who was now sitting in silence and staring at a point in the middle of the table as if studying the movements of a minute insect.

'Arthur's not too well,' said Billy at last, turning to me with a tactful wink. 'He's had to come out. Bit of a funny turn.'

Arthur looked up and, removing a well-pressed handkerchief from his top pocket, began to dab his forehead. He avoided eye contact with Billy and me, and when he spoke it was as if to some imaginary person situated somewhere in the space between us.

'I'm not one for crowds. Not a party person. Not now. Not after the do I had last year. By rights I should be at home resting, taking it easy. That's what the doctor ordered. But I came here today for Billy's sake.'

There was another brief period of silence, during which I speculated wildly. Was this an unlikely friend or an unloved relative? And what kind of *do* had he suffered? I looked expectantly from Arthur to Billy, hoping that one or the other would supply an answer. But Arthur remained sunk in self-communion and Billy was keeping up a discreet silence.

'Have you known Billy long?' I asked, hoping that this was a promising cue, one that might go somewhere.

'A good deal longer than you have, dear boy,' he muttered, a sort of dark frisson passing over his face. Still refusing to look anyone in the eye, he had fixed his sightless gaze at a spot just above my right shoulder.

I decided to persevere.

'I expect so,' I said brightly, provoked into adopting a jaunty tone. 'It must be less than twenty-four hours since Billy and I met.'

'So he tells me,' he said in a bitter monotone. He flashed a sardonic half-smile before his eyes moved off again, his attention apparently caught by something far more interesting in a distant corner of the room. But when he next spoke, his little show of indifference was betrayed by a depth of feeling, a shudder of animus, that seemed to erupt from his stomach and cripple his voice, making it rasp and squeak like a rusty old saw. 'Pretty sharp, are you, Matt? Nifty, like? Skilled at nosing your way, lifting the shirt, sniffing the goods?'

I stared at him in blank stupefaction. Indeed, so startling was it – this lightning transformation from frail invalid to foul-mouthed hobgoblin – that several moments passed before I was sufficiently composed to speak.

'I beg your pardon?'

'Myself, I'm not greatly fond of that place. Some nights

you sit in a corner, you can't hear yourself think. And let's face it, sunshine, the queens that go there are mostly shite.'

Billy threw me an anxious look and then leaped to his feet.

'Arthur, you've said it yourself, you're not well,' he said. His voice had acquired the tone of a nurse or minder. 'Come on, I'll see you home. We'll order a cab.'

Needless to say, it was a relief to see the back of Arthur, though it meant that Billy was gone for nearly an hour and I was again left to amuse myself in the company of complete strangers. When he returned, however, he was especially bright and attentive, so I said nothing about the incident, even though the event, to put it mildly, had rather soured the evening for me. Certainly I *wanted* to talk about it, but I sensed from his deliberate avoidance that the subject was taboo. This was puzzling, and all my efforts to enjoy myself after that were mixed with feelings of resentment. We strove to keep the conversation light, but we were aware, it seemed to me, that our talk had become trite and artificial.

When did we get to bed that night? I don't honestly remember, though it must have been sometime in the early hours of the morning. We were pretty pissed, of course – indeed, almost too wrecked to enjoy each other. Not quite, though, and we eventually succumbed to sleep as pale blue light began to spread across the glass panels of the roof, having soothed away the troubles of the night in gentle caresses and then drowned them in a bout of ardent activity.

So we again rose very late and went straight to Dylan's for lunch. We ate hungrily and chatted, carefully steering a course around the viper in the room. But when I got to the end of my baguette I sat staring at my empty plate. The moment had come, it seemed to me, to put the question.

'So what *about* Arthur?' I ventured.

'Meaning?'

'Friend or foe?'

He looked at me hard. 'Friend.'

I raised an eyebrow, noting the set expression, the firm control of his reply. Should I venture further? No, definitely not. We had clearly reached the end of this pointedly sparse exchange.

But by late afternoon curiosity had again got the better of me. We were lounging on a grassy mound under a tree beside a pond. I tossed a chunk of cake into the water and there was instant pandemonium as a dozen ducks fought over it with ferocious squabbling. A timeless scene lay before us. Mothers were chatting in sunlight, oblivious to the rough-and-tumble of their children in the play area, while in the distance some teenage boys, constantly pursued by a yelping terrier, were kicking a ball round a grass verge and booting volleys of shots at the hapless defender of a makeshift goal. Nearby, an elderly couple dosed on a bench, she protected by a straw hat, he by a handkerchief knotted at the corners; and in the otherwise blue sky a few fleecy clouds and vapour trails put some finishing touches to this familiar picture of Sunday afternoon in the park.

Conversation had reached a lull. I gazed into the middle distance and decided to be bold.

'So tell me some more about Arthur.'

'Such as?'

'Such as anything.'

'It's like I say . . . he's an old friend.'

'An old venomous friend.'

'Look, he's not always like that. He can be a laugh. He's up and down a lot.'

'You're very good to him.'

'He's very good to *me*.'

'In what way?'

He flinched slightly – and hesitated.

'It's like I say . . . he helps me out sometimes.'

I stared at him.

'Helps you out?' I could hear the edge in my voice. 'You mean – *what*? He gives you money?'

I was aware of the need to tread carefully, but the words simply broke from me.

Silence.

I was glaring at him. He was looking me in the eye. Calm, unruffled.

'Well . . . we all need a bit of that, don't we?'

A brief pause. The air vibrant with tension.

'What? You allow that . . .'

I wriggled uncomfortably; the word *reptile* was dancing on the tip of my tongue.

'Christ, man, it's not a picnic on a barman's wages.'

A burning sensation flared up in my chest as I struggled silently with powerful feelings.

'Well, if it's a picnic you need, come to me. I'll give you a goddamn picnic.'

'Matt, calm down.' He spoke gently, but in a commanding tone. 'And let's change the subject, shall we?'

We had found ourselves a secluded corner. I was sitting cross-legged on a mossy patch of ground. He was lying on his stomach, his head close to my knee. I finished my cake in silence, then reached out and caressed the back of his neck. But I was far from easy, and after a while I leaped up and walked to the edge of the pond. I stared down into the murky depths. A large fish was nosing calmly through weed. My mind was racing. I was astonished to find myself in such turmoil, my desire now mixed with strong surges of jealousy and protectiveness. The past forty-eight hours had changed me – or so it seemed. My life had overturned in a single weekend. It was no longer a case of wanting Billy. Now I needed him. Needed him badly. What had begun in pleasure was threatening to become painful.

'Billy, time's running out.'

'What, you think I need reminding?'

'Look, I'm tempted to stay over and drive back at dawn.'

He turned, looked at me and sat up. 'Oh, come on, that's crazy. You'll be in no fit state.'

I sat down beside him. Shook my head. 'Yeah, yeah, you're right.' He sighed and lay back on the grass. I clambered over him and knelt astride his body. 'But look, I'll phone you as soon as I get in.'

'Please, love.'
'And I'll be back soon.'
'How soon?'
'Next weekend.'
'Really?'
'Best I can do, I'm afraid.'
He flung his arms round my neck. Pulled me close.
'Can't wait.'

I'm not quite sure when or how the Gordon Street set-up started. At the time I met Billy it had been my home for three years, and my going to live there had happened as a result of Sonia, a work colleague, moving out and suggesting that I take over her room. She had decided to move back to New Zealand, and was hoping that I would be her link with the past, her means of staying in touch with the house and its occupants. I had to be interviewed, of course, and in spite of glowing references, it was not an easy ride. The panel consisted of Mary, Drew, Clare and Eddie, the others having agreed, apparently, to let these four represent them. Actually, I suspect that Andy simply couldn't be bothered. He always seizes any opportunity to bunk off meetings. And as for Dan and Boo Boo – well, it was too much to expect them to cut short their regular mid-evening fuck.

Eddie kicked off, naturally, and I hated him from the first. His opener was one of those smartass questions about why I thought I would make a better housemate than the other applicants for the room.

'Better?' I said. 'I've no idea if I'm better. I'm not competitive, I'm just *me*. An individual.'

'Okay,' he said. 'That's fine. So what *kind* of an individual? Give us the picture, warts and all.'

And that was just the start. He continued in similar vein throughout and completely dominated the discussion, even though the others did eventually manage to put in a question or two. They, as you might expect, were much softer. Drew and Clare even offered a friendly smile, a gesture that provided some relief from Eddie's hard-faced scrutiny. But it has to be said that Mary, in her spaced-out way, was occasionally disconcerting too. Throughout the interview she stared at me with great intensity, her eyes boring into me as if to penetrate every fibre of my being. Then, towards the end, she sat bolt upright and coughed to command attention, as if about to launch into a major speech. I turned to her and she asked me solemnly what my astrological sign was. I replied, with a smile, that it was Aries – though with the moderating influence of Sagittarius rising. At this she nodded sagely, and, to my alarm, proceeded to write a very lengthy note on her pad.

So, as you can imagine, I was amazed when Drew phoned me a few days later to break the news that if I was still interested the room was mine. I accepted at once, of course, although perhaps less warmly than might have been expected, because in the intervening period I had been debating with myself whether I *was* in fact interested. Did I really want to share my life with this awkward bunch of misfits, three of whom I'd not even met? I asked Drew if it had been a hard decision. 'Yes,' he said, 'but these things are usually a matter of compromise, aren't they?' I muttered assent, not wishing to put the poor guy on the spot by probing any further. But his reply has left me wondering ever since about the exact nature of the negotiations that led to my moving in.

Well, it could have been worse, all things considered. On the plus side, the place was never dull, that's for sure. But, then again – let's not blink the facts – it was often Heartbreak House. On the day I moved in, Clare came to my room. 'Did they tell you about the upstairs loo?' she asked. 'No,' I said. 'Is there one?' She groaned and buried her face in her hands. 'As you may have noticed,' she said, 'we have a problem with communication here. In short, no one tells anyone anything. Yes, there *is* one – and very handy it is if you feel the need during the night. It's on the landing below, next to Andy's room. It looks like a cupboard and there's no lock on the door. Someone has promised to fix one at every meeting I've attended, but it hasn't happened yet. There's also a problem with the ballcock. To flush, you have to stand on the seat and plunge your arm into the cistern.'

In many ways Clare was the best of the bunch. Although initially off-putting – she looks and sounds like a head girl – she's actually sympathetic, caring and practical. The others were always laughing behind her back, poking fun at her brisk, no-nonsense approach, but I didn't buy that. When I broke off with Dieter soon after moving there, she was my support, my rock. In fact she was, and still is, my best friend. At the time that I lived there she was writing a doctoral thesis on some obscure woman bard, an Irish mystic of the late seventeenth century, and, as she constantly reminded us, the end of the project, which had already occupied her for God knows how long, was not yet in sight. Consequently she also got criticised for being narrow, self-absorbed, sunk in her own tiny world – or, in Boo Boo's elegant phrase, half up her own backside. That was rich, coming from them – a case of blaming Clare for the faults they recognised in themselves. Who did we turn to when we want something sorted? Dan? Mary? Eddie? You've got to be joking. Those armchair critics didn't know their anuses from their genitalia. The person we all turned to was that burner of the midnight oil, our very own queen of the conference circuit, with her tea-time chats, her bone china and her 'nothing to do but bash on'.

It was after two when I got in. There was a light on in Clare's room – wouldn't you just know it? – but otherwise the house was a graveyard. I called the pub immediately from the phone in the hall. It was the only way to contact Billy; he didn't have a phone of his own. He said he would listen out for the extension on the top landing, and in the unlikely event that someone else answered, I should smack the receiver down smartly; a call to the pub in the small hours would not be appreciated. He took an age to answer, and in my agitation – should I hold on or hang up? – I started to kick the wall. Eventually he responded, but when he spoke he sounded like someone with brain damage.

'Uh . . . oozat?'

'Billy, it's me. Who d'ya think? I've just got in.'

'Christ, Matt, what time is it?'

'Yeah, I know it's late. I told you it would be.'

'What happened?'

'Nothing, love. It's a long journey.'

A brief pause.

'Great weekend.'

'Brilliant.'

'Sorry about Arthur, though.'

'Not a problem.'

'Bit of a sicko. Not his fault – know what I mean? He needs treatment.'

'Hey, let's not talk about this now. I just wanted to report that I've landed.'

'Yeah . . . Well, thanks for phoning, sweetheart. Been thinking about you.'

A smothered yawn.

'Look, dozy, love you to bits, but go back to bed. I'll call you tomorrow.'

I tapped softly on Clare's door on my way to my room. 'Entrez,' she trilled in her brightest executive tones. I found her bent over her desk, back towards me, writing in a notebook. Tower blocks of books, on upper and lower surfaces, formed a kind of cityscape around her. To me, her room had always suggested a desperate attempt to impose some kind of order on ever-threatening chaos. The neatly-stacked files with meticulous labelling stood shoulder to shoulder as if to form a defense against the engulfing tide of literary debris. 'One moment,' she said, clearly anxious to record some thought before it flew away, never to be recaptured. Then, turning abruptly on her swivel-chair, she greeted me with a smile.

I made a gesture of mock helplessness. 'Don't you ever shut up shop?'

'Well, what about you? What sort of hour is this to be phoning someone?'

'Ah,' I said with an embarrassed grin.

But she saw my discomfort. 'Don't panic,' she said,

holding up her hands. 'Didn't catch a thing. Not at this distance.'

'Look, you may as well know, it's no big secret. I've met someone.'

'Someone? Well, thanks a lot. I guessed as much. Anyone who gets a call from you at this ungodly hour has got to be *someone* at the very least.'

'It's difficult. I don't know where to begin. He's – oh Christ, let's leave it till the morning.'

'Oh, my pet.' She looked at me closely. 'This is clearly something very special.'

'So what's been happening here?' I said, seeking a swift change of subject. I could feel myself beginning to colour up.

'Lots. How much time have you got? First – and this may not be an event worth mentioning – Dan and Boo Boo have had another row and are not speaking. Next, Drew has been offered that job, but is in two minds whether to take it. Oh, and here's the really juicy bit. A colleague of Eddie's – a woman called Chester, can you believe? – has accused him of sexual harassment . . .'

As I say, the positive side of Gordon Street – Number 7, as we called it – was the unpredictability. Yes, there were patterns of behaviour, as in the case of Dan and Boo Boo, but no two days were quite the same. I loved the constant stream of visitors, even though some long-term crashers occasionally outstayed their welcome. The big communal spaces, the lounge and dining room, were the hub of the house and always buzzing with people and conversation. Television was banned from those areas, and remained in short supply, even though it was allowed elsewhere. In fact, the only television in the house during my stay was the old unlicensed box in Andy's room, which only he ever watched. Instead, there were spontaneous gatherings, social events, parties. We usually liked to eat together, though there was no obligation, and attendance at meals largely depended on who was the acting chef. If it was Mary, I sometimes ducked out. Now don't misunderstand me, I love vegetarian food. However, I draw the line at seaweed soup followed by a mound of old twigs fried in batter. Sometimes the guests outnumbered the places at table, in which case we moved to the sitting room, pushed the furniture to the walls and squatted in a circle.

Yes, there was a lot of coming and going at Number 7, but you grew to accept and even enjoy it – the casualness, the impermanence, the flow of human traffic. So one evening, say, you're preparing a meal with Eva, a lively young Venezuelan who beguiles you with rich tales of Caracas. The pair of you hit it off nicely, you warm to each other, you sense a bonding. But then the next evening there are new faces. And Eva? She's on her way to Madrid. You never see her again. Among the new faces is Mikhail, a suave young diplomat from the Russian Embassy. He's sort of attached to Mary, whom he met last night at a rock concert. Bulky and handsome, he's the hit of the evening, a natural entertainer with perfect manners, a sexy voice and a well-spun repertoire of tall stories. But that's it – he doesn't appear again, and Mary shrugs off all inquiries. He's passed through the house like a meteor.

It was perhaps a mistake to knock on Clare's door that night. She detained me longer than was good for me. In barely five hours I would have to get up to go to work. But when I eventually got to bed, I couldn't sleep anyway. I lay between the sheets, turning over recent events. I was missing Billy already. We were separated by just a few hours of driving time, yet there seemed a great gulf between us. My mind was haunted by a mass of images – people, scenes, faces, places – and dominating them all, looming out of the mass, was the image of Arthur. His narrow face and shifting eyes kept swimming into view, overlaid by the mutterings of his mischievous voice. I tried to blot him out, turn him off, but however I dodged, I couldn't rid myself of his dread presence. He was always there, squatting in the middle of things like an odious dung-beetle.

Dawn eventually came, but the night had left me utterly drained. What's more, a peek through the curtains as I dressed for work revealed that the day had broken grey and wet. My heart sank; I would have given anything to crawl back into bed. Nor did my mood lighten when I snapped on the radio and caught yet another report about the so-called gay plague. However, over a breakfast of burnt toast and some scrapings of marmalade from an empty jar, I made a positive decision: to cut out my usual walk to work and take the bus. The thought revived me and I was away by eight-fifteen. Actually, we don't open the doors until ten, but I always like to arrive in good time. I need to prepare myself mentally. Relax with a cup of tea, sort the mail, glance at the rota, that sort of thing. But if I had never felt less in the mood, there was at least a bonus on arrival: the regulars who normally gather outside the building, waiting to be admitted, were nowhere to be seen. Nasty weather has its benefits. I'm usually the first in, but this morning Maggie had got there before me. I wondered why. A disastrous weekend? A quarrel with the kids at breakfast? Work, for Maggie, was a refuge, as I knew from experience. I found her in the office, ripping up out-of-date leaflets and flinging them into the waste-paper basket with what looked like therapeutic abandon.

'Yet another uplifting start,' I said, shaking my rain-soaked umbrella over the sink.

She gave me a wry smile.

'And how was your weekend?' This, I knew, was throwing caution to the wind.

'You don't want to know. You really don't.'

'Try me.'

'Okay. You remember Dave had that crackpot idea about converting the loft?'

'Uhuh.'

'Not a professional job, mind. Oh no, DIY.'

'Uhuh.'

'Well, he made a start at the weekend, stumbled, and his foot came through the ceiling.'

‘Oh shit.’

‘But he’s fine, absolutely fine. And that’s the galling part. I wish he’d broken every bone in his body. What I want is my ceiling back.’

I made some tea and we exchanged some more scraps of news. She asked about the conference, how it had gone. I said that it had been okay, though dominated, as ever, by pushy types and high-handed know-alls. I said nothing about Billy or the events of the weekend. It wasn’t the time or place: the subject was too complex, my feelings were too involved, for the casual banter of tea-time conversation. At nine-thirty the telephone rang. We glanced up and nodded at each other with knowing apprehension. I lifted the receiver. Yes, it was Tony. Very sorry, he wouldn’t be in today. He’d been sick all weekend with a non-specific illness, possibly as the result of something he’d eaten.

‘Get well soon,’ I said, and replaced the receiver.

‘I knew he’d bunk off,’ Maggie scoffed. ‘Look at the rota. He’s on cleaning duty.’

We fell about laughing.

Staying in touch would not be easy, that was clear from the start. And anyway I sort of knew it in my bones. For a kick-off, we worked different shifts. He went on duty as I came off. When I most needed him, he was least available. Daylight hours? No chance. He was either in bed or at the pub. Our one opportunity to speak to each other was after midnight. We therefore seized this precious moment, milking it for all it was worth, though often conveying our eagerness, our need for such daily contact and renewal, through conversation that was incoherent and punctuated with yawns. So on the whole it was a frustrating business, a fragile connection that broke every night with a click at the end of the line. Our consolation was the thought that we would see each other again soon. I never finished a call without a solemn promise to drive up at the weekend.

On the following Friday morning I packed a bag with a change of clothing and stowed it in the boot of the Morris.

My plan was to set off immediately after work, and I was hoping that nothing would happen to prevent a quick getaway. As things turned out, though, it was a day of quite exceptional stress, when everything seemed to conspire to defeat me. First, Tony, now back at work after his weekend illness, insisted on taking two hours off in the middle of the day for an urgent appointment with his chiropractor. Then Nora, an elderly alcoholic who spends most of her days on park benches, had a spectacular falling-out with Maggie, which culminated in a shouting match, a can of lager being thrown at the wall and Nora herself being ejected. This led to agitation among the other clientele and ultimately to the collapse of George, a gentle soul with shattered nerves who is prone to hypertension.

By mid-afternoon it was clear that a change of plan was called for. I needed a break before taking to the road. In which case, to avoid the rush-hour traffic, there was no point in setting out until after six. This would put me back a bit, but had its positive side. It would give me an hour to unwind, and to grab a bite to eat as fortification for the journey. It would also allow me to give support to Maggie at the end of the day, both by lending a hand with the clearing up and in the form of companionship. After all, I could scarcely leave her to recuperate alone, Tony having agreed, in a rare moment of generosity, to see George to the hospital for treatment.

'Phew!' I called as I locked the front door. 'Fancy a brew, Mags? I'm gasping.'

'I thought you wanted to tear off,' she said.

'I did. But now I want to stay here with you.'

'Oh, how noble! Bless you, my sweet.'

I had said nothing to her about driving to Yorkshire, which would have meant telling her more than I was ready to tell. In fact, I'd given her no reason at all for wanting to get away early, and she must have been curious. She's got a sharp nose, has Maggie. Nor is she shy about asking a straight question. But on this occasion she seemed to sense my reticence and respect my right to silence. So we sat in the office, nursing mugs of tea, and though we talked all round the church, the question of where I was going never arose. It was a feat. I was impressed by the diplomacy, especially in one with such a love of gossip.

How dull, how interminable, the drive. I suppose I should have felt gratitude to the Romans for the straightness of the road – splendid work, you chaps! – rather than smouldering resentment. To be fair, there *were* compensations. The grey skies had cleared by late afternoon, giving way to a long, light-filled evening and eventually a pink afterglow in the west. But there was no escaping it, the travelling was a curse. However I looked at it, my most fervent wish was to get it behind me: to *be* there – and *now*, in an instant. I had no time for the adage about how much better it is to journey than to arrive. Who first came up with that half-baked notion anyway? Someone who never made the kind of journeys I make, that's for sure. Who never felt the pangs of separation. Who was never in an itch to be in the same room with someone. To have him – hold him.

Worst of all was the final stretch, when the light had all but failed and there was nothing but the road, the occasional looming vehicle, the beating on through the darkness. Confined to the cell-like interior of the car, the stretch of tarmac caught in the headlights, my mind turned in on itself. What exactly was I doing here? What impulse had led me to chase off into the night like this? Why was I not at home with friends, comfortably settled on my own patch of soil? What *was* this mad pursuit, this caper, this folly?

What was Billy to me, or me to Billy?

And yet, when I saw the lights of the Black Horse again (I arrived at around eleven-thirty, having found a handy parking space in the lane) I felt a renewed glow of pleasure and excitement. The warm night, the blazing windows, the heady crowd on the pavement, so reluctant to drink up and go home – all of it came flooding back with a sense of fond familiarity. My bohemian friend was there too, loitering at the entrance, still louchely attired in rolled trousers and gay bandanna, still shamelessly flaunting his halo of red hair. I smiled at him as I pushed past, which put him in a serious flutter. He flapped himself nervously, squinting at me closely with a look of half-recognition.

'Phew! Isn't it *hot* out here tonight?' he began, in a rerun of his former line.

I grinned and nodded. 'It certainly *is*. Positively sultry.'

I spotted Billy as soon as I entered. He was collecting empties with a clear show of purposefulness and issuing firm reminders to dallying customers to drink up. He was obviously busy and hadn't yet noticed me, so I held back; this was clearly the wrong moment to spring forward and claim his attention. But after a while, to hide my sense of awkwardness, I took a corner seat. From here it was possible to observe the whole colourful scene, to watch the rowdy gathering unnoticed and with quiet amusement. Still toying with their drinks, Giles and Big Ron were at their usual table, loud in conversation with some friends and showing no signs of calling it a night; and a look around the room suggested that several other groups were similarly unaware that closing time had arrived.

But my amusement was short-lived. Pondering how Billy was going to propel this crowd towards the exit, my glance fell on an overdressed figure at a nearby table who was hunched over an empty wine glass. The showy jacket was the instant giveaway, though he would have stood out even in the drabbest attire. My heart lurched. He was alone – what else? – and his eyes were fixed on me, which was all the more unsettling given that I'd never managed to command their attention before. Most disturbing of all, I had the sense that he had been staring at me for some time.

It was a moment of acute discomfort. The etiquette of the situation suggested that I should smile, show some acknowledgement, perhaps even go and join him, but I felt a powerful resistance to the idea and a kind of surly doggedness kept me rooted to my seat. To avoid further embarrassment, I looked away in a weak pretence of not having seen him, my mind wrestling with itself in a turmoil of hesitancy. Should I relent, keep my head turned, or simply get up and walk off? But soon he relieved me of the need to make a decision by taking the initial move himself. From the corner of my eye, I saw him get up and come towards me. I still kept my gaze averted, however, and for a while – moments that felt like aeons – he hovered around me, even hung over me, though I tried to show no sense of his looming presence. Then a sharp noise, as he scraped a chair across the floor to my table, made me turn in mock surprise and greet him with a strained smile. That was all I could muster; any further show of warmth was beyond me. So I left the first words to him.

'I heard you were coming.'

'And here I am. The rumour confirmed.'

He glanced at me, and then immediately looked away, as if in disgust. 'As you know, I'm not too keen on this place, but I like to look in now and again. Stay in touch. Patrol the estate. Keep an eye on things.'

'Keep an eye on things?' The phrase had an ominous ring; apart from which, I was amazed to hear that he could keep an eye on anything. However, as I now knew, he had, when unobserved, the steadiest gaze on the planet.

'About our last encounter . . .'

'Don't mention it. Best forgotten.'

'Not the sunniest of introductions, certainly. But then, I'm not in good health. I think you know that.'

'Billy said something of the sort.'

He threw me another glance. Then his eyes darted off again. 'Tidy old journey you've made.'

'Indeed.'

'Going to make a habit of it?'

'That depends.'

'Yeah, doesn't everything.' He shook his head and gave a hollow chuckle. 'Look, Nat.' His eyes were still scouring the room as if in search of someone, and he spoke quietly out of the side of his mouth. 'Mind if I call you Nat?'

'Not at all, but the name is Matt.'

'Some simple advice. I don't know what you're up to – '

'I'm not *up to* anything.'

'Just *listen*, for Christ sake.'

I flinched in the face of another bilious eruption, another quicksilver transformation just as startling as the former. Yes, the hobgoblin was back. He turned, our eyes met (almost for the first time) and he held me transfixed. Nailed me, in fact. For a few moments he seemed too rattled and discomposed to speak, as if the exertion of trying to keep some young upstart under control had left him breathless. But he made a conscious attempt to calm himself, and when he did speak at last, it was with slow, quiet deliberation.

'The thing is this. The lad belongs here. He's not what you think. He's not your type. He's one of us. And folks up here don't like folks down there . . . *interfering*. Poking their big eager . . .' He tapped his nose, brought his face close to mine. 'Know what I mean?' I made no response. Simply stared, spellbound. 'So why not do yourself a favour, snowflake, and just . . . *flake* off back to London.'

This last utterance was delivered with iron control and an unmistakably menacing articulation. At the same time, his chest heaved in the effort, betraying the passion behind the words. Too stunned to make response, I simply watched him in amazed stupefaction. He stared back at me with a hard look, as if willing me to challenge him. Then suddenly his face clenched, as though his body were racked with pain, and he clutched at his heart. I was alarmed – so alarmed, in fact, that my instincts overcame my feelings of repugnance and I reached out towards him in a gesture of support. He seemed not to notice, however. Instead, he rose unsteadily to his feet, belched, and without so much as a backward glance made for the door.

He left me in a state of considerable agitation. For a while the pub, its atmosphere still reeking of noxious fumes, seemed a quite different place, a hellish contrast to the one I had found so welcoming on my arrival. But eventually, with the help of some deep breathing, my jangled nerves began to settle down and I started to reconnect with the conviviality that was still pulsing around me. I decided not to dwell on what had happened. Well – for the present, at least. This was not the moment to try and make sense of it. I could catch up with that later. No, I was now more than ever in an urge to see Billy again. Had the crowd thinned? Yes, a bit – though the hangers-on were clearly in no mood to bring the party to an end. And this was encouraging. For some reason it was a comfort to know that the world spins on, cheerfully oblivious of the sordid little scenes being played out in its midst.

'Leave it to me. I'll have a word.'

'A word won't be enough. The man's cracked.'

It was the next morning. We had woken late again and were back at Dylan's for a midday breakfast. I had avoided the subject of Arthur until now, not wanting to sully the moment with unpleasantness. 'Avoided', though, might be an overstatement; it was not actually a matter of conscious avoidance. Until that moment the sight and sound of Arthur had been entirely obliterated by the thrill of seeing Billy again. And of course, let's not forget them, the engulfing, all-consuming pleasures of the night.

But now the man was back. Back to haunt me, back to haunt both of us. Here in the sunlight of late morning; here on the pavement outside the café.

'Look, leave it to me,' repeated Billy firmly. 'I'll tell him straight. He'll get an earful. I won't *have* this.'

We fell into silence. I was trying to master my feelings, prevent myself from blurting out things I would later regret. If the loathsome Arthur was hard enough to cope with, there was the even greater difficulty of handling myself. The vital thing that I wanted to say kept struggling to escape, and I strove to hold it back.

In the end, though, it was too strong for me, and suddenly it leaped free – like a dog that's slipped its leash.

'The thing is, I don't get it. I mean, I can't believe . . .'

'What?'

'That you and he . . .'

A fat snort. Then a bold, straight look. 'We don't.'

'Ah, come on. Don't lie to me, love, please.'

‘It’s true.’ The straight look again.

‘So what’s the deal?’

‘No deal.’

‘You keep him dangling. You’re a tease.’

A wry smile. ‘Yeah, I guess. Something like that.’

This cryptic response effectively drew a line under the conversation. Spoken in a firm voice, it delivered a clear message: press no further. I took note, swallowed hard and, seeing no other option, determined to forget and relax. After all, he had point; I should rise above these nagging obsessions and respect his right to privacy. Why not simply enjoy this weekend of pleasure? Why not simply cherish these carefree days of fine weather and bewitching company?

Or at least . . . for the moment.

‘Evening, William. So this is the latest, is it? Mm, what a catch. Lovely smile, nice teeth.’

The doorman was a heavyweight. Not from bodybuilding, but from too much food and lack of exercise. Lank black hair hung round his ears and he kept flicking loose strands from his face. His collarless shirt had become a damp rag, and the tiny floral waistcoat draped round his fat shoulders had burst open like a pod from the pressure of his massive frame. It was hard to imagine anyone less awesome or commanding, less suited to the role of doorman. Indeed, apart from his bulk there was nothing impressive about him at all, and certainly nothing to suggest that he might be able to ward off unwelcome intruders. He ushered us in with a bow and a curving sweep of his hand.

We were at basement level, having approached via a narrow flight of steps that descended steeply from the road. But beyond the squalid little entrance the scene was more promising. The place was busy, though not overcrowded, and newly furnished with bar tables, lounge areas and spot-lit walls. On the dance floor some female couples were swaying gently to some slow country music, while around them an assortment of men – mostly in couples, and many with arms flung round each other's necks – looked on languidly. Elsewhere, groups of drinkers, mixtures of men and women seated at tables or standing, produced a lively buzz of conversation that often erupted into noisy laughter. My eyes were immediately drawn to a figure in the background, a handsome dark-featured young man in a white sleeveless vest whose slim muscular arms were pinned to the wall by a mere boy, an imp who looked far too young to be here. It was a scene that was difficult to read. Was this love play, or the throes of a bitter quarrel? There was also the obligatory drunk – in this case, a man in frayed denim shorts and Docs, who was sprawled across the bar, his head cradled in his arms. An unsmiling barman was standing over him in a posture that was again hard to interpret. Was he about to offer words of sympathy, or issue a final warning?

A young woman, part of a group gathered round a table, spotted Billy as soon as we entered and rose from her seat. She fluttered her hand to attract attention.

'It's Terry,' he said. 'I knew she'd be here. Come on, I'll introduce you.'

I smiled and trailed along behind. Terry stood up excitedly as he approached and they fell into a fulsome embrace. When they broke apart, she took his face in her hands and looked at him searchingly.

'Haven't seen you for ages,' she said. 'Where *have* you been hiding?'

He shrugged. 'Oh, I dunno. Been a bit off the scene recently.'

She nodded vigorously, as if to suggest that she'd been a bit off the scene quite a few times herself. She then arched an eyebrow and gestured towards me. 'And other things on your mind, perhaps?'

He grinned. 'Well, something like that,' he said, before turning to introduce me.

Terry pressed my hand eagerly and kissed me on both cheeks with an effusiveness that I found rather sticky. She had a suspiciously easy gift for dispensing warmth and sincerity. Plump, round-faced and pretty, her most striking feature was her silky skin, although, as I discovered later, she also had one leg shorter than the other, which caused her to walk with a slight limp. At first, I seemed to fascinate her. Who was I? Where did I live? What did I do? How did I become involved with Billy? But then, in an instant, distracted by a remark she had overheard from the other side of the table, she seemed to lose interest and seek diversion elsewhere, as if she had wrung me dry of any entertainment value I might have. True, we did speak to each other again later that evening, but by this time she had changed. She was cooler and more distant. It was clear that I was now an object of sinking curiosity rather than the person she had greeted earlier as a long-lost friend.

Meanwhile, abandoned by both Terry and Billy, now sharing wild, weeping hilarity with a dragged-up young man who was clearly the hypnotic focus of everyone's attention, I took a moment to look round the table at the intriguing assortment of individuals who made up the rest of the gang. To my left, on the other side of Terry, sat a bulky young woman in a check shirt, her sleeves rolled to the elbows, her hair cropped to within a few millimetres of her scalp. Golden hoops the width of tennis balls bounced on either side of her impressively large head and her painted eyelids shone like mother-of-pearl. In her serious mode she had the dignified and imposing look of a Masai warrior, but every now and again her face would split with merriment and she'd let forth a blast of maniacal neighing laughter. Beside her sat two young men, who might or might not have been a couple, it was difficult to tell. They passed remarks to each other on occasion, but seemed otherwise detached. The near one was tall, his jet-black hair stiff and shiny with lubricant and brushed upward into a quiff. Paleness and fine bone structure lent him an angular beauty, and behind his rather blank look there was a suggestion of quiet inwardness. His mate, on the other hand, was a short, tousled urchin, as bright and cute as a jockey, who caught my eye at one point and gave me a friendly nod, as if to welcome me into the circle. The star of the group, however, was undoubtedly the aforementioned young gender bender, who was sitting to my right on the other side of Billy. Outrageously made-up, his eyes ringed with liner, his lips black, he too was wearing outsize earrings, but in this case long teardrops of glass like the pendants of a chandelier. A tight-fitting Alice Cooper T-shirt accentuated his skinniness. Sadly, his inexhaustible supply of camp chatter, though amusing for a while, soon wore me down and then turned me off completely. I found myself irritated by the amount of rapt attention he was getting, for it seemed to me he didn't deserve it. And so, partly to relieve the tedium, partly out of mischief, I finished my beer and strode off to the bar, in what was intended to be a rather pointed snub.

'So what'll it be, then? This one's on me.'

I was waiting to give my order, my head bent over the bar. The words were almost breathed into my ear. I turned in surprise. It was the little tousle-haired jockey. He had seen me depart and leaped smartly after me. The top of his head came barely up to my shoulder, but he was smiling into my face with confident self-assurance, as if bidding me to admire his bold opportunism. His best features, as he clearly knew, were more than adequate compensation for his lack of height, and along with his general air of glowing good health, I again noticed the bright hazel eyes, the dimples that formed brackets round his smile, the flawless white teeth.

'Well, thanks a lot,' I said, staring at him in mild confusion.

He grinned at me with an enquiring wide-eyed look.

'So what'll it be?' he repeated.

I hastily recovered. 'Well, make it a pint of this,' I said, pointing at one of the pumps.

He nodded and hailed the barman.

'It's Craig, by the way,' he said, shaking my hand firmly as we waited for the drinks to be served.

'Nice to meet you, Craig.'

'And you're Matt, I believe.'

'That's right. What keen ears you've got.'

'Razor sharp, mate.' He grinned, winked and flicked one

of his lobes. 'Cigarette?'

He held up a packet.

'Well, thanks a lot,' I said again, falling into a verbal tic that made me wince. I reached forward and removed one. There was a pause. We smiled at each other. 'So tell me, Craig,' I said, breaking in to cover the awkwardness, 'you and Billy – '

'Yeah, old friends. Same school, in fact.'

'Really? So you know each other well?'

'Oh yeah,' he said with a chuckle and a wink. '*Very* well.'

Unprepared for this, I fell silent. I stared hard at him, again wrestling with confused feelings and stabs of resentment. But why? Did I suppose that Billy was chaste? Surely I knew that he slept around like other guys, that he must have a history of lovers and one-night stands at least as long as my own. Well, of course; that was not the problem. Or at least not the main problem. No, it wasn't what I knew about Billy, it was what I *didn't* know. Craig seemed to speak about Billy as if he owned him. From a world of close knowledge that excluded me. The two of them seemed to share something: a bond, a secret understanding, an elusive intimacy that I could only dimly perceive, glimpse through frosted glass. It made me suddenly aware of my insignificance, my lack of worldliness, my flat-footed vulnerability. How remote I was from the streetwise culture into which I had become drawn. I had stumbled blindly into Billy's life, with flimsy notions about installing myself at the centre of it, and now I could see the truth. I was an absurd figure, hovering hopefully on the sidelines, a mere smudge at the edge of the photograph. Perhaps I should heed Arthur's vicious but clear-sighted advice and truckle off back to London.

Did Craig sense my discomfort? I was trying to hide it. Inwardly I was torn, feeling intrigued by this insinuating little bloke and keen to hear more, yet also vaguely menaced. Then the drinks arrived and there was no getting away; I was trapped. I wondered if Billy was watching us. And if so, would he conclude that Craig and I had contrived this little rendezvous by secret communication? I glanced across the room. But no, Billy was laughing and gesticulating and deeply absorbed in riotous banter with his mates round the table. Was he even aware that Craig and I had left the circle? Apparently not. With his attention still focused on the young man in the Alice Cooper T-shirt, he seemed oblivious to all else around him.

'Billy and Baz,' said Craig, noticing my nervous glance. 'They go back a bit too.'

'Baz?' I said.

'Guy with the black lips. Lad's a total gas. A scream. You'll have trouble breaking them up tonight.'

'Is that so?' Another incendiary remark. I carefully considered it and again fixed him with a hard stare. I could sense myself becoming edgy. 'So what is this, Craig? Come on, shoot it straight. What exactly are you driving at?'

'Driving at?' He shrugged and raised an eyebrow. 'Nothing, mate, nothing at all. Hey, come on, don't get the hump, what d'ya *think* I'm driving at?' His face lit up with wide-eyed innocence. I turned away and we fell silent for a while. Then he reached out and squeezed my arm. 'Look,' he said, 'I can see you've got a thing about Billy. I can see you're Billy's boy.'

I scoffed. 'Got a *thing*? Billy's boy?'

I turned away, took a long draught of the lager and fixed my eyes firmly on the picture of Nureyev pinned to the back of the bar. What was I doing here? I didn't have to listen to this. I could pick up my drink and return smartly to my seat. I wasn't under any obligation to stay here in return for a pint of lager. Yet something kept me rooted to the spot. Was it Craig's personal magnetism, the fascination of his approach, an itch to see which way he would jump? Most probably all of these. Yes, I had to give it to the lad, he certainly had technique and manoeuvrability. So I waited to hear what he would say next, never doubting that he would spring a surprise; that just when I thought I had him in my sights he'd leap like a grasshopper and appear on the other side of me.

'The thing is, Matt,' he said after a pause, 'as I see it, you're playing a losing game. Now don't take that wrong. It's just how it looks to me.'

'A losing game.'

'Wasting yourself.'

'Wasting myself.'

'I mean, *you're* hanging out for Billy, but ask yourself, is *he* hanging out for you?'

'I think he is.'

'Oh boy, is that wilful blindness. Take another look across the room, mate. Take another look at your own true love. Does he care that you're here talking to me? Is he even aware of it? Are you even a glimmer in the darkest corner of his sozzled brain? I don't think so. He's well away, he's had a few, and when they take him home tonight, he'll be scarcely conscious. If we drink up and go, you could be back and under his duvet before dawn and he won't have noticed a thing.'

'Drink up and go.'

'To my place . . . my warm nest, cosy sack, wrestling pit. Believe me, Matt, you won't be disappointed. I'll show you what this pint-sized guy is made of. I've got a rage on me you'll never forget . . . *and* some stuff will help us on our way.' He drew a box of pills from a pocket and flashed them at me, his face lighting up in mock delirium. 'So Matt, what d'ya say? Come on, let's go. Loosen up, jive a bit, get juicy.'

This was so preposterous, so wonderfully grotesque, that I started to giggle, though I managed to stifle an impulse to be openly derisive. Craig's gift for self-parody had now outstripped his offensiveness. The fast-working little man, the lightning Don Juan, had changed. His danger, his malice, had lifted, to be replaced by an appealing clownishness. I looked at him, coming on to me for all he was worth, beaming his most seductive smile, and felt a rush of tenderness for his swaggering cheek, his virile posturing, his bursting keen-eyed intensity. In fact, he was so irresistible that on an impulse that took both of us by surprise I leaned forward, took his head between my hands and, with a quick glance over my shoulder to make sure that we were not observed, kissed him gently on the mouth. He looked thunderstruck for a moment, and a flush of colour sprang to his cheeks as he gazed back at me with an expression of bewildered expectancy.

'Craig,' I said, 'you're absolutely gorgeous. In any other circumstances I'd love to see your place, share your sack, snuggle down with you . . . loosen up, wriggle, wrestle, whatever. But you've said it yourself, I'm Billy's boy. I'm hanging out for Billy. Can't take the risk.'

In the pause that followed, the gleam in his eye faded and turned to a wry smile. He shrugged, scratched his brow, shook his head. Then, with a small sigh, he reached out and patted me fondly on the cheek.

'Ah, that's sad. So sad. And what's the point? Like I say, it's all a delusion, Matt. You're wasting yourself.'

'Perhaps,' I said, 'but I want to give it a go. Can't know till I've tried, can I?'

Billy did not drink himself into a stupor, nor was it difficult to separate him from the others at closing time. We went home together, slept till noon and then made love. At which point the weekend was already drawing to a close, the sand in the glass running out. In fact, there was barely enough time to fit in an afternoon stroll to Kingsley Lodge, a modest stately home with well-tended flower-beds and an elegant tea room.

So Craig's prediction proved false – though his words stayed with me, shadowing my thoughts. I kept seeing the disquieting twist in his smile. He knew the score better than I. Should I respect his streetwise savvy, or dismiss it as mere machination? *Was* I deluded, chasing rainbows, or was *he* lying – putting doubts in my mind, pouring poison in my ear, for his own purposes? These questions nagged me as I drove southward through the night.

What a crowded weekend it had been. But then again, how brief. No sooner arrived than over. Were Billy and I any closer? Hard to say. So little time, so little space. Snatching at pleasure seemed to override any chance we had to get to know each other. And as the dazzling motorway lights sped past me, splintering in the refracting glass of the windscreen, I wondered how long this fragile arrangement could last.

It was on Clare's prompting that I acted to relieve the pain.

'So what do you want?' she asked.

'I want to be with him. And not just at weekends, but all the time.'

'Well, tell him that. Invite him to come and live here for a trial run. No one will object. And if it works out, you can then look around for somewhere more suitable.'

'But isn't it too soon?'

'Good God, man! Strike while the iron is hot. He who hesitates is lost, as Addison put it.' She reached for her dictionary of quotations. 'At least I think it was Addison.'

'You're absolutely right,' I said, kissing her warmly on the cheek. 'You *and* Addison.'

But I had worked it out for myself. It was simply a matter of testing the water. What I needed was for Clare to give the plan her blessing. With Clare behind me I could proceed with confidence. With her backing I felt licensed to speak to the others, to put the proposal to Billy. I was invigorated and immediately formed a plan of action. I would call an extraordinary meeting for the following evening and get the reaction of the others to what I had in mind. I was moderately optimistic. For, as she rightly said, who could reasonably object? After all, long-term guests were a regular feature of the place.

Well, Eddie would object, in all probability. But unfairly and just to be awkward. And the others would oppose him: largely in reaction to his provocation, though apparently on a point of principle and in pursuit of reason and justice. It would be a stormy session, but in the end his resistance would be worn down. I would then have the green light, the go-ahead to speak to Billy at the weekend.

We met at six the following evening. I had called for an early start, expecting a long, drawn-out affair. Dan and Boo

Boo were absent, as usual, but the system at Gordon Street was that decisions were carried if more than half the members were present. Absentees could of course attempt to reverse decisions at a later date. Those present listened to me in polite silence. In general, they seemed tired. Only Clare and Mary showed any positive response, nodding occasionally to signal their interest and sometimes managing a sympathetic smile. Eddie sat with his eyes closed and a look of stony indifference.

I gazed around after my little speech. 'Would anyone like to comment?'

Eddie got up. He rose slowly and expansively, with his usual theatrical self-display. 'Is that it? You called a meeting for *that*? Christ, I thought it was something important. Well, I've got fuck all to say. As a matter of fact, I don't give a gnat's bollocks. So if you don't mind, I'll get back to my salami sandwich and crossword.' And snatching up his newspaper, he stomped off to an exchange of amused glances.

Mary said: 'I'm sure I'll be fine with Billy – it is Billy, isn't it? – as long as we share the same karma.'

I smiled, she smiled. I cast my eye around the room for any further contributions. Drew shrugged, Andy shrugged. Clare beamed at me. It seemed the meeting was over. Class dismissed.

So far, so good. But then a setback occurred: the Morris failed its test. Extensive repairs were required to bring it up to standard; the necessary parts were not immediately available; it would not be ready for collection until after the weekend. So my plan to speak to Billy would have to be postponed. After all, we needed to discuss this matter face to face and in some depth, not by means of brief, late-night chats on the telephone. I was dismayed. In my keenness to know what his response would be, in my anxiety to get this thing settled, the ten-day separation seemed an eternity, the delay intolerable. Once again, it seemed, we were calling to each other across a wide gulf. I was full of fears. Between here and there, between now and then, great changes could occur. I had met Billy's friends, seen how potentially marginal I was to his life. I had to assert myself, make my presence felt. I had to act quickly.

But then it came in a flash. The solution lay close to hand. On my very desktop, in fact. Why had I not thought of it before? I could write a letter. I could make use of pen and paper, those old friends that had served so well in the past and withered in the age of the telephone. I felt inspired and began immediately. I wrote swiftly and spontaneously, the lines coming almost unbidden, the words gushing forth in an embarrassing torrent, an unimpeded headlong sprawl. And when I read over what I'd written, I was amazed. I could still do it; I'd not forgotten. The expression was not polished, but it had flow. There was scarcely a slip, a blot, a scratching out.

Dear Billy,

I'm trying to imagine where you might be as you read this. Are you in your room? That room that I'm so fond of? Perhaps seated at your desk, relaxing on the sofa, or even lying in bed? Oh God, how I wish I was there and not here. Or alternatively, that you were here and not there. I'm feeling so miserable at the moment as a result of this wretched car business – which I won't go into now because I intend to tell you about it when I phone tonight. But that's part of the problem, isn't it, love? The phone calls. Those few precious moments of conversation in the early hours. They're so brief, so meagre, so unsatisfactory. And you sound a million miles away. The phone is not the place to say what I want to say. I need space, I need room to expand. And that's why I've decided to write.

So then, what I want to say right off, love, is that I'm so happy when I'm with you. When I'm with you, I'm happier than I've ever been. I know we've known each other for just a brief while, but already I feel I can't live without you. Does that sound crazy, or do you have similar feelings? And could you imagine giving up your job, your room, the whole of your present way of life, to come here and live with me? I was speaking to Clare, the friend I mentioned, about all of this and her advice was not to hold back, but to act now, to tell you exactly how I feel and what I want. And what I want is for us to live together . . .

I finished the letter in a single sitting and posted it immediately. But when I phoned him later that evening I didn't mention it. To do so would have meant saying why I had written, and this was not the moment. It was ten to midnight. I didn't want to raise the topic against a background of smoke and noise from the bar. I wanted him to consider my proposal in tranquillity, not in his usual after-hours state of late-night fatigue.

'Hi, love. Got rid of them yet?'

'Have I hell! It's been diabolical here tonight. Hughie McNab got rat-assed and threw a punch at Patrick. We've had the police. They've just carried him off to the cells.'

'Oh no, what a drag!'

'Absolutely.'

'Well, in that case my news is even more unwelcome. Look, love, I'm afraid I can't make it at the weekend. The Morris has failed its test. It's at the garage and won't be ready for pick-up until next week.'

Silence.

Then: 'Wow, that's a bit of a blow.'

'I know, I know, it's a bummer. I'm as depressed as you are.'

A long pause.

'The truth is,' I said, 'I could do with a new vehicle.'

'Matt, love,' he broke in, 'I'm really sorry about this but I can't hang about. Patrick's gone home, I'm on my own and I'm already dead on my feet.'

'Okay, okay, that's fine. You get back to whatever you were doing and then get some sleep.'

'You too, love.'

'Sweet dreams, babe. Same time tomorrow night?'
'Yeah,' he said. 'And it's my turn. *I'll* phone you.'

The following evening Clare invited us all to listen to a play on the radio. It was a new play about the political troubles in Ireland. Clare's family are Irish, though they've been living in England for many years now and she herself was born here. She made the suggestion at supper, and there were nods of interest. So just before nine o'clock, when it was due to begin, about eight of us gathered in the sitting room, some curling up in armchairs, others squatting on the floor. The company included a couple of Australian women, friends of Mary who were crashing on her floor for a few days, and Drew's new girlfriend Bonnie. The old pine chest that stood in the middle of the room and served as a rough kind of table was laden with drinks and glasses, including several cans of lager and two half-finished bottles of Spanish plonk. The play focused on three characters who are caught up in the sectarian violence and whose families are torn apart by it. It was compellingly written and acted, and also blazingly topical: the troubles, given recent events, were especially hot news at the time. Yet I couldn't quite keep my mind on it. I kept thinking about Billy. Had he received my letter? And if so, how was he reacting? I looked around the room. Everyone was listening with fierce concentration, clearly absorbed by the drama and gripped by the taut, angry dialogue. Clare caught my eye. She seemed to sense that my mind was distracted, that I had 'troubles' of my own. I smiled at her, and she smiled back.

When the play ended we all glanced round, nodding silently.

'Powerful stuff,' said Drew.

We all murmured in agreement. Further comments followed, although the discussion soon broke down into smaller units. I remained detached, however; in fact, for much of the time I was preoccupied with my own thoughts. But then Clare got up to help herself to another drink and came to squat on the floor beside me.

'You're very quiet tonight.' She looked at me narrowly. 'What's going on?'

I flashed her a worried smile.

'I've written to Billy. And I'm wondering if I've scared him off.'

'So you've not heard back?'

'Well, I'm not sure that he's had the letter yet. It was only yesterday that I posted it.'

She patted my hand reassuringly. 'Look, you've done the right thing. It's better that it's out in the open. I'm sure no harm's been done. In fact, I think you'll be brought closer.'

Shortly after this she went off to her room, saying she must get back to work. And this seemed like an appropriate moment for me to leave too. So, excusing myself in similar fashion, I said goodnight to the others and slipped away. In my room I paced to and fro for a while and then tried to read the next chapter of my book. Finally, I stretched out on the bed and stared up at the ceiling with my hands behind my head. I was anxious to stay awake. Billy would call in the next hour and I needed to listen out for the phone in the hall – the only one in the house. I had left the door of my room slightly ajar, but probably someone would get there before me. Most calls to the house were followed by the sound of someone shouting up the stairs.

Eventually, out of concern not to miss the call, I went back to the sitting room, which was now empty. I flopped into the armchair nearest the open door and made myself comfortable by tucking my legs up under me. I had brought my book. The phone was just a few yards away, but in any case there were other people around. I could hear voices in the kitchen. Was that Andy and Mary? It was difficult to tell – the kitchen was some way off, at the end of the passage. So I tried to read; and this time, by some miracle, I succeeded. In fact, after a while I became totally lost, completely absorbed. It was Andy who eventually brought me back to my surroundings. Passing the door some time later, he peered in and raised an eyebrow.

'What this? No home to go to?'

'Expecting a call,' I grinned.

He gave a thumbs-up. 'Lucky old you,' he quipped as he trudged off up the stairs.

But I glanced at my watch. It was now twenty past twelve. The discovery came with an abrupt sense of shock. Billy was not going to phone. So what had happened? He had promised. And anyway we always spoke to each other at around this time. We had never missed a night.

It was my letter. That was the reason. What other could there be? He had received it today, it had thrown him into total confusion, he was thoroughly embarrassed by it.

But then again, maybe not. Perhaps he was simply reluctant at this late hour to talk about it. Perhaps he was tired, or not in the mood. This was a huge change that I was proposing, and he needed time to consider it. I understood all that. But why not tell me? Why leave me dangling? Why retreat into silence?

With these thoughts passing and re-passing through my mind, I sat for a further ten minutes and then took myself off to bed.

This was new territory for me. Oh, not entirely new – I'd passed through similar experiences, though nothing strictly comparable; nothing that involved anything quite so desperate as sitting beside a telephone, waiting for it to ring. But there had been hard times. When I was fifteen, for instance, my parents sent me away to boarding school. I'm not sure why; they could ill afford it. Was it to strengthen my character, or did they simply want me out of the way? Well, let's be charitable; let's assume they believed they were doing their best for me.

Wickham's occupies a large mansion, set in its own grounds, in a remote corner of Devon beside the River Tamar. I presume it's still there, though I've never been back. Parts of the main block date from the seventeenth century, but the current building is mostly made up of later additions, and the site as a whole is ungainly, a clumsy hotchpotch. The founder, Brinsley Wickham, died some years before my arrival and a portrait of him hangs in the entrance hall. It shows an austere, dark-suited greybeard with rimless glasses, sitting bolt upright in a book-lined study.

I hated the place: the mustiness, the broken furniture, the food, the cross-country running, the whole sadistic regime. The best of the teaching staff were eccentric, the worst were barking mad. Most of them were eternal schoolboys, whose chances of survival in the outside world were slim. I remember a newcomer, a bright young man who came to teach music after years of working in a bank. He was a breath of fresh air, but he didn't last long. In fact, he left after just six months. And where did he go? We never found out. According to rumour he became a travelling salesman. He was far too sane for us; or that's how I reasoned it. He lacked the required thick skin, the protective hard skull, the necessary brutality.

My life changed at this time. Up to this point, if not exactly a happy child, I had been at least reasonably gregarious and popular. Now I was a loner. Well, not a total solitary. Throughout those dark adolescent years I tended to drift along in the company of a tall bespectacled boy called Stebbings, a dedicated swot who was always known simply by his surname. Clever, capable, reserved, he too was out on a limb: an oddity with an aloof smile. We shared a love of books, a dislike of strenuous exercise and a hard sardonic attitude to pretty well everything. We were never really close, however, and sometimes I felt that he regarded me with deep suspicion. Well, I couldn't blame him for that, could I? After all, I was a mystery to myself. Why, for instance, could I not take my eyes off the back of Willoughby's neck? Why did I linger in the changing room whenever he was taking a shower? And why, to come to the fundamental question, was I so excited by the shape of his arse?

Meanwhile, I was learning. Oh, not from sex education or the media. This was 1972. News of the revolution had crossed the Pond, but had not yet penetrated as far as the Tamar Valley. No, I was picking up scraps of information from books, though admittedly anything substantial was in short supply. In the school library, for instance, I stumbled on a brief but fascinating profile of André Gide in an introduction to French literature – a frustrating discovery, as it turned out, for there were no books by Gide in the library, and apparently no other references to him. But the thing that really sticks in my mind is a novel, a dog-eared paperback that I picked up in a secondhand bookshop in Tavistock. It was a thriller, heavily indebted to Dostoevsky and Hitchcock, about two young men who commit a murder out of curiosity; and although somewhat disturbed by the story, I recognised the relationship instantly. 'So you're not alone,' I thought, relieved to find that I had an existence, if only in fiction.

A turning point came at summer camp. One evening we were seated round a fire, singing songs. There was a slight chill in the air, and after a while the boy sitting next to me – Harry Alderton, his name – drew me close, put an arm round my neck and wrapped us both in the blanket that was draped round his shoulders. This was no more than a friendly gesture, I now realise, and therefore a perfectly innocent thing to do. But whether or not it aroused suspicion, it certainly aroused *me*. So much so, that I found it alarming, if not impossibly daring, and from that moment I was Harry's devoted admirer. I mooned around him, always sat near him, sought any chance to be in his company. And after summer camp the worship continued. Back at school I would slip chocolate to him during lessons, follow him to the library, leave notes for him in his locker. Eventually, although we had little in common except a fondness for cats and a taste for chocolate, the friendship developed to the point where he took me home for the weekend. He had a large family, and as there was no spare room in the house, we had to share his small bed. Nothing happened, of course; he couldn't have been less interested. I simply remember the smell of him: the warmth that he gave off as he lay snoring beside me.

In the middle of the night he grew restless and eventually got up. 'Can't sleep,' he whispered, touching me gently on the shoulder. 'I'm moving to the sofa.'

But my attachment didn't cool. If anything, it increased. Back at Wickham's I continued to follow him around, doting in secret.

Then came grief and loss. The following term he suddenly left. His father, who worked for an insurance company, was posted to Chicago, and the family went with him. It was a blow from which I've never quite recovered. Though there was never any future in it, Harry was my first love. I still think fondly of him – of that whole time – and jealously guard the pain.

I was bad-tempered at work the following day. It was not just that I had a lot on my mind and had spent a sleepless night. No, the stresses of the working day were also higher than usual. First, Tony phoned in to warn us that he'd be late coming to work. His four-year-old daughter had a temperature and needed to see a doctor. He couldn't say *how* late, but from experience of this kind of thing Maggie and I estimated eleven-thirty at the earliest – which, as things turned out, was an optimistic forecast. Next, two inspectors from Social Services turned up on a surprise visit. Armed with notepads, they poked into every corner of the workplace, demanding to see accounts, records, files. Their unexpected arrival was bad news in itself, but to crown it all I couldn't lay hands on my diary. I found it later in the day, tucked down the side of the sofa in the tearoom. At which point it was far too late to soften their disapproving looks.

At home that evening, I flopped on my bed and fell asleep for about an hour, before being roused by the sound of someone knocking hard on my door. I sprang up and flung it open. Clare was standing outside, looking puzzled.

'Welcome to the land of the living,' she said, sounding slightly cross.

'Sorry, I'm shattered. It's been a really hard day.'

'Oh dear.' She tried to look sympathetic. 'Anyway, look, there's a call for you.'

'A call?' I came to my senses with a jolt. I planted a kiss

on her cheek and bounded down the stairs. 'Thanks a lot,' I threw over my shoulder. But as I approached the phone my excitement turned to apprehension. I hesitated before picking up the receiver.

'Hullo.'

'Hullo. Is that Matt?'

'Yes . . . Is that you, Billy?'

'Hey, whoa there. I'm afraid not. This is Patrick.'

'Patrick.'

I couldn't quite hide my disappointment, although, as he must have guessed, I was also burning with curiosity. What was I about to hear, good news or bad? And why was Patrick the messenger? Was I about to be brushed off by means of a third party? My mind was speculating wildly.

'Billy asked me to call you.' I felt my heart tighten, as if a fist were squeezing it. 'He told me to tell you that he's off work at the moment with a bug of some kind. Nothing serious, though . . . so not to worry.'

'Off work? So that's why he didn't call last night.'

'Yeah. He's sorry about that. He'll call when he can.'

'Is that it? No further message?'

'No . . . Why? . . . What were you expecting?'

'I wondered . . .' The news was frustratingly brief, tantalisingly incomplete. 'Oh, well . . . it's nothing. I mean, forget it.' I stumbled into silence, struggling to think what more I could squeeze out of this meagre exchange. 'Look, Patrick, you will keep me informed, won't you? My car's off the road at the moment, but if Billy needs someone to look after him, I'll certainly find some way to get there.'

'Sure, mate, no problem.'

'And give him my love.'

'I will. Must go now, Matt. The customers are growling.'

'Yeah, I can hear them. Bye, Patrick. Thanks for the call.'

The next few days were an absolute torment. In expectation of another call, I was on constant alert. But none came. Nor could I reach anyone at the pub. I rang every night at my usual time and held on, but I seemed to be trying to summon the dead. Then, on Sunday, in desperation, I rang at lunchtime. And on this occasion someone did lift the receiver. I held my breath.

'Black Whoorse.'

It was a man's voice, but not one I recognised. A deep husky voice, with a strong Geordie accent.

'Oh, hullo. Could I speak to Billy, please?'

'No, lad. Billy's not heah, Ahm afraid.'

'Well, in that case, perhaps I could speak to Patrick?'

'Ee, ya're clean ootta luck, man. Patrick's not aroond eetha. Can Ah tyek a message?'

'Er . . .' I hesitated. 'Well yeah, if you would. It's a message for Billy. Would you tell him Matt phoned.'

'Uhuh. Ah'll dee tha. Matt, is it?'

'And sends his love.'

'Sorry, Ah divvnae quite catch. Was that . . . ?'

'Yeah, that's right. As in Oscar and Bosie.'

'Gotcha . . . Areet, man . . . Is tha it, then?'

'Yeah, that's it. Thanks a lot. Bye.'

I replaced the receiver and sat for a few minutes on the lower stair, mulling over this conversation and the events of the past few days. What on earth was going on? Who was the guy I'd just spoken to, where was Patrick, and why was it so difficult to get anyone to answer my calls? Certainly it was a relief to have spoken to someone, even if a total stranger; phoning the pub recently had been a bit like hallooing the Marie Celeste. But I was not too confident that Billy would get my message, and disquieted by intimations that big changes were occurring in his life, over which I had no influence or control. One thing was clear, though: I had no option now but to wait. There was nothing more I could do. I chewed my nails for a while and then, weighed down with these depressing thoughts, got up and wandered, dazed and disconsolate, into the kitchen. Mary was there, removing a tray from the oven with the help of huge protective gloves.

'Good timing,' she said, 'I need someone to sample these peanut and cow-parsley cakes.' And she thrust them rather insistently under my nose. To tell the truth, I sometimes have doubts about Mary. Is she as innocent as she looks?

Anyway, I told no one about this recent breakdown in communication. As a way of ending the isolation I was tempted to tell Clare, but I didn't want to burden her again with my problems. Besides, it might be just a blip. Was I making too much of a merely temporary setback? I was conscious of being withdrawn and edgy, both at home and at work, but if anyone noticed this, they didn't say anything. Getting to work was a struggle too, although once there I found that the demands of the job took my mind off any personal concerns. On Monday I went to a late-night showing of *Red River* at the cinema on the far side of the common. I wanted to flee the house, lose myself, be transported. I was in danger of becoming a haunted figure, addicted to the sound of the telephone. Nevertheless, when I got home at half-past twelve, I checked hastily to see if there was a message for me, and found, to my bitter disappointment, just a few words scribbled on the pad in Andy's headlong scrawl: *Eddie, Pru says you still owe her for the meal at McGuire's*.

On Tuesday the garage phoned me at work to say the Morris was ready for pick up, and when I arrived at five that evening the mechanic went through the invoice item by item, explaining what he'd done to bring it up to standard. I was dismayed at the size of the bill, which came to just over two hundred pounds.

'It gets heavier every year,' I complained, adding in muttered undertones that perhaps it was time to take my custom elsewhere.

He shrugged. 'Or change your car. Actually, I could show you a nice little Peugeot. New in today. Low mileage. One lady owner.'

I gave a twisted smile and shook my head in despair.

When I got back to the house I met Clare in the hall. She was slipping out to do some shopping. She greeted me cheerfully and asked what sort of day I'd had. 'Best if we let that pass,' I said. We exchanged a few more polite remarks and then, excusing myself with as much grace as I could muster, I stormed up the stairs. In my room I ripped open an envelope addressed to me that I'd taken from the hall table and found myself staring at an invitation to join a sauna club in Surbiton. Singles welcome. I tossed it into the bin and then fell back on my bed. I was feeling hellishly low. In fact just about as low as I'd ever felt. Yes, I now had the Morris back and presumably in good repair, but would there be anyone at the Black Horse to welcome me when I got there?

Half an hour later my centre of consciousness had moved from my head to my stomach, so I got up and wandered downstairs in search of something to eat. But as I passed through the hall on my way to the kitchen the phone began to ring, and with casual off-handedness (there was a call at Number 7 every fifteen minutes, and it was usually for someone else) I reached out and snatched the receiver off the hook.

'Hullo.'

'Hi there. Could I speak to Matt, please? Is he around?'

The voice was unmistakable, but so totally unexpected that for a moment I was struck dumb.

'Billy?'

'Matt?'

'Oh, thank God! Where the hell have you been, love? I'm out of my mind.'

'Matt, it's a long story. You did you get my message, didn't you?'

'But that was last Friday. It's now Tuesday.'

'Yeah, I'm sorry, it's complicated.' He paused for a few moments. 'Look, the thing is, I'm at Arthur's. I've been staying here since the weekend.'

'Staying with Arthur?'

'Matt, I can't discuss this at the moment.' He paused again, as if waiting for my response, but I was too surprised and confused to speak. 'Anyway, the good news is I'll be back at work tomorrow, so I'll call you at the usual time. We could talk then. In the meanwhile, I just want you to know that I'm okay.'

'Billy, I don't understand.'

'Leave it, love, please. I can't talk now.'

Was Arthur within earshot?

'I realise that, but – '

'Matt, please, we'll speak tomorrow. Take care, love, and bye for now.'

A click at the end of the line brought the conversation abruptly to an end. And suddenly I was alone again, like someone waving from an empty platform at a train that had just disappeared into a tunnel. For a few moments I kept the receiver clamped to my ear, as if by doing so I could bring Billy back. I was aghast at the brevity of the exchange and almost mad with frustration. How could I bear another day of this waiting? There was so much to say, so much to hear, so much to discuss. I was distressed by what I'd heard, too. Staying with Arthur? Why turn for help to that insidious creep? Slowly, painfully, I replaced the receiver and went to sit on the lowest stair. Cradling my head in my hands as if nursing my churned-up thoughts, I stared dolefully at a point on the floor. And it was here that Clare caught me some minutes later on her return from the shops. I looked at her glumly.

'I take it your day hasn't improved,' she said. 'Come on, let me cheer you up with some jasmine tea and a slice of Madeira. You can tell me all about it.'

And after Harry, what? Well, quite a few years after Harry, there was Antonio. Not his real name, just my attempt to glamorise him. Actually I'm not sure that I ever knew his real name. The name he went by, I suspect, was an alias. He was a waiter, and not remotely Italian, I hasten to add, though he worked in a bright new pizza parlour in Kensington. No, he was unmistakably Anglo-Saxon and from Chiswick. And me? I was still a student when I met him, pursuing a qualification in social work. He was quite a bit older than me, and nothing special to look at, though his strong hairy hands and flirty eyes were irresistible.

We met on the tube one morning. The carriage was packed to the gills, we were crushed together, and I apologised for treading on his foot. He shrugged, fixed me with his slow mesmeric smile, and brought his hand into contact with mine by sliding it along the rail. My face went suddenly hot and I looked away. Then, at Waterloo, he followed me off the train. In the street I glanced over my shoulder and spotted him. He had me in his sights and was sauntering through the crowd just a few yards behind. He caught up with me as I waited at the crossing. Came and stood right next to me, in fact. I saw him arrive, glimpsed him from the corner of my eye, but ignored him. A few moments later he brought his mouth close to my ear.

'Anyone for tennis?' he breathed.

We went to a greasy spoon for coffee.

Here he told me a lot of things that were almost certainly untrue: that he was a blues guitarist in a small outfit; that he had once owned a nightclub in Finsbury; that he knew George Best. For, as I soon learned, he was a compulsive and inventive liar, always keen to impress and quite shameless. Actually, I'm not sure that I believed anything he said even at the time, but his boyish ways and rampant horniness made me forgiving and indulgent. So I accepted the invitation to eat at his restaurant that evening and afterwards we strolled back to my room. I was living in Fulham in those days, in a two-storey apartment that I shared with three other students.

Sex with Antonio was always hot and must have been audible throughout the whole house, a suspicion that was confirmed one morning when a fellow lodger asked, with a sly smile, if I'd had a good night. One thing bothered me, though: he always leaped from the bed, pulled on his pants and left soon after the climax. And though I showed my disappointment, pleaded with him to stay, he always ignored my protests. Nor would he explain his behavior; or, at least, not to my satisfaction. I simply didn't believe his claim that he was incapable of sleeping anywhere but in his own bed. At first I learned to live with it, but as my emotional attachment grew, the more acute the problem became. 'Okay,' I said one night (I used to meet him in a bar after work), 'you can only sleep in your own bed? So let's change routine and go to your place.' He frowned, looked uneasy, began to fidget. Oh no, that was not possible. His vigilant landlady lived on the premises and allowed no visitors. He couldn't take the risk.

Poppycock, I thought. But said nothing.

Then one night I surprised him. It was a night when we had arranged not to meet. He had some repairs to do on his bike – or so he said. I was deeply suspicious. Was he now tired of me and seeing someone else? I was convinced of it. So convinced, in fact, that curiosity drove me to spy on him. At closing time that evening I hid in the doorway of a shop opposite the restaurant, and when at last he emerged it was in the company of a woman and two small children. The group was full of excited chatter. They crossed the road, drew near and passed the doorway without seeing me or even glancing in my direction. I let them walk on for a while and then ran after them.

'Hi, Antonio,' I called.

They all stopped and turned.

'Antonio?' exclaimed the woman with a snort of amusement.

But he handled it superbly. He was Mister Cool – all the way from his arched brows to his suede boots.

'Sorry, mate,' he said. 'I'm afraid you've got the wrong guy.'

Shortly after this he and I broke up. Or rather *I* broke off with *him*. He, of course, was all for keeping the show on the road, but I was not prepared to be a late-night diversion from Marion and the kids. There's nothing in this for me, I told him. He didn't understand, though. He was genuinely baffled by all the fuss. Then, as the writing on the wall became clear, he tried to woo me back with a show of tenderness and affection. And when the final rupture came, he wept.

It was a wrench for me too. I was miserable for weeks. I missed him enormously and suffered sleepless nights, as well as bouts of self-pity. Nor could I concentrate. My studies became an intolerable burden and I came close to abandoning the course. In fact, everything lost its meaning, and for a while there seemed nothing to live for. Though I never again set foot in the restaurant, I was sorely tempted to go back: to plead, grovel, start afresh.

Then one morning in early March I woke feeling different. I got up and peered through the blinds. There was spring sunshine on the lawn, and clumps of daffodils in the flower-beds were fluttering in the breeze. I did some vigorous bending and stretching and tucked into a bowl of cornflakes. But it was not until I snapped on the radio and began to listen with interest that I knew.

Yes, it was over.

Billy called at just after eleven the following evening. He sounded tired, but relieved to be on the mend and much more relaxed than the night before. We began with an easy preamble, swapping bits of news but carefully avoiding any headlong plunge into the things that were most on our mind. He gave me a brief account of his illness. I asked after Giles and Big Ron, Terry, Craig and Baz, and we then fell silent. At which point we would normally have called it a night and looked forward to seeing each other at the weekend. But now the silence was pregnant, our consciousness of big things unsaid, of gaping holes in the conversation, palpable. I waited, feeling a need to tread warily, anxious not to sound too obsessive. And eventually *he* took the lead.

'Got your letter.'

'Ah yeah, my letter. Sorry about that.'

'Why sorry? It's beautiful.'

'Yeah, but . . .'

'No, it's me that should apologise.'

'Why should *you* apologise?'

'Because I don't know what to say, do I? I'm lost for words. I mean, no one's ever written me such a letter.'

'No need to say anything yet, there's no rush. I'm just asking you to think about it.'

'I *am* thinking. But you're right – I need time.'

'Sure. Take whatever time you need.'

'It's a big move, Matt. This is where I was born. My life, my friends, are here.'

'I know, I know. And it's too soon. We've known each other for just a few weeks. But I had to write, Billy. I'm quite sure in my own mind and I'd hate to lose you.'

It seemed an age before he replied; I waited nervously.

'Yeah, I understand. And like I say, it's a beautiful letter.' Then, after a period of silence: 'Look, it's been good to talk, Matt, but I'm dog-tired now. Honestly, dead on my feet. Can we continue this at the weekend?'

'Of course, love. Good night. I miss you so much. But it's been a great relief just to hear your voice.'

'Night, Matt. Sleep well. Missing you loads too.'

I waited, and after a pause there came the familiar click at the end of the line.

But if I usually dreaded this moment, this severing of our fragile link, tonight it was less painful. That final exchange, however brief and tentative, had raised my spirits. I felt suddenly better, better than I'd felt for days, and for several minutes I stood in the hall, rapt in thought. Then gales of laughter from the kitchen struck my ears and I looked up. Clare, Drew and Mary were having a lively midnight huddle. The noisy disruption shook me out of my trance and I strolled down the hall to join in the fun.

'Where for breakfast? Somewhere new?'

'No, Dylan's as usual. I'm thoroughly attached to the place. Fond memories.'

We were in bed, staring at the ceiling, enjoying a relaxed post-coital moment. His head was resting in the crook of my shoulder, and from time to time he'd kiss my neck or gently nick my earlobe. Yes, it was Saturday again, the sun was high, and our recent lovemaking had been all the more pleasurable for having been postponed. Eight hours earlier, passion had yielded to the need for sleep. Held up on my journey by a mysterious build-up of traffic, I had arrived at the Black Horse at around midnight. At which point I had been introduced to Stan and Betty, the landlord and his wife, who had just returned from a trip to Marbella. So it was not until two hours later, after much chat about the pros and cons of the Spanish licensing laws and the consumption of several ruinous glasses of brandy, that Billy and I had tumbled into bed and into a state of immediate unconsciousness.

At Dylan's, we decided that we were not hungry. Billy confessed to feeling slightly queasy, probably from the effects of the previous night, and I nodded in sympathy. We ordered a couple of strong black coffees, and the talk turned immediately to Stan and Betty, their habits and foibles, before moving on to Spain. Billy had never been to Spain. Would he like to go? Yes, certainly; to anywhere abroad, but Spain sounded ideal. The conversation shifted again, to food we'd eaten, films we'd seen, the kinds of music we liked. Meanwhile, the thing we had promised to discuss hung in the air, unmentioned. We seemed reluctant to speak about it. Was this the right moment? Probably not. Why raise it now? Why not simply wallow in the pleasure of being together? There would be time. Later today . . . or tomorrow.

Curiosity got the better of me on a quite different point, however.

'How's Patrick?' I asked.

'Patrick?' He sounded bemused. 'Oh, haven't I said? Patrick's gone. He went in a hurry. Stan accused him of putting his fingers in the till. Gave him the boot.'

'What?' I stared at him. 'Stealing from the till ? Do you believe that?'

He shrugged. 'Dunno. Stan believes it and that's what counts.'

'Well, what a turn!' I shook my head in a daze. 'How *is* Patrick? Have you seen him?'

'I've seen him a couple of times. He's angry and upset, of course. Bitter, in fact. But I've not really discussed it with him. He refuses to talk about it. I heard through the grapevine that he might go back to Belfast.'

We lapsed into silence, as if out of respect for Patrick.

'So what are we going to do with the rest of this day?' I said at last. It seemed a change of subject was needed to dispel the gloom that had come over us.

He glanced at his watch. 'There's the lunch-hour shift. But I'm off again at two. Perhaps you could pick me up? We could take a stroll through the market. It's a lively scene on Saturday.'

'How long have we got exactly?'

He grimaced. 'I'm back on at six, I'm afraid.'

The market was a permanent feature of Market Square, though much bigger and noisier on Saturdays than during the week. The long-established stallholders, dealers in local produce, cakes, books and hardware, were clustered around the central fountain. They were outnumbered, however, by the visiting traders, whose stalls were pitched on the outer edge and reached into the side streets. Here we found portable radios, clothes pegs, deckchairs, cigarette lighters, antique clocks and fancy crockery, although the stall that attracted most attention was a travelling joke shop, specialising in itching powder, plastic tarantulas and water-spouting bow ties. It was a pleasant afternoon, the heat of midsummer made bearable by a scattering of fleecy white clouds. We strolled around for a while and Billy bought a luxuriant pot plant for his room. We then sat at a table outside Goodman's, the café on the square, and ordered a pot of Darjeeling from a jaded teenage waitress who kept hitching up the skirt of her ill-fitting uniform.

'Well, well,' said Billy. 'Look who's here.'

I glanced round. It was Craig and Terry. Craig had a rectangular mirror in a pine frame tucked under one arm. Terry was hugging a large pink teddy bear.

'Still together then,' said Craig, tipping me a wink. 'How long is it now?'

Billy and I smiled at each other and shrugged.

Terry pointed to the bear. 'What d'ya think?'

'Absolute tat,' said Billy. 'You're a pathetic junk freak, girl.'

She and Craig threw back their heads and brayed loudly.

'Why not draw up some chairs and join us?' I said. 'I

could order some more tea.'

Craig glanced at his watch and threw an enquiring look at Terry.

'Better not,' she said. 'We need to get home and make ourselves beautiful. See you at the club tonight?'

'That depends,' said Billy.

'Ahah.' Craig tapped his nose. 'Say no more.'

Another gust of laughter and they moved off, chuckling and waving.

Billy and I smiled at each other and settled back into companionable silence. It was perfect bliss, this sunlit break, this lazy four-hour interval between shifts. I was keenly aware, though, that it would soon be over, that time's winged chariot was at our backs. With world enough and time, I thought, I could content myself with this unhurried courtship, but Billy was due back at work in an hour, which left me yet again reluctant to burden these precious moments with my pressing concerns. Would there ever be a right moment to discuss my letter? I feared not. I sensed that the weekend was destined to slip away without our talking seriously about anything at all.

The market was now at its busiest and after a further ten minutes of watching the bustle, we decided to leave and take a stroll through the park before heading back to the pub. I offered to pay for the tea and looked around for the waitress. She was elusive, however, and whenever she did appear she was looking the other way. Eventually I got up and went into the café. The woman at the till was gossiping, so I hung about patiently and then coughed to signal my presence. Instantly she turned and smiled, as if in response to some irritating interruption. I presented the bill mutely and she glanced at it. Then, oozing false charm and scarcely breaking the flow of her talk, she rammed it onto a spike and held out her hand for the money.

It was only then, as I was making my way out, that I spotted him. He was there, in the seat next to Billy. An inescapable, weaselly presence, brazenly ensconced in *my* chair. His back was towards me, however, so I didn't immediately recognise him. Indeed, my first thought was that this was one of Billy's friends to whom I'd not been introduced. But when the penny dropped, I froze. In fact, I had to fight an impulse to turn on my heel and leave the building by the back door. But after some moments of hesitation, I swallowed deeply and walked out. As I approached the table I feigned surprise and greeted him with a curt nod, which was as much civility as I could manage. In return, he flicked his eyes over me and raised a sort of wry, ghostly smile. He then looked away, as if unable to give attention to anything so obviously beneath his notice.

'Back in the saddle, I see.' Was he addressing me, or the pigeon that had just landed on the bollard across the street? 'I understood you were laid up.'

'Nothing serious. Just a small setback.'

He gave a hollow chuckle. 'That's a shame. Thought we were shot of you.' His tone was sinisterly jocular.

'Nope. You'll have to try a bit harder. I don't scare easily.'

A rich guffaw. 'Oh, now that's dangerous talk. Don't get cocky, big boy.'

Billy leaped to his feet and snatched up his plant.

'We must go. I'm on duty in an hour.'

He gave Arthur a hard look, nodded to me and we walked off.

'I thought I might look in later,' Arthur flung after us. 'Keep an eye on things.'

I glanced over my shoulder. He was leaning back, poking at a tooth with a wooden pick. His eyes were focused on the far side of the square. There was a smirk on his face, a look of showy self-approval that made my palms itch.

I dined alone that evening in a quiet cellar bar that I found tucked away in a courtyard just off George Square. It was a decent meal, seriously impaired by the lack of Billy's company. What did Billy do for sustenance, anyway? Did he eat meals? It seemed to me that he lived, quite literally, from hand to mouth. I stayed till nine-thirty, reading my book mostly, but also chatting to a lively Italian student, a tireless raconteur who had amusing stories to tell about his quarrelsome family in Naples. I then strolled back to the Black Horse and went straight to Billy's room. I had resolved to give the bar a miss tonight. I had no wish to meet Arthur again.

An archway at the side of the pub led to a metal staircase giving access to all floors. I let myself in with the keys Billy had lent me and easily found my way up to his room. I looked around. It was strange being there alone. The scene was a mess. Clothes were scattered over the bed and sofa, a discarded newspaper littered the floor and there were unwashed cups everywhere. Yet somehow the place seemed all the more endearing for it and I made no attempt to clear up. I simply fell into one of the armchairs and settled back, feeling drowsy from the glass of wine I'd taken with the meal. And when I came to consciousness about ten minutes later, it was to find Billy standing over me, looking worried.

'Matt, are you okay? Sorry to wake you.'

'Hi, love.' I smiled at him sleepily and tried to stifle a yawn. 'Yeah, fine. Sorry, must've nodded off.'

'Matt, I've got a big favour to ask.'

I froze. A big favour? I struggled to sit up. 'Uhuh.'

'It's Arthur.' The name fell on my ears with a thud. I felt a sudden heaviness in my limbs. What now? Dark thoughts filled my mind, but I kept my mouth shut for fear of saying something I would later regret. 'He's not well. He's had another turn. Look, I know it's a lot to ask, but I wondered if you'd drive him home.'

I stared in amazement. Had I heard him correctly? I was still half asleep.

'Drive Arthur home?'

'Yes.'

I continued to stare. Speechless, uncomprehending.

'Billy,' I said at last, 'Arthur and I detest each other. You *know* that.'

'Okay, so forget *him*. I'm asking you to do it for me.'

For *me*? Phew, that was a sneaky one. How to answer

that? It was unfair. I flinched, squirmed in my seat, huffed. 'So what's wrong with a cab?'

'It's urgent, that's the thing. He needs to get home soon.'

'Look, I don't get this. Not well? Had another turn? What's that supposed to mean? Are you sure he's ill? He's a devious little shit. He's doing this to ruin our weekend.'

'It may be mostly in his mind, Matt, but he *is* unwell.'

'Mostly in his mind? Well, in that case an offer of help from me is likely to bring on a seizure or something.'

'Please, love.' His face had taken on a pleading look. 'For me.'

I went silent and glanced away. I was pinned and wriggling.

Reluctantly I struggled to my feet. 'I'll fetch the car. Tell him to wait outside the front entrance.'

He searched my face and snapped a kiss on my cheek.

The car was parked some distance away in a quiet turning off Bridge Street, so I had a fair walk to pick it up and it was not until twenty minutes later that I returned and drew up outside the main entrance. Some of the hardier clientele were drinking on the pavement in spite of the cool night, but I had no need to look for Arthur. He was standing conspicuously apart from the others and raised a hand to draw attention to himself as soon as I arrived. Then, stepping forward, he yanked open the passenger door, heaved himself into the seat beside me and looked straight ahead, lips firmly compressed, as though I were his regular hired driver and communication between us unnecessary.

I switched the engine off and waited. We sat in silence. I had made up my mind not to speak unless spoken to; to do nothing except by request. We could sit there until Christmas if need be. And when at last he spoke, it was in a flat, expressionless tone. 'Straight ahead,' he said. 'Then left at the top to the roundabout.' I switched the engine back on and drove off. I was boiling, yet determined to stay in control. It was essential not to give way; not to let him see how I felt; not to give him the satisfaction. We drove on and from time to time he gave further directions, all delivered with icy precision; control was the keynote of *his* bearing too. 'Second on the left. Straight on at the traffic lights. Right at the T-junction.' We turned into a street of bay-fronted bungalows and he indicated with a hand movement that I should slow down. 'This is it. The blue door with glass panels. Number 13.' He gave a low hollow chuckle, the one human utterance he made during the entire ride. 'Unlucky for some.'

I pulled up at a convenient space, and, without turning, waited for him to leave. I gazed resolutely through the windscreen, my eyes fixed on a fluttering street lamp. He made no movement, however, and for perhaps half a minute – though it seemed an eternity – we sat motionless and silent beside each other, while the tension, particularly in the confined space of the car, seemed to increase to breaking point. It was a contest: whose nerve would give first? I considered the options. I could ask him politely to go; or lunge at him with an ugly face; or get out, open the passenger door and haul him into the gutter.

But then, to my great relief, he spoke, though what he said was very far from what I expected to hear. 'Matt, we need to talk.'

I turned to face him. 'Really?' A derisive snort. 'Why? What's there to talk about?'

'Not here. Come inside.'

'Come inside?' I was full of paranoid suspicion. 'I don't bloody think so.'

His face went a funny colour. 'Look, Matt,' he muttered, turning suddenly devilish in that now-familiar way of his. 'We need to fucking *talk*.'

I looked away, silently wrestling with confused thoughts and torn between contrary impulses. On the one hand, I was keen to get this odious creature out of my hair, yet on the other I was burning to know what he had to say and have things out with him. So my decision took a while to arrive, and when it came, it felt involuntary. I simply found myself, so to speak, nodding and muttering, 'Okay, lead the way, but don't expect me to stay long.'

I remember very little about Arthur's house; I was too angry and tense to take much notice. He lived alone, so Billy had told me, although he had spent most of his life in the company of his mother. She had recently died, leaving the house and its contents to him. Certainly the place suggested that nothing had changed for decades. It was cluttered with heavy, dark-stained furniture and on every wall there was a large gilt-framed picture of a coastal view or seascape. He showed me into the living room and invited me to sit, but I declined. I simply stood and looked him in the eye, challenging him to make the first move. He met my look head-on and we held our ground for a while, appraising and outfacing each other like a pair of he-goats.

'I'll come straight to the point,' he said.

'Good. Please do.'

'Stop messing with him. You're fucking his life up.'

'I'm sure he can decide that for himself.'

'All this pressure, this flannel, this soft soap – he could do without it. That letter you wrote, for instance.'

'What the hell do you know about a letter I wrote?'

'There's not much gets past me.'

'Or me, for that matter.'

'Don't kid yourself, chum, you don't know the half of it. You think that boy's going to give up a lucrative patch to go traipsing after you?'

'Lucrative patch?'

'Oh, come on, Matilda.' A dark chuckle. 'You know the score. Let's just say there are blokes up here who are not short of a bob or two.'

'And you're always there for the whisper in the ear and the notes crushed into the palm.'

A broad grin. Then, in a high mocking falsetto: 'Dear me, what *are* you suggesting, young man? I don't think I like your tone.'

So far I'd hung on to my cool by the merest thread. Now I lost it.

'You warped maniac.' I felt my chest heave. 'You don't fool me. You're not really ill. This is a manoeuvre. You've tricked me here to put the screws on. Well, don't kid yourself, chum. It'll take more than a squalid little louse like you.'

'Oh really?' The twisted smile had disappeared. He was no longer amused. 'Look, pal, I've given you fair warning.' He fished around frantically in his jacket pocket, found a piece of paper and held it up in front of my nose. The name written on it meant nothing to me. 'Yeah, that's right, I've been doing some research. Now it's *my* turn to write a letter. Is this the guy you work for? I'm sure he'd be very interested to hear what you get up to at conferences.' He was poking me aggressively now, jabbing at my shoulder with a savage scowl on his face.

And suddenly it was all too much. The face thrust close to mine, the jabbing finger, the repellent physical presence. I felt a surge inside me, as some force seemingly separate from myself welled up and took over. The room started to spin and in an instant it just happened: my fist shot out and slugged him in the stomach. I heard him gasp, saw him clutch himself, and slowly, in an agony of slowness, crumple and fall to his knees, his arms clasped round his waist, his face contorted with pain. I watched all this with mingled triumph and horror, my mind exploding in a turmoil of sensations. But when I came to myself a few moments later, I stood staring at his folded body in stunned disbelief. With a smart turn, I marched quickly from the room and out of the house, slamming the door behind me.

I drove back to the pub in a frenzy, all the while intensely aware that I ought not to be driving, but desperate to put some distance between myself and Arthur as quickly as possible. My hands were shaking, and I clutched the steering wheel with conscious firmness. I was hoping against the odds that the parking space I had vacated half an hour earlier would still be free. Fortunately it was, though backing into it in my current state required several attempts. I let myself into the pub by the back door and went straight to Billy's room. I tossed the car keys onto the coffee table and flung myself into a chair. My mind was a seething cauldron, a riot of wild and contradictory thoughts that chased each other and spun off in all directions. How to explain myself to Billy? How would he react? Should I apologise? *Why* should I apologise? And what about Arthur? Was he seriously hurt? Surely not. The man was a sham, a trickster. But what would he do now? How had I got myself into this mess? Should I drive home immediately, flee this nightmare?

I don't remember how long I sat there. It was perhaps half an hour or more, but essentially I was unaware of time. In fact, I was so consumed by my own thoughts that the sound of footsteps on the stairs took me by surprise and put me into a state of mild panic. I turned and saw Billy coming towards me. He was smiling, though as he drew near his expression changed to a worried frown.

'Matt, are you okay? How did it go?'

'Not well – not well at all. Look, Billy, sit down – something's happened.'

He sat down and without further preliminaries I went straight in. I kept my account of the incident brief and direct. He listened in silence. I didn't flinch during the telling, nor apologise. I was angry, heaving with anger, and he could see it.

I finished and there was a long pause. Then he stood up, came across the room and knelt beside me. He caressed the back of my hand.

'This is my fault,' he said. 'But please believe me, I *was* concerned about him.'

'*Your* fault?' I scoffed. 'Not in my book.' I was breathing deeply, unable to meet his look.

He kissed my smouldering cheek. 'Yeah, whatever. Anyway, look. Keep calm. I'll phone now. Just to have a word, make sure he's okay.'

I nodded, and he smiled briefly before slipping downstairs to the upper landing. He was gone for perhaps ten minutes, during which time I paced the room like a caged panther, my hands tightly clasped behind my head, my neck muscles tensed hard against them. I could hear nothing except the drone of Billy's voice on the floor below, which drove me to speculate wildly on what was being said. I was still a mass of conflicting impulses: anger, curiosity, guilt. What dominated, though, was a sense that they were discussing me as an intruder, an outsider, a trouble-maker, that the two of them were sharing an intimacy that was denied to me. It was the reappearance of that suspicion, that insecurity and resentment that I had felt in conversation with Craig.

When Billy returned, he looked quite relaxed and unconcerned. I scanned his face feverishly.

'So what's the news?'

'Ah, he'll survive. He's indestructible.'

'So no injuries?'

'Nah, not really. I was just a bit worried about his heart.'

'His heart? I thought you said his troubles were mostly in the mind.'

'Well, they are . . . mostly.'

'Christ, *now* you tell me.'

'Relax, Matt.'

'Relax? I've just assaulted the man. He might prosecute.'

'No chance. He'd never get involved with the law.'

'That tricky bastard? He'd perjure himself to get me put away.'

Billy moved in close and put his arms around me.

'Anyway, for the moment, let's go to bed, love,' he sighed. 'We can talk about this in the morning.'

I looked deep into his face and saw that he was tired. Very tired. He looked dead-beat, in fact. And it seemed to me that he was right; we should leave it until the morning. So I nodded.

'Okay, let's go to bed,' I said, though with mixed feelings and a vague sense of dissatisfaction. On the one hand I was relieved at this calm reception of the news; I had counted on some distress at the very least, perhaps anger, even a major row. Yet on the other, we had to have this thing out, and surely an honest confrontation was what was needed? There was a sense of unfinished business in the air. The problem of

Arthur had not gone away. On the contrary, it was now weighing on me harder than ever.

And it returned the next morning, during breakfast. As usual, we had woken late, after a night in which we had smothered our cares in the warmth of our bodies. The breakfast itself was fine, too. Billy, better prepared than on previous weekends, had forked out on a jar of special coffee, a crusty loaf and a pot of thick marmalade. The day started well, in fact. The room, flooded with light, seemed to float in an airy blue sky, and we began, quite deliberately, with casual, cheerful banter. But then, during a lull, just as I was wondering how I could bring myself to prick this warm evasive bubble, Billy beat me to it with a request that brought our situation sharply into focus.

'Matt, don't get mad, but I was wondering if you could drive me over to Arthur's. I need to see him. Check that he's still okay.'

I froze, lifting a slice of toast to my mouth. It hung in the air, a few inches from my lips.

'There's no reason for you to come in. You stay in the car. I'll just make a brief visit to see how he is.'

A long pause. I put the toast back on my plate.

'I'm sure he's fine,' I said, without turning my head. 'Isn't that what you told me? Why is this necessary?'

'Matt, he lives alone.'

'Is that surprising? The beast in his lair.'

'He's an old friend. He may need help. I need to do this.'

'Billy, can't you see what's happening? He's trying to break us up. The man's insanely jealous, or something. Actually, I'm not sure that I know what drives him. At any rate, he feels threatened. And he's not ill, he's a sham. Surely you can see that. Oh, he may be a bit groggy after last night, but he'll soon recover. If you go there now, you won't get away quickly and I've driven here this weekend to be with you. To talk to you. We've so much to talk about and so little opportunity. Billy, when are we going to talk?'

He was silent for a while. Then he got up, walked to the

window and stood staring out of it, his back towards me. 'Matt, I've told you, I need more time.'

'I understand that. I don't want a decision, I simply want to talk. This weekend is ours, Billy. It's for us. Don't let Arthur ruin it. Please.'

He continued to stare out of the window, silent and absolutely motionless. Then he turned to face me. His mouth was taut. 'I'm going to see him, Matt. Will you drive me to his place, or shall I walk?'

It was my turn to fall silent.

'If you go,' I said after a pause, 'the weekend's finished. He'll eat you up. There'll be nothing left for me.'

'I'll be back within the hour.'

'That's very unlikely. But in any case, I won't be here. The weekend's over. I may as well drive back to London now.'

He stared at me intently. I was trembling, teetering on the brink of tears, hoping passionately for a change of heart. I wanted him to embrace me, kiss me. I studied his face, but it was hard, unyielding.

'Matt, why are you being like this?'

'Why? Because I love you. Haven't I made that clear? I've said it often enough. I've put it in ink. What more do you want?'

'Love?' He scratched his head. 'Yeah, well, that's the problem. I'm not sure I can cope with love. That's something new.'

'New?'

'Well, what *is* love?' He shrugged. ' I don't think I know. All I've known is this bond with Arthur. I suppose that's a kind of love.'

'Love? You call that love? That's not love, that's ownership. You're in his pocket. You like it there. It's where the dosh is.'

I winced. This was way out of order. Quite unforgivable. I could have bitten my tongue off. I looked at him. His face was rigid, his lips compressed.

'Okay,' he said, 'I'm off. I'll see you soon – that's if

you're still here.'

He hauled on his jacket and hurried from the room.

The next twenty minutes were some of the most painful of my life. I was in an agony of indecision. To leave now was a drastic step and might lead to a break-up. On the other hand, I had no way of knowing when Billy would return. Arthur might keep him for hours, pouring poison in his ear. Why humiliate myself by skulking here? Why play hanger-on? It was abject and degrading. It was more than I could bear. My face burned at the thought of Arthur smiling at my defeat. I paced the floor. I flung myself into chairs and leaped out of them again, clutching my head as if racked by a stonking hangover.

I decided finally that I had to go. I gazed around, clenching and unclenching my fists. Was this the end? I consoled myself that there might be ways to repair the damage. I gathered up some things of mine that were lying around and threw them into a bag. I checked that I had everything I needed, that nothing was left behind, and pulled on my jacket.

So this was it.

I stood looking at the room for perhaps the last time. The unmade bed, the patch of sunlight on the rug, the coffee table strewn with the debris of breakfast are features of a mental snapshot that remain with me still. Then, hauling my bag onto my shoulder, I walked briskly down the stairs and let myself out.

How did I survive the following days? I'm at a loss to explain. Actually, they're not clear in my memory, and perhaps that's a clue. I think I willed myself into a state of numbness. Although I spoke to no one about what had happened, I threw myself into the life of the house. I went to meetings, sat up chatting to people till the early hours, and even volunteered to be chef on two occasions, scrawling my signature across the duty roster and surprising everyone with a couple of special dishes taken from one of the many books of worldwide cuisine that filled the shelves in the kitchen. I went to work earlier and left later than usual. I sorted files and brought reports up to date. I listened to Maggie's domestic problems and filled in cheerfully for Tony when transport problems made him late one morning. And that's how I got through.

The phone calls simply ceased, however, and the silence was almost unbearable. At nights I lay in bed wondering whether we would ever see each other again. I prayed that he would call, but didn't really expect it. Should *I* break the silence by calling him? I decided not to. It was partly a matter of pride, but also a sense that what I had to say could not be said by means of a late-night conversation on the phone. My message, my attempt to make amends, would get lost in the noise, the smoke, the fatigue. Instead, I began another letter.

Dear Billy,

Please read this and hear me out. I've thought about phoning you, but this way is best. First and foremost, I want to apologise for last weekend. I did and said things I now bitterly regret. Can you forgive me? The only excuse I have is the one I gave at the time – that I love you, and when we're in love we behave in extraordinary ways. I think I will always love you, even if I never hear from you again. But I still hope that we can come through this and continue to see each other. In fact, I still hope that in time you will come to live with me. I know I've put you under a lot of pressure and I promise to cool it in future. I can do nothing about my loathing for Arthur, and I hope I never set eyes on him again. Even so, I'm prepared to risk another collision, if there's a chance, even a slim chance, that we can stay together . . .

It was not an easy thing to compose. I laboured at it for three nights and posted it on the Friday. By then there had been no communication between us for almost a week. Would it produce a reply? I so wanted to hear from him that words of any kind would have been preferable to the insufferable silence.

On the following Tuesday a poster appeared on the kitchen noticeboard. Drew was planning a party for his thirtieth birthday. It showed a cake with candles, flanked by cork-shooting champagne bottles: *Please keep Friday free and bring a friend.*

'Can you come, or are you driving north?' Clare asked me.

I shrugged. She stared at me curiously. The moment had come, it seemed, to open up. We were alone, drinking coffee late at night in her room.

'Call him,' she said. 'Don't give up.'

'I can't. I would if I thought he wanted to speak to me. But he doesn't, does he?'

'You don't know that. You're both feeling bruised and shy at the moment. Anxious not to mess up, say the wrong thing. My guess is that he'll write. Mark my words, there'll be a letter soon.'

But by Friday no letter had arrived. If he was writing one, he was taking his time. I was wretched by now, convinced that he wanted nothing more to do with me, and at night sometimes overwhelmed by black thoughts. Yet during the day, whatever my mood, I managed to stay cheerful on the outside. I decided that if I had not heard from him by early the following week, I would phone. This was not much comfort. I was sure we were finished, but at least it might bring this agony of waiting to an end. Meanwhile, there was Drew's party. I was scarcely in the mood, but on the other hand there was no escape. Not to go would mean inventing excuses. In any case, the truth is I welcomed it. Now, more than ever, I needed company, friends, distraction.

After supper that evening, a few of us – Clare, Mary, Andy and myself – cleared away and helped Drew to prepare for his big event. We covered the dining room table with tinfoil, and Mary placed the cake she had made in the centre. It had a layer of white icing on top, thirty candles round the perimeter, and *Cheers, Drouis!* spelled out in chocolate buttons. It got a round of applause, even though Mary protested, perhaps a shade *too* insistently, that cakes were not really her thing. We surrounded it with an array of nibbles – crisps, nuts, olives, vols-au-vent, biscuits and cheeses – and then loaded the table with drinks. We put wine at one end, beer at the other, and in the middle a motley collection of glasses gathered from every part of the house. Mary disappeared after this, saying that she was going to slip into something more relaxed. The rest of us, pleased with our effort, toasted Drew and sat about waiting for the other guests to arrive.

We were soon joined by Eddie and his friend Eve. She was someone we had met before, though the friendship with Eddie was apparently an on-off affair, and actually more frequently off than on. She was a model, tall, svelte and peachy-skinned, who always wore tight-fitting dresses to show off her figure. How Eddie had met her was a mystery. He handed her something bubbly in a long-stemmed glass, as though he knew without asking what she wanted. Their settling-in was interrupted by the arrival of Dan and Boo Boo, whose early appearance was a great surprise since they could never be relied on to turn up to anything, and especially not on time. They came with their hair newly dyed, purple and green respectively, Dan in a sloppy pink sweater and plimsolls, Boo Boo in a waistcoat and khaki slacks. Smiling all round, as cool and amiable as ever, they helped themselves to a couple of glasses of brown ale from a bottle they had brought with them.

Minutes later the doorbell rang and four guests were admitted, all friends of Mary from her tarot-reading circle.

'Oops, were we restricted to one guest?' she asked, turning to Drew with a strained smile. 'As you can see, I put out a rather general invitation.'

'No problem at all,' said Drew warmly, pouring himself another monster glass of claret. 'The more the merrier.'

In fact, arrivals were soon so frequent that we decided to leave the front door ajar. We pinned a notice to it – simply

Drew's Do beneath an arrow – and by nine o'clock the place was buzzing. I drifted around from group to group, drinking a lot and talking too much. I seemed to be floating inanely across a great yawning chasm.

Clare pulled me into her circle at one point and introduced me to a couple of her friends, James and Antonia. I pumped their hands rather too forcibly, I think, and tried to engage them in conversation. Along with everyone else, I was not quite coherent, but no one seemed to mind.

'Are you alone?' Clare whispered in my ear.

'I'm afraid so.'

'Well, I'm pleased to see you're not slumped in the corner with a bottle of gin. What's happening?'

'Fuck knows.'

She smiled and kissed me on the cheek.

Shortly after this I fell into a vacant chair, closed my eyes and drifted off. I'd not intended to, but an accumulation of sleepless nights and the effects of drink proved too much.

I woke to the feel of someone shaking me. It was Andy.

'Matt, there's a call for you. Couldn't catch the name. Drowned out by the noise.'

A call? I felt a fluttering in the stomach.

I got up, dazed, and staggered into the hall. There were several groups out there, laughing and chattering, and music was thumping away in the living room – in fact, coming through the wall. I picked up the receiver as though it were a bar of hot metal.

'Hullo,' I said cautiously, listening hard with one ear and blocking the other with a finger.

What I heard was like the gurgle of water in a drain.

'You'll have to speak up,' I said. 'There's a party in full throttle here – the noise is deafening.'

This time the voice was a little more distinct.

And now I was sure.

'Is that . . . ? Is that you, Billy?' I gasped. 'Oh God, love, it's so good to hear your voice, but I can't catch a thing. Could you try again?'

I was speaking across him, my words stumbling into his.

This time I caught the name *St Pancras.*

'St Pancras,' I said. 'St Pancras.'

I kept repeating the name like a mantra, as if through repetition it would acquire meaning. Oh, for Christ's sake, what the hell's going on here? Why can't I understand? If only I weren't so fucking pissed.

'Billy, I'm so sorry, I've had a few. Could you repeat? Did you say St Pancras?'

More burbling, and just a few words breaking through the fog of my fuddled brain: '. . . decision . . . sooner . . . London . . . half an hour ago . . .'

There was also that name. Repeated over and over, punctuating the burble at intervals: '. . . St Pancras . . . St Pancras . . .'

Then suddenly I understood. It was a physical sensation, as if a bolt of lightning ran through me. For a few moments I was quite speechless: stunned into silence, as if someone had slapped me hard in the face. But could I believe my ears? Surely it was some kind of cruel joke. Perhaps I had misunderstood; I was scarcely clear-headed, after all. He was speaking again now, saying something more, though I couldn't make head or tail of it. Not in my overheated state. Not with the crackly line. Not with the noise all around me.

Never mind, self-possession and voice quickly returned.

'Billy,' I blurted out, almost shouting, 'I'll be there in half an hour. Stay where you are. Don't move.' Then, as if speaking to a child: 'Did you hear me? *Stay where you are. Don't move.*'

He said something in reply, but I haven't the least idea what. I replaced the receiver smartly and pounded up the stairs to my room. I snatched up my wallet and jacket, then thundered back down the stairs and out of the front door as if fleeing a house on fire. The chattering crowd in the hall must have witnessed all this with open-mouthed bemusement, though I was too intent on my purpose to notice or care. I made for the tube, and by luck a train pulled in just as I sprinted onto the platform. Opposite me, two richly-dressed Caribbean ladies sat calm and dignified throughout the journey, like glamorous guests at a royal wedding. In contrast, I squirmed in my seat, gripping the arms like a patient in a dentist's chair.

St Pancras was teeming, and as I hurried through the grandeur of the foyer, glancing anxiously in all directions, I must have looked like a gangster slipping the mob or a thief on the run. The sheer size, the vast din and commotion of the place was dismaying. How would we find each other in all this mass of humanity? What a fool I was! Why had I not specified a point of contact? I had fucked up. It was the booze, the excitement, the fuzziness in my head. I stood on a seat to gain a vantage point and swept my eyes over the entire scene. But that was tantalising; I seemed to see Billy in every set of features that passed. Should I call out? Draw attention to myself? Reveal myself in all my current madness? Well, no; I was desperate, but such exhibitionism was definitely a last resort.

A sudden inspiration. What about the bar? Where else would a barman with an hour to kill hang out? I sprinted across the forecourt and burst through the doors. Heads turned as I dodged through the crowd and circulated the room, scouring every corner feverishly. The place was heaving, but to my bitter disappointment there was no sign of Billy. Instead, I met a sea of curious faces – some neutral, some hostile, some smiling indulgently, as if wishing to offer kindly support to a distressed lunatic.

I wandered out, feeling utterly dejected and defeated. 'It's a nightmare,' I muttered to myself as I stood watching passengers hurrying to their trains.

Completely stumped, I gazed around blankly. What next?

And it was then that I spotted him. Wearing his rumpled grey T-shirt outside his jeans, carrying an old beat-up rucksack over one shoulder, he was strolling past me quite casually, drinking tea from a paper cup and glancing about watchfully, clearly unaware that I was standing just yards from his elbow. There was nothing at all remarkable about him, he was the picture of ordinariness, yet for me he had a glow of beauty, a translucence, that quite took my breath away, and for several moments I couldn't speak. I simply stood and watched him saunter past. Then my voice leaped into my throat, I called out, and he turned, saw me and grinned, his face splitting from ear to ear. And that moment, the moment his face lit up, is one I'll always remember. He was, as I say, quite perfect. As fresh as a snapshot.

PART TWO

August-November 1984

Dinna regret Rhian. Is that how it goes? Sorry, I never learned French. Anyway, Terry used to play that track on Sunday afternoons, and some of us would get up and mime to it. Gone now, most of it, though bits have stuck, and they come back to haunt me at times like this. You have to hand it to the great songs, the great divas, they speak for us all. Especially those of us who are not, as Matt would say, linguistically gifted. So no regrets, because chance doesn't come too often. Chance, as they say, is a fine thing, so when it does come you have to seize it. Sure, it might burn you, might freeze you, might turn you to dust and ashes. But it's the one thing that matters in the end, and you simply have to go for it. That's how I see it, anyway.

People are dangerous, though, aren't they? Matt turned my head, you might say. I was doing all right till I met him, bumping along very nicely in my own small world. I sort of liked it and had no notion of anything else. It was a rough old life, all about fun and getting laid. Life with the corners knocked off, as they say. Life seen through a haze of booze. And at first he was just another guy. I liked the look of him. His lean features, his smile, his voice. His habit of blowing smoke rings and constantly ruffling his hair. But then he seemed to creep up on me. I was flattered by the attention he showed, his always coming back for more, and I could feel myself being drawn in, my powers of resistance draining away. 'Is this what you want?' I kept asking myself. One strong effort and you could be off this hook. And I might have got free, but for the letters he wrote. That's what did for me. This is for real, I thought; this guy means it. You'd better not pass this up; it might not come this way again.

Not an easy move, though. They were all against it, all of them. Terry, Craig, Stan, Betty, the lot. Ooh, they said, Little Miss Superior. Getting a bit above yerself, dearie? You'll never make the grade down there, yer gormless twat. You'll come crawling back within a week. No, they didn't like it, not one little bit. No one cheered. No one wished me well. But it was what I expected. Any bid to escape always makes them mean and jealous. Climb out of the pit? Not without a fight. They'll haul you back by your ankles. And as for Arthur, he was vicious, murderous. He'd known all along, he'd seen it coming. I was a selfish little shit, after all he'd done for me. He'd find me, he'd track me down, I was not going to get away with it. Nor that toffee-nosed prick with the slick voice and the cheesy smile. He'd seek us out, he'd flay us alive. Yet all this helped me to make up my mind. The more dire the warnings, the bigger the threats, the stronger my resolve to get the fuck out.

No, I'm not a man of the world. In fact, I've not ventured much beyond my own backyard. A few years back five of us spent a weekend in Paris. We stayed in some poxy old place in Montmartre, where the sheets were thin and frayed, the mattresses like planks. The first night we all got extremely pissed, and the rest was a blinding hangover. The sights? Didn't see a thing. Or if we did, I don't remember what. And that's it. That's my knowledge of Abroad.

London. Just thinking about it was risky, exciting, scary. The great unknown, as far as I was concerned. I'd passed through it just once – as a kid on a visit to Margate to see Aunt Rose, who was ill in hospital. A fleeting impression, but I remember the crowds, the underground, the glimpse of St Paul's as we passed over the river at Charing Cross. The sheer bloody size was the most awesome thing. And looking at maps is no use to me. I can't stand maps. All those lines and symbols. I prefer to be up on my feet and walking.

The day I left home I stood alone on Norrie Station. The word must have got round that I was leaving on the 3.30, but there was no one to see me off. I should have caught an earlier train, but I knew I'd never make it; there was too much business to sort. Anyway, it pulled in on time and I was first through the door. I slung my bag onto the rack and settled quickly into a window seat. The platform was pretty busy, and I sat watching an elderly couple as they struggled on board with a heavy suitcase. There was no hanging about, though; a few minutes later the guard blew his whistle and we started to glide away. So that's it, I thought: I've done it. Whatever happens now, for good or ill, I've made my decision. And I felt suddenly better.

But then I glanced round. Someone was tapping at the window. It was Terry. She was running beside the train and shouting something. It sounded like 'stay in touch'. Tears were streaming down her face and she was waving pathetically. I smiled and blew a kiss. Well, I had to return some show of feeling, didn't I, if only for old times' sake. But really, I wasn't moved or anything. The dramatic last-minute arrival was so typical of Terry's play-acting. I was tired of all that and looking forward to something new, something genuine. The train was speeding southward. I settled back. Would I honestly give a fiddler's fuck if I never saw any of that lot again?

Fields, farms, towns and station platforms went flashing by, and as they flew past the old life seemed to recede with them. Then, an hour down the line, we crossed a wide glittering river and it was like a milestone. Suddenly I stopped looking over my shoulder and my thoughts turned to the future – to London, hurtling towards me, and to Matt, who might by now have become a stranger. It was a week since he had written, and for the past fortnight there had been no other communication between us. Would he still welcome me, or had I kept him waiting too long? I'd wanted to phone, I'd often been on the point of phoning, but confusion had held me back. The really pressing thing, as I'd seen it, had been to sort myself out, to be clear in my own mind. And I *was* clear now, but until the train had pulled out that morning there had always been the chance that I would pass it all up. That I'd go on clinging to the life I knew.

As the journey drew to a close in the dusk of mid-evening, the lights came on in the London suburbs and I caught fleeting glimpses of people at home, watering plants, petting the dog or settling down with the evening paper. I thought of all the flats and houses and families stretching for mile after mile in all directions, and it made me feel lost and lonely, like a pebble washed up on a beach. We passed through a tunnel, the train slowed and the passengers reached for their luggage. Then, as the vast cavern of the station eased into view, the doors swung open and people spilled out onto the platform, making for the exit even before the train had come to a standstill. Everyone looked brisk and purposeful. Everyone, that is, except me. I wandered along, looking around – dazed, uncertain, wide-eyed as a child in a fantastic emporium.

I was tempted to phone Matt immediately, but all the phones were in use. In any case, I needed to stop moving, get my bearings, think about what I was going to say. So I wandered into the station buffet, even though I'd eaten some sandwiches on the train and wasn't really hungry. Nothing looked particularly appetising, but I forked out for a plate of sausage and chips and a mug of tea, and then wandered over to a table where a young woman was sitting alone opposite a vacant chair. She glanced up as I approached, gave me a pinched smile and went straight back to her book. Not exactly welcoming, I thought. But anyway, I took it to mean that she had no objection to my sitting there.

I tucked into the meal out of bravado – as a way of fortifying myself, hiding my discomfort. After all, what *was* this mad venture? I was struck by the danger, the precariousness of my situation. I was nothing but a face in a vast crowd. Matt, the very reason for my being here, didn't even know that I *was* here. What's more, in view of what had passed – or rather, not passed – between us lately, he might have given me up for lost. I had no one but myself to blame. It was all down to my indecision. I had said nothing for fear of changing my mind. Indecision would be my downfall. Was there any going back? Had I burned my bridges? What *had* I done, in fact? I thought of London laid out under the stars, its twinkling lights stretching to the far horizon. Matt was out there somewhere. I needed to find him, speak to him. I had to make a go of this. I had to make it work.

So I can't describe the relief I felt when I heard his voice on the phone that evening. I knew that it was *his* voice, even though the circumstances – the noise at both ends of the line, the fact that he was obviously pissed and couldn't speak without slurring – made it sound not quite familiar and even slightly unreal. 'Stay where you are, don't move,' he said. And I knew then that things were going to be all right. There might be delay and confusion in all this hurly-burly, there might be frustration and disappointment, but eventually we would find each other. So I hung up briskly when I heard the click at the end of the line and strode off feeling a whole lot lighter. A weight had fallen from my shoulders and my feet found a new springiness. I went straight to the buffet and bought myself another cup of tea. Yes, I thought, as I strolled around the forecourt on the lookout, it's going to be all right. At which point a great rustling overhead made me glance up in wonder, and I stood staring at all those wings beating in the dusty rafters, like tokens of my rising hope.

Some moments later I came back to earth with a bump, startled out of this trance by some noisy passengers dashing for a train. I blinked, shook myself and strolled on. And shortly after this I heard him call my name. I turned, saw him standing there, and my heart flew out. He looked so fragile, so amazed, so thrilled, like someone in a state of happy shock. I wanted to embrace and hug him immediately, but shyness held me back. For some moments we simply stood there with stupid grins on our faces. Then we both stepped forward, our bodies folded into one another and we held on tight for a long time without speaking.

'I should have called earlier,' I began.

He placed a finger over my lips.

'Hey, no explanations,' he said. 'Come to the party. Let's celebrate.'

And that was it. The big things were set aside, no questions asked. We leaped onto a tube train and sat grinning at each other across the aisle. I caught another glimpse of the river, the blazing towers, the barges, the floodlit spires and domes, and suddenly we were there, in Clapham, emerging from the station into the noisy revelry, the cosmopolitan riot of South London. All of it perfectly familiar to Matt, but to me, fantastically new, strange and exciting. And my wonderment must have been plain to see because he glanced at me, put an arm round my shoulder and kissed me gently on the cheek. Then, as we trailed hand in hand through the streets, he pointed out the local landmarks: here the library, there the best hairdresser, and over the road the patisserie where the meringues and éclairs were irresistible.

Number 7, Gordon Street, the house where Matt lived at the time, is vast, believe me. And when we got there, the rave was at its raviest. We had to push through a crush of people to reach the drinks table in the back room, Matt leading me by the hand and hailing friends on all sides. I followed, smiling shyly at the flushed faces around me and trying to hide my sense of being the stranger, the interloper, the gatecrasher. But there was no need for shyness. No, not at all. Along with everyone else, it seemed, I was a familiar old chum. The drinks table, however, had been ravaged. Matt stared at it in dismay, lifting and inspecting bottle after empty bottle. Eventually he stumbled on something the colour of piss, which bore an unreadable label in some weird foreign lettering. So we poured some of this gut-rot into a couple of discarded plastic cups and used it to toast each other, our faces twisting all the while into hilarious grimaces.

Soon we were surrounded by a group of smiling, inquisitive faces. Matt slung an arm round my waist and pulled me close.

'Okay, guys and gals,' he said, 'this is Billy. And I don't know for sure yet, but I hope he's going to stay.'

'Yeah!' someone whooped, and there was a round of applause. Then Matt began to introduce me to everyone.

Actually, I've no idea who I met that night. Too many

faces, too much confusion. But I do remember Drew, because he stepped forward, rather unsteadily, and shook my hand first.

'This is the birthday boy,' said Matt.

'Nice to meet you, Billy,' said Drew in a swooping voice; he was extremely well oiled. 'And welcome to the start of my fourth decade.'

I feel sure Dan and Boo Boo were there, too. I mean, a couple with hair dyed green and purple? Who else could that have been? And probably Mary and Andy.

But the only other person I clearly remember from that night is Clare. Yes, she stood out. There was something impressive about her. Something solid, warm and real. Her piercing eyes were a bit unnerving, though. They seemed to see right through me. She squeezed my hand, kissed my cheek.

'Brilliant timing,' she said with a wink. 'Matt's so happy. Just look at him.'

And so my life in London began. Yes, a dazzling, head-spinning start – but altogether too much. At some point in the early hours I must have crashed, overcome with fatigue, knocked flat by the bombardment of new sounds and sights. And I'm not clear what happened next. Did I take myself to bed, or did someone carry me? I have a drowsy memory of lying half-awake on the sitting-room floor, surrounded by a few determined night owls, the party having thinned to a mere handful. But after that, nothing. Nothing, that is, until very late the next morning, when light, seeping round the curtains of Matt's room, trickled into my consciousness. I was confused at first, puzzled by the strange surroundings. Yet the unfamiliarity was not alarming. I felt secure and pleasantly relaxed, as memory and self-awareness slowly unfurled. Matt was asleep, snuggled up behind me, his arm round my waist, his breath gently fanning the back of my neck.

I lay there, reviewing my life – impressions, memories, the whole kaleidoscope of past, present and future passing through my mind. I thought of my parents. My mother weeping on my shoulder, all sentiment, not a shred of real feeling. My stepfather staring at me with his shrug of indifference, silent, contemptuous. I thought of Terry, Craig, Baz and the others, their twisted grins and jealousy, their snide remarks. And then Arthur, muttering abuse and threats – defeated, embittered, bilious with hatred. No, I felt no regrets for the passing of the old crowd. And as Matt murmured and grunted in his sleep, his chin nuzzling my ear, I pressed my rump deep into the warmth of his groin. Yeah, I thought, so far, so good. So far, a wholly satisfactory move. And to arrive with such a right royal fanfare!

There was movement in the house. I could hear footfalls on the landing, blurred conversations, people calling to each other. I unhooked Matt's arm, climbed out of bed and took a peek through a crack in the curtains. We were several floors up and I was looking down into a backyard at an old rusted bike leaning against a shed. It was a boisterous day with ragged white clouds and patches of blue. A clump of tall purple hollyhocks and a leafy horse-chestnut were tossing wildly in the bluster. Matt groaned and stirred. I climbed back under the bedclothes and he turned towards me, reaching out and drawing me into the naked heat, the earthy odour, of his body. I pushed my face deep into the cleft of his shoulder, and his hands slipped down and began to knead my buttocks. Our swollen cocks rubbed against each other in a rage of excitement.

It was midday before we emerged from the room. In the kitchen we found Drew, Mary, Clare and Andy, seated round the table and nursing mugs of tea. The room was littered with debris from the night before. As we came in, they all looked round and smiled. Drew's smile was more of a wince, though. His face was grey and he looked like a patient in a terminal care unit. Actually, I was surprised to see him there at all, late though it was. Andy pointed to a couple of empty chairs and there was a bit of shuffling to make room for us.

'I'll top the pot and make some more toast,' said Mary.

I gazed round the table and smiled shyly at everyone. Our arrival felt like an interruption. All eyes were focused on me and I wanted to hide. I'm not always shy, I should say. Admittedly I'm not a raving extrovert, but in the right company I can be quite boisterous. It was just the newness, the strangeness of the setting. I wondered if this place would ever stop feeling new and strange.

'We're discussing Natasha,' said Clare, coming to my rescue. 'How much nicer she is when she's spaced out.'

Natasha? I cast my mind back. Was she the woman in the rainbow dress with beads in her hair? I had a vague memory that I'd met someone of that name the previous night. Anyway, no one said anything for my benefit, and I was pleased about that. It felt like no explanation was needed: that I was in the swim, one of the circle.

In any case all further discussion of Natasha was broken off by the sudden arrival of Eddie, who burst into the room in a fury.

'Jesus!' he exploded. 'Where the fuck are they? Everything in this place walks.'

'Hey, what's up?' said Matt.

We all twisted round.

'The pliers! They were definitely in the toolkit yesterday morning. I put them there myself.'

Eddie threw an accusing look at every single one of us.

'Is this something urgent, Eddie?' said Clare, looking impish. 'Could it wait? Mug of tea, perhaps? Slice of toast?'

'You being funny, Clare? Tea and toast? For fuck sake! I've got carburettor trouble and Eve needs to get home. She's got a shoot this afternoon.'

'Oops,' said Andy, leaping up and running across the room. 'I think I may be the culprit. Yes, here they are, Ed, under the sink. I borrowed them yesterday to remove the top from a rather tricky bottle of fizz.'

Eddie stood stonily with outstretched palm.

'Thank you, *Andy*,' he said in icy tones.

'This is Billy, by the way,' said Clare. 'Have you met? Been introduced?'

Eddie glared at me, sprang forward and thrust out a hand as if about to run me through with a sword. I shook it limply. He turned and marched off. We heard the front door slam, and instantly everyone erupted. The hilarity must have lasted for several minutes. Clare and Mary wept, dabbing their eyes with some leftover paper napkins. Andy beat the table with his fists. Even Drew managed to crack his face into a painful grin.

'Welcome, love,' said Matt, hugging and kissing me. 'Welcome to the asylum.'

You may be thinking, who is this guy? Where did he spring from? What was his life before he met Matt? Well, that's fair enough; I often ask myself those questions. The problem is, I can't match those people who can recall every detail of their childhood in vivid technicolour. No, my early chapters are a bit of a blur. As I remember, it was mostly the four of us: Mum, Paul, Sandra and me. And yes, that was the pecking order: Our Paul, or Bully Boy, the eldest; me, the runt; and poor old Sandra battling it out in the noisy space between us. Dad was a shadowy figure who was rarely in the house. Most evenings, after supper, he disappeared, sometimes to meet his latest fancy woman, sometimes to join his mates at the Greyhound. Dodgy geezers, the lot of them: as dodgy as ever breathed. Eventually they got done for burglary, Dad included, and were put away for a few years. So after that we saw almost nothing of him, since on his release he and Mum had the mother and father of all rows and he slammed out, never to return. For a while he lived with Sheila, one of his girlfriends, but when they broke up, we lost all trace of him. It was only when Mum was seeking a divorce that his name began to crop up again. By which time we kids were not much interested; we had scarcely known him.

There were substitutes, of course; blokes moved in occasionally. None of them stayed, though – which, in most cases, was lucky. There was just one that I liked, and that was Ray. He was different from the others. He took an interest in us, for one thing, standing up to Paul whenever he got too cocky and treating Sandra and me to sweets and trips to the cinema. Mum was obviously smitten too, so his overnight runner is still a bit of a mystery. We begged her to tell us what had happened. Where had he gone? *Why* had he gone? Would he be back? But she simply shrugged and behaved as if she didn't know. All we could get out of her was some vague muttering about how he was not 'the sort to be tied down'.

Anyway, eventually one of these blokes did stay – and sadly it was Pete. He moved in, I remember, just after my sixteenth birthday, a great lumbering sack of lard. He sank deep into an armchair, poked his ears with a pencil, and spread his stockinged feet so wide they blocked the hearth. It looked ominous, and sure enough a couple of months later he and Mum were married. By this time Paul was inside, serving a six-month sentence for assault – the first of a chain. Sandra was still living at home, but stuck in a quarrelsome bind with Mad Mick, her current boyfriend, and deeply depressed. Things looked desperate.

One night, after a shouting match with Pete, I stormed out and wandered the streets, my hands thrust deep in my pockets, my hood hard down over my head. It was cold, and when it started to spit with rain, I decided to call on Craig, who was living up on Brunswick Hill with his dad. Craig came to the door, hauled me in and we bounced upstairs to his room. We sat on the floor, sharing a spliff, and I spilled out all my fucking grief and misery.

'Stay here tonight,' he said. 'Dad won't mind. He's easy.'

'Yeah, thanks,' I said doubtfully. 'But that's a temporary fix. What about the future?'

We formed a plan. We'd leave school at the earliest and get a job. Any kind of job: packing, shelf-filling, cleaning, anything. We'd take charge, live our own lives. Yeah, bollocks to the lot of 'em. We worked ourselves up, got pretty high, drank too much coffee. Later, we tried watching a stupid film on television – there was a flickering box in Craig's room – and then lay full stretch on the floor, listening to Pink Floyd.

I knew all about Craig, let me tell you. We'd wanked each other more than a few times in that very room, and even sucked each other off on one memorable occasion. But sharing his narrow bed was a new experience. Tons of guys go for him, of course. He's a neat little package. But the odd thing is I was never that keen. Don't ask me why. Was he too familiar, like a kid brother? After all, we'd been together all through school. I'd known him since he was an urchin with a snotty nose – a midget hanging about the playground in a torn anorak. Oh sure, he'd blossomed nicely, I could see that. I admired his small breastplate chest and tight rump. But perhaps something of that earlier image still clung to him? Anyway, let's be clear, it was a lively night, and he seemed to have no such reservations about me.

We stuck to the plan. Craig got a job as a hotel porter, I started frying burgers for the café on Station Road. Not a promising start, but I was chuffed. I now had money in my pocket and could afford to move out. So, at Craig's suggestion, I took over the spare room at his place. Nothing fancy – in fact, no more than a box with a busted window – but his dad let me rent it for a song. I moved in one weekend, bringing a few possessions in an old rucksack. These were all my worldly goods. I hung a poster on the wall, placed my cassette player on a chair, then lay on the bed for an hour listening to some Motown stuff through earphones. The following weekend I bought an old wardrobe from a local junk-shop, and hung my shirts and jacket from the bar-rail on twisted wire hangers.

For the first couple of weeks Craig came to my bed almost every night. Then the visits got fewer and eventually dropped off completely. We still hung out together, though – in clubs and coffee bars, or whenever we went to see a film. And we knew about the Black Horse. Who didn't? To tell the truth, we were madly curious about the place, though shit-scared of going there. Then one night we found the courage to pay a visit. We were under-age, but who was to know? We didn't dress up or anything; we wanted to blend in, look low-key, casual. We had no idea what to expect, but most of the crowd were friendly. In fact, some of them were all over us. We met a lot of people that first night, including Giles and Big Ron and a young woman who introduced herself as Terry. It was Arthur who stood out, though. He's the weirdest sod, is Arthur, but he knows how to impress. And it's not just the waistcoat and bow tie. It's the eyes that rove all over the place.

He shook our hands in a very formal way.

'First time?' he asked.

We nodded.

'Could be the start of something,' he said.

Yeah, too true; though that was not clear until the 'something' had already started. It began in the most casual way. I was sitting alone at the bar one night – Craig was somewhere else – when the guy on the next stool turned to me and smiled. He was well-dressed, perhaps in his early thirties, and quite a looker actually, though a bit smarmy, in the manner of a salesman. He had a flashy watch, and kept twisting a gold ring on his third finger. We got into conversation, and after a while his knee began to press into mine. He bought me a drink, and at closing time we went back to the hotel where he was staying. To be honest I was only half interested. It was curiosity more than anything else. I stripped down to my shorts and got into bed. He went to the bathroom, and when he came out he was starkers. He had a good fit body, with glowing pink skin, like a swimmer or squash player. He climbed in beside me, and lay some way off for a while, smiling and stroking my hair. Then he moved in and the show really began, though in a very gentle way at first, with lots of touching and nuzzling. But it got rougher as the action built up, and suddenly he was breathing heavily, pushing my legs back over my head and smearing my hole with something cold and wet. I closed my eyes, and when a searing pain shot through me I tried to push him off. 'Relax!' he urged, and minutes later we were thrusting together in synchronised movement.

I was thrilled. Thrilled to bits. I mean, this was it. My first fuck.

When it was over, we sat up in bed and he reached for his cigarettes. We lit up, and as we drew on the smoke he told me some more about himself. He was married, with two small kids, and worked as an advisor for a finance company based in Essex. He wasn't too specific, though; he kept himself well covered. So I lied about myself; I said I was an art student. He nodded as if impressed, but didn't show any further interest, and when he offered me his bed for the night, I stubbed out my fag and said I had to go. I pulled on my shorts, went to the bathroom, and a few minutes later I came out and found him sitting on the edge of the bed in a silk bathrobe. He pulled me close, kissed me, patted my bum. He said he was moving on the next day and didn't know when he'd be back. He told me to take care. You too, I said.

Twenty minutes later, standing on my own doorstep, I unzipped the inside pocket of my jacket, reached inside for my key and pulled out something I had no idea was there. Yeah, a small wad of notes. I flicked through. Five tenners. I stared in amazement. I mean, I never stow money in my jacket; I always use the side pocket of my jeans. I felt a burning in my chest, and for minutes I stood rooted to the spot. I let myself in and trailed up the stairs in a daze. I tossed the notes onto a chair and lay on the bed, turning things over. I worked out that he saw his chance when I made my visit to the bathroom. But I was still puzzled. Was this payment for services, a gift to a poor student, a bit of both? Whatever it was, I felt demeaned. It seemed I had slipped into a world of shady deals without even knowing.

I avoided the Black Horse for several days, and when I next paid a visit Arthur greeted me with a funny smile.

'Saw you depart the other night,' he said, breathing into my ear. 'I presume he tucked you up nicely?'

I looked into his face, read what was there, and somehow I knew that he knew. It was the leer on his lips, the cunning gloat in his eyes.

But even though I took my time, I couldn't think of a smart reply.

'None of your business,' I said.

'Exactly my business,' he chuckled. 'And where's my cut?'

After the riotous landing, the feel of solid earth. Yeah, it took some getting used to, this moving in with Matt. All my adult life I had lived alone. Now I had to think in a different way, be aware of others. No spreading myself, no dropping clothes on the floor, no strolling bollock naked to the bog. Oh sure, most of the time I felt good; glad to be with him, glad to be loved and fully alive. But there were these moments when I longed for some privacy, some corner to myself, some space to chill out. My room over the pub had been a refuge. Up there, above the fray, aloft in my perch, I'd been king. Here, as one of the crowd, I had to learn to fit in, or, as one of a pair, to string along, play my role. Sometimes, as I stood at the window, turning things over in my mind, or staring vacantly at a cat stalking a sparrow, Matt would creep up behind me, slide his arms round my chest and hug me tight, crushing my ribcage. And I'd feel my chest heave in sudden aversion, as if to snap the bonds, slip the chains, break free of all these niggling constraints.

'We don't have to stay here,' he said one day. 'We could look for something bigger. A small flat perhaps? Something on the north side?'

I shook my head. 'Let's not rush things. This is fine. For now.'

'For now? How long is now?'

'Matt, I've no plans to leave.'

'I want you to be happy.'

'I *am* happy. I like it here.'

'You will tell me, won't you?'

'Of course.'

And I spoke the truth. Mostly. In general, I *was* happy. I liked the house and the people we lived with. As a start, as a way of settling in, the arrangement was fine. No, what I needed more than extra space was money. What I needed was a job. And by the end of the first week I'd found one.

It happened so casually, so easily, that for a while I couldn't quite believe my luck. Walking back from the shops one morning I caught sight of a small handwritten sign. *Catering assistant wanted. Apply within*. I peered through the window. Small place. No more than a handful of tables. But bright, modern, jazzy, with an abstract mural covering the whole of one wall. Also crowded, lively and obviously popular. Worth checking out? Certainly. So I went in and sat down at a small corner table. But service was painfully slow. A cheerful young woman in a chef's apron kept appearing and disappearing. Eventually I caught her eye, but almost immediately she flew off again. At which point I sighed and went back to studying the menu, feeling neglected and slightly peeved.

Moments later I looked up to find her standing beside me, smiling and nodding, with pad and pencil at the ready.

'Sorry to keep you waiting. Bit understaffed today.'

'No problem,' I said.

'What can I get you?'

'Er . . . well, nothing, actually. The fact is I came in to speak to someone about the sign in the window.'

Her face lit up, keen with interest.

'Well, speak to *me*,' she said, dropping onto a chair. 'I'm Kika. This is my place.'

I liked her instantly. She was warm, easy-going, unaffected, her round face crowned by a close elfin crop. Twenty-five or so, I guessed. I asked about the job. She said she was desperate. She needed a dogsbody, but someone with catering experience. What was my background? I mentioned my training, my qualifications, my six months at the Cross Keys, my three weeks at Metcalf's, my past year at the pub.

'Fine,' she said briskly. 'Any references?'

I bit my lower lip. 'Sorry. Came away without them.'

'Hmm,' she said.

She sat back and appraised me with a searching look.

A customer snapped his fingers. She got up and brushed her apron. I thought she was going to apologise and walk off.

Instead of which she turned and smiled. A sort of slow, lazy smile.

'Tell you what,' she said, 'I'll give you a trial run. Dunno why. Must like your face or something. Come in tomorrow. About half eight.'

And I was there, of course. Oh yeah, I know mornings are not my style, but there was no passing this one up. I peered through the window when I arrived and Kika spotted me immediately. She let me in through the front door and led me through to the kitchen. Her hair was pushed up under a tight-fitting cap and her hands were floury.

'I'm making some quiches. I do this every morning, but I vary the recipe. Keep it creative, that's my motto. Anyway, hang your jacket up and find yourself an apron.'

She set me to work immediately. Preparing vegetables, grating cheese, washing up.

'We open at nine, but business is slow till eleven, so there's always plenty of time to get lunch underway.'

'What do you do besides quiches?'

'Take a look here.' She showed me a menu that was pinned to a board on the wall. 'Besides quiches, we always do soup, and today it's lemon and spinach. So that's the next task.'

We worked in near silence for the first couple of hours. Which was surprising. I thought she might want to chat, learn a bit more, ask a lot of questions. But no, she bustled about, preparing food, seeing to customers, giving orders whenever she saw me looking around for something to do. She was testing me, I could tell, so I made myself useful. I did everything in double quick time and let her see that I knew my way around a kitchen. Once, when she was called away to the phone, I rolled out a perfect sheet of pastry, filled a couple of dishes and trimmed the edges. Then later, when a delivery arrived, I rescued some cakes from the oven that were in danger of getting caught. On both occasions she nodded approvingly and I was pleased. I had earned myself some credit.

By mid-morning, just as she said, the scene was much busier.

'Let's swap,' she said. 'You take care of the café, I'll clear up in here.'

I nodded, glad of this chance to see the other side, pleased with this show of confidence. The place was almost full, but I moved around smartly, taking and delivering orders with speed and efficiency and without asking for help. The call was for coffee mostly, sometimes with cakes or croissants. Twenty minutes later I had everything under control and stood leaning against the counter surveying the happy scene. Kika joined me. She smiled and pinched my cheek.

'Good work,' she said. 'We're doing fine.'

The lunch hour was manic, though.

'If you get hungry, grab what you want, bring it here to the kitchen and take a bite between orders. Bit of a scramble, I'm afraid, but there's usually a chance to take a break later on.'

She was right. By two-thirty the rush was over. Custom had dwindled to a few latecomers and afternoon shoppers. In fact, during a particularly quiet patch, she made a small pot of tea and invited me to join her.

'Phew!' She dropped onto a chair and kicked off her shoes. 'Best bit of the day. We just need to keep an eye on things now.'

She stretched and leaned back, her arms behind her head. 'Well now, what's the news? Anything planned for tonight?'

I shrugged. 'That depends on Matt.'

'Who's Matt?'

'Matt?' I stared into my mug, then looked up boldly and grinned. 'Matt's the guy I live with.'

She nodded thoughtfully, her mouth settling into a broad smile.

'Ahah. Now I understand. That's why I like your face. Story of my life. I always go for the guys who are unavailable.' She paused to take a swig of tea. 'Been together long?'

I shook my head. 'Just a few weeks.'

'Ah yeah, that's springtime.' She began to hum a waltz tune, a secret smile playing on her lips. 'The only pretty ringtime.' She flapped a hand as if to dismiss her own silliness. 'Anyway, how's it all going?'

I shrugged. 'It's okay,' I said. 'So far.' I hurried to change the subject. 'And for you? How's *your* life?'

'Thierry and I have been together for four years,' she said with a giggle. 'And yeah, it's sort of – okay – so far.'

Her giggle turned to wholesale collapse and I simply joined in, swept along by her infectious laughter. It seemed beside the point to ask *why* we were laughing. It was just a great moment of fun and shared lunacy; a bonding; a moment to be enjoyed rather than understood.

'Anyway,' she said, 'you be careful.'

I looked at her and raised an eyebrow. 'Careful?' I chuckled. 'What's that supposed to mean?'

'I mean there's a lot of sick people about.'

I turned suddenly sober and lowered my eyes. 'Yeah, I know. But don't believe everything you read.'

'So what do *you* believe?'

'Dunno. I'll wait and see.'

She nodded and looked thoughtful. 'All the same,' she remarked, 'you *should* be careful.'

I drained my mug. 'Yeah, thanks.' I flashed a smile. 'I will.'

After that, the day wound down quietly as far as custom was concerned, although the final stretch called for one last heave in view of all the clearing up. Kika, being a stickler for order, insisted on every fork being washed and put away, ready for the morning. We started in good time, though, and most of it was done before we saw off the final customers and switched the sign to *Sorry, we're closed*. Fifteen minutes later we turned and looked at each other. Kika sighed, pulled off her apron and glanced around, nodding with satisfaction at the gleaming pots, the stacked shelves, the spick surfaces.

'Ya done well, mate. So what's it to be? Stay or quit?'

I grinned and nodded. 'I'm on if you're on.'

'Great!' She stuffed a wad of notes into my hand. 'Now

you get off, I need to count the takings. But I'll see you tomorrow and we'll sort out your hours and pay.'

The sun was still high when I left the café that evening. The busy street outside was a scene of shimmering brilliance. I was in a such a state of exhilaration, my spirits so high, that I seemed to be floating. I almost danced home. Matt was in the kitchen with Clare, Mary, Drew and Andy. They were sitting round the table sharing a pot of tea. I came in briskly, and must have looked flushed and exalted or something because they all stared at me in expectation.

'You seem to be bursting with news,' said Clare.

I nodded and looked at Matt. 'Got it,' I blurted out.

He leaped up and put his arms around me.

'Got what?' said Andy.

'Some of the ready.' I waved my wad of smackers. 'Found myself a job.'

I sat down. Drew slapped me on the back and there was a round of applause. I felt, and probably looked, a bit dazed. Andy patted my head and Clare poured me a cup of tea. There were lots of questions and I found myself giving a blow-by-blow account of the day.

'We should celebrate,' said Clare.

'But not here,' said Drew. 'The larder's bare and it's my turn to cook. I vote we go out.'

'Yeah,' said Matt. 'Somewhere sparky. Who's for Daniela's?'

This suggestion was greeted with vigorous nods on all sides. So Mary went off to prepare a poster inviting anyone to join us. We pinned it to the noticeboard and Drew added a postscript, warning all stop-at-homes that he was bunking off as cook for the night and consequently they would have to fend for themselves. But when the time came there were no other takers and in the end it was just the six of us.

Daniela's is a small place in a back street, specialising in pizza, pasta and atmosphere. It's intimate and welcoming and nearly always full. Fortunately Drew had phoned ahead and booked a table. This was my first visit, but the others were regulars, and Pietro, the head waiter, greeted us as old friends. He ushered us to a corner table and handed us copies of the menu. It was a warm night, so we removed our jackets and rolled up our sleeves. There was a lot of excited chatter as we glanced through what was on offer and tried to make choices. Drew groaned with delight, kissed the tips of his fingers and strongly recommended the Pizza Napolitana. Mary, on the other hand, declared a strong preference for the tortellini. In the middle of our noisy discussion Daniela herself arrived. A large, olive-skinned lady with a pumpkin face and an infectious laugh, she shook hands with us all, passed on news of her family and wished us all *bon appetito*. There were a couple of musicians too, adding colour to the evening: Sylvie, who played gypsy airs on a fiddle with bags of theatrical flourish, and George, her accompanist, who moved between accordion, concertina and keyboard.

We were a snug group, seated round a rectangle, Matt at one end, Drew at the other, Andy and I facing Clare and Mary across the middle. The place was buzzing, but Pietro was soon hovering over us, pencil and pad at the ready, and after we'd given our orders the conversation slipped into easy banter. I was the quiet one, of course, still the newcomer, still slightly shy and awkward, the listener rather than the talker. Andy may have noticed this because at a certain point he turned to tell me an amusing story about a bloke he knew who ran a bric-à-brac stall in Camden Market. He then started to question me. Where exactly was I from? Was I homesick? What did I think of London? Did I know Northumberland, where he had once taken a girlfriend on a cycling holiday? All this was intriguing. I mean, I hardly knew the guy. Until this point no more than a few brief words had passed between us. He stood slightly apart from the others, it seemed to me. Bright, self-contained, a bit of a mystery, he worked for a finance company in the City. He hated his job, he told me, but his plan was to make money and then go travelling. He was keen to see India and South America, though in the long run he might go back to his roots and rejoin his family in New South Wales.

It was a funny experience, talking to Andy. It made me feel odd. I saw how remote I had already become from my own roots. Andy was nice enough, but educated, confident, secure in his well-paid job. We had nothing in common; we were from different planets. So what was I doing here? I gazed around at the group. Who *were* these busy chatterboxes, these smart talkers with smooth accents? Was this my scene? Too soon to say, of course. But could I honestly imagine being part of this circle? I looked at Matt, Clare, Mary and Drew. They were in noisy, heated debate with each other. Something to do with the rain forests. What could we do to save them? Did anyone care? What would happen if we did nothing? I looked on, blank and bemused, a mere observer, detached and unobtrusive. In fact, I rolled up inside myself and shrank to nothing at all. I became a shadow on the wall, a blur in the corner. And there they all were, and on they went, chattering excitedly, perfectly absorbed, utterly wrapped up in each other.

My mind flew back to Terry, Craig and the others. True, I sometimes hated that crowd, but at least we spoke the same language. At least we were involved, if only on a basis of hatred. Here, I was a fish on dry land. Learning to survive in this element would take millennia. No, I was not homesick. At least, that's what I told myself. But actually, in a bizarre kind of way, I was. At that moment I had a depressing need to be back with all those old familiar faces, yabbering, squabbling and shrieking to the rafters. I longed to be back at the centre of things: not here, skulking in the wings. As I say, I'm not shy. Give me the right setting and I'm not tongue-tied at all. Quite the opposite. Quite the little show-off at times. But here? Well, these people were matey and likeable, but a bit full of themselves. They left me no room; they cramped my style.

In the middle of these thoughts the food arrived, and since we had all chosen something different, there was a dizzying variety of dishes, everything piping hot and colourful and spiced with a heady mingling of aromas.

Marco, a very young waiter – Daniela's grandson, in fact, and no more than a boy – uncorked a bottle of Chianti with cool professionalism and poured a measure into Matt's glass. Matt took a mouthful, rolled it round his palette and nodded his approval. Marco, looking secretly pleased, topped up the glass and then moved around the table, displaying the bottle with quiet pride and offering the wine to the rest of us.

Clare raised her glass. 'To the café,' she said, looking at me and smiling. 'Buona fortuna!'

Everyone around the table had started to eat, enticed by the sight and smell of such food. But now they lay down their irons to toast me, echoing Clare with murmurs of congratulation and good wishes.

Matt reached out to me. I slapped the palm of his hand and we locked fingers in mid-air.

'To Matt and Billy,' said Drew, raising his glass again.

'Yeah,' someone whooped.

'Hey,' said Andy, nudging me. 'He's a changed man since you came.'

I smiled and looked at Matt. He was beaming, his face flushed. There was a gleam in his eye and wine was spilling down his shirt front. And suddenly I realised why I was there, what it was all about. I couldn't let him down now, could I? I was in this too deep. In any case, he was my own best chance, the lightning that might never strike again. How could I pass him up?

Talk of getting in too deep brings me back to that toe-rag Arthur. The truth is, I don't need to say it, the man was a heap of trouble. I could see that from the start. So how did I get drawn in? Ah, don't ask. I guess I was fascinated. So much so that after a while the fascination overcame my repugnance. I mean, there was always the promise of the next encounter, the lure of easy money. Life became an adventure, a leap in the dark, a roller-coaster ride. I always kept a certain distance, though. Always looked after my independence. And that didn't please him. He hated me choosing my own bedmates. But I stood my ground and turned down many an offer, including quite a few from the old reprobate himself.

Was he a friend? Yeah, in a way, though a pretty weird one. I mean, he was always keen to fix me up with a trick, yet sometimes as madly jealous and possessive as a lover, especially if I spent more than a night with anyone. Madly jealous? Well, let's just say he was mad. And actually that's no exaggeration, he *had* been inside a few times. Physically, too, he was a complete wreck. He was always calling the doctor, and there were more pills in his bathroom than in a dispensary. He grumbled about being hard up, but I'm convinced he had a secret hoard under the bed as wide as a suitcase. Anyway, he could usually manage a handout whenever I needed one.

One other thing I have to thank him for is my job at the pub. He was always pretty thick with Betty and Stan, being a regular of theirs for God knows how long, and when the vacancy came up he put in a good word for me. Well, it suited him to the ground, having me there on display every night of the week. But he could still get upset about the guys I chose to speak to, and especially those I took home at night. What he really wanted, I could see, was absolute control, and that made me even more determined to resist him. In fact, it roused the devil in me, so that I would wave blokes in front of his eyes, flaunt my freedom like a harlot, in order to show that I was not his bloody glove-puppet.

I'll say this, he was never dull. Sometimes he made me laugh like a drain. He had a dark, sick sense of humour, which, strange though it sounds, sort of humanised him to some extent. It was hard to relax with him, though, because he was so unpredictable and could turn funny in an instant. This bugged me at first. That is, until I learned to bite back. Yeah, we had some spectacular rows. Once I kicked him so hard that his shins turned black and took weeks to heal. So why didn't I just knee him in the nuts and wave goodbye? I don't honestly know. I suppose our fighting grew into a wary kind of respect, even affection. I mean, it seems odd to say this, but before I met Matt, Arthur was the pivot of my life, even though we were never sexually involved and sometimes couldn't bear the sight of each other.

A night at Daniela's. A night on the town. Yeah, great when you can lie in, but how did I get to work the next day? And more to the point, how did I make it on time? Well, to tell the truth, that's because I didn't sleep. Matt and I were otherwise engaged. And after the action, when Matt had drifted off, I was still awake, listening to the dawn chorus. So at seven-thirty I got up, pulled on my jeans and T-shirt, and padded down to the kitchen where I sat alone, sipping tea, nothing astir except next door's ginger tom, rubbing itself ecstatically against the window-pane.

At the café Kika was kneading dough. She gave me a cheerful greeting, and then looked at me closely. 'Forgive me, but you look terrible.'

'A wee celebration,' I said.

'Shouldn't have paid you. Knew the money would go to your head.'

'Yeah, my head. Wish I could lop it off.'

'Oh dear, will you last?'

'I've known worse.'

'Leave it to Auntie. I know just the thing.'

She flew off and mixed up something with a raw egg. I pushed it away.

'I'll be okay,' I said with a weak smile.

I was beyond conversation, though, and for the first two hours we again worked in near silence. In fact, if anything, the silence was even deeper than the day before, all communication between us kept to a bare minimum. To be precise, she gave me instructions from time to time, to which I responded with a grunt. But by late morning the thick grey fog in my head had begun to lift. I even managed to raise a painful smile at one point. This was when, hurrying in from the restaurant, she slipped on some spilled water and sent a tray of crockery crashing to the floor. Luckily, she was as amused as I was. In fact, she went into fits. She then came up behind me and began to rub my temples. Even so, I turned down her offer of black coffee, settling instead for a mug of peppermint tea. Just an experiment, of course. Normally I wouldn't touch the stuff.

This being Saturday, we were busier than usual and what lulls there were came at unpredictable times. During one of these slack moments I noticed that Kika was sitting in the restaurant. She was deep in conversation with a tall handsome guy whose curly black hair was thick on top and ran all the way down to the base of his long neck. He was dark-skinned and wore rimless glasses. I couldn't hear what they were saying, but it was clear that their head-to-head was not a happy one. There was not a flicker of a smile on either face and the tension between them was clearly displayed in their body language. Words seemed to be spilling out in short angry spats. I busied myself with the washing up and a few minutes later I saw Kika march back into the kitchen. I glanced at her, but she didn't seem to see me. She looked taut, strained, preoccupied. She yanked a box across the floor and began to load the fridge with yoghurts. Shortly, the man wandered in after her and hung about, leaning against one of the worktops.

'So what shall I tell them?' he said. He had the faint trace of a foreign accent.

'Oh, tell 'em what the fuck you like,' she snapped.

The man was silent for a bit and then suddenly flung off, almost colliding with me as I crossed the room to wipe my hands on a towel. Kika sniggered and shook her head. She watched with a wry smile as he barged through the café and out of the front door. Then she turned to me.

'That was God,' she said.

'Thierry?'

She nodded.

'Nice name, Thierry.'

'Nothing wrong with the name,' she said with a rich laugh.

For me, though, things were looking good. We were well suited, Kika and I, and within a week I knew the ropes and had completely settled in. The money wasn't so hot, but there was enough to get by, and I was allowed one day off in the week. So what to do on my days off? Not a problem. The great unknown lay all around me, waiting to be explored. I studied maps and routes, and leaped onto tube trains and buses, always carrying my old canvas rucksack slung over my shoulder, packed with chocolate, a bottle of water and Matt's dog-eared streetfinder. I did a lot of walking too. In fact, I must have covered vast distances. Sometimes it seemed to me that I had tramped the length of every street in London. I wandered across parks and over heaths, beside canals and through long straggling street markets. I watched the riverboats from Westminster Bridge, I climbed St Paul's, I stood awestruck on Primrose Hill. The others at the house were impressed. After a couple of these trips I could show a knowledge of London to match theirs, and even mention places they scarcely knew existed.

And what about that crew? They were certainly not your average housemates, as you've gathered. Take Dan and Boo Boo. Oh yeah, amiable, but remote. We scarcely ever saw them. And what did they do all day? No one seemed to know for sure, and it became a running joke. They didn't have regular jobs, that was clear. The rumour was that Boo Boo was some kind of part-time masseuse, but no one could quite confirm this. And Dan? According to Clare, he worked in a one-room office in Chalk Farm, fixing gigs and designing posters for a rock group, but she never let on how she knew. Mary insisted that they were well-off. She had a theory that Boo Boo had inherited a fortune from an elderly relative who had died. But most of the stories about them seemed based on guesswork. Then there was Eddie, whose life was similarly shrouded in mystery because he was such a liar. Well, no one actually used that word – he was usually called 'an unreliable narrator'. He was always getting into scrapes and flying into rages. But he certainly had great entertainment value.

In the main, it was a household of politicos. Oh, it's true that Andy and Drew wore suits to work, but they were always dead keen to join any kind of anti-government protest. Everyone hated Thatcher, and I wasn't exactly mad struck on her myself. But I couldn't work myself into a state like they did, going insanely ballistic and pop-eyed and frothing at the mouth. As a matter of fact I'd never given much thought to her at all. The miners had been on strike since March, and the dispute was coming to a climax. So we collected for them and sent food parcels, and even joined the protesters outside the Commons on one occasion. All this was new to me; I'd never taken much interest in politics. And it opened my eyes. I'm more aware now; more inclined to swing a rattle, blow a whistle, shout.

To be fair, the Gordon Street crowd were fine on the whole. Clare was a staunch friend, and Drew, Mary and Andy were good mates too. One thing that bothered me, though, was my status. Except for Eddie, who tended to ignore me, they treated me like one of the gang. But after all, I wasn't, was I? Not really. I was just a guest. I didn't attend meetings, for instance. Well, it seemed obvious to me that I had no right, though no one except Eddie would have been likely to object. The rules of the house were vague and only Eddie ever questioned what went on. Eddie had the mind of a lawyer and was always seeking clarification on some point of order. But even he said nothing about my staying long term, presumably because he'd housed quite a few long-term guests himself. Eddie was a stickler for the rules except when he had an interest in breaking them. So the issue never arose; it was a hornet's nest that he wisely left undisturbed.

So far, so good, then. I had a lover, a home, a job. Yet there were doubts. I wasn't quite easy. Where was this venture going? How long could it last? Nothing's for ever. Yeah, I know that; I can cope with that. Go with the current, ride the wave, that's my instinct. But could Matt cope with it? Could we travel together? It was certainly great at times. At times I was flying. I loved him, and still love him, as I've never loved anyone. But I could feel change in the air, creeping in at every corner, whistling overhead, flapping round the ankles. I could feel movement in every living, breathing moment. And the ripples you can ignore, but then the ground shifts slightly.

The date is tattooed on my memory. September the twenty-first: a mere four weeks after I'd started work at the café. The weather sticks in my mind too, since it was thundery and teeming with rain that morning. Luckily, as I now had a key to the side door, I was able to let myself in when I arrived. To my surprise I found the kitchen empty, though I became immediately aware of voices on the other side of the wall. I stuck my head round the door. Kika and Thierry were sitting in the café, facing each other across a table. They were having another intense head-to-head, and were so deeply engrossed that they showed no sign of having noticed my arrival. Not wanting to intrude, I stole away and left them to it. In the kitchen I glanced at the menu, which showed that there was plenty to keep me busy. So I set to work on the soup of the day.

Fifteen minutes later Kika bounced into the room and began to roll out some pastry that she had prepared earlier. She was closely followed by Thierry, who hung about awkwardly, shifting from foot to foot and rubbing his temples as if to soothe the shooting pains in his head. Neither of them greeted me or seemed remotely aware of my presence. The air was humming, the atmosphere so thick you could touch it.

'Ah, this is stupid,' he said at last. 'You're so pigheaded.'

'Look, why don't you just fuck off, Thierry?' She was rolling out the pastry with increasing vigour. 'You can see I'm busy. I've got a business to run.'

He made as if to leave and then turned back. 'Okay, I'm off. We can talk about this tonight.'

'Talk?' she scoffed. 'What's the point? Haven't we talked enough?'

Still he paced the room, reluctant to give up, and by now I was feeling acutely uncomfortable. So it was a great relief when the milkman arrived with a delivery and I could escape the kitchen for a few minutes. When I returned Kika was alone. But she was silent, the tension from the spat with Thierry still hanging in the air, and we worked on without speaking for the next hour or so. She even managed to avoid eye contact, though I caught a glimpse of her tear-stained face from time to time. It shocked me to catch sight of something else, too. Yeah, a couple of small bruises, one on the left corner of her mouth, and another on the cheek above, just below the eye. Anyway, it must have been mid-morning before there was any real communication between us. At which point, around ten o'clock, she suddenly appeared at my side, holding two steaming mugs of coffee. She banged one down in front of me and gave me a weak smile.

'And how are you?' she said bravely.

'Still wet,' I said, pointing to the legs of my jeans and my discarded socks and shoes.

She looked tired and washed-out. Her eyes were dark and heavy, and her face was a sorry sight, particularly with that hint of bruising. There was no sign of her usual sparkle.

'Not the best of starts,' she said. 'Sorry about that business earlier.'

'Never mind that, are *you* okay?'

'Hmm,' she mused. 'On the ropes perhaps, but not yet on the floor.'

When I laughed at this, she brightened a bit and even managed to produce one of her old infectious giggles.

'So we'll go the full ten rounds, will we?'

'You betcha.'

She kissed me on the head and moved off into the café.

And with that, no more was said about the incident. In fact we got through the day as usual, with casual remarks and cheerful bits of banter. But I felt quite anxious for her at closing time. What was she going home to? Did she need help? As I pulled my jacket on, I looked at her closely, and she seemed to sense my concern.

'Look, don't worry,' she said. 'I'll be fine. I've arranged to stay with my friend Dot tonight. I'll talk things over with her.'

*

What Dot said I never found out. Over the next couple of days life at the café resumed its usual pattern, and the place ticked along merrily without any hint of trouble, just as if the disruption had never happened. So I tactfully avoided any mention of the subject, especially since Kika seemed determined to put it all behind her. She seemed as sparky as ever, throwing herself into the work with all the old briskness and energy. But then, after closing time on the Saturday, she invited me to sit down at a table. She said she had something important to tell me. I sat down slowly and warily. I guessed what was coming and looked hard at her. She seemed to read my thoughts and nodded gravely as if to give warning.

'Do I need to say? I can see you know.'

I stared at her and shook my head. 'I can't believe it,' I said. 'It's been so good.'

'I know, I know. And I'm so sorry. But I've made up my mind. I'm going to travel. The Caribbean and South America. I need to get clean away. Dot's coming too. We're going to break out together.'

I felt suddenly hollow. As if my stomach had dropped to the floor. As if everything had fallen out of me.

'Oh God,' she said, clutching her head. 'You look devastated.'

And I was. Really upset. Too upset to speak. I got up and turned my back on her, trying to hide my feelings. She waited silently, as if in respect for my grief.

'I know you have to do this,' I said at last, 'but I don't think you realise. This job means a lot to me. I'm trying to make a new life for myself. It's helped me to settle in.'

I heard her get out of the seat. She came up behind me and put her arms round my shoulders. She held me silently for several minutes.

'Believe me, I do realise. I feel sick about letting you down. But I've got to do this. It's the only way to shake him off.'

And she was right; she had her own life to think about. Yet I still felt resentful, as if the injuries were all mine.

'So when are you planning to close?'

She hesitated, drew a deep breath. 'Ah, yeah. Now we come to it.'

'Go on. I'm ready.'

She unclasped me, as if to allow me breathing space.

'Look, forgive me, there's no way to break this gently.' She paused. 'Tonight, actually.'

'What?' I turned to face her. ' Are you serious?'

She sighed and slapped the side of her face, as if gently chiding herself. She looked pale and worried.

'I talked it over with Dot last night and finally made up my mind. I would have told you this morning, but I didn't want to ruin our last day. I'll pay you to date, of course, plus a week's notice.'

'But why so soon?'

'Because I need a quick, clean break. I don't want to hang about here where he can find me. Sure, I owe rent on this place, but it's money well spent if I can be shot of him.'

We were silent again. And now it was my turn to clutch my head. I was dizzy with shock.

'It's all so sudden,' I said.

'I know, I know. And I'm so sorry.' Her voice broke slightly. 'But look, something will come along. I'll write you a great reference.'

I smiled wryly. 'Thanks, but it won't be the same.'

She bit her lower lip. I thought she was going to cry.

'Yeah, I'm going to miss you too.'

As I say, sometimes the ground shifts. The next few weeks were hard, some of the hardest of my life. The loss of the job made me dull, moody, restless. Starting again was not a cheerful prospect. I had begun too high, that was my problem. But then again, I blame myself to a large extent. I should have had more grit, not caved in at the slightest setback. Oh, I made some attempt to find work. I flicked through the papers, I glanced at windows and noticeboards, I followed up anything that looked at all promising. But my heart wasn't in it and I always gave up after a few inquiries.

What did I really want? I was confused. I knew what I didn't want. I didn't want bar work. I was out of that game and determined to stay out. No, I needed to move on. I needed a complete change. But what kind of change? Catering offered my best chance of finding work, but nothing I saw seemed attractive. Not after the café. Not after the experience of the past few weeks.

Frustration made me irritable. Matt went off to work during the week, and I lazed about in his room, trying to read or listen to music. Thank God I had my own music. Matt likes Bach, blues and bebop, and nothing much in between. As for his books, they had absolutely no appeal. They split basically into two types: novels by dead writers and tomes with titles like *Homelessness and Social Policy*. Fortunately, there was a collection of tatty old paperbacks in a bookcase on the first-floor landing. So I rooted around in this lot and pulled out a few cheap thrillers and crime novels. But time hung heavy and I couldn't always concentrate. Sometimes I just flopped into an easy chair and stared vacantly at the ceiling. The great unknown lay all around me, yet I'd lost interest. I had no wish to jump on a bus or a tube train. My bag hung from a peg on the wall. Lopsided, abandoned.

Nor did I want to meet the others in the house, even though there was plenty of opportunity. Believe me, the place wasn't exactly silent during the day. Voices, familiar and unfamiliar, called out to each other, droned away in the distance, or sometimes came near, as people crossed the landing and went buzzing past the door of the room. But for some reason I didn't want to join their chat circles and discussion groups. It was the return of the old outsider feeling that had been with me since I came to live in the house, the sense of estrangement that had flared up quite fiercely at Daniela's some weeks before. It was the return of the homesickness I mentioned earlier, which is so hard to explain, especially after all that slagging off of the old crowd. Perhaps they were right and I *was* overreaching myself. Perhaps I'd never make it down here. Perhaps I'd go crawling back. I felt ashamed to be thinking like this; to be wavering, giving in without a fight. But I could feel myself crumbling.

Of course I always brightened when Matt came home from work. In fact, it was the thing I lived for. I loved the way he used to burst in eagerly. The way he crushed me, smothered me with kisses. He was so keen, it was frightening. And like I say, I had to go with it. I saw it as my one chance to fly, get high, lose myself. On the other hand, another part of me wanted to wriggle free, bail out, shoot it down. Sometimes I thought, I don't know who he thinks I am. Hey love, I wanted to say, it's no one special, it's just me. Remember? Little old Billy?

Yeah, as you've gathered, one part of me is a bit wary of this love thing. Sometimes it seems no more than a mirage, a misty phantom, something deep and weird in the head. You make a grab and it vanishes. I can see the appeal, though. It has a strange kind of magic and takes you to somewhere you've never been, like smoking a joint or even reading a book. Which is appropriate, really. Because didn't someone say that it's all down to reading? I mean, this notion of love. That it all comes from books?

Talking of books, I met Clare one afternoon on the stairs and she invited me to tea. Christ, you should see her room – they're everywhere! And even the titles are beyond me, never mind the insides. Apparently, she's writing a book herself. It's all about some mad Irish woman, a poet who was thought to be a witch or something. Clare serves tea in these bone-china cups that once belonged to her grandmother. They have a blue willow-pattern design on them. Cute, but a bit posy. And the tea was something herbal and scented. Not really my thing. Made me gag, but I tried not to show it.

Clare's nice, but she's full of questions; she wants to know everything. She tends to mother you, like an older sister. Now I don't mind opening up in the right company, but I always like to keep a bit of myself back. Leave me alone and I might just creep out a bit; crowd me and I'm likely to clam.

‘Such sad news about the café,’ she said.

‘Yeah, bit of a setback.’

‘Loss of work is so unsettling. You must feel quite dashed.’

‘Yeah, something like that.’

‘Still, you and Matt seem made for each other. I’m so glad you’re here for him. He was heartbroken when he thought he’d lost you. Out of his mind.’

‘Yeah, I know.’

‘Anyway, I do hope something turns up. Can’t live on air, can you? Or love.’

She asked about my background, my family, my previous work. She asked about the Black Horse. She asked about my friends. She asked what I missed. I didn’t spill a lot, though; I told her what I wanted to tell her and no more. And when I got back to Matt’s room an hour later I felt moodier than ever. All the old doubts came back with a vengeance. I was feeling boxed in, squeezed by too many expectations. Could I live up to all this? Did I want to? Was I losing control, yielding to how others saw me? I could feel myself resisting. Tensing. Tightening like a coiled spring.

But none of these events had anything like the impact of my next encounter, which occurred just three days later. Again, I remember everything vividly. I woke late and lay dosing in bed, so that when I next looked at my bedside clock, it was mid-morning and Matt had been at work for several hours. I stumbled out of bed feeling bad. My life was sliding into decay, crumbling into ruin. I pushed an arm through a sleeve of my shirt and a button flew off and rolled under a chair. In despair I fell back onto the bed, clutching my brow. I considered crawling under the duvet again and then rejected the idea. The next forty minutes were spent looking for a needle and thread. Luckily Clare’s basket contained every size and type, though by this time I was sick of my dreary, shuffling existence. So this is it, I remember thinking: fixing this button will be the summit of this day’s achievement and perhaps the high point of my entire week.

To dispel the gloom I decided to go for a walk. It was an overcast day, but warm and pleasant enough, if slightly sultry. I thought I might call at the supermarket and pick up a few bits for the kitchen. Cheese and fruit were running low and we were clean out of bread. I might also buy a paper and stop off somewhere for a coffee. The very thought bucked me up, so I hauled on my jacket, grabbed my keys and wallet, and cantered down the stairs and out of the front door. It was mid-autumn and the trees and flowers were now blowsy and bedraggled, especially in those truck-laden streets. The school term was well underway too, so the pavements were no longer buzzing with parents and kids. Still, it was good to be out, to be sharing life with others rather than turning things over between the walls of Matt's room. I didn't hurry, I sauntered, stopping to peer in the windows of my favourite shops: the rag-trade place, full of colourful T-shirts printed with every kind of logo; the patisserie, where cream cakes were displayed on those elegant tiered stands you see in fancy hotels; the antique shop called Selby's, with its gallery of Victorian prints and crowded assortment of bric-à-brac.

What happened next is difficult to describe. I started to feel uneasy in a vague sort of way. But the funny thing is I don't know why. That sense that someone is following you, where does it come from? Do you catch it from the corner of your eye, pick up patterns of movement that worm into your consciousness and gather into a suspicion? I honestly haven't a clue. I only know that after a while I became convinced that it was happening to me: someone was definitely dogging my steps. The feeling was so strong that once or twice I stopped and looked round, only to find myself staring into a stream of blank and unfamiliar faces. I slipped into a newsagents. Would anyone follow? I bought a paper and a packet of fruit gums, all the while glancing over my shoulder. Apart from myself, though, the place was empty.

So it was all a delusion? A trick of the mind?

Well . . . probably.

Yet when I walked on, the uneasiness was still there.

Eventually, in my madness, my determination to confront this thing head-on, I dodged into a churchyard. The church itself was locked up, so I sat on a bench in the porch and waited. And sure enough, within a few minutes I heard footsteps crunching over the gravel. Yes, someone was approaching, though I couldn't see who it was; the path ran beside the church and was hidden from view. My heart was beating fast, my hands were shaking, and I was suddenly in a panic. I was trapped and had to get away. In an instant I leaped up and rushed out, colliding full pelt with a figure who was just a few paces away and lurching towards me. Our heads smacked together and the force of the impact knocked the man to the ground. I saw him fall and heard him cry out, though for several moments I was too stunned to take in the situation or speak. I simply stared down at him in astonishment. And even in the unlikely setting of that churchyard the form was unmistakable.

'Christ, I don't believe this!' I gasped, when I finally got my breath back. 'But yeah, it makes sense. I might have known. I mean, what the *fuck*?'

I had knocked him onto the grass verge. He lay sprawled on his back, speechless from shock and winded by the fall. I glared at him angrily, still in a state of shock myself. He was moaning gently and at the same time lifting, bending and stretching his right leg, which seemed to have been injured in the fall. My strongest instinct was to walk away and leave him there. But after a while I went forward, reached out an arm and hauled him to his feet. Looking round for a seat, I spotted a rectangular tomb nearby, hidden in a cluster of yew trees. I guided him towards it, brushed off some dried crow-shit, and we sat side by side on the flat surface for a few minutes, silent and still dazed. He pulled a large white handkerchief from his breast pocket and began to dab his brow, all the while taking deep breaths and heaving huge sighs. He was piling on the agony, tragedy written on every feature.

'Well, well,' I said. 'No real surprise, is it? The proverbial bad penny.'

‘Oh, thanks,’ he croaked. ‘That’s nice.’

‘Shake you off? No chance. You’re the little old guy in the story. The one who squats on your back, his legs gripping your neck.’

‘God Almighty, give me a break, will ya? I hope you realise you knocked me nearly senseless. I may need treatment.’

‘Yeah, from a shrink. And it’s not a matter of *may*, it’s a bloody certainty, ya mad bastard!’

‘’Ere, mind yer language.’

‘Oh, don’t start all that. Let’s have some explaining, shall we? What the hell are you playing at?’

He looked around furtively, and even glanced up at the trees, as if spies might be hanging from the branches.

‘We can’t talk here,’ he said.

‘Why? What’s wrong with here? This is perfectly fine.’

‘I haven’t come all this way to skulk in the back-end of a churchyard.’

‘Oh really? Couldn’t be more suitable, actually. Remember the last time we spoke? That dignified little speech about the next time you saw me you hoped it would be in a box?’

He went silent for a while, staring ahead, mopping his brow.

‘William . . .’

I scoffed bitterly. Christ, how did I ever get mixed up with a toad like Arthur?

‘Don’t William me. You can cut that out, I’m not impressed. This is my turf, not yours. You don’t own me. You never did.’

My voice was rising, which seemed to make him uncomfortable. Suddenly he leaped up, and with surprising sprightliness. The injured leg, as I suspected, was mostly sham.

‘There must be a place around here,’ he said. ‘Come on, let me treat you to a late breakfast. I’ve come all this way. I need to talk to you, Pixie. Hey look, you’re not going to slam the door on me, are ya?’

Pixie, yeugh! He's the only one who ever calls me that. It's short for Pickering, my surname. He uses it whenever he's feeling generous. It's supposed to be chummy, affectionate. I've always hated it, and actually I think he knows. So I didn't reply. Instead, I got up and walked off. He followed me, crunching over the gravel just a few paces to my rear. But as I left the churchyard and turned into the street, he suddenly appeared beside me. I made no acknowledgement and we walked along in silence. My mind was in turmoil. Part of me wanted to throw him off, toss him aside, disown him altogether, but curiosity and insecurity were getting the better of me. And he knew it. He sensed I was wavering; he's a cunning, manipulative sod.

Halfway along the next block, he clapped a hand on my shoulder and brought me to a halt. We were standing beside a burger bar. Bright plastic tables, padded bench-like seats.

'How very convenient,' he said.

He flung an arm out in front of me and held the palm outstretched, as if to invite me in. I faced him with a straight, no-nonsense look.

'For you perhaps, but not for me.'

'What? You won't even share a pot of tea?'

'It's not the tea, it's what goes with it.'

'Look, no pressure, no hard sell. I just want to talk.'

'Yeah, *talk*. Depends where it goes.'

He went silent. We stood awkwardly on the pavement. He stared hard at me and I outfaced him.

'I can't believe this,' he said after a while. 'I can't bloody believe it. How long have we known each other?'

He looked genuinely hurt. And it was all show, I knew that. But whether real or not, I fell for it. That's my problem, I let people get to me. Even shits like Arthur.

I glanced at my watch.

'Make it quick,' I said. 'I can't be hanging about. I've got shopping to do.'

They say the closer you are to some people, the more you want to wound them, cast them off, fling them aside. Seeing

Arthur in London, his turning up like that, was a weird experience, believe me. I can't quite describe what I felt. I suppose I was secretly pleased in a daft sort of way. I felt grounded again, back on familiar soil. Yet I also wanted to drive a stake through his heart. Oh yeah, that day I discovered depths of feeling in me I didn't know I had. A while back I mentioned my insecurity. There, in London, I was still wobbly on my feet. I'd not been around long enough to feel certain of my bearings. I imagine I had the dazed look of a visitor, of someone just passing through. I knew that he could see all this, that he was there to make use of the situation, and I hated him for it. Yet my hatred was mixed with a kind of nostalgia, of fondness for the old antagonism. Besides which, I was curious. Arthur and the old crowd were part of myself; forgetting them, tearing them out, was an act of self-mutilation. Like lopped-off limbs, they were there and not there; ghostly presences in the mind, still tangible though unseen.

He knew all this, of course. So feeding my curiosity became part of his strategy, part of the subtle approach he adopted to start with. Softly was the watchword. He carefully avoided a full-frontal attack; he knew that would be disastrous. It was an amusing act to watch.

'Terry sends her love,' he began, pouring the first cup from a stainless-steel pot.

'Well, you can take that back. I'm through with plastic sentiment.'

'Aw, come on, that's not fair. A few weeks in the city and you've turned as 'ard as nails.'

'That girl's so shallow, if you breathed on her she'd evaporate. And that goes for all the rest of ya.'

'Oh dear, is this to be the tone? Civility's not too much to ask, surely to God?'

'Civility?' I laughed harshly 'What do you know about that, Arthur? Where was civility a few weeks back? Do you recall that poisonous little diatribe? The one about coming after me and flaying me alive? What a conveniently short memory you've got.'

'Look, I'm not here to pick a fight. What I said then, that's all in the past. I was a bit upset, remember. So let's try to put it behind us.'

'So what *are* you here for?'

'I was coming to that. I'm down on a spot of business. Thought I'd look you up.'

'Look me up? Spying, hiding in doorways, following at a distance. Excuse me, but that's a bloody funny way to look someone up, wouldn't you say?'

'Just surveying the scene, that's all. Wanted to catch you alone. Couldn't knock at the door, could I? Not too sure of the reception, so to speak.'

'Spot of business? *What* spot of business, exactly?'

'Christ, give us a break. What *is* this, the Inquisition? If you must know, I came to see a specialist. About my problem. Someone the GP recommended.'

'Let's not play games, Arthur. We both know why you're here. You're here to persuade me to come back. Turn the screws, twist my arm, make me weaken.'

He looked comically indignant. How could I think such a thing? And I had to smile. I'd seen that look of wounded innocence, oh, so many times before.

He shook his head sorrowfully. 'Not at all, my unworthy friend, you do me wrong. Like I say, I was in London and thought I'd pay you a visit.' He paused, as if almost too choked to carry on, but I was watching him closely. I could see him preparing to launch his next manoeuvre. 'I'll say this, though, Billy Boy, you've still got friends up there. Oh yeah. I was speaking to Stan and Betty just last Sunday and they were singing your praises, in spite of all the grief you've caused them. They'd take you back any time. You were well set up at the Black Horse. Nice comfy room, and some of the clients were very partial.' His mouth curled into a sly smile and he rubbed his thumb and forefinger together. 'And what about your ma and pa? What about your family, eh? They'll be missing you.'

'Nice try, Arthur, but I don't think so. We're not exactly close, me and that lot, remember?'

‘How’s Lover Boy?’

‘The name is Matt and he’s fine. So if you were hoping he’d caught malaria, I’m sorry to disappoint you.’

‘Not too well off, though, is he? I’ve seen where you live and it’s not exactly Buck House, as the duchess remarked. And we thought you were off to join the nobs.’ He scanned my face for some sign of agreement, some indication that living with Matt had not come up to expectation. ‘Look, matey, if you come back, things’ll be different. I know I’ve been a grouch, I know there’s been words between us, but we can draw a line under all that now, can’t we? You can return on your own terms. We can start afresh. And like I say, the clients still remember you.’

‘I’ve no interest in the clients, Arthur. I’ve found something else.’

‘Something else, pah! You honestly think you can stand the pace down here? Oh yes, it’s fine now, everything hunky-dory. But what happens when the bread goes stale? What happens when the cheese turns green and furry? What happens when the oil runs out?’

I was silent. He fixed me with a hard stare, as if demanding a response.

‘Don’t let me stop you in full flood,’ I said. ‘The floor’s entirely yours.’

He sat back with an exasperated sigh. ‘What I’m saying is, you don’t know where your own best interests lie.’

I sat back too, with another harsh laugh. ‘Where’s that, then, Arthur? With you? You have my best interests at heart, do you? Of course you do, I’m so sorry. What an ungrateful sod I am to question your kindly advice, especially when you’ve come all this way on my behalf.’

The smile had left his face now. In fact, he was looking distinctly rattled. The soft approach was about to turn very hard indeed. Oh yeah, Arthur can turn funny in an instant. As I should know better than anyone.

‘Something else, you say? Oh yeah, the name is Matt, I remember now. Fresh face, soft floppy fringe, wet behind the lugs. Oh sure, that’s something else, and no mistake. But I thought your skin was a bit tougher. I thought you knew the score, how to handle yourself. Look again, ya sad sap, it's all a bloody dream, a mirage, a bubble. Can you hear me? Rub your eyes, shake your head a couple of times and it will all vanish.'

I smiled wryly. 'Oh well, thanks for the tea, Arthur, I think I'll be off now.'

'This Matt, does he know the history? Have you told him?'

'Have I told him what exactly?'

'You know bloody well what. That those wide eyes of yours are not as innocent as they look. That that sphincter of yours has been punctured more times than I've had hot dinners? That the sighs of the heart mean less to you than the size of the wallet?'

He was breathing heavily now, his face was red and he seemed to be heading for another of his breakdowns.

'This is the rant of a desperate man, Arthur. Cool it, or we might have to send for the boys in white coats.'

'So he doesn't know. That's not quite fair, is it? That's deception, that is. Perhaps someone should drop him a hint, a line or two in the post. And perhaps that someone should be me. I'll give it some thought when I get back. Dig out the old pad and envelopes. Got the address right, have I?'

He pulled a piece of crumpled paper from a pocket and held it out to me. I snatched it and read it quickly. It was correct in every detail, right down to the postcode. I ripped it apart and stuffed the pieces into my pocket.

'The act of a desperate man, William. I know it by heart. Yes, it's stowed away in the portable filing system.' He pointed to his head. 'I've also given it a special entry in here.' He pulled a small notebook from his inside pocket and flashed it in front of my eyes. 'Just to show how much I treasure it.'

My mind was racing. Of course it was no surprise that he knew the address. How else had he found me? No, what intrigued me was *how* he knew. Where exactly had I slipped up? Had I been careless? And why had I given so little thought to any of this before?

'Snouty as ever, I see. So how did you find it?'

He smiled. 'Oh yeah, I was wondering when we'd come to that. Thought you'd never ask.'

'Okay, so I'm asking.'

'Stan and Betty, of course. You sent for your cards, remember?'

I nodded and went silent for a while. Then I stood up, straightened my clothes and brushed myself down. He glanced up at me expectantly, a little smirk at the corner of his mouth.

I fixed him with a deadly stare. 'If you ruin this for me, you sick bastard, I'll never forgive you. *Never*. I'll come for you, just as you once threatened to come for me. I'll smash up that cosy little nest of yours. I'll knock you to the floor and kick out your slimy yellow guts.'

I turned and walked briskly out. I was trembling like a leaf in a force-ten gale. I imagined him sitting there with that funny smile still stamped on his face.

'Ooh, tough talkin', Pixie,' I heard him call after me.

Most of my dreams, however vivid, fade immediately on waking. Not this one. I woke with a start that night, bathed in a cold sweat. It took a while for me to realise, with relief, that I was in Matt's bed. The room was not quite pitch black. Pale light of some kind was fringing the curtains. Matt was asleep. I could hear his gentle breathing. I lay there on my back, glad – oh so glad! – to be awake, but not sure if the world I'd escaped from was not more real, even now, than the world I'd woken to.

In one part of this dream I was wandering alone through a walled churchyard. Yet not quite alone; I was aware of some menacing, unseen presence. Some way ahead a snarling dog had blocked my path. To escape, I plunged into a patch of dark undergrowth and stumbled across a grave. There was no inscription on the headstone, but the blank slab was burning vividly, flames licking the edges. The image is branded on my memory. And now someone was drawing near. Or was it some *thing*? In rising panic I started to run like a hunted creature, the breath of the hunter scorching my neck. All at once the churchyard became a vast lake. I was swimming in a tangle of choking weeds. Some people were rowing in a small boat, far off in the distance. I called out to them – called with all my might – but no sounds escaped my lips. I tried again; tried with every breath in my body. The person in the stern stood up. He looked around. It was Matt. Had he heard? Apparently not. I was dumb, impotent, helpless. The oars dipped, the boat glided on. It became a speck on the horizon. The weeds closed over me.

On waking, I lay still for some time, breathing hard and staring into the solid blackness of the room. And after a while I realised that my throat was dry. So I got up and went to the bathroom. I gulped back a glass of water and splashed my face several times. But the person in the mirror sneered at me. You're a fraud; you've never really owned up to who you are. You'll be found out; the world hates a cheat and a liar. I stared back. I opened my mouth to defend myself, but my tongue was as heavy as lead. It stuck in my throat: dumb, impotent, helpless. I wandered back to bed in a daze and crept stealthily under the duvet. As if trespassing. As if I had no right to be there. But for all the care I took not to disturb, I failed. Matt murmured, turned sleepily towards me and wrapped his arms around me. His warm breath fell on my cheeks, his wet mouth crushed against mine, the heat of his body enveloped me.

'Hi, gorgeous,' he said. 'You're *so* nice. Have I ever told you that?'

I was close to tears, afraid of breaking down.

'Hold me tight,' I said. 'As tight as you can.'

Yeah, hold tight. We come now to the hard bit. Hard in all senses. The ride from now on is bumpy and I'm not sure that I can say what happened. I'm not even sure that I know what happened. Fear, insecurity, lack of confidence, low self-esteem, they were all in there somewhere. And losing the job didn't help. I had too much time to sit and brood. Oh, that sod Arthur had his own devious motives, I knew that. But was he right? Was it all a mirage? A bubble that would soon burst? Now let's be clear. The threatened letter, that was nothing: an *empty* threat. He would never write it. No, Arthur was more subtle than that. He knew how to get under one's skin, sow seeds in the mind, erode from within. He didn't need to write that letter; it was enough to mention it. Its power was symbolic. And the target was not Matt; the target was me.

The following week was so painful I can scarcely speak about it. I rarely went out, and then only to the shops. I moped about in the room, turning things over in my mind. And my thoughts always came back to the same question: what am I doing here? Well, I knew the answer: I had been seduced by this thing called love. And what *is* love? I still don't know. I can only point to my life with Matt. If the word means anything at all, then that must be what it means. If love exists, then that's the nearest I've come. But how to live with anything so fragile? The responsibility was too great. Sooner or later I was bound to slip up, let him down, let everyone down. 'He's so happy with you, he's a changed man,' they all said. So his happiness depended on me? That was frightening, that was awesome. I mean, I'm no one special, I'm just a bloke. Would I be to blame when the oil ran out?

What Matt was thinking I don't know. Did he sense my doubts? I think he did, though I tried to disguise them. Every evening he would look closely at me, search my face for signs, reach for my innermost thoughts. He would embrace me from behind, hug me, bite my neck. His worst fear was that I would leave him. I was always aware of it. I knew it in every fibre. And sometimes I couldn't stand it. Sometimes I wanted to slip from his grasp, dodge the fierceness of his gaze. Sometimes I would invent an excuse to escape the confinement of that room. Usually I pretended that I was off to the shops, that there were things I needed to buy. And the freedom of the streets was welcome, though sometimes it seemed to make the predicament starker. It was good to know that I could bust out, but then the real situation felt more oppressive by contrast.

A few days later Matt came home from work in the early afternoon. He found me sprawled on the bed, reading the final chapter of *Sharp Practice*, a lurid crime thriller full of sex, violence and drug dealing. He was in rather a jaunty mood. He explained that he was using up some annual leave and had taken the rest of the day off. Brilliant sunlight was slanting through the window – we were enjoying a few days of Indian summer – but the room, I'm sorry to say, was a bit of a mess. There were unwashed plates and mugs lying around, some crumbs had been crushed into the carpet, and one of the chairs was draped in a heap of tangled clothes. Yes, I was moving downhill rapidly, slipping back into my old slovenly habits.

He rattled his car keys. 'Come on. Let's go for a drive.'

My eyes flew open. This was such a change of routine; leaving off early had transformed him. He was usually drained when he got home. I could sometimes revive him by massaging his neck and rubbing his temples, but it was often an hour or more before he was fit to do anything.

'Go for a drive? Hey, what's got into you?'

'I think it's this room. It's becoming a pit. We need to get out more.'

I felt a surge of resentment; it sounded like a rebuke. 'So what have you got in mind? Beer and crisps at a country pub? A stroll on the sands at Margate?'

He paused. 'No, what I'm proposing is a trip to Sevenoaks.'

I was intrigued by this, but rather taken off guard. I knew that his parents lived in Sevenoaks. He had spoken to me about them on one occasion, though he didn't often do so. He had a sister too, who lived in Sussex, but he mentioned her even less.

'Sevenoaks?' I said. 'What's this? Meet the family?'

He threw me a challenging look. 'Well, why not? We're a couple now, aren't we?'

I didn't question this. Instead, I got up, wandered to the window and stared out. 'So what are they like? You've never said much about them.'

He hesitated, and then shrugged. 'They're fine. Oh, I can't deny that we have our differences. We don't always see eye to eye. But they're decent enough. They mean well. They'll love you.'

It was now my turn to hesitate.

'Look, I'm not sure. Is this the right moment? I'm not on top form today.'

He came up behind me and threw his arms round my neck. 'You'll be splendid,' he said, kissing my cheek.

I turned and cocked an eyebrow. 'Hmm.'

I didn't feel splendid. Anything but.

However, I decided to smother my doubts. I hauled myself off the bed and snatched up my denim jacket from the back of a chair. At the very least a drive into the country would lift my spirits. Or so I told myself.

Despite Matt's familiarity with the back routes, it took us an hour to hit the open road. But when we did, the rush of cool air that wafted over us as we emerged from the stagnant fumes of the city had just the exhilarating effect I'd been hoping for. We stopped en route to buy some plums from a wayside stall as a gift for Matt's parents, though we immediately munched our way through half of them, which rather defeated the purpose, so we stuffed the rest in the glove compartment for finishing off on the way home. Shortly after this I snapped on the radio. I was in the mood for a blast of loud rock. What emerged, though, was an operatic aria from a diva in full flood, every vocal chord stretched to the limit and an orchestra surging in the background. I turned to Matt with a snort of laughter, but just at that moment, intent on his driving, he swerved off the main road into a suburban estate, and after a few turns brought the car to a sudden halt.

We had pulled up outside a handsome mock-Tudor lodge, with crossbeams and leaded windows. The place had the look of a showpiece home from a property magazine. Two abandoned deckchairs stood on a cropped lawn, surrounded by poplar trees, acacia bushes and a bright white fence with arrow-tipped slats. I surveyed the scene and then glanced nervously at Matt, who had turned off the engine and was watching me closely.

'Wow,' I breathed. 'Classy or what?'

He took my hand and squeezed it. 'Hey, relax. They'll love you.'

We got out, adjusted our clothing and strolled slowly up the path with pretended casualness.

'I'll take you round the back,' he said. 'Mum doesn't like me to ring the doorbell. I'm not a visitor, I'm family. She insists I treat the place like home.'

But the front door opened before we reached the house, and there stood a slim, elegant lady in a pale-blue dress, her tanned face slightly lined, her dark hair stylishly cut and flecked with grey. She greeted us with a smile, and almost immediately a figure appeared behind her, peering over his glasses and clutching a newspaper. He was tall and slightly stooped, with a fringe of cropped hair round his bald head and a neat grey moustache.

'Matt,' he gasped.

'Typical,' said the lady, shaking her head. 'Descend without warning.'

'Sorry,' said Matt. 'Came on impulse. Such a lovely day.'

She turned to me, still smiling, but with a quick penetrating look that seemed to strip me naked.

'Mum, Dad,' said Matt, leaping in to cover the slight awkwardness. 'This is Billy.'

They had firm handshakes, and I tried to match the firmness. I was conscious of being judged, and acutely aware that handshakes, for these people, were a sign of character.

'Penny,' said the lady.

'Charles,' said the man, coming forward and thrusting out an arm, military-fashion. 'Nice to meet you.'

'Yes, indeed,' she said. 'Now come through to the back. What will you boys have? Some wine? We've just opened a bottle of Chablis. Or there's beer, if you'd rather.'

The house was as immaculate inside as out. We were led into a spacious sitting room, tastefully decorated in red and gold, its soft furnishings scattered with fat, newly-plumped cushions. I can still feel the impressive spring of the carpet. From there, we passed into a handsome conservatory, a riot of white tracery and flowering plants. A picnic table lay just beyond, marooned on a wide expanse of lawn. It sheltered beneath an ample pink shade, its gleaming white linen encircled by wicker chairs. Penny invited us to take a seat and then slipped off to fetch some extra glasses. Meanwhile, Charles adjusted the height and angle of the shade. The sun, though sinking, was still quite powerful and dazzling.

'How strange, your turning up like this,' he said. 'We were saying only last night that we hadn't seen you in a while. Yes, Georgie looked in to cut your mother's hair and was asking after you. Ah, she's such a lovely girl, isn't she? Always bright and cheerful.'

Matt turned to me with a large wink. 'Georgie's unmarried and about my age. And of course she'd make someone a charming wife.'

'Ah, come on,' protested Charles. 'That's not what I meant at all.'

'What this?' said Penny, returning with a tray of drinks and glasses. 'Quarrelling already? For heaven's sake, Matt, you've only just arrived. Now, have you boys eaten? Should I make some sandwiches? Whip up an omelette?'

'We're fine, Mum,' said Matt. 'If necessary, we'll grab something on the way home.'

'We've been snacking on plums,' I said sheepishly. 'We bought them from a stall. They were meant for you.'

She shook her head at this and broke into fits of warm laughter, though it was difficult to tell whether she was genuinely amused or simply keen to create a bond between us. I'd been silent until then, and she seemed relieved, not only to hear my voice but to share a moment of humour.

'This boy's not from round here, Daddy,' she said. 'That's for sure.'

'No, by 'eck as like,' said Charles. 'Come on, woman. Surely you recognise a Yorkshireman?'

He leaned forward to refill his glass. Despite his gangling, dishevelled look – khaki pants, open-neck shirt, sleeves rolled to the elbow – he had the distinguished air of a family solicitor, though he was, as I knew, a retired architect.

'So tell us about yourself, Billy,' he said. 'How did you become entangled with our Matt here?'

'Entangled!' scoffed Matt, shaking his head and turning to me. 'Take note, love. This is the kind of language I have to suffer in this place.'

'Oh Matt,' pleaded Penny. 'Don't start all that now, please.'

'Entangled?' said Charles, glancing around at all of us with a look of bewildered innocence. 'So what's wrong with entangled, may I ask?'

'Look, we're not a couple of college dudes. We're not buddies hanging out. We're not Tom Sawyer and Huck Finn. We're lovers. We live together.'

There was a moment of stiff silence. Penny took a large gulp of wine.

'Of course,' she said, smiling all round. 'That's what I assumed.'

'Me too,' said Charles, with an edge of resentment. 'It was a fair supposition and now you've confirmed it. But how were we to know? We're not telepathic.'

'Anyway, it doesn't really matter where we met,' said Matt. 'But if you must know, it was in a bar.' He turned to me with a smile. 'Yeah, one very hot crowded night and Billy in a muck sweat.'

'In a muck sweat?' said Penny, with a hint of amused distaste. Her eyes were boring into me, avid with curiosity.

'Pulling pints,' I said.

I didn't flinch. I looked her straight in the eye and spoke in a flat voice. The truth would come out sooner or later. And anyway, why hide it? I wasn't ashamed of what I did. After all, it was useful work, unlike some. Why put myself down?

Charles nodded and looked a bit uncomfortable. He glanced at his watch. 'So not on duty tonight?'

By God, they're quick, these two. Rip you open, flush you out in minutes.

'I left my job to come and live with Matt,' I said.

'So you're unemployed?' said Penny.

I nodded, not feeling up to further explanation.

'Look, it's been a difficult time,' said Matt. 'Billy had a job, but then the business folded.'

In the silence that followed Penny and Charles looked at me critically. I was again being judged, not the slightest doubt about that, and I could feel them becoming distant. They were smiling with kindly interest, but I withered a bit under their cool appraising eyes, sensing that I didn't quite measure up.

'I suppose,' said Charles at last, 'there's always the dole to fall back on.'

I shifted in my chair. 'Not really. I've been hoping to avoid that.'

'Hmm,' he mused. 'Well, it's a matter of finances, I suppose.' He was staring at the floor, speaking to no one in particular.

'We're okay,' said Matt edgily. 'We'll manage till something comes along.'

'Bar work,' said Penny. 'Is that hard to find?'

I met her steely gaze. Why don't you just out with it, ma'am? Barmen? Ten a penny.

'Billy's trying to move into a new area,' said Matt. 'And I approve of what he's doing. It shows resourcefulness, in my view.'

Thank you, Matt, I'll conduct my own defence, if you don't mind.

'Yeah, I'd like a change of scene,' I said.

Silence. Unspoken attitudes hanging in the air. I was waiting for Charles to say that I should play to my strengths; that a job of any kind was better than no job. I could almost feel what he was thinking; his thoughts seemed to block the space between us as solid as bricks. If you were really resourceful, his frown said, you'd know the shame of being a kept man; you'd get off yer arse, hop on yer bike, roll up yer sleeves. That's what his face said. But actually, of course, he said nothing, making his attitude all the more deafeningly clear. Silence, as they say, speaks volumes.

But then Penny broke in with a tactful change of subject. 'So you've moved in with Matt,' she said. 'A bit cramped for the pair of you? That room?'

'Nonsense,' said Matt. 'It's not a room, it's a shared house. Anyway, how would you know whether it's cramped or not? You've never been near the place.'

'Well, I've never been invited,' she said, looking hurt.

'Because I know you'd disapprove. You abhor dust. You loathe mice. You shudder at the sight of stains in a toilet bowl.'

'Dear me.' She smiled and shook her head. 'I'm sure that house is nothing like as scarifying as you make out.'

'As a matter of fact, we have discussed making a move,' said Matt, turning to me with a smile. 'And I'd go tomorrow, but Billy has doubts.'

Penny and Charles looked at me curiously.

'Early days,' I said. 'Don't want to rush things.'

Charles nodded. 'Sounds very sensible to me. Don't be swayed by Matt's impulsiveness.'

'Sensible!' Matt leaped up, his whole body trembling. 'Bah! I've had enough of this. Come on, Billy. I'll show you my old room.'

I glanced at Penny and Charles, and we smiled at each other with bemused shrugs. Matt's tone was that of someone calling a pet dog to heel and I was unsure how to react. Should I resist or trot along behind? Compliance seemed necessary to preserve the peace, so I stood up. But I rose very slowly, with a pointed glance at Matt to make clear my unwillingness, my displeasure at this treatment. Matt's troubled relationship with his parents was now all too obvious. I had had doubts about the wisdom of this venture from the start, but now I was beginning to ask myself about the purpose of it. Why were we here? Was this a social visit or a mission? And what about me? What was *my* role in this awkward scenario? I was beginning to feel less like a person in my own right than a pawn in a game.

Matt's old room was upstairs, at the end of the landing. A small ceramic plate reading *Matthew* was still attached to the door. It had a sterile, unlived-in look. Everything spotless and tidied away.

'Isn't this sad?' he said, strolling about. 'I mean, nothing's changed, and yet – I dunno – everything's different. It never looked like this in my day. The place was a stinking mess.'

It was a fair-sized room, the walls decorated with posters of wildlife and postcards from foreign destinations. A single made-up bed, covered in a striped counterpane, stood against one wall, and a desk, facing the window, looked out into the branches of a luxuriant conifer. A dozen or more naked clothes-hangers hung from the bar of a free-standing metal frame, and several cardboard boxes were stacked in one corner. Containing what? Matt's old clothes? Discarded playthings? Most surfaces had been cleared of debris, but a framed photograph of Matt in his graduation gown had been placed centrally on the chest of drawers. I cast my eyes over the half-dozen books standing upright on the shelf above: a child's one-volume encyclopedia; a world atlas with a torn back and split spine; an abridged version of *Ivanhoe* with a frayed and faded dust-jacket. The whole scene spoke of adoring parents, failing to adjust to the departure of an only child.

I glanced around silently. I was still feeling quietly nettled about Matt's recent high-handed behaviour. Did it show? I think perhaps it did, because shortly afterwards, as we stood side by side gazing out of the window, he slid an arm round my waist, then turned and planted a soft kiss on my cheek. After a while, though, he pulled away, crossed the room and opened the door of a built-in cupboard. He fetched the chair from his desk, stood on it and reached deep into the back of the upper shelf.

'Ah, yes,' he said. 'This is what I really came to see. This is what I really wanted to show you.'

And what he really wanted to show me was a large golden teddy bear. He was holding it aloft, displaying it proudly. It was certainly a fine specimen. True, it had a few bald patches and had lost some of its sheen, but otherwise it was in good nick. He stepped down and sat the bear on the bed, its back propped against the pillows.

'Meet Wilfred,' he said.

I nodded and stared at the bear with a kind of vague hostility. I've always had an aversion to teddy bears, I don't know why. Do I simply hate the mawkishness that surrounds them? Yeah, I think it must be that; it's not the bear itself, but what it represents. And what did Wilfred represent? I'm not sure. Anyway, I looked at Matt and his eyes were shining. Glistening, even. And in a flash I saw, as never before, that we came from very different worlds. That deep gulfs lay between us, spaces that perhaps we could never cross. I saw that it was not just Penny and Charles who had failed to adjust. Matt was clinging to the wreckage of his old life too, even as he strove to kick free. It was a defining moment. I saw in an instant what this whole visit was about. It was about home. It was not about me and him, but about him and them. About how he needed them and didn't need them. About how rebellion is often a sign of dependence.

We left Wilfred sitting upright on the bed. On departure, Matt stood for a few minutes, his hand on the doorknob, looking back fondly at the room and the cherished bear. To me, the creature looked horribly smug and I wanted to shy something at it. A rotten apple-core perhaps, or a gnawed bone.

In the kitchen we found Penny, uncorking a new bottle of wine.

'I've just remembered, you boys,' she said. 'There's a punnet of strawberries in the fridge and some chocolate ice cream. You know, Matt. Your favourite.'

We looked at each other, grinned and shrugged.

'Well now, what a treat,' he hummed. 'Yeah, that'll do nicely, Ma.'

And I nodded in agreement – though with a secret smile, of course. I mean, you had to give the old girl credit, she knew a trick or two. Strong, skilful, tenacious.

Two weeks later, on Black Thursday as I now call it, I woke to the loud rattle of my alarm. I smacked it smartly on the head and lay listening to the sound of rainwater spilling heavily onto the sill from the broken guttering. It was half-past nine, Matt had gone to work, the house was as silent as the grave. Setting the alarm had been Matt's idea. He saw it as a way of pulling myself out of sloth and dissipation. Mornings were the best time to look for work, he said. Getting up would invigorate me. Give me a sense of purpose.

But getting up had no such effect. I felt as heavy as lead and slightly sick. This was partly the result of over-indulgence the night before. A woman called Carmen, who was staying for a few days as a guest of Clare, had volunteered to act as cook. Carmen was from San Diego and her prize dish was a rich fish casserole, which we'd eaten in large quantities and washed down with several bottles of wine. But of course that's not the whole story. Food and drink won't fully explain the way I was feeling. As I knew, and as you've guessed, it had much more to do with my state of mind.

I stood in front of the mirror and was dismayed by what I saw. The person staring back at me looked lost and miserable. So I tried straightening up and stretching my face into a smile. But that seemed to make things worse. The smile was cheap, fake, painted-on. So I turned away, and it was then that I spotted the note. The blue paper and round script were unmistakable. Prominently displayed, it was propped against a mug on the desk and held in place by a glass paperweight. I snatched it up and read it quickly.

Good morning, love! Or should that be afternoon? (Only joking.) Anyway, on second thoughts, not Scotland. Too cold. How about Italy or the south of France? Think about it. Love, M.

Italy? The south of France? I stared at the words blankly, and then tossed the note aside with a faint sense of nausea. No, it was no use, I simply couldn't relate to these sudden crazes. At that moment both places seemed as remote as the moon.

The kitchen was strewn with the remains of breakfast. Unwashed plates and mugs were everywhere, and in the middle of the table a long-legged insect was thrashing about in a pool of milk. I felt the teapot. Tepid, ycugh! But hold on, what's this? A fag packet, apparently discarded and sheltering a single broken-backed ciggy? Oh boy, just the ticket. Just what the witch doctor ordered. Now, I'm not a regular smoker. I've never been a baccy fiend, a nicoteeny. In fact, at that time I hadn't lit up in months. But for the next few minutes I sat and drew deeply on that busted stick, staring vacantly at the wall, watching the smoke drift lazily upward as I waited for the kettle to boil.

Vacant? Well, that may be how I looked, but actually I was not in the least vacant. No, I was anything but. I was a battleground. A field of conflict, overlaid with fear and guilt. And my fear and guilt were related, as I well knew. They came from the same place: a dim corner somewhere in the back of my head, where they'd seen an unspeakable truth crouching in darkness. A truth that was only just now, at this very moment, beginning to emerge into the cruel light of morning.

Now let's be clear. Matt's still there, right at the centre: the focus, the core, the Pole Star of my life. Yes, he's the one. Always will be, now and forever. Spiritually, we're inseparable. In every other way, though, we're worlds apart. A clumsy fit, an ill-matched pair. And so – how to explain this? – I sort of judged that in the long run our planned life together was a doomed project, a dream-scenario resting on shaky foundations. In the long run he would find me out; I would fail him; we would hurt each other.

I see that visit to Sevenoaks as the turning point. Not that I can say exactly what happened. On the surface, nothing really did happen. All I can say is that a light seemed to come on in my head, throwing up angles and corners, revealing cracks and crevices, creating odd perspectives and shadow effects. And afterwards, everything in the landscape looked the same, yet slightly different.

So yeah, the thing was decided, my mind made up. It was as good as made up the night before, in fact. I thought, if it's going to happen, and it *is* going to happen, it might as well happen now. But all the same, to simply sneak away? Without word, without warning? Oh no, that was too cruel. That was cowardly, that was evil. How could I live with myself? Just thinking about it made me flinch. My body convulsed. I writhed in my seat as if stung by hornets. The proper thing to do was to face up to it, I knew that. To tell him, face to face. But tell him? How could I tell him? I had thought and thought about it. There was no way to tell him. Even if I could find the words, they would still be useless. He would plead, he would beg me to stay, he would turn me inside out. There would be anger and tears. It would be too painful. It would be unbearable.

On my way back to the room I met Clare. She came hurrying down the stairs towards me, stuffing a reporter's notebook into a bag slung over one shoulder.

'Are you all right?' she asked with a searching look.

I smiled weakly and nodded, feeling uncomfortable, distant, anxious to avoid her piercing gaze.

'I'm just off to the library for a few hours,' she said. 'What about you? What are you up to? Perhaps you'd like to come round for tea later on?'

Again I smiled weakly. Dumbfounded, utterly at a loss.

'Great,' she said. 'I'll tap on your door. Say, around four.'

She flew off and I trudged on up the stairs with a sinking heart and a lurching stomach. I seemed to be wading into a dark swamp. When I reached the room I shut the door firmly behind me. I glanced around at the shabby furnishings, the peeling paintwork. The place was a far cry from what I'd imagined the day I'd set out for London. Matt was educated and well-spoken, yet he lived in this ramshackle warren. Oh,

I knew that social workers were not exactly rich, but nevertheless I'd expected something a bit grander. How naive I'd been, and how far I'd come in a short period. Still, what did the state of the room matter? It had been home for the past few weeks, home in all senses, and I was seeing it now for perhaps the last time. My nausea flared up again, worse than ever.

My first consideration was money. I snatched my jacket from the peg behind the door, reached into the top pocket and tossed the contents onto the bed. I had about forty pounds. Well, it wasn't my money. Not really. Not money I'd earned. Oh, I liked to think it was. At the time I thought of it as the remains of my final wage packet from the café, but that had drained away long ago. I was now living on handouts from Matt. Anyway, whether mine or not, it wasn't enough. To get home and avoid starvation, I needed more. So I started to ransack drawers, reach into back corners, explore all possible hiding places. Nothing came to light, however. Not a brass farthing. Nothing, that is, until I turned to the bedside cabinet. Here, in a lower drawer, I discovered a small hardback notebook, its pages ruled horizontally and vertically and scrawled all over with lists and figures relating to purchases and expenses. Then, between the pages containing the latest entries, I found what I was looking for. Three worn and dog-eared tenners. I lifted them out and kissed them. Silently, guiltily, eagerly. Like a miser reviewing his hoard.

The next stage was easier. As a matter of practicality I packed my bag with just the strict necessities: toilet bag, towel, a change of clothes. To my view, in any case, it was part of the simple logic of the situation that I should take with me only the things I'd brought a few weeks earlier. Then I sat on the bed and looked around. So this was it. The moment was on me, the fire licking my ankles. Still time to change my mind? Not really. I knew now, in the core of me, there was no turning back. No, there was really only one thing left to do. I moved to the desk and ripped a sheet from the pad. Though words are not my bag of tricks, I had to break the news. I had to leave a note. Some words of explanation, however brief.

Dear Matt,

Don't be mad, please don't be mad, but I've gone back to Norrie. I can't stay, I really can't. I'm ashamed to sneak away like this and I'd like to talk, but I'm scared. Scared of upsetting you. I love you and always will, but I'm no good for you. We're different – very different – you and I. You must see that. I've taken some money, which I promise to pay back. I'll phone you sometime when I'm settled. And who knows, maybe someday I'll manage to explain myself. . .

I glanced through what I had written and shook my head. It was mean, shabby, paltry. It would have to do; it was the best I could manage. To hide my sins I pushed it into an envelope. My shame was for Matt's eyes only. I wrote his name on the outside in that big ugly sprawl of mine, stuck it down and left it on his desk in the very place where he had left his note to me.

At St Pancras I bought a ticket and made inquiries. Forty minutes to kill. I went to the buffet, dawdled over a cup of tea, tried and failed to eat a sandwich.

We pulled out at around midday. It was also midweek, so not exactly busy. I found myself sharing the carriage with perhaps a dozen other people. I slung my bag onto the rack and hunched myself against a window, staring out wanly at the receding suburbs. Rain was slanting down heavily out of a grey sky. I tried to deaden the pain, close down, go numb, but no amount of trying could smother my fear and loneliness. I felt sick to the pit of my stomach. Fields and houses flashed by, and with every mile that we crossed I had a sense of falling backward down a hole. We entered a tunnel, and I watched the light at the end shrink to a pinprick and then vanish. I thought of Matt, still at work, happily oblivious. I saw the envelope lying on his desk, now out of reach, now beyond recall. I watched it burst into flames, curl at the edges, shrivel to cinder. I could hear the bedside clock, ticking away relentlessly. I snatched it up, hurled it against the wall. But the sound went on; there was no stopping it. I twisted and squirmed in my seat, clenching my fists, tensing like a person electrified by a chain of brutal shocks.

I leaped up. I had to shake out of this. I needed air, exercise, a change of scene. Above all, I needed a drink. Where was the bar on this train? I turned to the guy swigging beer in the seat behind me. Up at the front end, he indicated. I snatched up my bag and stormed off.

At the bar I joined a short queue, and within a few minutes I was at the front. The lanky barman had a weird lopsided face that made him look stupid and aggressive, so it was a relief when he served me with a smile. I bought a can of lager and went to a seat at a nearby table. Someone had left a newspaper behind and I flicked through it, being too self-absorbed to take much interest. Nor was I much aware of my fellow passengers. I cast a weary eye round the carriage, without feeling more than a fleeting curiosity about any of them. There was just one person that caught my notice. This was a young soldier, who was leaning on the end of the bar, clutching a can of brown ale. Was it perhaps the uniform? After all, his looks were not immediately striking, although on closer inspection he was not unattractive in a rough, mean-eyed kind of way. His expression was hard and coarse, but he was lean and fit and lightly tanned, with a brush of wiry black hair. Perhaps, though, it was neither the uniform nor the looks. Perhaps it was the fact that he was alone and obviously hungry, his eyes forever flicking around the room looking for contact. And perhaps, above anything else, that they kept straying back to me.

At first I reacted by looking clean away. I was feeling far too anxious, raw and tender to be interested, let alone excited. I didn't want adventure; I wanted warmth, security, consolation. Or that's what I told myself. And I was right: that is what I wanted, but loneliness can sometimes make us desperate. Anyway, to make my lack of interest quite clear I shifted my attention to the other side of the room and focused my gaze on a young couple who were trying to manage their little boy, a toddler bouncing with excitement. But I couldn't quite stifle my curiosity, and from time to time I stole a quick glance at the soldier, only to find, with a sharp thrill, that his eyes were always there, trained hard on mine and searching for contact. Several times I snatched away before deciding to have this thing out. On the next occasion I fixed him with a bold stare. But he didn't flinch. No, he outfaced me until I became quite hot and nervous. This is ridiculous, I told myself; the last thing you want now is to become involved with this guy. So I finished my beer, leaped up and, without looking back, made off.

But I knew it wouldn't be easy; this jock was clearly very persistent. And my suspicions were quickly confirmed. Somewhere in the middle of the next carriage I glanced behind and saw that he was following me. I flung myself into an empty seat, and seconds later he came by and dropped into the seat just across the aisle, so that we were sitting almost face to face. He drew a packet of cigarettes from his top pocket, pulled one out and lit up. He offered me one, I shook my head and the eye-catching game continued. But I refused to be drawn. I stayed detached, never fully engaging with him, observing him only with brief, sidelong glances. And we kept this up for quite some while. I was expecting him to speak; to say *something* at least. But he didn't. This was a wordless game.

Eventually, in a final attempt to shake him off, I went to the toilet. I took my time, hoping to find that he'd gone on my return. But vain hope. When I opened the door, he was there, leaning against the wall, drawing deep on his cigarette. And this time there was no escaping that hard look. My eyes sealed onto his and I noticed a faint smile pass over his lips. I hesitated for a moment and he came quickly forward, forcing me back into the cubicle. Then he stepped inside and pulled the door behind him. We stood gazing at each other for a few moments before he reached around and snapped the lock.

Neither of us showed even the flicker of an expression. Up close, though, I became more aware of his appeal. He had a wide shapely nose, dark growth on his chin and upper cheeks, and a warm reek of sweat. He stubbed his cigarette out on the washbasin. Trails of smoke curled lazily upward from his thick tawny lips.

His mouth looked achingly kissable, but the sex began without preliminaries of any kind. He simply unbuckled his belt, dropped his trousers and pulled up his shirt. Then, thrusting out his hips, he slapped his taut belly and snapped the band of his shorts. His blank face was quite inscrutable, but his hungry eyes were trained on mine and he kept flicking them downward in invitation. He was wearing baggy white boxers with large red polka dots. The crudeness of his approach alarmed me, yet the speed of his operation was so overwhelming that any resistance I might have had wore away in an instant. He locked his eyes onto mine with such force, held me so transfixed, that I simply stared back, fascinated, hypnotised, ready to obey. I had become a slave, a creature without self-will. Slowly, with trance-like concentration, I sank to my knees. I pulled his shorts down over his hips and his prick lobbed out – thick, brown and fringed with black hairs. I licked the foreskin and instantly he started to stiffen. I pushed my face into his groin and snuffled around. I kissed his tight scrotum and began to run my tongue up his shaft, now broad, erect, tall as a column. But before I reached the tip he came. In thick creamy cascades. In a rich lava overflow that burst from his slit and left both of us draped in white gummy threads.

Almost immediately his lust turned to annoyance. With me? With himself? From disappointment, self-disgust? It was difficult to tell. Anyway, his hard face now became angry and contemptuous. He looked with a grimace at the mess he had made. But his eyes avoided mine. I was no longer there; I had ceased to exist. Without speaking, without even glancing at me, he reached out, tore some sheets from the toilet roll and cleaned himself up, wiping the stickiness from his belly with determined thoroughness and flinging the wet tissue into the bowl as if burying something vile. Then he quickly hauled up his pants and trousers, buttoned up and brushed himself down, all the while checking his uniform for any stains. I watched all this from my knees, my shirt bespattered, a globule hanging from my chin. I was hoping for a word or a look at least. Was this *my* fault? Surely not. Yet I felt that it was. Guilt, in my current state, was not far from the surface. Finally he did fling a look at me, but it wasn't one to enjoy. More a kind of sneer, followed by a short hard laugh. I had become an insect.

Moments later, having delivered his parting shot, he turned and left swiftly, slamming the door behind him with a crash.

The rain got worse. It was teeming when we arrived in Norrie. In fact, the weather conditions were almost biblical. The town was shrouded in murk, a dark pall lay over everything, and it was hard to believe that it was only late afternoon. The station bar was brightly lit and crowded, perhaps because it offered warmth, company, refuge. I examined the loose change in my pocket and decided that I could just about afford to buy myself a Scotch. I was almost destitute, but care with money had never been my strong point and right at that moment I needed comfort, fuel, fortification. I also needed time to think. Now that I was here, what was the next move? I had only the vaguest notion. Not difficult to predict what kind of reception I'd get at the Black Horse. Would things be any better at home? Hard to say. We'd never been close, that's for certain, and I'd not stayed in touch since moving to London. But surely they'd not deny me a bed for the night?

The cabbies were obviously benefiting from the extreme weather. There was a queue at the rank in front of the station. I hung about, watching rain cascade in curtains from the roof of the awning. The gloomy scarface who eventually picked me up seemed to recognise me. Certainly his mug was familiar; I'd probably travelled in his cab before. 'Been away?' he said. 'Yeah,' I said. 'Been working down south.' I was watching the fare ticking up on the clock. This was a luxury I could ill afford, but the leather upholstery was doing wonders for my self-esteem. I needed to arrive home in style.

But on reaching Stone Street, style gave way to practicality. I paid the cabby, pulled my jacket over my head and made an undignified dash for the porch. I then took a deep breath and slammed my thumb on the bell with great force. Moments later the door flew open and there stood my stepfather, frowning and looking irritable. In short, the way he usually looked. But I was taken aback to see him at all; I expected him to be at work. At first he stared blankly as if he scarcely recognised me, and his frown intensified. So I lifted my jacket higher to reveal more of my face, and his head jerked back in recoil.

'Oh, Christ!' he groaned.

'Who is it?' called my mother from within.

'Come and see for yourself.'

I loathed the man. Always had. I've said it before, but I can't say it enough. And now my hatred welled up in a flash. I wanted to smash his stupid ugly mug. My mother came hurrying to the door.

'Billy!' she gasped. She looked bewildered, caught off balance, thrown into sudden confusion. In short, not exactly pleased to see me. I mean, she didn't clasp me to her bosom or anything. No, she was all dithery, as if uncertain how to react. But after all, what did I expect? 'Well, well, this *is* a surprise. Look, come in out of the rain. Don't stand there on the doorstep. Pete, why can't you ask the boy in?'

My stepfather turned and disappeared. I shook myself off on the mat in the hall, then followed my mother into the sitting room. She flopped onto the sofa with a nervous smile and invited me to sit. I perched on the arm of the chair opposite her. I felt awkward, uneasy, unwelcome. The atmosphere was heavy with the need for explanations, and I wasn't sure that I was up to giving them. I smiled back at her, stupidly. Where to begin? I couldn't seem to collect my thoughts, find the words, spit it all out. And Pete's hostility, rumbling in the background, wasn't helping matters. In fact it was seriously interfering with my composure. I could hear him crashing away in the kitchen, banging pans and crockery around, apparently preparing a meal. A meal that was likely, when presented, to burst into flames.

My mother looked at me closely. 'So what's the news, then? Are you back?'

I nodded. 'It's a long story,' I said.

She shook her head. 'I've been worried sick about you.'

That's stretching it, I thought; it's rare for you to give anyone more than a passing shrug.

'You never phoned, you never wrote. We feel neglected, your dad and me. Left in the dark. Can't understand what's going on at all. Who's this bloke, anyway? You've never said much about him.'

I studied the floor, swallowed hard. 'He's just someone – a guy I met. Came to Paul's wedding, remember?'

Pete had appeared in the doorway.

'Betty's been here telling me stories,' she said. 'She and Stan are furious about the way you flounced off like that. Dropped them in the thick, good and proper. The things she said about you.' Her voice was beginning to falter. 'They're not true, Billy, are they? They can't be true. Tell me they're not true.'

I stared at her silently. Her eyes were brimming, though I wasn't much moved. She has a way with tears, my ma.

'Of course they're true, woman,' snarled Pete. 'You 'eard what she said. He's been going with men for years.' He turned to me with a withering look and his voice fell to a dark mutter. 'And some of 'em pay for it.'

I gazed at him in horror. Or rather, horror mixed with hatred. It seemed to me I ought to speak, explain, give an account of myself. But there it was again, that great stone in my throat. Sudden panic and nausea welled up in me till I thought my heart would burst. I leaped to my feet as if my clothes were on fire and snatched up my bag. There was no staying here. Much more of this and I'd commit a murder. I stormed out of the house and down the garden path.

My mother flew after me. 'Billy!' she screamed from the

doorstep. But I didn't look back. The only response was Pete's growl. 'Leave him go, woman. The dirty sod!'

At the end of the street I stopped, leaned over a fence and was violently sick into someone's front garden. Then I sat on a wall and tried to collect myself. The rain was still falling in rods but I scarcely noticed it, even though I was soaked to the skin and globules were rolling over my scalp and trickling down my neck. I had other things on my mind. In fact, my head was pounding. Betty, that evil bitch! I'd settle with her one day. I'd never go back to the Black Horse, never. Not even if she came begging on bended knee.

But what now? Everything looked bleak, in ruins. I was homeless, jobless, destitute. I stared into the black night and a sense of desolation stole over me. Where could I turn for help? Well, there was always the old crowd, of course. Would they come through? Could they be relied on in an emergency? And I saw that belief in the old crowd had never quite deserted me. Or at least, never until that moment. For now, up against it, faced with brute reality, I had doubts. In any case, could I swallow enough pride? Could I crawl to them after all that had passed between us? I trudged through puddles to the public phone box on the other side of the street.

I flicked through the pages of my address book.

Terry? I started to dial her number, then lost my nerve and dropped the receiver back on the hook.

Craig? I held on till someone picked up at the other end, then cut the line dead.

Baz? I shook my head. Why bother?

This is desperate, I thought, butting my head against a metal plate advertising emergency phone numbers. Numb with indecision, reduced to utter paralysis, I watched the rainwater flowing down the panes. A drunk loomed out of the darkness, pressed his nose against the glass and passed on. I shivered. Yeah, utterly desperate. Absolutely rock-bottom desperate. Well, did I deserve friends? Had I ever been a friend to anyone?

Time to grasp the nettle. I turned to a new page in the

address book and dialled the number swiftly, before I had time to reconsider. Any port in a storm. Or to put it another way, there are nights when a bed, however unsavoury, is better than a park bench.

'Come on, shitface,' I muttered aloud. 'I know you're there.' The phone was ringing, but no one was picking up. I hammered the wall in dismay. This was it, after all. The end of the jar, the floor of the barrel, the bottom of the bucket. 'Come on, shift yourself. Always there to interfere, ya bastard, never around to help. Stubborn as a mule, deaf as a fucking post!'

At that moment, as if in angry response, the receiver was snatched up.

'Yeah, 'ello?'

It was the old familiar growl, of course. Yet somehow – in a way I can't quite explain – somehow oh-so-welcome, even endearing.

'Hullo, Arthur,' I said hesitantly, trying to hide the catch in my voice. 'It's me.'

There was silence for a few moments. A crackle, some wheezing, a grunt or two. Then:

'Well now, what a turn-up!' He was almost purring. 'Yeah, skip the introduction, old chum, I'd know that voice anywhere.' A rasping chuckle. 'So the prodigal returns. And didn't I tell ya? Anyway, what can I say? Don't hang about on a pisser like this, ya dickhead. Come on over.'

PART THREE

October 1985

It's been thoroughly weird right from the start, and it's getting weirder.

To tell the truth, I don't know what it's all about. It's not about sex. Not really. I mean, don't get me wrong, we do *that* frequently. Oh yeah, every damned night with oyster sauce and all the trimmings. The thing is I'm not sure *why* we do it. I mean, it could be a turn-on. He's a nice-looking bloke, and I'm – well, okay, I'm not exactly cat-walk material, am I? I could do with an extra couple of inches. And I *hate* my arse, which I'm trying to firm up at the gym. But the left profile's not too bad, as Petra often remarks. And let's be fair, I've got my little band of admirers.

The problem is, with this guy it feels like work not pleasure. He's not really *there*, if you know what I mean. So where is he? God knows. It's the same when we're chatting or holding hands across a table. He seems to look straight through me. That's what I say, it's weird. It's been thoroughly weird from the start.

Take this trip, for instance. We meet, oh, perhaps half a dozen times and suddenly he wants to whisk me off to Yorkshire. Yeah, he's dead keen. But me, I'm a bit cool. I hardly know the guy. He says, 'We'll drift up through the Welsh borders and perhaps take a look at Chester first.' I says, 'Eh, hold on, this is all going a bit too bloody fast for me. I'm not sure I can get the time off, for a start.' Well, I'm usually easy-going, me, but I don't like it when people *assume*. In fact, I can be quite firm when someone gets pushy or tries to take advantage. So he says, 'Okay, but give it some thought.' Which I do. And I think, yeah, well, could be nice, a little autumn break – especially if the weather's good and the trees are still in flaming leaf.

So here we are, in a teashop in Conway. And yes, the weather is mild, crisp and bright and the trees are a riot of colour. We've just been to the castle and Matt is telling me all about Edward I and his ring of fortifications. I listen politely. Matt knows a lot, and knows he knows a lot. Presently he gets onto Edward's son, who, it seems, was as queer as the crew on a cross-channel ferry. This king, Edward II, had the hots for one of his courtiers – Piers Something? Anyway, he came to a truly sticky end in the dungeon of – oh, again I forget the name – but anyway, another castle not unlike the one we've just been visiting. The details of his murder are too indelicate to relate aloud, so Matt whispers in my ear; the teashop is full of elderly ladies, some of them wearing hats. I feel a teensy bit queasy afterward, and rather *off* my scone and cream.

'Sorry,' says Matt. 'It's just that some of the history books blink the facts.'

Am I building up a picture? What I'm saying is, the attempt is there, but we don't really *connect.* Oh, occasionally there's a spark, but if we do share a laugh, it's a bonus. Most of the time he seems elsewhere. Actually, I have this sense of something gnawing away at him. The long silences, for instance. The intermittent bursts of forced laughter. The strained conviviality. The often obsessive behaviour.

Let me illustrate. Yesterday morning a young bloke in a Rolls overtook us on a bend and had to swerve sharply in front of us to avoid a truck coming the other way. Matt raged and wouldn't let the subject drop. Further down the road, at a small market town, we spotted the Rolls parked in a lay-by. Matt, still fuming, pulled in behind. The owner was nowhere to be seen. 'We'll wait,' he said, and I stared at him. 'But he might be gone for hours,' I said. He was silent, his jaw set, his expression grimly determined. Twenty minutes later he ripped a sheet from a notepad and began to write a message. But before he'd finished, the guy turned up. Matt leaped out like a member of Special Branch. I watched the scene from the passenger seat, rolling the window down to try and catch what was said. But words were superfluous: the body language – the wild despairing gestures, the tossing heads, the jabbing fingers – said it all. In fact, the whole charade was coming close to a prize punch-up until I intervened by leaning heavily on the car horn. At which point Matt flung himself back into the driver's seat and we tore off, though not without both men letting fly some final terms of endearment.

Yes, something's gnawing away, but don't ask me what. Story of my life. Why do I always wind up with these dark horses? As I say, I hardly know the guy, and there are no signs that things will change. Oh, I know what he does, I've been to his place, I've met a few of his housemates. But beyond that, nothing. What's he thinking, feeling? What's his history? There are these no-go areas, these mysterious black holes. For instance, there must have been guys before me. Who were they? When I ask about them I get the vaguest of shrugs. Are these a glimpse of the future? Hmm, well, it sure as hell looks like it. That's *your* destiny, honeybun, I tell myself. That's where you're headed, better get used to it. This week you're sort of special, this week you're the boyfriend, but somewhere down the line you'll wither into a vague shrug.

Tuesday morning, and I'm not struck on this place. The lime-green wallpaper in the dining room is shuddersome and the service painfully slow. *His* choice, of course; *I'm* never consulted.

When we checked in last night, the receptionist was rather prim. 'Twin beds?' she asked, glancing down at her desk book. And Matt comes back, bold as brass: 'No, no, certainly not. A large double, please. And preferably one that doesn't squeak.'

Well, really! . . . I could feel the pink spreading to my furthest extremities.

Anyway, more good weather and it seems we're off on

another long hike. Matt has a book called *Walks in the Dales*. He's very pleased with it. It's stuffed with information and has pull-out maps. He's disgusted with my footwear, though, and stares in horror at my slatted slip-ons.

'Haven't you got anything stouter than that?'

'Where are we going?' I reply. 'Up the Amazon?'

He clutches his head in despair and falls back on the bed. 'Well, we're certainly not going for a stroll on the prom, or for that matter, a bloody ballet lesson.'

It's our first major row. As I remarked earlier, Matt is a bit obsessive.

I suppose I should have been on my guard from the start. It's a sign that something's not quite right, isn't it, when blokes come on strong like that? I mean, I'm sitting there on the sofa at Mim's little birthday soirée, twirling a bowl of pale pink bubbly and minding my own little packet, when up strolls Matt, plonks himself down and starts rattling away to me as if he's known me all his life. And I'm typically English, me. A bit buttoned up. A bit skirt down and knees together. I mean, in general we don't take to that kind of pushiness, do we? I remember thinking, well, I don't much care for your style, but I must say you've got a nice row of even white teeth and a rather fetching forward-flop. And to be fair his arrival did promise to spice up what had so far been, for me at least, a disappointingly flattish evening. So I smiled a bit, and flicked the flecks from my cashmere, and tried to give him a discreet glimpse or two of my left profile.

He said, 'Sorry, am I invading your privacy? Sometimes I see it as a sort of mission to coax flowers off walls.'

Yeah, no kidding; I'm not making this up. That's honestly what he said. Can you believe it? I mean, the sheer bloody arrogance. It flashed out instantly. Oh, take my word, the charm of the man is sometimes, as they say, highly resistible.

I said, 'Well, don't put yourself out on my account. Some of us love walls.'

And that set the tone really. How we ended up between

the sheets is still a mystery. For the past few weeks we've been stumbling along together like participants in a three-legged race. So this trip to Yorkshire is a risky project, a kind of testing period. Will the friendship survive? Hmm. Well, frankly the odds are getting longer by the minute.

As I say, I've not been too successful with guys. I could reel off a list of names, but I won't bore you with the whole history. I don't think it's luck, I think it's *me*. But what's my problem? Do I set my sights too high? Or is it that I bring out the worst in people? That's what Petra thinks. She says I've got a negative outlook. That I look for the worst and always find it. Actually, last year there was a near success. I moved in with a sweet man who worked in soft furnishings. The sex was particularly good and I've never been laid on a better sofa. He was also very affectionate. Well, *too* affectionate. Monogamy, shall we say, was not his style. He'd bring guys home and invite me to join in a threesome. A threesome, me! No, I'm sorry, that's not what I do, that's not my thing at all. Now don't get me wrong, I'm not a prude. I like sex, but strictly of the one-to-one variety. And in these scary times, what with the flying rumours and everyone, it seems, turning celibate, it's just as well perhaps. Anyway, we paddled along together for a bit and then sort of drifted apart. Shame, really, I was fond of him. In fact, I still hear from him. I had a postcard just last week, suggesting that we meet up again one evening.

Oh yeah – me, him and who else?

Wednesday? Is that all? Surely we've been slogging over field and moor for months. And what have we seen? Or should that be, what *haven't* we seen? Anyway, ruins. Heaps of them. We've tramped around many a decayed building, scrambled over the trodden stones of this or that abandoned abbey or monastery. Teashops? Not in the desolate regions we explore. More likely stiles, dry-stone walls and sheep droppings. Now, don't get me wrong, I love a nice view. But from behind a plate of glass.

Still, this place – The Wheatsheaf – has its attractions.

Wooden beams, quaint old furniture, decent beer. Yeah, in the absence of a teashop I'm prepared to settle for a quiet pub with horse-brasses, ploughshares and a generous expanse of leg-room. In fact, the only thorn in my butt at the moment is Matt. His mood at present is – how shall I put it? – skittish. Listen, that's him now, sharing hearty bonhomie with the landlord. Can you hear? And five minutes ago he was yammering away to that couple over there in a fit of excitement that was almost embarrassing.

These mood-swings are a feature, as I've already hinted. Have they always been, or am I to blame? Ah well, I guess I'll never know. This guy is inscrutable. So why inquire further? Why torture myself? Yeah, swing to the left, swing to the right, life is a square-dance, after all, so why not shrug and simply swing along too?

Oh no, what's happening now? He's inviting that couple to join us in a game of darts. Challenging them to a contest – them against us. Jesus, this is *truly* terrible. Has he any idea how useless I am? I haven't slung a dart for decades. I'll be lucky to hit the wall, let alone the board. But Doug and Juanita (Is that really her name? She sounds from Bolton) look delighted – even eager. Oh, this is so cruel. And don't tell me my scheming partner here doesn't know what he's up to. I'm not a juggins. This is all a low plot to humiliate me.

Well, thank God that's over. Still, as things turned out, it was nothing like as shaming as expected. Pathetic player though I am, I'm in a different league to Juanita, who hurls a dart like a javelin, with a sense of direction that's often lethal. So here we are again, striding the footpaths, leaping over streams, slashing through briars with the aid of Matt's trusty stick. Our destination now is that derelict farmhouse on the brow of the hill over there – from which vantage point, it seems, we'll be treated to a quite stunning view of Ribblesdale. Hallelujah!

Oh look, I must snap out of this. I mean, I'm curious as to what impression of me you may have picked up from the foregoing; what sorry self-portrait I may have painted from all this jaded blithering. Perhaps you agree with Petra, that I'm negative? That I look for the worst and always find it? If so, then let me hasten to correct the image that I've created. Yes, I do sometimes enjoy life, I do sometimes let my hair down. Oh, it's true that I don't have an immense appetite for this rough old business: I'm not Dickens or Balzac or Tina Turner. It's just that sometimes, when I'm with someone special, or watching a great musical, or preparing mushrooms à la grecque to the strains of Ella or Sarah, I think that maybe, along with Cole Porter, I too have a capacity for getting kicks.

So what's my idea of a holiday? I can answer in a flash. A few years back I went flitting off to Berlin for a weekend binge with my old pal Dodie. She used to be Dennis before the change, which I must say she's managed with amazing aplomb. We both love five-star luxury – grand staircases, flunkies, that kind of thing – and the place we stayed in, let me tell you, had all that in spades. And don't ask where the money came from, I simply refuse to think about it. Anyway, our suitcases were bulging so much we could scarcely lift them. Honestly, you'd have thought we were staying for a month at least. We hit one of the high spots on the very first night, a club in Kreuzberg called Marlene, which was cool and lively and brazenly wicked. The barman was Karl, a blond Nordic giant with high cheekbones and bronzed arms that rippled out from a sleeveless white vest. We couldn't snatch our eyes away and clung to the bar, perched on stools, chatting him up till closing time. So that set the pattern really, we just kept going back. Of course, there *were* developments. One night Dodie disappeared with a monocled Viennese roué, a gracious, silver-haired gentleman in skin-tight leather who claimed to be related to royalty. On another, I was taken home by an alarmingly wayward insurance salesman from Potsdam. But these were mere diversions: our real devotion was to Karl, and we spent the last night cosying up to him and getting steadily legless as we slung back the cocktails.

*

I'm often like this on holiday: that's to say, wide awake, fresh as a daisy, at three in the morning. Is it the unfamiliar bed? Hmm, perhaps. Lack of exercise? You've got to be joking; these past few days I've been walked off my poor blistered feet. Well, then, too much exercise? The stimulation? The cheese I ate earlier? No, no; all of these things may have had their part to play, but the main reason I'm lying here as bright as a bar of strip lighting is because of what happened today. Yeah, it's been full of hairy moments, this thing with Matt, but today delivered the *coup de grâce*.

So what exactly *did* happen? Actually, I'm not sure that I know. What I do know is that we've now turned a corner – a very sharp corner – and to be frank I can't wait to get home.

Anyway, let's go back and start at the beginning. After breakfast, Matt said he wanted to take a drive across Keighley Moor and drop in for lunch at a place called Norfield. He'd been there before, he said, and knew the town well. In fact, last year he'd spent a whole week there – a particularly fine week in June – attending a conference. He said he wanted to take another look at the splendid old town centre, full, apparently, of fine Victorian buildings and worth a second visit. Again, no consultation with me about any of this. No 'by your leave' or 'how does *that* suit?' or 'what have *you* got in mind?' To be fair, though, the drive was pleasant enough, and we had an enjoyable break at a bar in the middle of the moor, where we got into cheeky repartee with a couple of brawny bikers from Pontefract – gorgeous, weather-beaten lads in studded leather, whose thick accents brought me out in goose pimples.

And so to Norfield. Well, that's a quite different story. To be frank, I wouldn't give you tuppence. At the time I couldn't imagine what we were doing there – though I know *now*, of course. Matt went into ecstasies over the Town Hall. But the muck, the grime, the pigeon shit! It quite spoiled the view. I said, 'That might be a nice piece of Neo-Gothic or whatever you call it, but someone needs to take a polisher to it.' No, sorry, I can tolerate the old stuff as long as it's clean.

And the market in the square? Well, that's nothing but a litter-strewn fountain and a heap of stalls peddling cheap junk. We strolled around for a bit, and I did my best to stifle the yawns. But Matt – well, he seemed utterly absorbed, and gazed round the whole while in a sort of meditative trance.

I guess by this time we were both feeling a bit peckish and ready for a spot of lunch, and Matt mentioned a pub that he knew where you could usually pick up a decent cheese roll and a pint.

'Suits me,' I said. 'Lead the way.'

And he did, without the slightest hesitation or uncertainty about direction. In fact, he clearly knew the route, if not the town, like the back of his hand. But having found the place, I couldn't begin to understand what all the fuss was about. It was an old, perfectly ordinary, rather dingy backstreet tavern. The White Horse, Black Horse, Dray Horse? Something like that. Anyway, Matt glanced around nervously as we entered and received a curt nod or two in return. I also heard a few mumbled remarks and saw a smile pass between some of the customers. There were perhaps a dozen or more men in the room and just two women, one with her head lolling on the other's shoulder. He then put an arm round my waist – a gesture which took me by surprise, since he rarely touched me except in bed – and steered me rather awkwardly towards the bar. The barmaid was an ample young woman in bulging skin-tight jeans, who turned to us with a routine smile as we cast our eyes over the lunchtime specials chalked up on the board. We ordered a couple of ploughman's, with Wensleydale, pickle and a garnishing of salad, and then carried our drinks over to a corner seat.

Here we sipped our beer in silence while waiting for the food to arrive, though from time to time I would steal a glance at Matt, who was studying the scene intently, with a kind of electric alertness.

'The local queer bar, I presume,' I remarked in an aside, though the comment scarcely needed an answer; I was just musing aloud to break the silence. Actually, what I really wanted to know was why he hadn't let on before.

'Yeah, absolutely,' he muttered, still preoccupied, his eyes fixed steadily on a group of card players seated round a table on the other side of the room. 'No doubt about it. Queer as *fuck.*'

Yes, just like that. Right out of the blue. Emitted between clenched teeth, so to speak. I looked at him, a bit taken aback by this abrupt evisceration, and we again lapsed into silence.

'Do you know some of these people?' I said after a while. We were obviously the focus of some interest, and the atmosphere was beginning to make me feel distinctly uncomfortable.

'Ha!' he scoffed. 'You betcha.'

I made no attempt to follow this up. Okay, I thought, so play mysterious, if that's your game, but don't expect me to jump.

So it was a relief when the food arrived. True, we ate in silence, but getting stuck in at least partly covered the sense of awkwardness. Matt tore off hunks of bread and cheese, and gulped them down like a wolf. I consciously took my time, and returned the plates to the bar when we had finished.

Shortly after this, however, one member of the card-playing group detached himself and strolled across the room towards us. His eyes were lowered as if searching the floor for something. Without a word passing his lips he drew a chair up to our table and sat down directly opposite us. Then he looked up, leaned back and clasped his hands loosely across his stomach. He paid no attention to me whatsoever. Instead, his gaze flitted all round the room for a few moments before coming to rest on Matt. The two men locked eyes instantly, and for several minutes they looked hard and steady at one another, squaring up like sheriff and outlaw in the final showdown of a western. It was a fascinating scene to watch, the pair were so intensely self-absorbed, apparently totally unaware of anyone else in the room. They were well matched too – the man's posture was grimly defiant, but Matt stared back with equal force, fixing him with the same hard look. They had these funny smirks on their faces, as if taunting each other.

'Well now, if it's not my old sparring partner,' said the man. 'I was wondering when you'd show up.'

'Hullo, Arthur,' said Matt coolly. 'How are you?'

As I say, this trip has been pretty weird from the start, but looking at this guy Arthur, I wondered just how weird it could get. He was so freakish, so shifty-eyed, so sickly-sweaty that I'm lost for expression. The most noticeable thing about him was the creepy way he spoke. Words seemed to slide from the corner of his mouth like poisoned pellets. In spite of the snappy turnout – the jacket, waistcoat, spotted bow tie – there was something seedy and deeply repellent about him. In fact, I'm amazed that Matt should be acquainted, even on speaking terms, with such a creature. There's obviously more beneath the surface than I could possibly imagine, a dark side to his character that exceeds even the alarming revelations of the past week.

'I'm extremely well,' came the reply, in a tone that sounded like a jeer. This was so obviously untrue it was laughable; the man was a wreck in every sense, and clearly in need of urgent medical attention. 'Back to the scene of the crime, then, Matt?'

'That's right,' said Matt, flashing a horribly false smile. 'Can't stay away. You know how it is. Memory Lane. Fond associations and all that.'

'I hope you're not here to upset the boy. He's back where he belongs. Do not disturb, remember?'

Matt lifted his spread palms in a gesture of astonishment. 'I only looked in to say hello,' he said.

Oh, such guilelessness, such sweet innocence. Didn't fool me, though, not for a moment. I had no idea what was really going on, but it didn't need Sherlock Holmes to see that this visit was more than a mere social call. Upset the boy? Scene of the crime? I juggled with all these clues, my nose twitching, my ears flapping, my mind racing.

Arthur gave Matt a harder, even more searching look. He clearly didn't trust him any more than I did. It was obvious, in fact, that whatever little scheme Matt had in mind, it was going to face some tough opposition. So the response, when it eventually came, was surprising.

'Okay, I'll speak to him – but if there's any hint of trouble . . .'

'Trouble?' said Matt with a sly smile. 'Dunno what you mean.'

Arthur ambled back, his deliberately slow gait almost insolently casual, and we simply sat there, sipping our beers in silence, the air clamouring with unanswered questions. But when I cast an eye at Matt, he looked deep in thought, self-absorbed, tense, like a witness in a court case about to give testimony. What about *me*, though? Can you imagine how *I* was feeling? I mean, what the hell was going on? Who was this guy Arthur? And who was 'the boy'? I was flushing hot and cold all over with anger and confusion. How dare Matt bring me here without preparation or warning? How dare he involve me in his secret manoeuvres? How dare he *use* me in this way? I kept glancing across at the group, who were huddled together in a low buzz of conversation. And suddenly the tension got the better of me. I leaped up and, without a word, stormed off to the gents. I didn't need a piss, it was just a place to cool off. I filled a basin from the tap and splashed cold water on my face. Then I peered over my shoulder. There was a guy there, standing at a urinal, pulling at himself and glancing around, just as there always is. Anyway, I hung about for a bit, but eventually the atmosphere became uncomfortable, so I went into a cubicle and slammed the bolt. I pulled down the toilet seat and sat on the edge. My mind was writhing like a snake-pit. Someone knocked on the door. 'Fuck off!' I shouted.

Matt was in close conversation with a young man when I returned. Yes, a slim, attractive, open-faced lad with a thick brush of sandy hair and the hint of a freckle or two. They were leaning towards each other, intensely absorbed, the intimacy between them plain to see. So here was 'the boy' – who could doubt it? – and I had no trouble in seeing what all the fuss was about. Yes, the mists were beginning to lift and it was now clear to me why I had never been, nor ever could be, anything more than rear-end Charlie – if you'll forgive the expression. Anyway, I sat down and the young man turned to me with a worried half-smile.

'Clint,' said Matt, who suddenly condescended to notice me, 'meet Billy.'

And I saw immediately that this introduction was not for my benefit, but for his – for Matt's. Indeed, the picture now sprang into focus and I saw what my function was, my part in the whole equation.

Meanwhile, could Billy trust his ears?

'Come again?' he said cautiously – just as they all do.

I smiled. 'A nickname,' I said. 'The family's called Eastwood.'

He nodded and grinned, though in an instant he became shy again and turned back to Matt. And watching them closely, I saw again how enwrapped they were, how consumed by each other. So farewell, murky obscurity. Yes, the central mystery of this autumn jaunt was now over, and everything about this odd little fling was at least crawling into daylight, if not into crystal clarity. Actually, I had two functions: I was here as a cover, a front to hide behind; and as a buffer, a means of absorbing the emotional charge between Matt and his ex.

'So, as I say, we fancied a trip to the Dales,' said Matt, 'and, as we were in the area, I felt we couldn't drive past without dropping in.'

This sudden stress on 'we' was amusing; it was not, as you might say, a feature of his language that I had noticed before.

Billy said nothing, simply looked uncomfortable. He kept shifting in his seat and his eyes flicked away shyly whenever they met mine.

'Anyway, tell me more,' Matt said. 'You're working *here* again, are you?' He swept his eyes round the room with a look of mild disparagement.

Billy gave a nod. 'Yeah, I'm on duty now, in fact. Karen's just filling in for ten minutes to give me break.'

So the talk went on and I listened; and some bits of what they said made sense and other bits were totally opaque. But I was learning fast, and with every exchange some more fragments of the mosaic fell into place. I also watched, and the vibes that passed between them were unmissable. I was way off on the margins, of course; I barely existed. They were the players, I was the audience. They were playing to each other, though, not to me; and they spoke in undertones, their heads close together. It was scarcely the most private of settings, but they seemed unaware that anyone else was present. They were in love, these two, that was obvious. But the thing was too strong, they couldn't stand the heat. They were hurt and unhappy, the pair of them. It was a fascinating little drama; I lost myself in it. The hero was Billy. I liked him instantly. A straightforward lad, sensitive, troubled. Matt, though, was like a coiled spring. His speech was too deliberate, dangerously controlled and verging on insult.

'I've still got it,' he said. 'Yeah, I kept it.'

'Kept what?'

'That note you left.'

'Ah.' Billy lowered his eyes and shook his head. 'Sorry about that. As you know, I'm not good at explaining myself. I *have* tried to write to you since. Several times, actually.' He looked up and shrugged hopelessly.

'But?' Matt's eyes were hard, unyielding.

'But . . .' Billy again shifted uneasily. 'I tear up everything I write.'

There was a pause. I studied the pair of them. Billy looked close to tears. Matt was staring at him. Closely, quizzically.

'You OK?'

Billy wiped his eyes with the back of his hand. 'Yeah, fine.'

'What I mean is, how are you managing, you know, in general?' The softened voice was full of concern.

Billy was silent for a moment. Then he looked Matt full in the face and spoke with slow deliberation. 'Yeah, I know what you mean. And I'm fine. Honestly.'

'Oh really?' said Matt, turning hard and edgy again, one of his legs jiggling convulsively. 'You're quite sure about that? Because I can't *honestly* believe – '

He was interrupted by the reappearance of Arthur, who stood behind Billy and gripped him by the shoulders. 'As I was saying, Matt, I hope you're not here to upset the boy.'

The flatness of the utterance, apparently made without moving a muscle, was chilling. I was also struck by the movement of the eyes, the constantly shifting gaze that always returned to Matt without once deigning to light on me.

Matt scarcely stirred, though tension was visible in every limb.

'I'm sure the *boy*,' he said icily, fixing Arthur with hard concentration, 'can take care of himself.'

'He certainly can. And what did he say? He's fine. You heard it from his own lips.'

'I don't need you to tell me what I heard, thank you.'

'Hey, come on,' said Billy. 'Just cool it – the pair of you.'

'I gave you warning,' said Arthur.

'And who are you to give warnings?'

'Matt,' said Billy, 'this has gone far enough. I think it would be best if you left now.'

'Absolutely,' said Arthur. 'Couldn't put it better myself. On yer bike, matey. Skedaddle and toodle-pip.'

Matt leaped up, eyes flashing.

'What?' he spat at Billy. 'You chose to give up all we had for *this*?' He flung his wrist at Arthur in a gesture of contemptuous dismissal. Then he turned to me. 'Come on,' he said, as if to a dog. He nodded towards the door. 'We're leaving. Now.'

'That's right,' brayed Arthur. 'And don't forget to take your spaniel.'

Matt ignored this. Instead, he threw Billy a final despairing appeal.

'I'll be in touch,' said Billy, meeting his gaze with brimming eyes. 'I'll write – or phone.'

Matt snatched up his jacket and made to leave. I

followed. There was a huge scuffling of chairs. I could see the turning heads, hear low rumblings of disapproval, feel the scorching eyes. And the drama wasn't over yet. At the door, Matt turned and stalked back into the room. He pulled out his wallet, fished inside and flung some notes onto the table.

'I'm not sure who I owe,' he said, looking first at Billy, then at Arthur, an evil grin on his face. 'But sort it out between yourselves.'

The entire pub fell silent. The place froze, in fact, stunned into immobility. Every eye was trained on Matt, the focal point of the action, and for a moment the scene resembled a dumbshow in a waxworks museum, all stiff and statuesque, yet vibrant with feeling and tension. I was appalled, of course. And so, it seemed, was everyone else in the room. Everyone, that is, except Matt. But was he quite sane? His face had a transfigured look. He seemed to be beside himself, floating above it all, driven by some kind of monstrous demon. I watched and waited, mesmerised and horrified. With a swift, half-crazed glance round the room, he turned, strolled back and kissed me hard on the mouth. But this was too much, more than I could bear, and in the tension of the moment I flinched and pulled away. He seemed not to notice, however. Instead, he slid an arm round my waist, in the same showy way that he had when we entered the pub, and guided me out into the street. There was absolute uproar as we left.

Four o'clock? Is that really the time? They're cruel, these church clocks, aren't they? They strike the hours like a death knell. No rest for the wicked. But wait a minute, *I'm* not the sinner. He's here, stretched out beside me, vibrating to the deepest snores that ever shook a bed.

Anyway, to resume. We scarcely spoke on the drive back. Matt sat at the wheel in a smoulder of dark heat; I could feel the waves coming off him. I had precious little concern for his feelings, though, since I was raging myself. We drove straight here, so that we arrived by late afternoon when the sun was still fairly high. I had no idea how we were going to spend the rest of the day, let alone what was left of this so-called holiday. My little autumn break had become a nightmare. Matt demanded the key from the girl at reception with not even a token smile and trudged off up the stairs. I dogged his heels, as my role demanded. He let us in, flung himself into an armchair and closed his eyes. But this was not an afternoon nap; he had no need to catch up on sleep, I was sure of that. No, he was simply sealing himself off from me. And that was absolutely fine; I didn't want to talk any more than he did. Oh yes, there was plenty to talk about, but this was not the moment. I gathered up my book of crosswords and quietly let myself out. I smiled at the girl at reception to make up for Matt's surliness, though she showed not a flicker of response and simply stared at me as if I were soft in the head.

The high street was buzzing. I wandered to the top, bought a cup of tea from a man in a kiosk, and joined a group of people sitting around the plinth of the war memorial. The square was still awash with warm sunlight and the scene here was relaxed and friendly. In fact, it represented the very reverse of the way I was feeling at that moment. I glanced at the young man beside me. He was superb: tight jeans, black boots, check shirt rolled to the biceps. A builder, perhaps? A trucker? Anyway, bouncing fit and attractively rough round the edges. I simply couldn't take my eyes off him. He turned, noticed my admiring look and smiled. Yeah, transfixed me: pierced me to the core with a broad heart-stopping grin. Oh, I thought, if I could just take you home, my lad, what wouldn't I do to you? But first I'd scrub those fingernails. Just look at the state of them.

Matt was in the hotel bar when I got back. He was toying with a gin and tonic while flicking through a restaurant guide. He seemed calm, if subdued, and greeted me with the ghost of a smile. I asked how he was and he shrugged. Actually, I didn't give a damn how he was, but I chose to maintain decorum for the moment. Timing, after all, is crucial, and the showdown was for later. Anyway, he expressed no interest whatsoever in *my* state of mind, or indeed where I had been for the past hour. So I called the waiter over and ordered a dry sherry. Eventually the silence became so awkward that I pulled out my book and started on a crossword. Shortly after this I became aware that he was pushing the restaurant guide across the table towards me, his finger pointing to an entry that he'd ringed with a ball pen. I glanced at it, barely able to disguise my indifference. The favoured place was described as an attractive country inn, with a varied menu and a choice of fine wines.

'I thought we could eat there,' he said.

I nodded. I mean, what else? The moment to turn rebellious would arrive in its own good time.

And so it did. The Orchard turned out to be quiet, softly-lit, intimate – ideal, in fact, for the kind of frank tête-à-tête that I felt the occasion demanded: the honest set-to that I was absolutely itching to have. The waiter led us to a side table, immaculately laid and discreetly separated from the other diners, and we nodded our approval. We both went for the Dover sole and Matt insisted on paying for a rather special bottle of chardonnay. 'That's fine,' he said to the waiter at the tasting. Then, turning to me with a wink, 'I think you'll approve.' Oh no, Sonny Jim, I thought, you won't get away with that. It'll take more than an ice bucket to make up for the mill I've been dragged through today.

In the lengthy wait before the meal arrived we sipped at the wine and cast glances round the room. Don't break the silence, I thought; let him do it.

And after a while he said: 'The Morris is performing rather well. Much better than expected, actually.'

'Yes, and lovely weather for the time of year,' I said in a pointed voice. So heavily pointed, in fact, that I could scarcely believe it was mine.

He studied me closely, clearly thrown off balance by my funny remark. Then he started to fiddle with the cutlery. 'Okay, you're right. It's been a freak show today. Sorry about that.'

'Is that it? Anything more you'd care to say?' As hinted

earlier, I sometimes surprise myself.

'Look, none of that was meant to happen.'

'Oh no? So we wound up in that bar by accident, did we?'

'Like I said, we were in the area – '

'In the area, my sweet arse. Let me give you my version. That visit was the whole purpose of this trip.'

'What?. . . No, no . . . Look, you've got it all wrong.'

'Okay, so put me right.'

He sighed, shifted nervously, glanced away. 'I admit I wanted to look in again. See Billy, sure. But I swear I never intended – '

'Well, whatever you intended, would you admit that you've been less than straight with me?'

'Look, I've said I'm sorry.'

'In fact, would you admit that you've used me?'

'Oh Jesus, come *on*.'

'Yeah, I've been mystified by this thing from the start. But now I get it. Today the shells fell from my eyes. Now I know why you never look at me, but *through* me.' I could feel myself getting hot. 'In fact, now I know what happens in bed.' I lowered my voice to a whispered hiss. 'It's not me you fuck – it's that boy.'

He got up quickly. 'Ah, this is crazy.' He tapped the side of his head. 'Anyway, can't stay, I've lost my appetite.' He fished in his wallet and tossed a heap of notes onto the table. 'That should cover the meal and the taxi.' And without a backward glance, he threw his jacket over his shoulder, marched for the door and vanished into the night.

So there I was, alone and exposed, thrown into sudden confusion, my face burning. I became aware of other diners looking over their shoulders and staring at me. Our little scene had created a flurry of interest. I sat for a while, trying to compose myself and wondering what to do. Should I pay up and leave, or stay and eat? I decided to face it out. Why let a minor embarrassment ruin the whole evening? I was hungry after all, and someone else was paying. I removed the money from the table and stuffed it into my pocket. Tossing out notes must be an expensive habit, I thought. Especially for someone who shares a house with a bunch of hippies.

When the waiter arrived, he glanced at the vacant space, then turned to me with a lift of the eyebrows. I explained that my friend had been taken ill, but that I would be staying and dining alone. He nodded, said how sorry he was, and placed a consoling hand on my shoulder. Though not quite my type, he was a big handsome guy and my heart melted. But don't fancy your chances, I told myself; keep your eyes on your plate and avoid disappointment. Anyway, men are trouble, men are heartbreak. So wise up and chock it down, Dizzy Lizzy; it's your own half of the bed tonight and more barren hours with Two-Timing Tim.

After the meal I phoned for a taxi and had a smooth and luxurious drive back to the forecourt of the hotel. I tipped the driver generously and watched him depart. I'd not wasted a drop of that chardonnay and was feeling rather heady to say the least. I glanced at my watch. It was only ten o'clock and such a lovely evening that somehow I was in no mood to turn in early. So why not take a stroll? I wasn't exactly keen to rejoin my tricksy travelling companion. No, let him rot in hell. And with sudden resolution I blew a kiss to the moon and wandered off into town with a slight lurching motion. It was surprisingly mild for October and the streets were alive with noisy groups of revellers. I strolled around for a while observing the scene, and then, on a whim, disappeared into a small cinema where there was a late-night showing. The film was a silly screwball comedy about a disastrous boy-meets-girl relationship. I arrived in the middle and when my eyes had adjusted to the darkness I could see that the place was almost empty, the audience no more than a few sad loners and some necking couples separated by acres of vacant space. I lolled in my seat, constantly shifting position, propping my head first on one arm, then the other. After a while I glanced behind. The couple devouring each other in the back row looked like two young men, though it was hard to be sure in the half light. Anyway, I wished them well, all the pleasure and happiness I've never had, and in my mind I saw them float up on a magic carpet, lift clear of the cinema, hover over the town and then glide the global airways, fucking like rabbits.

I left before the end and drifted back to the hotel. I came straight here to the room and found the door unlocked. I entered quietly and peered into the darkness. There was a hump under the duvet and the place was shaking to Matt's snores. So I crept to my side of the bed with the aid of light from the hall and snapped on the overhead lamp. Matt was lying on his side, his back towards me. He woke with a start, glanced over his shoulder and gave a faint groan. Then, turning away, he thrust his head deep into the pillow. I undressed, climbed into bed and snapped off the light.

But sleep was a long time coming.

Actually, I'm not sure that I've slept at all. I seem to be abnormally aware of every creak in the building. Yes, the place is astir in every limb. Listen. Can you hear the tread of feet in the hall, the blur of voices in the next room, the gurgle and clatter of the plumbing? Even if I do drift off from time to time, I soon wake in mild alarm, creepy ideas passing through my confused brain as I stare fuzzily into the darkness: *Where am I? How have I ended up in this box? The bastards have buried me alive*.

Anyway, that was today. That was the climax, the destination, the final revelation of this magical mystery tour. And what a humdinger. What a turning point in all senses. Now for the downward run. But at least the day has banished all doubt. No ifs or buts, I *know* now. And thank God this merry little prance is almost over. I tell you, I can't wait. Can't wait to get home.

Not pretty, this part of the country. Well, not from the M1, anyway. In other circumstances I might have suggested turning off and heading for the Peak. Some nice teashops in the Bakewell area. But no, in the current climate, I'm all for bashing on. And that goes for Matt too. The sooner we get home the better, as far as he's concerned. One look at the set of his jaw makes that clear. The original plan was to head back tomorrow, but that was before things took this cute little turn. It's a crying shame, though, because the weather is holding. Also, it's odd, but I'm as bright as a bunny now, when by rights I should be a dishrag. He, however, is deeply morose. I could scarcely squeeze a word out of him at breakfast, and it's been no better since.

Yesterday? I've not mentioned it. Best avoided. And when he suggested cutting the trip short, I readily agreed. Well, let's face it, there's no mileage left in this comic caper, is there? Except of the literal kind, of course. God, how many more hours of this? As I say, not exactly heart-lifting, the view from the motorway, particularly when you're trapped in a frozen block of silence that not even a sword could cleave, let alone a knife.

Still, I'm glad I took my stand. He's used me, strung me along, treated me shabbily. Essentially, he's not been honest. And I'll put up with a lot from people as long as they're honest. I'm not awkward or pushy or aggressive. In fact, I hate rows. But I won't be done down. Won't be screwed, if you take my somewhat dubious meaning.

What does that sign say? London 54? Oh, thank God. I just can't wait to turn the key of my own dear little pad, snap on the kettle and sink myself deep in cretonne. After which – yes, I've been planning this for the past several hours – I'll take a long relaxing bubble-bath, dense with muscle-soothing salts and minerals. Then I'll make a few calls, and I hope my friends have all removed their ear-plugs because I need someone to *listen*.

'So you don't think you'll see him again?' says Petra.

'Of course bloody not.' I'm a trifle tetchy. 'Not in the sense you mean. It's over.'

A pause.

'So another failure. Well, you know my theory.'

'Oh, don't start that. There may be a pattern, but this was something different. The man's a headcase.'

'Well, let's face it, you do meet a surprising number of those.'

'I know . . . I know . . .'

'Phone him now. Try again.'

'For God's sake . . . He's in love with someone else.'

Silence. I picture her – sort of *hear* her – stroking her chin.

'What you need is a boost,' she says. 'A change of outlook. A self-assertion class, perhaps.'

'Oh, do stop wittering,' I say, clutching my head, snatching up another peppermint cream. 'I don't know what I need. I only know it's *over*. And I repeat, it was weird. *Weird*, do you hear me? Thoroughly weird from the start.'

PART FOUR

April-September 1986

Clare Cavanagh peers through the slats of her blind. The day looks promising. Pearly light is spreading from the east, and the trees of the city – some with fresh young leaves – are silhouetted against the pale-blue vault of the sky. The air is alive with birds, noisily flitting from branch to rooftop or scampering through foliage. Her heart misses a beat as a gull swoops down onto her sill. Such a large, bold, confident creature. It treads around with martial strut before gliding off again. Then, looking up, she spots them. The swifts! Yes, gliding in wide arcs on sleek, outstretched wings. So here it is, she thinks – the moment we've all been waiting for – the first heart-lifting hint of summer.

She returns to her application form. *Please give details of any other experience that might be considered relevant, including unpaid work.* Well, she thinks, I've been mother, elder sister and nurse to this wayward family for a number of years. That must count for something, surely. But how to convey this other experience in one short paragraph. She chews the end of her pen.

Hullo, what's that? Creakings overhead, footfalls along the upper landing. She glances at her watch. Up and moving? At this hour? Unusual, to say the least. In fact, almost unheard of. She hears the approach, turns on her swivel-chair. A scuffling outside the door. A period of silence. Then a soft, tentative knock.

'Entrez, mon chou.'

A head appears. 'Sorry, Clare, I know you're busy.'

She smiles. 'Well, Cherub, what can I do for you?'

The cherub frowns and runs a hand through his hair.

'Er, I was wondering – could you spare a minute? Or even a couple?'

Ah, she thinks; so not on the cadge. Something serious, needs to talk.

'Tell you what,' she says, 'put the kettle on and I'll join you downstairs.'

'Only if you're sure. I don't want to be a distraction.'

She throws him a pained look and tosses her application form in the air.

'Tedious bloody thing,' she says. '*Please* distract me'

They sit facing each other. The teapot squats on the table between them, wrapped in the ribbed cosy that someone brought back from Windermere. He takes from his back pocket a sheet torn from the phone pad in the hall and pushes it towards her. She reads quickly the brief message scrawled across it in Eddie's blend of tortuous loops and spiky capitals. *Matt, Craig called. Coming to London next week. Any chance you and he could meet? If so, please call back*. The phone number printed beneath is heavily underscored. Clare frowns, wrinkling her nose, as if offended by the untidiness of the script. Then she looks up and stares at him in puzzlement.

'Craig?'

'One of Billy's friends. You remember.'

She shakes her head.

'Randy little bloke. Five foot nothing. Very cute and bold as brass.'

'Ah, yes.' She nods vigorously. 'Gave you the come-on.'

'That's the fella.'

They laugh.

'So what's the problem?'

'Good question.'

'Do you want to meet him?'

'I do . . . and I don't.'

They laugh again, then lapse into silence.

'I'm not sure that I can help here, can I?' she asks.

He smiles sheepishly. 'I guess not. I think I just wanted to share the problem.'

She nods thoughtfully. Then, jumping to her feet, she brings the kettle to the boil and refills the pot.

'Well, whatever you decide, you must respond,' she says, changing abruptly from giggling confidante to house mistress. 'It would be churlish not to.'

Back in his room he can't settle. He paces the floor and turns on the radio. Someone is giving his personal account of the Normandy landings. He snaps it off. This Craig thing is nagging away and he simply can't focus on anything else. The stumbling block is pride, he realises. He doesn't want to soil himself again. No, he'd like to stay aloof. But he's also avidly curious. What exactly is Craig up to? Playing the field, as usual? Some dodgy errand? Ah well, never mind. Whatever his motive, Craig will have news of Billy. And that, above all, is what he wants to hear.

It's been a hard six months. Six months of trying to forget. Of being haunted by the shock of events, the perversity of life, his own lack of control and sense of guilt. He's had six months to ponder his own behaviour and he'll never forgive himself. But then, nor can he quite forgive anyone. Not deep down. Remorse when it begins to rise is trounced by pride.

Clare is right, though. It would be churlish not to respond. So what's it to be? Yes or no? Pride says no. On the other hand, simply to meet Craig would be neither to humble nor commit oneself. So why not be gracious, and at the same time satisfy one's curiosity?

'Just a moment.' A woman's voice at the end of the line. 'Who's calling, please?'

'It's Matt.'

Some scuffling, then a long period of silence. More sounds of movement. Someone thunders down the stairs.

'Matt, old cock. Good to hear from you.'

'Hi Craig, lad. How ya doin'?'

'Fine, mate. Never better.'

'Really? That's good. Anyway, got the message. So what's all this?'

'Ah, nothing much. Just a spot of business.'

'Spot of business?'

'Yeah, you know.'

'Actually, I'm not sure that I do.'

'Anyway, look, I'll be there on Wednesday and staying overnight. Could meet you for a drink.'

A short pause.

'Er . . . yeah . . . okay. Anywhere in mind?'

'D'you know the Earl of Southampton?'

'Er . . . not personally, no.'

'Corner of Frith Street.'

'Well, I'm sure I can find him.'

'How about Thursday? Half eight?'

Not a hint of hesitation. Everything under control. You had to admire it. The chutzpah, the speed, the agility. Quite staggering.

'Er . . . mmm . . . okay, you're on. Thursday, half eight.'

'Great news.'

'We'll catch up then.'

'We certainly will. See you soon, babe.'

A click at the end of the line. Matt replaces the receiver and smiles. The reek of Craig has travelled the distance and hangs in the air. And did he imagine it, or did the phone wink?

Oh hell, he's not suitably dressed for this heavy squall. He ducks, pulls his jacket over his head and makes a dash for it. He's already spotted the pub from the other side of the street. In the doorway he shakes off the drops and runs a hand through his hair. But once inside, he's struck by a feeling of mild panic. The place is heaving. Will they find each other in this tight crush? Indeed, what does Craig look like? Can he recall after all this time? Well, broadly, he's neat, wiry, built like a jockey. But can he recall his features in detail? No, he can't. In fact, he has this nagging fear that he can't remember what Craig looks like at all. Or at least, that he won't be recognisable in this context.

There's also something deeply uncomfortable about searching for someone in a crowded place. People turn and stare, you feel intrusive. Matt glances round the main area and peers hastily into the room at the back. If Craig is here, it's not obvious. Best order something now. Holding a glass makes you feel less lonely, pointless and conspicuous. But then, just as he catches the barman's eye, a hand falls on his shoulder.

'Matt.'

'Ah, there you are, Craig. Couldn't spot you. What'll you have?'

'Just arrived, man. This fucking rain. Anyway, good to see ya, mate. Yeah, a gee and tee, thanks.'

They carry their drinks to the middle of the room and look for somewhere to sit. The only vacant table has a single chair, but Matt manages to persuade a guy to part with the spare that he's using as a foot-stool. He and Craig then settle their backs to the wall, turn to each other with a smile and raise their glasses. Matt notes again the features that he's been unable to recall from memory: the shiny pink forehead, the long lashes, the small brown mole on the neck. He also notices the gear. Yes, the lad's well turned out and fits very nicely into his white v-neck and faded blue jeans. A thick black belt with a steel buckle draws attention to his slim waist, and his jeans are rolled up a couple of inches at the bottom, so that they just clear his heavy-duty boots. Some music is playing, but at so low a volume that it's drowned out by the rumble of voices in the bar. Matt produces a packet of fags and offers one. Craig reaches across the table. They light up and blow rings for a few minutes.

'Well now, Matt.' Craig breaks the silence. 'What's the buzz? How's this naughty old world been treating ya?'

'Mm, hard to say. Bit of this, bit of that. You know.'

Craig nods. 'Yeah, tell me about it.'

'Anyway, speaking of naughtiness, Craig, I'm not sure that I've ever found out what exactly it is you do.'

'Well, like you say, bit of this, bit of that.'

'Is that so? Fascinating.'

'It's a long story. Don't let it bother ya.'

'I won't.'

A lengthy pause.

'So what *is* this, Craig? A social call? Or have you got something else in mind?'

'Like I say, I come on a spot a business, thought I'd look you up.'

Matt smiles and takes another swig.

'Hey, what's so funny?' says Craig with a grin. 'Don't tell me I'm trespassing again. I thought you and Paddy O'Reilly was finished.'

Another lengthy pause.

'Finished? I'm not sure that we'll ever be finished.'

They stare ahead, in silent meditation.

After a while Matt says: 'So nothing to tell me?'

'What? Regarding . . . ?'

'Who else?'

'Well, not a lot. He's still at the pub. Where else? Back in the groove.'

'How's he doing?'

'Seems okay. Don't see a lot of him these days. He needs to get out more.'

A long pause. Matt clears his throat.

'Does he ever mention me?'

'Not when *I'm* there.'

'Who's he with now?'

'No one, mate. No one I know of. That old buzzard Arthur still hangs around, of course.'

'So no big changes.'

'Nah, the scene's much the same. Well, there was a ripple back along. Terry started seeing this nurse from St Stephen's, a woman with two teenage kids from a broken marriage. But then the kids turned funny and it all fell apart. Baz is doing fine. His band has been booked for several gigs this year and they look set to get a recording contract.'

Matt shrugs and stares at the floor.

'Ah well, there you go.' Craig leaps up. 'Funny old life. Same again?'

Matt gives a glum, distracted nod, and when Craig returns a few minutes later he's still meditating, staring glassy-eyed at the pattern in the carpet.

'Hey, dreamer, warm yer cockles on that.'

'Yeah, ta.' Matt shakes himself out of his trance and reaches for his drink. 'So, Craig, you thought you'd look me up, is that it?'

They clink glasses.

'Well, you know me, always there for my friends.'

'A strictly social call, then.'

'Look, no conditions. This can go wherever you like.'

Matt snorts loudly. 'Oh yeah? Some neck you've got, Craig.' He smiles and shakes his head. 'Still, full marks for persistence, lad.'

Craig grins. 'Thing is, Matt, it's a different ball game, yeah? I mean, at this distance, who's gonna know?'

They meet Clare on the first-floor landing. She greets them with a smile and Matt, feeling rather light-headed, introduces her to his bright-eyed visitor. He'd been hoping they could sneak in unseen. But why, for God's sake? Some obscure embarrassment he feels about the situation? Anyway, here they are, the thing is out and there's no reason to be coy. On the contrary, be bold, confident, upfront. Clare, showing not a hint of awkwardness, nevertheless quickly excuses herself, saying that she must get back to work. She departs with another smile and a tiny wave of farewell that feels like a blessing.

In the room, Craig moves around, lifting and inspecting books and bric-à-brac. He seems particularly taken with a tiny figurine of a Chinese water-seller perched on a ledge above the desk. Matt follows, hovering just behind him and breathing gently onto the nape of his neck. After a while Craig turns to face him. Their heads move closer and they kiss tentatively, bringing their lips together with extreme delicacy, as if expecting the other to explode or dissolve into dust. But when Craig removes his jacket and lets it drop to the floor, Matt pulls him close and buries his face in the faintly perfumed hollow of his shoulder. The soft, scented skin is intoxicating. Reaching under Craig's belt, he pulls the T-shirt free and lifts it over Craig's head and raised arms. Then he sinks to his knees, planting kisses over the small, compact chest and dragging his tongue over the hairless flat of Craig's stomach.

And now the gloves are off. Or more accurately, shoes, socks and trousers. Craig slips his thumbs under the band of his undershorts.

'No,' begs Matt. 'Allow me.'

He draws them down with painstaking slowness, indulging a fetish. Craig's swollen lob flies up, bouncing like a rubber truncheon. But then, suddenly aware that the room is ablaze and the curtains drawn back, Matt leaps up and reaches for the light switch. In an instant the room shrinks to a bar of moonlight and their bodies become wraiths. At the same time Matt, hobbled by the pants round his ankles, loses balance and falls over backward. He stretches out full-length on the floor and lies on his back, giggling. Craig, chuckling lecherously, leaps onto him and squats astride his chest, pinning his arms to the floor.

An hour or so later, Matt, reaching for his cigarettes, glances at the clock on his bedside table. It's ten past two, and the alarm will go off at seven. Christ, he'll have to give it up, this helling around at all hours with the boys. It's been good, though. He and Craig light up and sit naked, their knees crooked, their backs propped against pillows. The duvet has been kicked off the end of the bed and lies in a heap on the floor. After a while they turn to each other and grin. Yes, it's been good. *Very* good. Bloody fantastic, in fact. Matt looks down at his cock, now limp and wrinkled, and shakes his head in amused disbelief. No doubt about it, this guy is an ace, an expert, a virtuoso. In his own word, a hotshot. But enough of all that, take a look at the time. With another swift glance at the clock, Matt stubs out his cigarette and plants a tender goodnight kiss on Craig's left cheek.

'Must get some sleep,' he says. 'Some of us have to work in the morning.'

They reach over the end of the bed and retrieve the duvet. Then Matt, turning his back on his bedmate, rolls into a ball and snuggles his head into his pillow. Craig finishes his cigarette, turns off the light and sits motionless, staring into the dark.

A few minutes pass.

Then, in an undertone: 'Matt, you still awake?'

'Uhuh.'

'There's something I need to say.'

A pause.

'Okay, I'm listening.'

'It's about Billy.'

Matt snaps on his bedside lamp and sits up.

'Billy? What about Billy?'

Craig is picking at a toenail, eyes averted, and continues to do so for some time, apparently absorbed.

'*What* about Billy?'

Craig reaches nervously for his cigarettes. As he fumbles, Matt knocks the packet from his hand and it flies across the room.

Craig rounds on him. 'Hey, cool it, man.'

'*What* about Billy?'

Craig sighs heavily. 'Okay, I should've said before.'

'But . . .'

'But . . . well . . . oh Christ, look, I dunno. Anyway, the thing is – he told me to tell you he'd like to see you.'

'Oh yeah?' Matt looks narrowly at Craig. 'Go on.'

'Well, that's it. As I say, I had to come down on a spot of

business. Billy asked me to look you up. And that's what he told me to say. He'd like to see you.'

'Oh really?' Matt gives a fat snort and stares hard at Craig, who is still visibly squirming. 'Well, isn't this just one helluva dandy time to tell me.' Craig, his face set hard except for a slight twitch in his cheek, says nothing. He looks away, avoiding the blast of Matt's eye. 'Never let an opportunity slip, eh, Craig? Never pass up on a fuck.'

Craig has a short spasm of amused head-shaking. 'Well, I didn't see *you* holding off.'

Matt is silent for a while, his chest heaving in angry confusion. Then suddenly he flings himself from the bed and stands staring down at Craig, eyes glittering with rage, mouth clenched. Craig, cowering beneath the duvet, looks up transfixed, as if threatened by an armed intruder.

'Get out!' Matt snarls.

Craig's mouth cracks open. 'What?'

His voice is weak with shock.

'You heard me.'

'You want me to leave?'

'Yeah, bugger off.'

'What, now? Walk the streets?'

'Bingo!'

'Aw, come on. This is crazy, man.'

Matt marches to the other side of the bed, throws back the duvet, and grabs Craig's arm as if to haul him to his feet. Craig leaps up angrily and pushes Matt away with a hard thrust to the chest. Matt glares and responds with a shove so violent that Craig topples over backwards. He then leaps onto Craig, straddles his body and pins his arms to the floor. Craig struggles furiously, staring up into Matt's flushed face with stricken eyes. In terror, he crooks a leg and knees Matt in the crotch. Matt flings back with an agonised cry, and Craig, slipping swiftly from beneath him, scrambles to his feet. Matt, groaning and clutching his balls, remains kneeling, his slumped body bent almost double. Craig stands over him and, reaching down, clasps his head in the crook of his arm. But Matt, thrashing like a tiger in a trap, seizes Craig's right ankle and hauls on it sharply. Craig falls over sideways with a cry and is forced to release his grip. In an instant Matt pounces on him, rolls him onto his stomach and slams his arms up behind his back.

'Shit, man! Give us a break.'

Matt says nothing, and only relaxes his hold when Craig stops struggling. They keep quite still for a while, all passion spent. An exhausted calm settles on the room. Shortly Matt stands up. He glances down at Craig, still lying prone in a state of apparent surrender. Then, with a faint harrumph, he strolls back to bed.

Craig, unsure of his next move, plays dead for several minutes, before rolling over, sitting up and squatting cross-legged on the floor. He gazes nervously at the hump beneath the duvet. Alert to any flicker, any hint of a snore or growl, he approaches with great caution and climbs in beside Matt. They lie in silence, as if wondering how to call an end to this interminable night.

Then Craig clears his throat. 'Like I say, Matt – '

'Can't think what possessed him.'

'Excuse me?'

'To entrust a message like that to a raving whore like you.'

Matt sits up and throws Craig a deeply deploring look. Craig shrugs and scratches his ear. His face is a cocktail of defiance and sulkiness, mixed with a twinge of guilt.

'Look, I'm sorry, okay? I'm sorry. You're right, I guess, I should . . . but then, like I say, who's to know? I mean . . .'

Matt turns away, snaps off the light and slams back into his pillow.

'Ah, forget it! Stop blathering and let's get some bloody sleep.'

Betty Trott, standing in the hall of the pub, dumps her shopping bags on the table and grapples impatiently with the knot of her headscarf. Raindrops fall steadily from the hem of her plastic raincoat, making puddles on the lino. She flings the scarf over the rail of the bannisters and then struggles with her umbrella, which has blown inside out. Yes, there's stormy weather, as forecast, and all over the country, apparently. Anyway, what's this? Some post has arrived. Nothing of interest, though. A bank statement, some promotional thing from the brewery, and Eileen's promised invitation. Well, they won't be going to *that*. She'll think up some excuse. Never did like the woman, and her marriage is a sham anyway.

Stan, in pyjamas, appears at the top of the stairs, yawning and scratching his head. His hair is an unsightly mess, a straggling gorse of thick grey tufts. Gawd, look at you, she thinks, and we open for lunch in twenty minutes. Still, don't say anything, it'll only make matters worse.

The phone rings suddenly with a loud tone that makes her heart jump. Who the hell, at this hour? She waits for half a minute to regain her composure and then snatches up the receiver.

'Black Horse.'

'Oh hullo. Is there any chance I could speak to Billy, please?'

'I'm not sure. Who's calling?'

'It's Matt. Is that Betty?'

Oh Christ, she thinks, that guy. I thought we'd seen the last of him. This is tricky. She hesitates.

'Oh hullo,' she says in her telephone voice, deliberately cool and distant. 'Actually, he's off duty at the moment.'

'Off duty?'

Again she hesitates. I don't know why I'm lying, she thinks. I might as well come clean; he'll find out sooner or later.

'Well, that's not strictly true. He's a bit unwell, actually. Not been too good for the past week. Perhaps you could call back again? Say, in a few days?'

'Not well?'

'Nothing to worry about. Just been a bit low, I think.'

‘A bit low?’ Matt pauses, desperate to hear more, but nothing more comes. ‘So can you tell me . . . I mean, what exactly . . . ?’

‘Look, I don’t know.’ She’s trying hard not to sound snappy, but damn it all, she’s not managed to take off her raincoat yet. She holds on through a period of awkward silence. ‘As I say, perhaps . . .’

‘Yes, okay, Betty, I will. I’ll do that.’ He speaks in rapid staccato. ‘I’ll call again, in a few days.’ Another pause. Has he finished? She’s got no time to stand and chat. ‘But Betty, before you go.’ She takes a deep, audible breath. ‘Could you do me a favour?’ No response. ‘Could you tell him that I called?’

‘Yes, of course,’ she says with exaggerated sweetness. ‘I’ll tell him that. No problem at all.’

She replaces the receiver with a firm click. Oh yeah? You’ll be lucky, lad. I’m not your go-between. Not after the trouble you’ve caused. Sort yerself out, sweetheart.

‘Sorry to pull you up, sir,’ says the young policeman, ‘but I couldn’t help noticing that your windscreen wipers are switched on.’

‘Er . . . I don’t understand.’

‘Well, sir, it’s not raining.’

‘So what’s the problem? I passed through rain a few miles back and forgot to turn them off.’

‘Could I see your documents, sir? I need to ascertain that this *is* your car.’

‘Please, constable, is this really necessary? I’ve somewhere to go.’

‘And that’s another thing, sir, you do seem to be in a great hurry. I couldn’t help noticing the way you took the last bend.’

Matt produces his licence and slaps it into the outstretched palm. The policeman scrutinises the document as if bent on committing every detail to memory.

‘Bit of a problem, sir. I’m afraid this licence has expired.’

'What?'

'It should have been renewed ten days ago.'

'Oh Christ!'

'I'm afraid I shall have to report this, sir.' Lifts little black book from top pocket. 'And now, sir, do you have the documents pertaining to the vehicle?'

'Not on me, no.'

'Then I must ask you to produce them at your nearest police station in the next few days.'

'Oh no.' Buries face in hands.

'It's in your own interests to comply, sir.'

'I mean yes, certainly, no problem.' Straightens up, smiles. 'Thank you, constable.'

'Not at all, sir. Very sorry to have detained you. However, perhaps I could advise you to take the rest of the journey with a bit more care and a little less speed.'

Yes, the journey, as ever, has been a curse. On arrival, though, his heart lifts. The good old place seems quite unchanged, and he speeds through the centre in defiance of the law, noting with relief the familiar landmarks: the Town Hall, St Peter's Church, George Square. Back again, he thinks. Back to where it all began. And no regrets, as Billy would say. Certainly life would be much easier if he'd never set foot here. But then, how dull and empty! There are just a handful of people on the streets, all of them wrapped up against the chill. It's still April, after all. But the pubs are brightly lit, and the Friday-night revellers, he guesses, are mostly inside, taking advantage of last orders. The Town Hall clock shows five to eleven. Not bad timing. With a bit of luck he too might squeeze in a drink before closing time.

But the crush in the pub is tremendous. There are two new barmen, pulling pints with vigour and joshing with customers, their shirtsleeves rolled to the elbows. Matt glances around. No sign of Billy, but he spots Betty at a table with a group of friends. Fortunately she doesn't notice him; she's in no state to notice anyone. Her face is flushed, and she's talking and laughing loudly. Indeed, everyone is thoroughly tanked up and preoccupied. Good, he thinks; and without hesitation or the slightest hint of furtiveness he heads straight for the door beside the bar, marked *Private*. He passes through with an air of bold nonchalance, and on the other side pauses briefly. Will anyone follow and question him? It seems not. Probably no one has even noticed.

Best not hang about, though. He hurries up two flights of stairs and hesitates briefly before tapping on the door to the attic room. His stomach is churning, he's full of apprehension. Billy may not be here; he may have moved. Or if here, he may not be alone. Anyway, Matt waits and listens . . . and fancies he hears . . . the sound of movement? Yes, someone's astir . . . footfalls on the stairs . . . some mysterious scuffling and fidgeting . . . and a narrow crack opens between door and jamb.

Then a face appears . . . shy, half-hidden.

At first they just gaze at each other. All words seem inadequate. In any case they can think of nothing to say except to murmur each other's name. Billy is the first to find voice. 'Matt,' he breathes, in the merest ghost of a whisper. He looks pale and cold. Dressed only in singlet and shorts, holding a quilt round his shoulders, he might be a refugee, or a child in a nativity play nervously awaiting his entrance. Matt moves closer. 'Billy, love.' Billy reaches out and touches his face. The quilt slides to the ground. They fall together, lock in a tight embrace and hold on in silence for several minutes. Then they break apart and gaze at each other again.

Matt takes Billy's hands and rubs them.

'Hey, you're cold.'

Billy smiles thinly. 'Yeah.' He ruffles Matt's fringe. 'You look fine, though. Just the same. You haven't changed a bit – and I'm so glad.'

'Oh God, Billy, I've missed you so much, so much. I can't tell you how much.'

'I'm sorry, love. Sorry for everything. So sorry, honestly.'

'No, Billy, no . . . it's me, it's me . . . I'm to blame.'

Matt, still rubbing Billy's hands, speaks in a crooning lullaby, as if to a child. He lifts the quilt from the floor and drapes it around Billy's shoulders. Billy takes him by the wrist and they mount the stairs. The room is in semi-darkness and full of shadows. The only bright spot is the central pool of light thrown by the standard lamp. They stand, holding each other in wordless communion, half in shadow, half in light, their bodies pressed together, their heads gently nudging. Matt strokes Billy's back, nuzzles his ear.

'So who let you in?' Billy murmurs.

'No one . . . I slipped in unseen.'

'From the bar?'

'Well, that's where I expected to find you.'

'And no one noticed?'

'Blind drunk . . . the tosspots.'

Billy chuckles. 'Anyway, thank God you're here. I've never been so glad to see anyone.'

'Nor I. The past months have been hell, sheer hell.' Matt pulls back. 'I would have come earlier, but . . .'

Billy presses a finger to Matt's lips.

'Not now,' he says. 'Save it. Let's have a drink.'

He leads him across the room and pushes him back onto the sofa. A small bottle of vodka, half consumed, stands on the coffee table. He takes two small tumblers and pours a large measure into each.

Matt wakes and glances up. Morning light is pouring in through the rectangle of blue in the ceiling. Pigeons – or perhaps gulls? – are clattering across the roof. Billy is asleep, lying on his side, his face to the wall. Matt snuggles up and gently kisses the nape of his neck. Billy wriggles and gives a moan: a drowsy, do-not-disturb moan. Matt bestows a final kiss, rolls away and gets out of bed. He does some bending and stretching, and then sits naked on the edge of the sofa, picking the flecks of white fluff from his navel and inspecting his feet. His toenails could do with a snip. He walks sleepily across the room and peers into the kettle. Just enough to make some tea. He pulls on his shorts, wanders back to the sofa, lights a cigarette.

The room is unchanged. It's the old familiar place, just as remembered, and it feels so good to be back. So very good that he seems to be reliving that first weekend, to be feeling the buzz again, the flush of pleasure and excitement he felt on that June night almost two years ago. But Billy. What about Billy? Now Billy *is* changed. He looks skinny and undernourished. He needs a good meal. So, first things first: before anything else they must go for a meal. And after that they must talk. They must talk till their tongues ache. Because of course there's so much to talk about and last night was not the moment for talking. No, last night was for body language: for skin talk, not words. Even so, Billy was disappointingly reticent. Matt wanted to make passionate love, go the whole distance, but Billy complained of tiredness. An odd reaction, given the warmth of his welcome and how special the moment felt. Ah well, a minor setback: there's plenty of time to put things right. A whole weekend, in fact.

Billy rolls onto his back and looks up. He sees Matt and smiles. A taut, washed-out kind of smile, Matt thinks. So what's behind it? But now the kettle is steaming. He wanders off and fills the pot. Returning with two mugs of tea, he sits on the edge of the bed and hands one to Billy. They clasp the mugs for warmth and sip in silence.

Then Matt says: 'We've been here before, haven't we? Isn't this where we came in?'

Billy looks at him shyly and grins. 'So you got my message?'

'From Craig? Oh, sure. Craig delivered the goods.' Matt searches Billy's face. 'In his own inimitable style, of course.'

Billy nods thoughtfully.

‘I had to use Craig. Couldn’t do it myself. I mean, I didn’t know how you felt about me. But I wanted him to speak to you face to face, not on the phone. Not much intimacy on the phone, is there?’ (Well now, thinks Matt, don’t underrate the lad; our Craig, let’s face it, could be intimate in semaphore or Morse.) ‘So when I heard he was taking a trip to Bermondsey – ’

‘Bermondsey? Well, I guess you know more about his trip than I do. Anyway, I take it you didn’t get *my* message?’

‘*Your* message?’

‘I phoned yesterday. Spoke to Betty.’

Billy snorts and shakes his head.

‘I knew when you didn’t respond,’ says Matt.

It strikes him again how thin Billy looks, how tightly his pale skin clings to his ribs and collar-bone. He reaches out and touches the ridges on Billy’s chest and shoulders.

‘Billy, what’s wrong? Betty said you’ve not been well.’

Billy leaps out of bed as if stung. He snatches up a T-shirt from a heap of clothes tossed on the floor and hauls it over his head. ‘She had no business saying that.’

Matt, shocked and puzzled by this sudden touchiness, sits and watches in silence, unsure how to respond.

‘Look,’ Billy says, ‘I’m fine, absolutely fine. I’ve just been a bit low recently, that’s all.’

He glances at Matt as if to gauge his reaction. Matt shrugs.

‘Okay, I know what you think. And you’re right. I drink too much and I don’t eat properly. It’s the job.’ Billy shakes his head. ‘And it all gets much worse when I’m depressed.’

‘Depressed?’

‘Look, love, I’d rather not talk about this now, if you don’t mind.’

Matt gets up and crosses the floor. He kisses the bridge of Billy’s nose and then enfolds him in his arms.

‘What we need is a hearty breakfast. Now remind me, what’s the name of that place on the Square?’

‘Dylan’s.’

'Yeah, that's it, Dylan's.' As if I need reminding; God, what a fraud I am. 'Come on, then, get yourself decent. Pull some pants on.'

In the street, Billy looks up and squints, dousing his face in sunlight. Simply being outside, after the confinement of the past week, feels good, but in such fresh spring weather it's exhilarating. Colour returns to his cheeks. Matt notices the change and grins. The transformation is so pleasing that a surge of warmth gushes through his own veins. He throws an arm round Billy's neck and gives a squeeze.

At Dylan's there are no tables on the street, and that's a shame because it's warm enough to sit outside. The arrival of spring has clearly taken the management by surprise. Never mind, it's reasonably early, there's plenty of room inside and they easily find a table near the window with a fine view of the Square. Here they tuck into scrambled egg and mushrooms, toast and marmalade, and wash it down with a pot of coffee. And as they eat, the sun moves higher until a beam of golden light breaks over the rooftops and floods in upon them.

They finish eating and settle back. Matt reaches for Billy's hand. He holds it tight and looks at him meaningfully.

'So what now?'

Billy shrugs and shakes his head.

'Billy, we *must* talk.'

Billy stares ahead, silent for a while, then turns and looks at Matt. 'Yeah, we must,' he says, with slow thoughtfulness. 'And we will. But not now, eh?'

Matt nods with quiet disappointment and looks away, his unfocused eyes coming to rest at a spot in the mid-air. But he's not permitted to sulk for long, for his mood is soon cut short by the sound of distant music. Yes, a brass band is playing in the street and seems to be getting nearer. Heads are turning, a crowd is gathering. Matt and Billy look at each other and grin. The excitement builds, there are cheers and shouts, and suddenly it bursts onto the scene: a ragged procession of men and women in colourful, gold-braided uniform, marching to a loud beating of drums, blare of trumpets and clash of cymbals. In an instant it's over: they've passed, the crowd is dispersing, the music fading. But the sheer physical impact has produced a rush of adrenalin, dispelling the earlier mood. Matt is buoyed up again, and once more reaches for Billy's hand.

'The other thing we need is a holiday. I mean, just look at this spring weather, for God's sake. Can't we take a short break? Shake off the winter gloom? Take the car to Cornwall, or a flight to Paris? What do you say? Can you get some time off?'

Billy smiles weakly. He squeezes Matt's hand and looks troubled. 'Hey, hold on. Don't rush me. This is too sudden. I'm not sure about this. I need to think. I've got a lot on my mind at the moment.'

Matt sighs and looks at the floor. 'Okay, I'm sorry, love. I'm getting carried away.' Then, raising his head, he gazes deeply into Billy's face. 'But what's going on in there?' He knocks gently on Billy's brow with his knuckles. 'I'd love to know.'

Billy shifts uneasily and turns away. 'I'll go for a refill. We need more coffee.'

'Oh, is that what we need?' says Matt, raising an eyebrow.

Billy is silent. Push no more, thinks Matt. You've pushed too far already.

At Benny's, the basement club on Market Street, there's the usual crowd. Matt and Billy arrive early, hoping to settle in with a quiet drink before the latecomers arrive. They nod at a few faces in passing and park themselves on a couch in a dim corner.

'Terry's put on weight,' says Matt. 'And I can't say I approve of what she's done to her hair. I guess she'll toddle over here for a chinwag soon. Her nose must be twitching for news.'

'Unlikely,' says Billy. 'She's off me and distinctly cool these days. But that's fine. The feeling is mutual.'

Matt volunteers the first round and strolls up to the bar. Almost instantly someone is nudging his elbow. He turns. It's Craig Ogilvie.

'Well, well,' says Matt stiffly. 'Would you believe it? Never thought I'd run into you.'

'Matt, put it there, mate.'

Matt, with a stony stare, ignores the proffered hand.

'Aw, Matt, come on. Not still sore, are you? I thought we were over that.'

Matt leans close and hisses into Craig's ear. 'I presume you mean to keep that fat gob of yours firmly fastened?' Craig nods vigorously. 'Good. And if there are any further twitches in that restless libido – '

'Matt, what d'ya take me for? Would I intrude at a moment like this? Believe me, I'm glad for the boy's sake that you're here.'

Matt cocks an eyebrow, then pays for the drinks and carries them back to the couch. Billy, half-hidden in shadow, is quietly surveying the scene. He looks up with a weak smile and that air of remoteness that he's had all weekend. Matt wonders again at the strangeness of his mood. A young man with jet-black hair sculpted into a rhino-horn – a fantastic creature whose fabulous appearance, Matt thinks, must require hours of devotion – pays them a fleeting visit and exchanges a few snippets of gossip, but otherwise they speak to no one. Craig, duly warned, keeps his distance, and Terry, settled with a group on the far side of the room, confines her communication to a ghostly wave, a brief fluttering of fingers. To Matt's relief, there's no sign of Baz.

'Same again?' he says after a while.

Billy shakes his head.

'You okay?'

'A bit tired. Shall we go? I could do with an early.'

'Yeah, sure. Whatever you say. A bit tired? Is that all?'

'Not now, love.'

Back at the pub, they stumble up the stairs to Billy's room feeling rather woozy. They've had no more than a large whisky at Benny's, but during the whole evening they've consumed – oh, can't remember – a few beers, some vodka mixes, that cocktail thing. Anyway, a fair amount. Matt glances at his watch. It's half-past twelve. He undresses slowly, fumbling for buttons and sometimes losing balance. He has to sit down to remove his socks. Billy falls back, fully dressed, onto the bed. Matt, naked, lies down beside him.

They lie there for some while in a stupor. Then Matt begins to unbutton Billy's shirt. 'What you need, my lord, is a valet. But remember, this kind of service will cost you.'

Billy lies inert. Matt tweaks his nipples, and then plants kisses all over his chest and abdomen. Billy moans, but scarcely stirs. So Matt tries to rouse him by unbuckling the belt of his jeans. And when there's still no reaction, he presses on, drawing down the zip of Billy's fly, slipping a hand into the gap, squeezing the bulge in his crotch. At which point, Billy, eyes firmly shut, gives a small grunt of disapproval and, reaching down, removes Matt's hand with great delicacy. Matt, disconcerted, sidles in and snuggles up with a nervous laugh, wrapping legs and arms round Billy and pulling him close.

'Hey, love, you're not going to shut me out again are you?'

Billy turns away, disentangles himself and stumbles off the bed. He crosses the room somewhat unsteadily and throws himself onto the sofa. Matt sits up with a look of confusion and studies him closely, noting his distressed look.

'Billy,' he calls softly, 'what *is* it? Tell me, please.'

Billy sits motionless. His face is frozen, his eyes are turned inward. Matt waits for a while and then jumps off the bed. He kneels at Billy's feet, reaches for his hands and looks searchingly into his face. Billy crumbles.

'Matt, I'm sick,' he blurts through tears. 'I'm very sick.'

Matt stares blankly, too stunned to speak. Sick? The word

strikes him physically. Like a blow to the stomach. Like a sword ripping through his body, leaving him hollow. His mind breaks into riot. Has he misunderstood? There's more than one kind of sickness, after all. Billy looks thin admittedly, but not otherwise unwell. Perhaps . . . but no, it can only mean one thing. It can only mean . . . yes, of course, how blind he's been! News of the sickness is everywhere. Yet somehow distant, muffled, from the far side of the Pond. He's never thought of it as something that might affect *him*.

'Sick?' he says. 'You mean . . .'

Billy nods.

Matt stares in dismay. His limbs turn leaden, and a kind of horror creeps over him. He feels himself being drawn down, spun in a vortex. He casts around for some straw to clutch. Perhaps Billy is mistaken? Deluded? Paranoid, in the current fearful climate?

'Are you quite sure about this? I mean, have you . . . ?'

Billy smiles sardonically. 'Been tested?' His tone is flat and hopeless. 'Yeah, of course. What are you thinking? That this is some kind of morbid fantasy?'

Matt gets up, utterly dazed and confused. He lowers himself onto the sofa beside Billy and sits in silence, numb with shock. His head is buzzing with questions, his mind leaping across chasms: *When? For how long? Is that why you left?* And further off, the mutterings of other questions: *So what now? Where does this take us?* And beneath them all, throbbing insistently: *And me? What about me? Am I sick too?* Billy reaches for Matt's hand and stares silently into the centre of the room with stony gaze, wiping the tears from his face with the sleeve of his shirt. After a while Matt puts an arm round his shoulder and they lean together, their heads touching. But Billy is shivering, so Matt fetches the duvet and they snuggle under it. And there they sit, saying nothing, deaf to the creaks and groans within the building, the sounds of voices from the street, aware only of the voices in their own heads.

*

Matt listens to the dialling tone, praying that Maggie will answer. She does.

'Maggie, it's me.'

'Hullo, sweetheart. Now let's see, you've caught this thing that's going round and won't be in for a few days.'

'Er . . .' Matt makes an odd noise, somewhere between a gulp and a splutter. 'Well, not exactly. It's complicated. Actually, I'm in Yorkshire.'

'Oh really? I thought that was all over.'

'Long story, I'm afraid. I'll explain later. But in the meanwhile there's a bit of a crisis here. Billy's in a spot of trouble. He needs help and there's lots to sort.'

'Lots to sort?'

'That's right, all kinds of stuff. Look, I'm really sorry, Maggie, I know this is inconvenient. I'll call again tomorrow. Can you cope?'

'Cope? An old workhorse like me? Well, I guess so. Heigh ho, cope with anything. No, that's absolutely fine, sweetheart. You get it sorted.'

Matt wakes suddenly, his limbs stiff, his left arm dead, crushed beneath him. He rolls over, stretches painfully, and when the blood returns, reaches for his watch. Ten to four. Soft moonlight, and Billy fast asleep. Well, that's good. Sleep has been in short supply for both of them recently; they must grab it while they can. He's caught up a little himself and is pleased about that. But will he get off again tonight? His mind is already spinning, taking up where it left off just a few hours ago. The shockwaves, though two days old, are still with him. His body has scarcely begun to absorb them.

His body, what *has* it absorbed? He gazes at the sleeping form beside him, which shows no hint of the worm that slinks through the night: no trace of the dark, secret love that destroys. He examines his own naked torso, presses the firm flesh of his forearm, touches the lightly-tanned skin of his chest. What lurks beneath? What lodges within this smiling shape? A stroll to the clinic will reveal. A mere pinprick pass sentence. Nevertheless, he must screw up his courage and face the music. Billy has led the way.

One thing is clear: they must brave this thing together. It's a heavy responsibility, the challenge is awesome, but he's ready to meet it. For Billy has called out to him, and to him alone. He, Matt, is the sole confidant; no one else knows. So whatever comes, they must shoulder it between them, share the weight. They must make a home, they must prepare. For they need each other now, he and Billy: now more than ever. Billy must come back to London. Not in a week, not in a fortnight, but today. They must return together; it must not happen again; they must not be separated.

He rolls over, smashes his head into the pillow. Will he ever get off? He must try. There's a long day ahead, many things to sort, a journey to make. His thoughts trail, grow straggly, and come to rest on a loud snore.

Billy wakes now and lies motionless for a while, listening to Matt's heavy breathing: not quite aware of himself, light with forgetfulness. But then his mind clenches on a rock. A rock that's lodged in the pit of his stomach. A rock that's been lodged there for weeks and can't be shifted. A rock that will lodge there for ever. His mouth is suddenly dry. He desperately needs a drink. He slips quietly from the bed and down the stairs to the bathroom.

This is now the way of his life: the way that every day begins.

He drinks from a plastic beaker and glances in the mirror. He sees a bright young face glancing back, a face he scarcely recognises. Can this be me? I feel so old. How can this face belong to someone so old? It's a trick, a deception. I'll wake up soon, the mirror will shatter. He pinches his cheek, punches his arm, feels the pain. No, the mirror is not lying. And yet, in another way, the image it reflects is a sham. For one thing seems certain: there will be no final reprieve. This glowing, solid flesh will one day – how soon? – turn skinny, blotched and racked with disease. It's true that the doctors at the clinic talk only in terms of treatment, but Billy is not by temperament an optimist. In his view there are no flights out of here, and any attempt to flee must soon default to base reality.

How strange and cruel life is: that pain and happiness are inextricably mixed. How perverse that he and Matt should be brought together again only by the threat of being parted for ever. His love for Matt never went away: it has been the one fixed allegiance of his life. Always strong, it became stronger in separation. Now fiercely passionate, it hangs over a pit of despair. Can it survive the dread times ahead? How short those times? Years, months, weeks? Pray God we're never separated. Please, dearest Matt, stay with me. Don't let me face this alone. Stay with me now to the end. To the bitter end.

In the spacious, five-storey house in Gordon Street known to its tenants as Number 7, the circle of young people seated cross-legged on the floor of the lounge are finishing a meal of potato fritters and spinach. The group, made up of permanent residents and their guests, is in lively mood, and the centre of attention is James, Mary Trimble's latest boyfriend, an engaging young man who works for a film company and has no end of stories to tell about the famous people he has met. Mary herself, smiling with quiet indulgence, gazes at James with pride and fondness. She has great hopes for this relationship and feels sure, though no inquiries have yet been made, that it will reveal compatible star signs.

Seated beside Mary is Clare Cavanagh, whose doubts about James are veiled by her laughter and warm show of amusement. Loads of charisma, for sure; but would you trust him with your cat, let alone your grandmother? No, this genial poseur is never right for Mary, who should know better by now, her fingers having been burnt many times. And where does she find these blokes, anyway? Surely not at her T'ai Chi class? James, a follower of the eastern arts? Well, it's all a head-scratching business, but fortunately not *her* problem. In any case, she's feeling buoyed up. A letter arrived this morning from the University of Kent, inviting her to an interview for the post of Lecturer in English Studies. Yes, she's in a quiver about it, but hasn't yet told anyone, afraid that the news will make the others in the house feel insecure. Actually, she hopes to stay on here even if she gets the job, assuming that that proves practical. But of course it's not yet clear how things will turn out.

'Hi, everyone,' calls a voice, breaking into her thoughts and interrupting the general chatter.

All heads turn and smile. It's Matt, peering round the door. He smiles back.

'I'm home . . . and I've brought someone with me.' Reaching behind, he pulls a shrinking figure into view. 'I think most of you know Billy.'

They gaze in surprise and bemusement. Billy's brief stay happened so long ago that memory has begun to fade. So what's this? The return of the lost one, or just passing through? Ah well, they shrug it off. It's a mystery, but simply part of the rich tapestry of this place, where people come and go all the time.

'Hi, Billy,' they sing out in ragged chorus.

Billy smiles and nods shyly.

'Come and join us,' says Drew. 'There's plenty of spare supper keeping warm in the oven.'

'Thanks,' says Matt, 'but we've already eaten. Besides, we need to unwind. We'll join you later.'

He and Billy disappear, and attention in the room immediately shifts back to James, who now provides further diversion by attempting a headstand.

'I learned this in class after school,' he announces from his inverted position. 'I can juggle and ride a monocycle too.'

'Please be careful,' says Mary, glancing round the room in mild embarrassment. 'I mean, is there really enough space in here for this kind of thing?'

Clare watches these antics with a wry, wincing smile, though her thoughts are elsewhere. So Billy is back. What a bolt from the blue! Oh, she knows about the Yorkshire trip, of course, but nothing has prepared her for this. So what's going on exactly? Is he back to stay? It certainly seems so. Looking up, she catches Drew's eye and guesses from his puzzled look that he's having similar thoughts. They smile at each other with shrugs of bemusement.

Upstairs, Billy drops his rucksack and gazes around. Matt snatches it up instantly and stows it in the cupboard, as if afraid that Billy will turn on his heel and sneak off again. Smiling, Billy wanders across to the window and looks down into the backyard. He's glad to find the view unchanged, grateful for its comforting familiarity. The rusty bike is still leaning against the shed, and next door's tom is still sharpening its claws on the fence. As he stands there, Matt comes up behind and clasps him round the middle, pulling him close, and Billy, feeling no inclination to pull away, leans back, rubbing his head against Matt's chin. That former sense of constriction, of being too close for comfort, has gone; he feels now only a welcome sense of security and peace.

'Good old Gordon Street,' he murmurs, still gazing fondly at the view.

'Good old what?' Matt chuckles. 'How long since you fled the place?'

'Yeah, okay, let's not go over that. That was then, this is now.'

'But, love, we can't stay here. We need more space.'

'Do we? . . . If you say so. But where do we look?'

'Oh, heaps of places. And put the word around.'

They fall silent for a while. Then Billy turns to face him. 'Matt, are you quite sure about this?'

'I've answered that already.'

'I know, but . . .'

'The very first thing we need is medical help.'

‘Well, that goes for *me*, certainly.’

‘And perhaps for me.’

Billy shakes his head. ‘Jesus, if I thought . . .’

‘Billy, we’ve discussed this. There’s no blame here. In any case, whatever the situation, it’s *our* problem now. We’ll see it through together.’

A clear, slightly chill morning in early May. Matt and Billy, having crossed the Heath and admired the view, are threading their way through the streets of Highgate with the help of a streetfinder. They climb a steep, cobbled lane and stand at the railing of a ramshackle house. The white paint is peeling, the roof slates are mossy and the strip of front garden is wildly overgrown. The nameplate on the gate is so weather-worn they can barely read it, though on closer inspection they can just make out that this is Hollyhocks, the house they’re looking for. Turning to each other with a nod and a smile, as if to say *Eureka!*, they push through the squeaky gate and advance up the path. At the door they take a moment to brush their clothing and adjust their jackets. Then, on a signal from Billy, Matt lifts the horseshoe knocker and gives three firm raps.

They wait, listening intently, feeling slightly nervous. And they continue to wait until doubts begin to form. Is anyone there? Yes, eventually they catch stirrings from within, a curtain twitches, there’s a scratching noise from the other side of the door, a slow sliding of bolts. Then a face appears. The face of a very old man with a mane of white hair, a jutting beard and thick spectacles pushed to the end of his nose.

‘Archie?’ says Matt.

The old man glares as though affronted: as though accosted on his own doorstep by confidence tricksters who have somehow discovered his name in order to swindle him. Matt decides to leap in with a swift introduction before the door is slammed in their faces.

‘It’s Matt and Billy. Do you remember? We rang last

evening to say we were coming. We're friends of Alistair Robey.'

The old man cranes his neck, cups his hand to his ear. 'What's that? Did you say friends of Alistair?'

'That's right.' Matt speaks distinctly, in a raised voice, remembering Alistair's warning that Archie suffers from deafness. 'We're Matt and Billy.'

'The chaps who rang yesterday?'

'That's right.'

'Oh, my dear boys, do come in. Please forgive me. You're so fresh and spruce, the pair of you, I thought you were calling on behalf of some cranky religious sect.'

They step into the hall, which has all the appearance of a small, very cramped art gallery. Paintings and drawings, originals of every description, cover the walls almost from floor to ceiling. Matt stops to admire an oil painting, a splashy impressionistic study in shades of blue, suggesting a wild seascape in the manner of Turner. Then, further on, he squints closely at a cluster of small abstracts, strikingly monochrome and Cubist in style. His eye is also caught by a delicate pencil sketch, a fine portrait of a handsome black youth in a check shirt, with a large gleaming hoop hanging from his left lobe. Meanwhile, Archie is tottering away down the dark passage, urging them to follow. They pick their way carefully, but the house is so full of hazards, the floor so littered, that Billy stumbles twice, first into a pair of Wellington boots and next into something that flies off with a scarifying feline squawk.

'Oh, take no notice of *her*. She *will* park her fanny in the most ridiculous places.'

They emerge at last into a sort of back parlour, a room that's slightly chilly in spite of the fire roaring in the open grate and the sunlight streaming through the rickety patio doors. It's a living area that seems to function as study, library, dining room and lounge. Books are everywhere, lying open on table or sofa, in towers mushrooming out of the floor, in crammed bookcases reaching to the ceiling. In fact, the amount of clutter here is shocking. Several parts of a Sunday broadsheet are scattered round the base of an old leather armchair; a dish of porridge, half-eaten and congealed, has been abandoned on a footstool beside a large wicker basket of washing; and a rosewood piano, displaying a nocturne by Field, is almost hidden behind a pile of cardboard boxes.

'Oh dear.' Archie surveys the room with dismay. 'Hard to find a place to plonk yourself some days. Total bloody shambles. I had this woman in for a while. Olive, her name. She was a treasure. But then I got rid of her. She was getting far too interfering and bossy. I rely now on my dear neighbour Charlie, a lovely lady who looks in occasionally, though I don't like to put her to a lot of trouble. Anyway, look here, remove that box of electrical gear, if you will, and make yourselves at home on the sofa.'

Matt and Billy are quickly settled. Archie, however, takes much longer. He potters around, makes a token attempt to tidy up, punches a few cushions and finally falls back into the old leather chair that is clearly his permanent niche. There follows a pause, during which he peers at them hard, as if they are specimens at a horse fair.

'You seem a couple of nice lads.' They turn to each other with a shrug and a grin. 'The thing I said to Alistair is this. I need someone to lend a hand. Someone I can rely on, someone I can trust. And I'm not bothered about the money. No, you can have the place for the merest peppercorn. But I do need someone who knows how to hammer a nail into a wall without causing a leak.'

Matt and Billy smile and nod, although somewhat diffidently, as if recalling a secret history of causing leaks.

'So how does that kind of arrangement strike you? Would it suit?'

'Absolutely,' says Matt. 'It sounds fine. Ideal, in fact.'

'Ideal?' chuckles Archie, throwing his head back. 'Oh, my dear boy, calm yourself. You haven't seen the place yet.' He struggles to rise. 'So let me show you.'

He looks in danger of collapse, so Billy leaps forward to lend a hand. Then, holding back patiently, they follow him into the hall and up the stairs, a steepish flight that he climbs with painful slowness and immense effort. On the landing he turns to face them.

'I converted this floor into a flat – oh, years ago. So it's all a bit shabby, I'm afraid. I've had a string of rent boys, if you'll excuse the expression. And mostly fine, except the last. Snifter, he called himself. Oh, good fun, but it was the bike, the music, the parties. No, I'm too old for that kind of thing. I showed him the door. Bit of a messy end. I said get the fuck out and take your Frank Zappa with you.'

He leads them into a room with a large double bed and an enormous wardrobe in polished, dark-stained wood. A recent, rather overworked view of the Piazza Navona hangs lopsidedly over the headboard. Bending down with wheezing breath, he rips off a strip of damp, peeling wallpaper and shakes his head.

'Badly needs a face-lift, as you can see. You boys any good with paint – or paper and brush?'

The boys again turn to each other with a shrug and a grin.

'We'll certainly have a go,' says Matt. 'We like a challenge.'

Billy nods. 'Yeah, great opportunity.'

The rest of the flat, comprising sitting room, bathroom and kitchen, is equally spacious, although Archie seems anxious to draw attention to all the defects. One of the rings on the gas cooker is faulty – and isn't there a problem with the plumbing up here? He turns on a tap. A fearful knocking shakes the pipes and water spurts out in angry spasms. He agrees that someone needs to be called in about it.

Back in the parlour, he offers them mugs of thick strong coffee, which he pours from a green enamel jug. The stuff is barely drinkable, but they thank him anyway, making warm compliments. Matt sips slowly, and to hide his discomfort pulls an envelope from the main compartment of his shoulder-bag. Inside, he explains, is a reference from his employer. Archie casts an eye over it, and then waves a hand dismissively. A good word from Alistair, he insists, is recommendation enough. But now, is this thing settled? He fixes them with an enquiring look, peering over the top of his specs. Oh yes, certainly; they meet his gaze with keen smiles and nods.

'Splendid!' Beams of satisfaction all round. 'In that case, we must discuss dates and arrangements.'

'Could it be soon?' asks Matt. 'I mean . . .'

'Whenever,' says Archie decisively. 'At your convenience. But the sooner the better, as far as I'm concerned.'

He struggles to his feet again. 'Oh now, where are they?' He crosses the room with faltering steps and begins to rummage through a desk drawer. The boys glance at each other, bemused. They're kept waiting an age. But at last, with a shout of triumph, he snatches up a set of keys – a rather weighty, long-handled bunch, held together by a length of twine – and holds them aloft.

'The only spares.' He totters across the room and tosses them with inconsiderate force into Matt's crotch. 'So if you need any more, you must have them cut.'

Matt, smiling bravely through eye-watering pain, nods and gathers them up.

Archie, still standing as if waiting to see them off the premises (though in fact wisely avoiding the effort of having to rise again from a sitting position) throws a glance from one to the other.

'Well, then, are we concluded?'

'Looks like it,' says Billy, with a grin.

'Excellent.'

Matt gets up and grasps Archie's hand.

'Yeah, feels good. So thanks a lot for everything, and we'll probably see you again very soon.'

'Looking forward to it.'

Archie kicks a book under a chair, bends slowly to lift the cat's bowl onto a table and leads them through the hall to the badly-fitting front door.

'Needs a chippy, this.' He yanks it open with great force and winces at the squeal it makes as it scrapes the step. 'Don't know of one, do you?'

Matt shakes his head. 'No, but it shouldn't be difficult to repair. Leave it to us.'

'Well, well, what a rare find you boys are. And how lucky we are to know Alistair. He and I met during an air-raid, you know. I think he was working for the government at the time. Then, after the war, he opened that little gallery in Chelsea and started to paint. I've got some of his stuff on the walls here, which is probably worth a bob or two these days. He's got a fair reputation, you know.'

The boys stand on the step, listening politely.

'As you see, I tend to rattle on disgracefully. So if I get to be too much, just tell me to shut up. Now it's a bit chilly for May, so don't hang about and catch your deaths. And remember me to Alistair, if you see him before I do – which seems pretty likely, since I see him all too rarely these days. And thank him for sending me two such lookers. Always had an eye for a face, did Alistair.'

The boys grin and turn down the garden path. They wave from the gate and watch the door close. Then they hug each other and head smartly for the high street, where they celebrate with a spot of lunch at a wine bar, all the while making plans and talking excitedly between mouthfuls.

'We'll move in at the weekend. We'll buy some paint and brushes and start to get the place shipshape. I'll tell the others tonight and offer to keep the room on until they find a replacement.'

Billy nods, and smiles musingly. 'Yeah, and let's start with the sitting room. I can't wait to get my hands on it. Strip away that dingy paper and slap up something bright and cheerful.'

'It's such a stroke of luck.' Matt shakes his head dreamily, 'I can't quite believe it.' He lifts his glass of Chianti and gazes deep into Billy's eyes. 'Anyway, cheers, love. Here's to the new life.'

Billy meets his gaze steadily for a while, then raises his glass and stares hard into its wine-dark centre.

'Yeah,' he says, his smile turning wry and meditative. 'To the new life.'

The car coughs a bit and then perks up, as if to acknowledge that a show of effort is needed on this of all days. It's not the brightest of mornings, but cracks of misty light suggest that the greyness might burn off. At Bryson's, the DIY store, where they seem to be the earliest customers, the assistant is helpful, offering expert advice and finding a box for their purchases. Traffic is also lighter than expected, so that by mid-morning they arrive at Archie's and let themselves in. Strains of music on scratchy vinyl greet them as they enter – some Brahmsian stuff for cello and piano – but there's no sign of Archie, so Matt calls out a greeting, for fear that the old boy might suspect burglary or something worse. There's no response, though, and Billy, keen to unload, returns to the car. Matt, however, strides down the hall and, popping his head round the door, peers into the back parlour. There's not a soul in sight, but plentiful evidence of recent occupation. Indeed, the room resembles an encampment from which squatters have fled. Matt, struck again by the staggering amount of clutter, imagines the frustrating search for missing items that must fill Archie's days. Then, through the window, he spots him, a tiny figure at the end of the garden, tearing up bread and tossing it onto a stone birdbath. The day is still dull, but sunlight breaks through at this moment, causing Archie to glance up, his snowy mane catching fire like a cresting wave.

Upstairs, in the kitchen, Billy is on his knees, inspecting the contents of the cupboard under the sink. Three decent pans and a fourth one with a dodgy handle. And here it is – the very thing he's looking for – an electric kettle. He peers inside. Needs a good rinse, but otherwise just the job. Matt enters, carrying a box of essentials: tea, coffee, milk and biscuits. Dumping it on the table, he gazes round with a show of satisfaction. But almost immediately his look changes to a frown. Crossing the room, he squints up into a corner near the ceiling, where an abandoned spider's web is collecting dust. He leaps and scoops it down with his hand. Billy, still on his knees, is exploring another cupboard full of cleaning materials. He tosses Matt a yellow duster.

When the kettle boils, they move to the sitting room and sit on the sofa, their hands clasped round mugs of coffee. They stare for a while at the house opposite, where the curtains are drawn, and wonder about the neighbours, the new life, the days to come. To Billy the move feels like a dreamlike interruption from which he will soon awake. The buzz he's getting now is good, but how long will it last? Yeah, he thinks, don't be deceived, Billy Boy. There's no escape, no hiding place. The thing is there, ticking away, and sometime, probably soon, the countdown will begin. So steel yourself and prepare, tell friends and family, don't cut yourself off. He turns and smiles at Matt. Thank God for you, love; you've come through for me. You're my prince, my last chance to snatch some happiness. Matt smiles back and squeezes Billy's hand. His thoughts, like Billy's, rattle around, rub and scrape each other. He's in the clear himself; the results of his test came through last week. But the relief he feels is mixed with guilt. Billy has never shown anything except relief, of course; yet the news seems to draw a line between them, to mark a point of separation. In any case, this period of false calm is unnerving. When will the storm break? Today? Tomorrow? Next week? Next year? How strange this thing, this dread we live with, which has brought us together again, yet threatens to blow us apart. And how will we cope?

A rich, warm, elderly voice breaks in on them.

'Welcome, honeybuns. How settled you look, and scarcely an item unpacked.'

They twist around. Archie, breathless from the climb, is thumping his chest in the doorway and clutching a fulsome spray of pink blossom snipped from the garden.

'A modest house-warming gift,' he says, holding it aloft.

When they invite him in, he enters rather unsteadily and stands for a few minutes to catch his breath, clutching the back of the sofa to prop himself up. He then falls back with a great sigh into the snug hollow of the armchair.

'Ah, that's better. Can't quite manage the wooden hill these days. I mostly confine myself to the lower quarters. But now, this room has distinct possibilities, don't you think? Anyway, I imagine you've got bold and exciting plans for it. I used to spend hours up here at one time. It was my writing den. I thought of myself as a poet, you know. Even published a slim volume, as well as a brief life of Marcus Blaine. Have you heard of him? No, of course not. No one has. But he had bags of promise back then. That's until Eugene threw him over for a younger boy. Absolutely broke his heart. Turned to drink, and then a very slippery slope. The funeral was spectacularly awful, what with Eugene sobbing shamelessly at the graveside and that shrill wife making bitter accusations and howling like a banshee. To be frank, I wish I'd stayed at home . . .

'But now, listen, I'm having a wee celebration. Oh, nothing much. I mean, this old place has seen many a rollicking bash, rooms heaving with bodies – and what the inside of that broom cupboard has witnessed doesn't bear telling. But I'm afraid I've left my wilder days behind. No, this is just you and me and a few friends – about six of us – for dinner. That's a fortnight today. So I do hope you can come. You can? Oh, I'm so delighted. That's really bucked me up . . .'

The smart Fiat coupé that has just drawn up outside Number 13 has been spotted once or twice before. The curtains of Fairview twitch convulsively, as the retired postmistress who lives there takes further avid note of her neighbour's comings and goings. A new one virtually every night, she thinks. Round and round they go, spreading disease like wildfire. It's a plague, according to the papers. In any case, it lowers the tone; the street feels vice-ridden. And him with a heart condition. You'd think he'd know better at his age.

The driver of the car keeps the engine running and turns to face his passenger. He feels a hand drop on his thigh.

'Look, I won't come in, Arthur. Got an early start tomorrow.'

'Ah well, please yourself.' Arthur reaches for the door handle. 'Anyway, see you at the weekend?'

'Doubt it. Same old floorshow?'

'Yeah. Sloppy Sue and the Slappers.'

'In that case, you won't. Not for dust.'

Arthur sighs and nods in agreement. 'Nah, you're right. It's not the place it was.'

No, not since the boy went.

He struggles out of the car, then hovers on the pavement.

The driver rolls down his window. 'You take care now, and don't do anything to frighten the horses.'

He speeds off. Arthur watches until the tail lights disappear.

Tonight, as he enters, the bungalow feels even darker and emptier than usual. He bends to pick up something from the doormat, and is relieved to see that it's a leaflet from the Mormons and not another of those anonymous death threats. He begins, as he always does, by inspecting the place room by room; after the last burglary he lives in dread of a return visit. Back in the living room he goes straight to the drinks cabinet and pours himself a large Scotch. He knows he should lay off, especially in his condition and especially after what he's just had, but damn it, he needs a drink. He falls back heavily into an armchair and sits staring at a photograph of his mother, a studio portrait that's been staring back at him from its place on the mantelshelf ever since her death almost twelve years ago. Taken on her sixtieth birthday, it was his gift to the old bitch. Why has he never removed it? He's not sure. Does he still sense her presence, fear her disapproval? Probably. But that has never stopped him, as now, pulling faces at it.

He glances round the room. What a tatty old box. What an anal cavity. Is this all he's got to show after thirty years of slaving at the MOD? The walls need repapering, the carpet needs replacing, the furniture should be chucked. Everything, after all, is a reminder of *her*. Perched on every ledge, smiling from every niche, sown into every stitch of the claw-footed sofa, she's everywhere. And what did she ever do except sit on his life? Ruin him, smother him in her own selfish interests? But for her, he could have travelled the world, instead of wasting his days in this mean, one-eyed hole. But for her, he could have been someone, instead of an obscure dogsbody traipsing the corridors of a government office.

An acid taste comes to his mouth and his face screws up in disgust. At the same time he feels a great surge in the veins, and in a flush of panic he struggles to rise from his chair. Something tugs at him, however, and he falls back, clutching his heart.

His eyes flit round the room and come to rest on another photograph, a snapshot of a toddler building a sandcastle on the beach at Blackpool, sunlight irradiating his golden locks. Yeah, bright day, bright start. So where did it all go wrong? Hard to say, but in general you could put it down to getting mixed up with a string of first-rate bastards. Harry, for instance. Harry, supremely. Harry, who delivered the first and deepest cut; who flung off to Dundee with that kilted clod. Yeah, no doubt about it, that's where the downward slope began. But his father's death the following year, from a faulty ticker that he generously passed on to his son, was another shock to the system. It upped Her Ladyship's dependence on him, tightened her grip, so that one vague morning he awoke to find himself forty-something and trapped. Fate had crept up on him without his knowing.

It was shortly after this that the 'business' started. And if Arthur is hazy here about the exact sequence of events, he's sure about one thing: it was Adam who put the idea into his head. Yeah, Adam: that mercenary tyke last seen pampering elderly gentlemen in a hairdressing salon in Bootle. Still, you had to hand it to the little shit, he knew how to flaunt his assets. Arthur remembers as if it were yesterday the night that Adam first entered the Black Horse. Clad in slacks and a white sweater and groomed to perfection, the boy looked glossily gorgeous. So, moving quickly into position, Arthur introduced himself, saying that he'd like to take the young man out for a meal – an invitation that, much to his surprise, was graciously accepted. After the meal they went for a walk, and Adam allowed himself to be groped on a park bench. But then the cheeky young beggar turned funny; he said he wanted payment. Arthur was taken aback; he'd never paid for it before. He jumped up, adjusted his clothing, and reminded Adam that he'd just stood him a lavish dinner at a posh hotel. A lavish dinner, plus cocktails, to put the record quite straight. He then marched off. Adam was decidedly cool after that, but the event bore fruit. It was, as Arthur became fond of saying to all his newcomers, 'the start of something'.

And once the idea had lodged, it was remarkable how easy it was to launch the 'firm', how quietly susceptible the boys were. Not that it was all plain sailing; keeping that lot in line called for a frequent crack of the whip. Craig was unreliable, Mitch deceitful, Curly a mental case. And Billy? Stubborn as a mule, never easily managed, sexually elusive – and yet – gifted with a boyish grin that could knock you flat and in the end probably the best kid of the lot.

Yeah, in spite of all the grief, the fondness remains.

It's a hard life, though; get onto a good thing and some bastard moves in. That prick from London had trouble written all over him, you could see it from the start. It's never a good sign when guys stick around. Still, don't give up without a fight. The boy came home after a chase. Could it happen again? Nah, too late; his head has been turned, the rot has set in. Arthur is seized with agitation. It's too much to bear. Once was humiliation, but to lose him twice.

He twists in his chair, squirming in every limb. Yeah, chopped down by one bastard after another. They've done for him nicely; tossed him on the heap and left him to rot. They need whipping, the whole bloody pack. No, whipping's too good; it's time to repay seriously; time to smash 'em up proper. He flings his empty glass at the wall. Yeah, starting with *her*.

Struggling to his feet, he stands unsteadily for a few moments, staring with fierce resentment at his mother's photograph. Then, taking a few tottering steps forward, he lunges. But before making contact, he feels a sharp pang in the left breast that twists his face into an ugly shape. His eyes fly open and a small gasp escapes from his gaping mouth. A gasp that sounds like the final flap of a deflating balloon.

The boys arrive first and look around with murmurs of admiration. A dazzling white cloth covers the table, which is set with gleaming cutlery and tall wineglasses. Archie calls to them from the kitchen, where he's stirring something in a pan on the cooker. They put their heads round the door.

'I thought we'd start with a nice clear soup. A little recipe I picked up on the Côte d'Azur – oh, centuries ago – before the war, when I was living down there with a very dear friend – chap called Freddie – who sadly shuffled off this mortal coil – now, let me see, was it last year or . . .'

Matt is holding a brick-shaped parcel in silver wrapping, Billy is holding an envelope. They wave them at Archie.

'Happy birthday!'

'Oh my dears, you *are* naughty. I did my best to keep it quiet, so I can't understand how you found out. Anyway, put them on the side, I'll open them later. Is that someone knocking? Do keep an ear cocked, because I'm apt to leave people standing on the step. Could that be Brice and Charlie?'

Matt goes to investigate. And yes, it *is* Brice and Charlie, who announce themselves confidently. But what an odd pair they are: he, short, plump and bald; she, tall, stooped and dangly, like a bankside willow. They beam at Matt, thrusting out hands in greeting. Brice smiles with sensuous lips that flick up into a bow; Charlie, on the other hand, is all teeth. Matt, hot and flustered after a struggle with Archie's door, introduces himself and waves them into the hall.

'Here they are,' shouts Archie, emerging from the kitchen in his chef's apron. 'The neighbours.'

'Happy birthday!' sings Charlie, embracing him.

'Yes, many happy returns,' says Brice, reaching into a carrier bag and drawing forth a bright parcel tied with pink ribbon and smothered in rosettes. 'Now, what is it we're celebrating? Your twenty-first?'

'Oh, you tease,' says Archie, slapping him on the shoulder.

'Don't listen to him,' says Charlie. 'You're still a boy.'

'Indeed I am – although some days I feel a hundred.'

Archie asks Billy to take charge of the drinks. For, after all, who more suited than an experienced barman? ('I wonder you don't inquire at the place up the road; they're always looking for people.') Yet care and experience are not enough: the cork flies out of the bottle with a loud pop, hitting the ceiling with force, and the bottle itself erupts, champagne gushing forth like lava. An explosion of merriment follows, in the middle of which Archie shouts 'Listen!' with such dramatic force that the hubbub dies in an instant and everyone turns to face him with a look of astonished inquiry.

'I thought I heard something. If that was a knock, it could be Oz. Would someone go and see? We mustn't neglect the poor man. He's not in the best of health.'

'Oh yes, Oz,' says Charlie. 'We've met Oz before. Super chap. Well, this is a growing band. Who else have you invited, Archie?'

'No one else,' says Archie, flapping his hands in dismissal. 'Half a dozen of us – that's more than enough at my advanced age.'

But it's not Oz. In fact, not anyone; the 'knock' was just a trick of the mind. Archie shrugs and looks a bit concerned, for it's very unlike Oz to come last. On the contrary, he's usually one of the first. Ah well, too soon to send a search party; so the guests, at Archie's invitation, make themselves comfortable in easy chairs, while he himself returns to the kitchen to take another look at the soup.

Charlie declares how pleased she is that Matt and Billy have moved in. The old boy needs someone on hand for companionship and in case of emergency. She's eager to know about them: what they do, where they're from, how they met. And her easy conversational manner disguises the sharpness of her nose. Oh yes, there's no doubt about it, she's good at sounding them out, at listening and smiling in a reassuring way, at drawing forth confession and making a mental note of everything she hears – or so they surmise. But still, they like her; shrewd and keen-eyed she might be, but she has warmth. She studied at the Royal School of Music, they learn, and now teaches piano and flute.

'Yes, and my professor was Henry Dilkes, who composes a bit and has a modest reputation. Have you heard of him?'

'For God's sake, they won't have heard of Dilkes, darling,' Brice breaks in. 'Hardly anyone has, and I'm not surprised. All those whimsical little exercises with titles like "Sarabande" and "Gay Galliard" and "A Musette for Meg".'

Brice, as they soon learn, is a dry wit, his habitual manner characterised by a sort of good-humoured peevishness. So what does he do? He's a writer, they discover. A writer? Yes, yes – for his sins. And what kind of thing does he write?

'Well, many kinds of thing, I suppose. That's to say, I'm a general hack, although I like to call myself a biographer.'

'Oh, away with such false modesty,' scoffs Charlie. 'General hack indeed! His life of Eugene O'Neill won an award.'

'A runner-up award, my dear – just to put the record quite straight.'

Archie appears at the door of the kitchen, wiping his hands on his apron.

'Take your seats, please, all of you. We must begin, otherwise the meal will spoil. I can't imagine what's happened to Oz.'

The guests rise with a buzz of excitement and Archie directs them to their places. The chairs at the ends are reserved for himself and Oz – if Oz ever appears – while the other four guests are positioned facing each other across the table. Billy again takes charge of the drinks under further orders from Archie, and restores his reputation by avoiding any spillage on the expanse of white linen. A short wait, some lively chatter, and then the host reappears in the kitchen doorway, holding, somewhat unsteadily, a large willow-pattern tureen. Matt leaps to lend a hand.

'No problem, I *can* manage,' Archie insists.

The guests watch his faltering steps with barely suppressed anxiety, however, and when the bowl gains *terra firma* there's an almost audible sigh of relief. The crisis is not quite over, though, for in the middle of ladling, Archie utters a small strangled cry and claps his hand to his mouth. Some rolls are warming in the oven, he tells Matt. Go quickly, dear boy, or they may scorch.

Billy watches Archie with fascination, marvelling at his alertness, independence and vivacity. Yeah, he thinks, you have to admire the old boy, still pushing the boat out after all these years. And how many exactly? That seems a closely guarded secret. Anyway, not in the full flush of youth, to use his own expression. And what a fund of memories he must have. All those years of living abroad, all that time at the BBC and the British Museum. He's survived most of his friends and he'll probably survive *me*. What's the chance that I'll be around at his age, entertaining tenants and neighbours, looking back over a long life? And with that thought, a change comes over the room. As Billy gazes on the scene before him, a screen falls, sealing him off from the action and transforming the others – Archie ladling soup,

Matt hurrying in with hot rolls, Brice and Charlie laughing at some joke – into figures in a giant shadow play. At the same time, an ice-cold feeling, starting at his feet, spreads upward through his body. The others, noticing his white face and glazed-over eyes, stare at him, and he becomes dimly aware that Matt, now back in his seat and assisting Archie, is offering him a bowl of soup.

Charlie, reaching out, snaps her fingers in front of his nose. 'Come back,' she says. 'Look, nourishment.'

There's an eruption of laughter, and Billy raises a rather weak smile.

'That's much better,' says Archie. 'My dear boy, where *have* you been?'

Matt, reaching under the table, squeezes Billy's hand. 'He's just recalled his promise to paper the bathroom ceiling,' he says, provoking another burst of laughter.

Just before the gathering up of the empty soup bowls and the arrival of the main course, a face appears at the side window. A huge face, red, crumpled and topped by a brush of thick grey bristles. Charlie spots it first and gives a little scream. Archie follows the direction of her quivering finger.

'At last!' he exclaims. 'What *has* the old bugger been up to?'

'*I'll* go,' says Brice and moments later returns with Oz, who tips in, holding aloft a bottle in one hand and a bunch of carnations in the other. Oz is an imposing figure and cuts a dash in his red velveteen jacket, although his speech and movement are not quite co-ordinated, as if from some disease of the nervous system. Words seem to stick in his throat or come all in a rush.

'So s-sorry, Archie, love. Unexpectedly delayed, I'm afraid.'

Archie flings his arms wide. They embrace and kiss.

'What a fright you gave us, appearing like that.'

'Couldn't m-make you hear. Too much m-merriment. Actually, I thought I was banished. Latecomers will not be admitted. That kind of thing.'

'My dear man, what elderly rubbish you talk. Now come and meet Matt and Billy, who are busting to meet you. And you remember Brice and Charlie, of course.'

The introductions over, Oz quickly settles in, slurping away at a bowl of soup with his napkin tucked into his collar and talking volubly between mouthfuls. He explains that he's been to see a friend who is sick. Hence the delay.

'I drop in about three times a week. I'm a sort of unofficial b-buddy.'

'Buddy?' says Brice. 'So . . . your friend . . .'

'All a bit hush-hush, I'm afraid. I shouldn't be t-talking like this. But yes, it's the big one. Last year he was a fit young guy, tanned and robust. Now he's a scarecrow, his skin dry and g-grey.'

Matt tenses and reaches under the table. His hand meets Billy's and clutches it. Billy holds on tight, his palm cold and slightly damp. His face, which Matt glimpses from the briefest of sidelong glances, is rigid, a stone-carved image betraying no emotion.

'That's terrible,' says Charlie. 'It must be very distressing for you.'

'I never know what I'm going to find,' says Oz, pushing his empty bowl aside and wiping his mouth with his napkin. 'His m-mood is so changeable. Some days he scarcely speaks. We sit on the sofa listening to the wailing of some soul singer and I think what in G-God's name am I d-doing here?'

'Hasn't he any family?'

'Not really. His p-parents are separated, and he only ever speaks to his mother. She knows, but rarely visits. I'm his f-family. I'm all he's got.'

'The *secondo piatto*,' says Archie, 'is fish. Salmon, actually. And very fresh. Delivered this morning by Dullingham's boy. Not a problem for anyone, I hope? Fish-bones are a fearful trial for some people, I know. But it should be very nicely cooked by now, if I've got the timing right. And I shall need a hand, please.'

Billy leaps up and begins to gather up the soup bowls, his movements so sudden and impulsive that they take everyone by surprise. He and Archie then move off to the kitchen, where the buzz of their conversation is overheard as a distant hum behind the continuing table talk.

Minutes later they return, processing as in a medieval banquet, Archie in the lead, bearing a silver salver, Billy with a napkin draped over one arm. The salmon is enormous: a stranded, pink monster, almond chips and sprigs of parsley sprinkled over its body like petals at a funeral. The others gasp with admiration and break into a warm round of applause. Standing proudly at the head of the table and basking in the appreciation, Archie takes charge of the carving-up ceremony, skilfully removing the flesh from the backbone and serving up fat slices onto plates handed to him by Billy. Matt, at a request from Archie, slopes off to fetch two bowls from the kitchen: a ceramic one, full of new potatoes tossed in oil and chives, and a wooden one, sprouting fresh green salad.

'Don't hang about,' says Archie. 'And help yourselves to vegetables. Matt, uncork that bottle, please, and top up those glasses.'

Brice, tucking in heartily, smacks his lips. 'Done to a turn,' he declares. 'You're a genius, man.'

Archie waves his hand airily, in a gesture of modest dismissal.

'You were saying, Oz?' says Charlie, lifting a fork to her mouth.

'Saying? Was I?'

'About your friend? His love of cemeteries?'

'Mm, well, yes. I say to him, you need to g-get out more. It's a lovely day. Now where shall we go? He says Highgate. And I think, oh n-not again. All that Gothic gloom. All those sarcophagi. What *is* this n-necrophilia?'

Matt, chewing with relish on a succulent piece of salmon, glances swiftly at Billy with a fleeting smile. Billy is eating extremely slowly: picking at his food, in fact. He glances back at Matt and smiles weakly. His face is pale.

'One day I put my f-foot down. No, I said, what *you* need is a sniff of the ozone, we're going to Southend. He was very reluctant at first; I had to drag him to the station. And scarcely a soul on the b-beach when we got there, it was the middle of winter. Great grey blustery clouds and spits of rain in the wind. The sea was a bit choppy too; we tried skimming stones on the surface without much success. But then he took off his shoes, rolled up his t-trousers and went paddling up to his knees. Not me, I declined. It must have been b-bone-freezingly cold; he was shouting from the shock. In fact, he did a lot of shouting on the beach, like an excited kid. I was embarrassed at first, people looking on and all. But I didn't try to stop him. I thought, you shout, man. Shout all you want. Shout your f-fucking head off.'

'More wine, anyone?' calls Archie, glancing round the table. 'Please help yourselves. Don't be shy. Another potato perhaps, Charlie? No? Absolutely not? Oh yes, I know, naughty of me to suggest it. Billy, what's wrong? You're not eating. Is it the fish? I must remember to ask in future. Some people have great difficulty with fish.'

'It's not the fish.' Billy smiles tightly. 'I'm not sure what it is. I've not been too well just recently.'

Sympathetic noises and anxious inquiries follow, and he immediately regrets the remark; a low profile is what he needs at this moment, and with almost any other excuse he might have avoided this unwanted attention.

The conversation moves on. Oz, now retired from his post in local government, is planning a visit to Rio, where a friend will join him on a short exploratory trip to the jungle. Charlie and Brice sound envious. They've booked a five-star week in Antibes, but they admit that this pales in comparison. Archie says how pleased he is not be going anywhere. He's seen many parts of the world and at his great age has no wish to travel by land, sea or air again. Brice ribs him with the taunt that, but for a twinge of rheumatics, he'd surely be off like a shot. Archie hold up his hands in horror, but then confesses to a longing to return to Capri, where he once spent an unforgettable week with the love of his life.

The salmon has now vanished, its bones picked clean, and all plates are empty except Billy's, much of which is untouched.

'I hope you've all got some room left,' says Archie. 'There's a further course to come. Matt, could you do some gathering up and give me some assistance.'

The two men disappear and soon return bearing dishes, which they place in the centre of the table to squeals of delight. The main attraction is a creamy cheesecake ('made by my own fair hand') which sits nicely on a terracotta plate. Beside it rises a hill of gleaming strawberries. The guests are invited to help themselves, and Oz, taking the initiative, moves in on the cake first, slicing off a sizeable hunk with unapologetic greed and a loud, deep laugh, his hoggishness made all the more noticeable by the conspicuous restraint of Billy, who helps himself to a mere sliver and three small strawberries.

'Oh, my dear boy,' says Archie. 'I'm quite disappointed in you. But eat whatever you can, and don't feel you must.'

When the meal is over, the guests sit back with satisfied smiles and make appreciative noises. Then, during a lull in the conversation, Archie claps his hands.

'Charlie, my love,' he says, looking pointedly at her, 'can I broach the subject? Would you entertain us with a little of your artistry? Or is that an unreasonable request after the third glass of wine?'

Charlie smiles graciously, in a way that suggests that she's been waiting for this moment all evening and would be offended if *not* asked.

'My pleasure,' she says. 'A little recital to enliven your birthday?'

'Precisely. How well you put it. Come along, all of you, gather round. Matt, would you kindly clear a space for Charlie. The instrument has been recently tuned with this very event in mind.'

Charlie adjusts the stool and sits there for a few moments, bending and stretching her fingers showily. 'Something vivacious to start with,' she says. 'How about a *valse brillante*?'

And with no more ado, she plunges into a stirring fanfare and a dazzling ripple of notes that quickly settles into a seductive waltz rhythm. Archie, seeing the lilting melody bring a smile to every face, glances round with pleasure. Even Billy looks captivated. Charlie, playing with shoulder-heaving, head-tossing *élan*, looks radiant, and the music spins on and on, gathering more tunes in its progress, until it begins to suggest a chain of whirling dancers. But then, on a sudden fortissimo, it splinters into a shower of falling sparks, fragments of the melody that cascade to earth and slowly fade away, before two loud chords bring the piece to an end with a grand flourish. Rapturous applause follows and Charlie looks round to receive it with a broad smile and a slight inclination of the head.

'Brava!' calls Archie, clapping vigorously. 'What a gift!'

'Splendid!' Matt exclaims.

'*I* was put to the p-piano' – Oz turns to Brice in mid-applause – 'but I never t-took to it.'

'Nor me,' replies Brice. 'No, I love the tenor sax. Jazz, you know, that's *really* my thing.'

Charlie, as if to respond on cue, glances round with a smile and breaks into a little ragtime piece by Joplin.

'Oh no. I'll have to abandon that. Not really my style. Anyway, I've not played it for years and can't recall how it goes. So how about a complete change of mood? Here's a little something, courtesy of Domenico Scarlatti.'

The audience, falling quite silent, waits expectantly. She pauses, hands on knees, focusing her attention, and when at last she strikes up, the opening bars, as in the waltz, are a kind of fanfare. Yet they dispel the previous mood utterly. For the trumpets now sound distant, like a retreat, and when the next phase of the music arrives, it has a plangent air, an aching undertow that drags at the heart. Unlike the waltz, with its dance-provoking swing, this piece freezes the listeners, fixing them in a concentrated trance. Passing through changing keys and mounting tension, it moves swiftly to a climax – a grinding crunch of notes that groans with pain – and then falls back into a state of quiet resignation. There are some moments of silence when the end comes, and the applause that follows, befitting the mood, is more restrained and reflective than earlier.

Matt, coming out of his meditation, glances around. So absorbed he's been, so lost in the performance, that he doesn't immediately notice the absence. But then – where? He stares at the other guests with a look of puzzled and embarrassed inquiry. And when Archie, who has witnessed the departure, points to the door, he speeds away, taking the stairs two at a time.

On reaching the landing, he spots the figure just ahead of him. 'Hey!'

Billy spins round like a startled ghost. His paleness has returned and his face looks shockingly washed-out under the landing light. Wiping a hand across his brimming eyes, he smudges his face, streaking both cheeks. Matt, touched by his lonely terror, moves forward to embrace him; and Billy, clasping him tight, breaks down utterly, sobbing convulsions racking his small frame, fiery tears spilling onto Matt's shirt. Matt cradles his head, pushing the hot face against his shoulder.

Down in the sitting room the gathering is somewhat discomposed. The guests turn to Archie with questioning concern.

'Don't look at me,' he says. 'I haven't a clue. But I do hope it wasn't the fish.'

'Hmm,' Brice muses. 'Not something he ate, in my view. More like something's eating him.'

'He was fine until you came,' says Archie turning to Oz.

Oz looks aghast. 'Something I s-said?'

'Oh, who knows?' says Brice. 'Let's not accuse ourselves.'

'Quite right, please forgive my careless remark,' says Archie, touching Oz on the shoulder. 'And yes, Charlie my love, on with the music. An encore or two, if you will.'

'In that case,' says Charlie, turning to the piano and stretching her fingers, 'how about something brisk and modern? This capricious little march by Prokofiev, for instance.'

She strikes up, her hands leaping off the keyboard like lively crabs.

'Anyway, quite a catch,' Brice whispers in Archie's ear.

'Oh, the lads, you mean. Yes, such fine boys, both of them. But not my doing. *They* found me.'

'Oh, well, very convenient, I must say. Wish I had your Midas touch.'

When Matt returns to the sitting room half an hour later, the guests have returned to the table, and their languid voices, bleary faces and drooping postures, pointing to the effects of good food and wine, suggest that the evening is winding down. They greet him warmly, doing their best to rouse themselves from the torpor that has come over them, clearly pleased to welcome him back and full of solicitous curiosity about Billy.

'Nothing to worry about,' Matt assures them. 'I'm sure he'll be fine in the morning. He's a bit – well, let's say under pressure at the moment.'

'Under pressure?' says Charlie, fixing him with a hard look.

'It's personal,' says Matt, meeting her gaze full on. 'Not something I can blab about.'

Archie leaps in to cover the mildly-strained atmosphere. 'Anyway, nothing to do with fish?'

'No, nothing at all.'

The old boy claps a hand to his heart, sighing with relief.

'Won't you join us, Matt?' says Brice, pointing to a chair. 'Some coffee and liqueur perhaps? Or a spot of this excellent cognac?'

*

The following day Matt and Billy call on Archie and find him deep in late-morning slumber. Lolling on the sitting-room sofa, head thrown back, mouth wide open, he looks too peaceful to be disturbed. They decide, through an exchange of whispers and mimes, to back off quietly, but just as they're tiptoeing away, he wakes. At first he blinks and stares at them blankly, but then his face lights up with pleasure and he reaches out, grasping their hands and inviting them to sit. They've come to apologise, they explain. He insists, however, that there's nothing to apologise for. These things happen.

'But you will tell me, won't you, if there's anything I can do to help.' He throws Billy a meaningful look. Billy nods shyly, his eyes searching the ground, and Archie turns to Matt. 'And that goes for you too.'

The boys smile at him and then at each other. Canny old bird; they don't come much sharper. How much has he guessed? Their minds buzz with the same thought.

The other reason they've called is to offer help with the clearing up. Archie is appreciative, but wonders if they will regret their offer when they see what needs to be done. He confesses that clearing up is a task he never tackles the same night; it would spoil the evening. Simply walk away, he advises. He struggles to his feet, moves towards the kitchen and beckons them to follow, indicating the litter-strewn table as they pass with the airiest of gestures. The sights of the table, however, are as nothing to those of the kitchen, where tins, jars and spilled ingredients hide between stacks of dirty plates, bowls and pans. Matt, glancing round with some amusement, rolls up his sleeves and slips an apron over his head, while Billy, looking rather lost at first, eventually goes off to fetch glasses, which Archie insists must be washed before anything else.

An hour later, the end in sight, they sit down at the old pine table in the kitchen, its rough surface deeply scored with knife marks and mottled with stains, and take a coffee break.

‘You know what *I* think?’ says Archie, snapping into a biscuit.

The boys tense and fix their eyes on him. Is he going to put them on the spot? Ask an awkward question? Venture into private territory?

‘Not a clue,’ says Matt with a tight smile. ‘Tell us.’

‘I think the pair of you need to get away. I think you need a holiday.’

The boys relax; they nod and grin.

‘Mmm,’ they sigh, almost in unison.

‘And I suggest the Riviera. Such charming places in the south – the cafés, the bougainvillea, the palm-lined sea-fronts. I simply love Saint-Tropez, you know, but also Rapallo, where so many writers and artists gathered in the nineteen twenties – though just before my time, I regret to say . . .’

Billy pictures these places in his mind’s eye. Apart from that bleary weekend in Paris, he’s never been abroad. He sees the tall, airy room, Matt and himself lying on cool sheets, the sun-drenched balcony, the glittering sea beyond. And he sees now how important it is – now more than ever – to seize the moment, how precious the moments have become. Yes, Archie is right, bless his thick woollen socks. They must go and share this experience. They must live all they can. They must burn with a bright, gem-like flame.

A few days later Matt returns from work hugging a pack of brochures. He’s feeling bright and energetic, and whistles a snatch of Handel as he pushes through the garden gate. On entering the house he catches a glimpse of Archie sitting in the parlour at the end of the passage and calls out a greeting to him before bounding up the stairs. Then, tossing the brochures onto the kitchen table, he goes in search of Billy. He finds him painting the frame of the bathroom window. He creeps up on him and hugs him from behind. Billy half-turns and kisses him on the cheek, though he seems subdued and quietly preoccupied.

‘Spotting the celluloid queens at Saint-Tropez, or strolling with the arty-farts at Rapallo. Take your pick, sir.’

Billy lays his brush down on the upturned lid of the pot and unhooks Matt’s arms. He turns slowly, and it’s clear from his expression that there are other things on his mind. Matt looks at him curiously.

‘There’s been a phone call.’

‘Uhuh.’

‘From Clare.’

‘Oh really?’

‘Yeah, with a message from Craig. Apparently he called Number 7, thinking we still lived there.’

‘Well, if it means giving that crowd the slip, thank God we don’t. Anyway, what’s the message?’

‘It’s about Arthur.’

Matt buries his face in his hands and falls back against the wall. ‘Oh Jesus!’

‘Hey, let me finish, will you?’

‘Look, you know how I feel about that vile creep. I never want to set eyes on him again.’

Billy chuckles darkly. ‘Well, there’s no chance of that, so you’ve got your wish.’

Matt uncovers his face. ‘What?’

‘Yeah. How to put it? The man’s no longer with us.’

‘No longer with us? Christ, get to the point. You mean – ’

Billy nods with a grim smile. Matt’s eyes grow wide with astonishment.

‘Apparently he collapsed at home just recently. Not sure *when* exactly. A neighbour noticed that his curtains hadn’t been drawn for days and called the police. They broke in and found his body on the sitting-room floor. Looks like his heart gave out.’

Matt stares hard at Billy, silently absorbing the news, wary of showing any reaction and wisely refraining from comment.

‘The service is next Sunday. Two-thirty at the crematorium. Craig thought I might like to know.’

'Who's going?'

'No idea. Craig said to call back if I wanted to hear any more.'

Matt shakes his head and sighs, the initial shock having given way to a sense of relief. Of course Arthur has long ceased to be any kind of threat, his dread presence eclipsed by a far more potent kind of menace. Nevertheless, his shadow has always lurked somewhere in the background, so it's good to learn that the man's fragile heart has finally put paid to the possibility of his reappearance. Billy, however, as Matt knows, must be experiencing quite different feelings. He and Arthur had a history, after all. However fraught their relationship, the event is the close of a chapter in his life. Perhaps, too, he sees it as a portent of his own mortality? Matt looks steadily at Billy and a crease appears in his brow as he struggles to find something appropriate to say.

'Well, well . . . what a bombshell.'

'What's that supposed to mean?'

'Look, I'm sorry . . . I'm stuck for words.'

'I knew he'd go suddenly.'

'Never gave it a thought, me.'

'Sad, too. No one there for him at the end.'

'Hey look, don't ask me to shed tears, love. I mean – *please*.'

'I'm not . . . I'm just saying . . .'

Matt reaches out and takes Billy's hand. Billy is silent, his face pale and grave, his thoughts turned inward. He sees the slumped body on the sitting-room carpet, the sprawled helpless limbs, the trickle of blood from the head, and the image holds him transfixed, becomes the focus of his confused feelings. Should he raise the dead man, lift him to a chair, dignify him, or kick him where he lies? Arthur, the sad monster, the pathetic bogeyman – insinuating, persistent, repellent. Too twisted to be lovable, too close to be ignored. Billy can no more reject him than discard his right arm. Shaper of his life, sealer of his fate. And that lonely end: a foresight of his own?

He clutches Matt's hand. Matt responds with a firm squeeze and holds on tight.

'So will you go?'

'Only if you'll come too.'

Matt snorts and shakes his head in amused disbelief.

'Christ, the things you ask.'

Piped organ music, soft and soothing, moves along to a steady baroque tread, creating a suitably contemplative mood as mourners arrive and take their seats. Billy, Matt at his side, glances about from a pew at the back of the chapel. Not a bad turnout for someone who died alone, his passing unknown until discovered by accident. All the expected faces are here, as well as a few that are unfamiliar. Family, perhaps? Old work colleagues? Friends from the Masonic Lodge? Craig, sitting beside Terry at the front and clearly noting every arrival, soon spots Billy and Matt. He nudges her, and both turn and smile. There's also a tight nod from Stan and Betty, sitting some way off on the other side of the centre aisle.

The service begins and runs along with the smoothness of a well-oiled machine. The chaplain is short, round and bald, a Friar Tuck figure whose voice is comforting and warm, yet somehow chillingly bland and remote. His address to the congregation, sandwiched between hymns, prayers and responses, is faultlessly researched and delivered, yet curiously empty and impersonal, like an entry in a biographical encyclopedia. In the chaplain's account, presumably based on testimony supplied by people who knew him, Arthur is remembered as a loyal son devoted to an ailing mother, and as a generous friend and colleague, honest in his dealings. Matt, avoiding eye contact with Billy, grips his hymn book and grinds his teeth in an effort to prevent himself from crying out.

Shortly after this the chaplain touches a button while intoning a prayer, and the coffin, conveyed by a moving belt, glides away into a curtained recess. For Matt, this is the moment that exposes the theatrical illusion of the occasion, for behind the recess, he imagines, are workmen seated around a table with fags and mugs of tea, playing cards, filling in football coupons or scratching their heads over crossword clues. The vanishing casket, passing from earthbound care into eternity, is in reality just another box awaiting dispatch.

Outside the chapel Billy and Matt are besieged by well-wishers, who shake them vigorously by the hand and then quickly disappear. Most are old customers of Billy from his time at the Black Horse, though some are people he knows from his association with Arthur. Nor do Stan and Betty, who also engage them in polite conversation for a while, show any inclination to linger. Pleading the call of the evening shift, they excuse themselves with smiles that are understandably lukewarm and distant. Indeed, only Craig and Terry show any interest in getting beyond routine pleasantries, though Terry's inability to speak in a natural voice makes Billy shudder. Rushing up, she kisses them both with an extravagant pout.

'Ah, what a sad reunion,' she sighs, her head inclined at a girlish angle. She takes Billy's hand. He regards her with withering dryness. Silly prat, what did I ever see in her? Is this the mate I used to drink with almost every night for years? So fake, so creepy. But who's changed, me or her? It must be me. Such a short journey, but what a distance.

'Good to see ya,' says Craig, beaming at them both and slipping Matt a wink. Matt responds with a grin. Randy little beggar; never pass up, even at a funeral. Basically decent, though; no chance he'll split. Gorgeous eyes. Nice smile too. Still, don't give an inch, avoid confined spaces and try to keep your pants on. 'So where are you staying? You're not booked in anywhere, I hope. Plenty of room at my place and you'd be more than welcome.'

Yeah, you betcha.

'Thanks,' says Billy, 'but we're driving back shortly.'

'Oh, what a shame,' says Terry. 'I was hoping we could

have a drink together.'

'There's a buffet reception at the Lodge,' says Craig. 'For relatives and close friends. Didn't I say? Arthur's mate Wesley arranged it.'

'Ah, sorry, we can't,' says Billy firmly. 'We'd like to, but it's a long journey and I want to pay a visit to Stone Street before we leave.'

'Oh really?' says Craig with a dubious look. 'That sounds like a hard one.'

Billy nods. 'Well, it's Mum I want to see, not Pete.' No, certainly not him; I'd cross the road rather than speak. And would I lose a wink if I thought I'd never set eyes on the brute again? May lightning strike; and when it does, I'll bath in pink champagne. 'Anyway, you know the score. Duty calls and all that.'

Craig and Terry look disappointed, but they nod understandingly and the talk breezes along for a while with some news of the old crowd before sputtering out. In the silence that follows all four turn and smile awkwardly.

'We must go,' says Matt, pointing to his watch.

'Stay in touch,' says Terry, flinging her arms wide and pouting her lips.

Craig holds up the flat of his hand in a farewell salute and the boys watch them depart. They leave the building hand in hand, and Billy, noticing for the first time the strange formality of their dress, stifles an impulse to giggle. Craig in pinstripe and Terry in a two-piece is a sight so rare as to be almost grotesque. If I didn't know better, he muses, I'd take you for a married couple.

In the car Matt turns to Billy with a searching look. 'Are you quite sure about this?'

Billy nods. 'Yeah, I need to see her. Throw out a line at least.' He shrugs. 'I mean, who knows? Might be the last chance.'

They gaze at each other with wry smiles, then lean forward and embrace.

*

Number twenty-four is situated on the ground floor of an ugly block of flats. They stare at it from the car for a while, and it seems to Matt that Billy has lost his nerve. But no, suddenly he flings out of the car and strides up the garden path with Matt following close behind. On the doorstep he flashes Matt an odd look, a mixture of jitteriness and resolve. Then, filling his chest with air, he raps hard on the knocker.

To Irene Cresswell, slumped in an armchair, the sound is like a rifle shot, shattering her afternoon nap. Her eyes fly open, her mouth snaps shut and she clutches at her heart, glancing round in bewildered panic. Who the blazes? Someone at the door on a Sunday afternoon? She stares at Pete, slumped and open-mouthed in the chair opposite. He's totally oblivious; his *News of the World* has slipped from his lap and he's snoring like a pig. Not surprising, after the half-dozen he put away at the Swan this lunchtime. Still, she's hardly in a fit condition herself after all those pink gins. Well, that's Reggie Clark's fault, forcing them on her. The rap comes again. She casts an eye over the room in horror. The state of the place! Breakfast dishes still on the table, piles of damp washing on the sofa. She struggles to her feet.

'Pete, we got visitors! Rouse yer bloody self!'

She shakes him roughly. He grunts, half-wakes and stares at her like a patient emerging from anaesthesia. As she moves towards the door she hastily adjusts her hair in the mirror and brushes flecks of dust from her dress. She opens the door with caution, peers through the narrow crack and, catching sight of two young men in dark suits, has a fleeting impression, in the fuzziness of her current state of mind, that she's about to be invited to a spiritual awakening.

'Oh no, my darlings . . . No, I'm sorry – I don't mean to be rude, but we don't go in for that kind of thing.'

'Mum,' says Billy.

She claps her hand to her mouth.

'Oh my Gawd,' she gasps.

Billy smiles at her with dismayed embarrassment.

'We've just been to Arthur's funeral and we couldn't

drive past the door, could we?' She gives a weak, befuddled smile. The boys stand awkwardly on the step, waiting for some further response. 'This is Matt, by the way.' She shakes the extended hand limply. 'Can we come in?'

She flinches, coming suddenly to her senses.

'Well, I should certainly hope so.' She steps forward and clasps her son in a rather clumsy embrace. 'It's lovely to see you. *Both* of you. But promise me you won't look round. I mean, you might have given some warning – we're in a fearful pickle. And take no notice of Pete, he's three sheets in the wind.' She ushers them into the sitting room, where her husband stares at them blankly. 'Pete, look who's here.' He looks, but his face is suffused with a bleariness that seems to prevent recognition. At any rate there's scarcely a flicker of response beyond a low growl, or possibly a clearing of the throat. Irene shrugs, and dismisses him with a toss of her hand. She too has a whiff of booziness about her, and her movements seem not quite under her control. But she struggles to take charge of the situation, whipping the breakfast dishes from the table and clearing up the scattered parts of the Sunday paper. Then, snatching up the piles of washing, she invites the boys to sit.

'We heard about Arthur,' she says. 'There was a short piece in the Gazette. I thought you might come up for the funeral, but I wasn't sure. I mean, I know you fell out with him recently. Of course, we didn't really know him like you did.'

Matt, suppressing a smile, studies the pattern in the carpet.

'He had a decent send-off,' says Billy. 'Stan and Betty and some of the regulars were there.'

'But you must have lost touch with that crowd, you're a Londoner now. Where is it you live again? I've got the details in the book and I've been meaning to call. But you know me, I'm no good on the phone. And as for writing – well, I was never a dab hand at that, was I?'

'We live in Highgate,' says Matt.

‘Highgate? That sounds posh.’

‘In a ruin,’ says Billy.

‘A partly renovated ruin,’ says Matt.

But it’s clear that Irene, smiling and regarding them intently, is not really listening.

‘Paul and Gail are doing well. They’ve got a kiddie now, a lovely little boy called Gareth. Yes, I’m a proud granny. And he’s growing *so* fast – well, she was pregnant at the time of the wedding, of course. I baby-sit for them sometimes. I know they’d love to see you. They often ask after you. I could give them a call. They might come over.’

‘Mum, we can’t stop long. We have to get on the road.’

‘What? Not even a cup of tea?’

Billy turns to Matt, who shrugs.

‘Okay. Just one . . . and then we’re off.’

She gets up, but Pete, staggering to his feet at the same moment, pushes her back into the chair. ‘I’ll get it.’

He shambles off and they watch him depart. Irene shakes her head. They hear him clattering about in the kitchen, to a background of pop music from a radio.

‘Bit rough on the outside,’ she says with a weak smile.

‘Aw, come on, Mum, don’t make excuses. Why do you stay with him?’

‘Oh Billy, don’t start that. You *know* why. Anyway, he’s not as bad as you think. He’s been good to me.’

‘He knocks you about.’

‘He does *not* knock me about.’

‘Don’t lie, Mum.’

‘Billy, spare me this, please. If you think I’d allow that, you know nothing about me.’

‘I know a black eye when I see one.’

‘Black eye? What are you saying? Do you see a black eye?’

‘I *have* done. Many a time.’

When Pete returns, the tray that he’s carrying suggests that he has handled the tea-making with surprising competence. Irene, noting the milk-jug, the sugar bowl and plate of biscuits, gives a faint nod of approval. He pours immediately from the stout china pot into four matching mugs and then settles back into his chair, still without uttering a word.

'So, Pete, what's the news?' says Billy. 'You're still at Mosley's, I take it?'

Smug git. I'm fucked if I'll let you sit there looking down your nose at us. I'll make you open your mouth if I have to force it with a crowbar.

Pete nods and looks away with a sour, half-sneering expression. Billy regards him with equal contempt and then comes back.

'Excuse me, Pete, something wrong? Cat got yer tongue? A slight touch of laryngitis, perhaps?'

'Oh no, 'ere we go,' groans Irene.

'Billy, cool it,' Matt urges.

'Hey you, smartass.' Pete jabs a finger at Billy. 'This is *my* house. Don't come here telling me how to behave.'

'It's also my mother's house, if you recall.'

'Oh Christ, that's a good one. You've not been near the place for fuck knows how long.'

'Is that surprising? The doormat doesn't exactly read *Welcome*, does it?'

'Stop it,' demands Irene. 'The pair of you.'

'Don't look at *me*, woman.' Pete throws up his arms in a gesture of innocence. 'It's him, your precious son. He bleedin' well started it.'

Billy shakes his head in disbelief. 'A bit of basic civility,' he says, blindly recalling a line that he's heard elsewhere and struggling to keep his voice under control. 'Is that too much to ask?'

'I'll tell you what,' says Pete, 'I'll be extremely civil. I'll take myself off. I'll go and finish my snooze upstairs and leave you three to jaw in peace.'

'No need for that,' says Billy flatly. 'We're leaving very shortly.'

He takes a large slurp of tea and pushes the cup away.

‘Oh no,’ wails Irene. ‘This is awful. Don’t go like this.’

‘It’s not your fault, Mum. It was a mistake to come. I should’ve known better.’

Pete leaps out of his chair and stands with his back to them, staring into the garden. Billy pulls a notepad from his bag and scribbles on it hastily. He tears off the sheet and hands it to his mother.

‘There’s the address and phone number. Perhaps . . .’ He hesitates as if struck by a troublesome thought. ‘Well, who knows . . . perhaps we could meet in London sometime.’

White walls, tiled floors, clack of heels. Square patch of sunlight, pot of hyacinths. This way, Mrs Cresswell. Smile, try to look cheerful, be upbeat. Not too lively today. Look, Billy, it’s your mother. We do all we can, of course. It’s so peaceful here, don’t you think?

Irene is in tears. She kisses the boys at the door.

‘I’ve not been a good mother, Billy, have I? I’ve done my best, but it’s been a hard life. Too many problems of my own, that’s the trouble.’ She lowers her voice to a murmur. ‘You’re right. Pete’s an oaf and I hate him sometimes, but I can’t leave him, can I? I need him. Or *someone*, at least. And who else is there?’ She wipes another tear from her eye. ‘Look, I’ll try to make it up to you. I’ll stay in touch, and maybe . . .’ Her voice trails away, as if not convinced by her own promises.

She comes down the path to see them off and stands at the gate, waving and wiping the stains from her cheeks.

In the car Matt says nothing, sensing the need for quiet reflection, and ten minutes into the journey it’s Billy who eventually breaks the silence.

‘Thick, brown and acrid. He never could make tea, stupid hulk. And those bloody biscuits. I hate soggy ginger snaps.’

Matt, at the wheel, turns his head briefly and grins. ‘Yeah, anything short of arsenic to drive us away.’

‘Short of?’ says Billy, slumping to one side and clutching his stomach.

They shriek from released tension, and the laughter that

erupts from them both rattles on for several minutes, far in excess of the joke.

A fringe of haze in the distance, but otherwise a clear, warm day with a touch of breezy freshness. Clare, reaching a high point, settles for a few minutes on a bench that a couple have recently vacated. The view is breathtaking and there's a fascination in trying to identify the scattered landmarks. She congratulates herself on making a wise choice: on rejecting the quick route in favour of the scenic one, an option she took on Matt's recommendation. She's always loved the Heath, and any opportunity to cross it, especially in such fine weather, is simply too good to miss.

She moves on, intrigued by the wide variety of life she encounters: birds, squirrels, joggers, pram-pushers, swimmers, sun-worshippers of all kinds – including pagan ritualists – and of course men. Scores of men. Men everywhere. Men alone, men in pairs, men in groups, men seeking men. And she feels concern for them. Are they careful? Alert to the dangers? Aware of the dire climate, the calamitous times we live in? She hopes so, and realises immediately that this hope is related to her affection for Matt and Billy. She assures herself that her concern has nothing to do with moral judgement.

At the edge of the Heath, just before entering Highgate, she pulls a book from her bag. It falls open at a page from which a folded sheet of paper escapes and flutters to the ground. She retrieves this, opens it and studies it carefully. It's a sketch map that Matt has drawn to supplement the information in her streetfinder. Aligning it with the one in the book, she compares the two. Then, with a much clearer notion of her bearings, she steps out again, noting with delight – as she always does on her visits here – the rough, countrified look of this corner of London.

And when twenty minutes later she stumbles on the house she feels immediately assured, for it corresponds in every way to the mental picture she has formed of it from the description she's been given. Yes, right down to the mossy slates, the blue shutters and the faded sign on the gate. But before she can lift the horseshoe knocker, Matt, who has seen her approach, thunders down the stairs and flings wide the door. They embrace and there's a rich exchange of compliments, as he makes admiring remarks about her cool blue dress and she comments on how handsome he looks in his white collarless shirt.

Billy, who is resting in the bedroom, hears her arrival. He swings his legs off the bed, struggles into an upright position and sits on the edge, holding his head in his hands. This tiredness is worrying. He's had several attacks recently. The effect of hot, sleepless nights, or symptom of his underlying condition? Despite weekly visits to the clinic, regular check-ups and reassurances, he's keenly aware that he doesn't really know. Consequently panic flares up in his chest at the slightest sign of trouble, the merest deviation from routine. Never before has he been so conscious of his body. He studies it obsessively, remorselessly, listening to every tick that it makes. And all this care, all this vigilance, is futile, he thinks. Somewhere in the dark wood the hungry wolf is waiting, ready to spring and devour. Someday he'll leap from the bush, teeth flashing. Not today perhaps, and not tomorrow – but *some* day.

He stands, fills his lungs and loosens up with some bending and stretching. Soon he hears the distant clink of crockery. Matt and Clare are making tea together in the kitchen. Their excited chatter, punctuated with bursts of laughter, resounds through the house, though he can't quite make out what they're saying. Still feeling heavy and dazed, he drifts across the landing and stands at the kitchen door watching them, his shoulder resting against the jamb. But so deep in conversation, so self-absorbed are they, they don't immediately notice him. 'Hi,' he calls in a soft voice, a near whisper; and they turn to greet him with little gasps, their faces breaking into delighted surprise.

'Behold the sleeping prince,' says Clare, leaping forward

and taking his face in her hands. 'Will my kiss awaken him?' Doubtful, she thinks; very doubtful. He's more than tired, he looks pale and wan. I noticed the change on his return from Yorkshire. He's lost his bounce. Is he unwell perhaps? Even very unwell? Could it be? But no, don't go there. Ignore these fantasies of an overheated brain. And yet?

They carry the tea through the house and into the garden. The house is entirely theirs today; Archie is in Chiswick with Oz, visiting the gallery of an old friend. They arrange themselves on wooden chairs around a table, and sit for a while soaking up the sunlight and admiring the plants, flowers and trees, especially the great spreading chestnut that fills the central space.

Clare tests the pot. 'What superior china. You do live in style these days. Milk for everyone?'

The boys nod.

'I hope you like marzipan,' says Matt, handing her a plate of cakes. 'These are from Harrison's, the local bakery.'

'Mmm.' She pats her waistline. 'Unfortunately I *do*.'

'So what's the news? Got yourself a job yet?'

'No, not yet. Shame about Kent. But several applications are still in the pipeline and I've been called for another interview, this time at Sussex. I've got great hopes for that, because if it comes up, I can again consider staying on at Gordon Street.'

'Gordon Street,' muses Matt fondly. 'So what's going on at Number 7?'

'What's *not* going on? How much time have you got?'

Matt's eyes light up. 'Whatever it takes. I'm all agog.'

'Well, first, the big news. Eddie is leaving us. At least he says he is, though no one quite believes it. He's back with Eve, it seems, and she's agreed to his moving in with her, but no date has been fixed and the theory is that they'll have another falling-out before it happens.'

Matt and Billy laugh. That's better, thinks Clare, studying Billy's face closely and responding to the change in him; there are these moments when you remind me of your old self. And Billy, noting her puzzled scrutiny, glances away.

The big news? The big news, let me tell you, is here inside me, and actually very small. Strange how big the smallest things can be. And I'd like to share this news with you, for then it might shrink and lose its power. But I'm not yet ready for that. Although perhaps in time . . .

'There's also a chance that Drew might leave. His parents are old and frail, and he's debating whether to move to Somerset to be closer to them. On top of that, Dan and Boo Boo want to sublet their room for six months to subsidise their trip to Nepal.'

'So we're talking about a whole new scene,' says Matt. 'Are you sure you want to stay?'

'Well, probably none of these things will happen. They're all speculative.'

Isn't everything? I speculate all the time. The future, after all, is guesswork. Even the experts know nothing. Well, nothing for certain. They juggle with probabilities, speak with maddening caution. Take Dr Martineau. What's he really thinking? Never drops a hint. Quite inscrutable.

'Hmm. So what else?'

'Oh yes, what else? Well, Andy has given his room a complete makeover.'

'And Mary?'

'And Mary – you've guessed it – '

'Has a new boyfriend. Say no more. This is Miguel, a flamenco guitarist from Cordoba. Or perhaps Lucien, a limbo dancer from Trinidad.'

'No, no, this is someone real. This is Lenny from Brixton, who unblocks drains.'

'Wow, that sounds pretty solid. So what's the verdict? Promising?'

'More so, in my view, than anything yet.'

Dawn. A blush of light, spreading upward, throws into relief the dark hinterland hills. The sea stirs, turning in its sleep. Ripples slap the quayside, boats jostle and creak. A fading moon hangs over the twinkling houses on the far side of the bay. On this side too, the village is waking. Two men, stowing boxes and fishing nets, nod at Billy as he passes. At the edge of the village he stops and peers down into dark, limpid water. Down to where shoals of small fish glide in glassy worlds of their own and an ancient barnacled crab makes its way resolutely across the seabed. He moves on, past the straggle of sheds and warehouses, to the point where the road runs into a short jetty and comes to an end. Out at sea, far beyond the winking harbour lights, a passing ship of some kind – ferry or cargo vessel – is just visible on the brightening horizon.

Back in the rented room, Matt, lying at full stretch on his stomach, a sheet covering the lower half of his naked trunk, his head thrust deep into a pillow, is struggling with dreamlike thoughts and images, the kind of phantasmagoria that invade the mind in a state of half-sleep. He sees a handful of people on a strip of beach, backed by high cliffs and wheeling birds. He and Billy are strolling by the edge of the sea. At a headland they fling themselves from rocks into shivering jelly and float on their backs in the vast unending blue. But they soon become separated, and Matt glances round to find himself alone. All at once a change comes over the sea. He feels himself tossed like a cork amid a huge swelling and sinking. Gripped by sudden panic, he beats with all his might in an urgent dash to the shore. But he makes no progress and the final stage is a terrifying, exhausting battle against a powerful undertow. With grazed knees, he scrambles over an avalanche of stones and eventually gains dry land. He staggers to his feet and looks around for Billy. To his horror, the beach is now deserted. He calls out in vain. Calls until he is hoarse. Then he sets out on a search. At the foot of a cliff he stumbles on a body sprawled beside a rock-pool – dashed and broken . . .

Aaagh! Writhing convulsively, he wakes with a strangled cry. He rolls onto his back and stares at the ceiling. Relief floods over him. Turning, he reaches for Billy, only to discover that the other side of the bed is empty. He sits up quickly, and looks around in mild anxiety and puzzlement. At almost the same moment the door opens and the stray returns, slipping in quietly so as not to disturb.

'Billy, thank God.'

Billy stares at him, faintly amused at this over-reaction.

'I woke early. Slipped out for a stroll. You okay? I heard a cry.'

'Yeah, yeah, I'm fine. Just a bad dream, that's all. Come here.'

Billy kneels beside the bed, and Matt, pulling him close, hugs him with a rare intensity that takes him by surprise.

'So, come on, tell me. What was the dream?'

'Oh nothing. Can't remember now. Come to bed.'

Billy smiles and shakes his head.

Matt watches him undress. And the slim, boyish figure, newly tanned, seems to him more achingly desirable than ever. Is this the beauty that grows stronger the more mindful we are of its fragility? He reflects, too, on the thin line between beauty and danger, of the threat that lurks beneath the seductive image: 'O Rose, thou art sick'. But no, no – that way madness lies. There are safe ways to make love, after all. He pulls Billy close, smothers him with kisses and finds himself recalling some other lines – lines that seem to well up in his mind involuntarily:

Let the winds of dawn that blow
Softly round your dreaming head
Such a day of sweetness show
Eye and knocking heart may bless,
Find the mortal world enough.

Billy gets in beside Matt and kicks away the sheet. Then he lies back, his arms behind his head. Matt turns, climbs across Billy's body and sits back on his haunches, his knees straddling Billy's hips. Billy grins and cocks an eyebrow: the stiff pole rising from Matt's groin is blocking his vision.

Leaning forward, Matt drags his tongue over Billy's nipples and then in a straight line from throat to abdomen. Billy's body convulses, and he emits a low sound, halfway between a groan and a giggle. Matt makes his way back slowly, and the opening round of foreplay ends when their mouths meet in a lingering kiss. They roll over and begin again in reverse, though Billy allows himself to go further, sliding his tongue to the base of Matt's shaft and gently nipping his scrotum.

On the next rollover, Matt reaches for a condom. He fumbles with it and Billy comes to his assistance, fitting the device over the slippery column with impressive expertise. Looking pleased with himself, Billy bestows a kiss on his handiwork and then lies back. Matt enters him carefully, pushing with slow tentativeness; but his thrusts build up, becoming gradually longer and harder until his frame starts to shudder. He climaxes with a great shout of release, and a few moments later Billy, pulling hard at himself, shoots in spasms, splashing himself generously from belly to upper torso.

Matt withdraws and collapses onto the bed. They turn to each other and kiss, then lie on their backs, breathing heavily and staring at the ceiling. After a while they drift into sleep, their limbs entwined, their bodies splayed like corpses on a battlefield. And when they wake the sun is quite high.

The waiter at Yannis's, the café on the quayside, is a contradiction. His flashy T-shirt, loud with images of footballs, tennis rackets and racing cars, is brash and sporty, yet he himself is quiet and shy. But if they found him rather distant at first, familiarity has overcome his former reserve, and these days he always appears promptly and greets them with a smile and a nod. His name is Yiorgos, as they discovered in conversation a few days ago, a conversation which also revealed that his English is much better than he usually lets on. He is tall, with a strong face, dark eyes and a crown of tight black curls; and his beauty is all the more attractive for being casual and quite unselfconscious. They guess he's about sixteen, though in general he gives the impression of someone older.

'Kala mera, Yiorgos.'

'Morning, my friends. And how are you today?'

'We're absolutely fine. How about you?'

'Hmm.' A shrug. 'So-so.'

'Only so-so?'

Another shrug. 'You want breakfast? Coffee, toast?'

Matt turns to Billy for confirmation. 'Yes, please.'

'Greek coffee?'

'Of course.'

'Sugar?' A mischievous grin.

'*No* sugar.'

He disappears, and Matt, diving into his bag, brings forth a dog-eared paperback. He found it this morning propped on a shelf in the room, among some other books discarded by previous tenants. It's called *The Good Soldier*. The title is familiar. He reads the blurb, thumbs through the pages idly and decides to give it a go. Glancing at Billy with the briefest of smiles, he instantly buries his nose, becoming oblivious to everything around him. The pages flick over briskly as he breezes through the first chapter. Billy stares ahead, captivated by the play of light on water, the soft bloom of clouds over the hills. Once again he is struck by the absolute peace and quiet of the place. There's scarcely a soul about on the quay, though out on the jetty two small boys are fishing for crabs, and after a while an old woman in black walks by, very slowly, holding a wicker shopping basket.

Yiorgos returns with a tray. He sets before them two small white cups of thick brown liquid, crowned with a thin head of froth, and two glasses of water.

'Only so-so?' repeats Matt, glancing up from his book.

'Please.' Yiorgos puts a finger to his lips. 'I don't talk. Not now.'

Matt nods, and glances to the rear of the café where the owners, Yiorgos's parents, are exchanging sharp words. He thinks back to what Yiorgos has disclosed in previous conversations: that he wants to leave the island and join his girlfriend in Athens; that he'd like to finish his education there; that his parents, having mixed feelings about this, have become irritable and quarrelsome, both with him and with each other. Matt shakes his head and smiles at Yiorgos, catching his eye with a look of silent understanding. Yiorgos, smiling back, spreads his hands in a gesture of quiet despair.

Although the village has nothing that you could call a beach, there are a handful of places around the bay where swimming is possible. Beyond the boatshed on the far side, for instance, there's a thin strip of stony shingle from which you can stumble painfully into the clearest water. Alternatively, at this site, you can launch yourself from the remains of a ruined wooden jetty, green and slimy with seaweed, but still used as a mooring post for small craft. This is the route taken by Matt and Billy, for by the time they arrive in the late morning the stones are uncomfortably hot as well as sharp. They have the place almost to themselves. Indeed, the only other people here are a dark, lank-haired woman and a skinny teenage boy: rough-looking vagrants that they've seen before at other places in the village. The woman is inspecting the boy's ears, pulling them open with a harshness that makes him flinch. She glances across at Matt and Billy, but does not smile.

They shake out their bright beach towels and spread them on the shingle. Then, stripping to their bathing shorts, they pile their clothes into clearly visible mounds. The slow, torturous hobble to the jetty makes Billy yelp, though he's the first to get there. With support from a rickety handrail, he walks to the end and peers over the edge, down into the clear coolness. Though the water here is too deep to stand in, the seabed is quite visible, and immediately he spots an almost stationary lone fish, suspended midway in the glassy iridescence. Slowly he lowers himself onto a wooden ledge a couple of feet below the surface, and the electrifying collision of cold seawater and hot suntanned legs makes him gasp. Matt, with supersensitive caution, is still creeping towards the jetty, his twisted face suggesting the squeamish horror of someone watching open-heart surgery. Suddenly Billy crouches, raises his arms to shoulder height and slides gently away. Matt hears him shout from the physical shock, then watches his head dip and rise as he swims out into the bay with strong breaststrokes. He sees him plough on into dark waters, disappear beneath the wind-ruffled surface and then shoot up again, flinging off bright drops with sharp flicks of his head. Matt creeps on over the stones, frustrated by his slow progress.

Out in the bay, Billy feels a great sense of freedom and exhilaration. Only rarely has he swum in the sea, and then not in conditions such as these. Treading water, he turns and looks back at the shore. Sea, land and sky hover before his eyes, and he feels no longer earthbound. The solid world has dissolved, releasing him from restrictions of time and space. So why not keep on going? Let it all sink away? What better moment to finish the show? Strike out into the blue vastness and let the tides carry me off? Draw me down into deep, deep nothingness? Roll me over, pick my bones? He glances round at the endless stretch of wetness. He feels the yawning abyss beneath his feet. And a sudden sharp chill strikes him to the marrow. Then, turning his gaze back to the shore, he sees Matt, a tiny figure on the end of the jetty, peering out to sea with hungry eyes. Dear Matt. Dear loving, loyal Matt. His one guard against nothingness, his reason for living. Billy longs to feel the clasp of his arms, the warmth of his chest. He raises a hand and waves. Matt waves in return. And with powerful overhead strokes, the dark waters sliding beneath him, Billy beats a path back to him over the salt-spray surface.

The general store is also the post office, the ferry agency and the *kafenio*. Three elderly men in caps, their lined faces mostly hidden under grey moustaches and stubble, sit outside all day and night, or so it seems, their sticks hooked over the backs of chairs. They talk endlessly, and from time to time throw back their heads and break into deep guffaws. Occasionally they are joined by a fourth elderly man, who is also the store-owner. His wife and daughter, however, are seldom seen out front, for the *kafenio* is mostly a male domain, though in the afternoons it becomes the village community centre, and fills up with locals of both sexes, drinking, gossiping and playing backgammon.

It's not an easy store to find your way around. To help yourself to a tin of sardines or a couple of large tomatoes you may have to reach behind a stack of metal buckets or remove a tray of loaves. Nor is assistance readily to hand; everyone seems too busy to offer help, and the only recourse is to keep searching until you stumble on what you want. In the process, you might find something you could well do without but are too weak to resist: a bright pink baseball cap, perhaps, or a guide to the island written in hilariously muddled English. Moreover, purchasing goods can be a lengthy transaction since the owner's very elderly father-in-law, who handles the till at the checkout, is slow, methodical, sometimes grumpy and often confused.

Matt and Billy enter. They take a basket and drift around, peering into corners and trying to read labels in Greek. En route they collect a white floured loaf, some hard yellow cheese and a tin of stuffed vine leaves. Billy holds up a bunch of dark blue grapes and regards them lovingly, but Matt reminds him that they already have some at home in the fridge, as well as a couple of very ripe peaches. When they arrive at the checkout, they are obliged to wait; the owner's father-in-law, writing long columns of figures on a notepad with a ballpoint pen, is clearly preoccupied. They unload the goods onto the counter, and after a while the old man looks up and glares at them as if they are bandits with raised shotguns. They smile and point to the goods. He lifts each item, squints at it and pushes a few buttons on the ancient mechanical till. Then, in his confusion, he reaches for a packet of washing powder that has been placed on the counter by another customer, a woman who has just joined the queue behind them. Matt wags a finger and smiles. The old man stares, looking again bewildered and hostile. Then he rings up the total, writes it on a scrap of paper and, still glaring, slides it towards them. They pay up and exit hurriedly.

They emerge to a quayside half in shadow, the sun partly obscured by a small cloud. And this brief escape from its harsh brilliance is welcome since it allows them to see the colours and contours of the island without squinting. The boats in the harbour, the domed church on the hill, the straggle of houses across the bay, usually washed out in the midday dazzle, have acquired, paradoxically, a new bright intensity. They saunter past Yannis's and spot Yiorgos, who is holding a cup in one hand and wiping a table with the other. They call out to him.

'Hey, Yiorgos.'

'Hullo, my friends. Good swimming?'

'Mmm, wonderful.'

'You want to eat? Some little fish perhaps? Tzatziki?'

'Not now. But we'll see you later.'

'I hope so.'

Back in the room they unpack the food and carry it on plates to the terrace, where the table is shaded by a wide umbrella. For a few minutes they sit, aware of their hunger, each waiting for the other to make the first move. But eventually Matt, breaking the deadlock, leans forward and saws the loaf in half. Then, tearing off chunks, they attack the cheese and vine leaves voraciously, washing it all down with some chilled retsina, the remains of a bottle opened the previous evening, now deliciously sharp after a night in the fridge. The view from here is across fields and gardens, but a thin strip of glittering sea is also visible between gaps in the quayside buildings. The terrace, ablaze with light and shimmering with heat, is alive with insects: tiny delicate butterflies, monstrous dragonflies, and lizards that flash over paving stones and walls and vanish in the flicker of an eyelid. The land beyond falls away to a sloping bank of vines and olive trees. A tall man in a straw hat is moving between the crops with a watering can, while his dog noses back and forth among the furrows.

Having stayed his hunger, Matt returns to his book, though from time to time he reaches for his glass of wine or a grape. Billy, feeling drowsy, begins to nod, though he continues to gaze at the crowded scene before him, restless with busy insect life, until his mind starts to teem like the swarming world around him. His attention is captured in particular by an exquisite blue butterfly in its unsteady progress from plant to flower; and he marvels at all that brief vibrancy, all that intensity of being. The thrilled creature, quite unaware of its short span, is in a quiver of ecstasy. This is how to live, it says; this is all we have; take it while you can.

In a trice it's gone; and Billy, his eyelids drooping, drifts into a present that looks neither to left or right; where the past is abandoned, the future disregarded. A present in which everything surrenders to the pleasure of now.

The part of the village that lies on the other side of the bay has a taverna and a *kafenio*, but no shops. It's the sleepiest of settlements. Indeed, the *kafenio* has only three or four tables and about a dozen rush-bottom chairs, most of them in dire need of repair. But this, together with the impressively large tamarisk tree that shades its terrace, is precisely its charm. Today a handful of customers are lounging here, talking and drinking through the deep quiet of the mid-afternoon. Billy, looking for somewhere to sit and sketch, surveys the scene as he passes and is tempted to stop. But after some consideration he decides to move on. The half-dozen fishing boats rocking gently by the sea wall are not sufficiently inspiring; nor is the shaggy dog, asleep in the dust beneath the tree. In any case the *kafenio* does not offer him the kind of privacy he needs. He likes to sketch in places where there is little chance that someone will peer over his shoulder and make faint murmurs of approval.

Beyond the *kafenio* the narrow road branches into a maze of twisting lanes as it snakes between the huddle of cottages. But soon it emerges into open countryside, where it winds on past the village cemetery to the end of the headland. The cemetery is enclosed by a low, dry-stone wall, and a sturdy, weather-beaten church stands beside the gate. To Billy, there is something romantic about its location here, high on the bare hillside overlooking the sea. He stands looking over the wall for a few minutes and then decides to explore further. Lifting the latch of the wooden gate, he lets himself in and wanders along the avenues. The rows are short; there are probably fewer than thirty graves here. But he finds them all intriguing, and from his scanty knowledge of Greek he can just make out some of the information. The headstones are mostly simple, though sometimes, in addition to name and dates, there's a photograph and a brief quotation. One in particular holds him transfixed. This is the grave of Alexis Ninou, who died at the age of twenty-seven. The handsome young man in the photograph, his dark eyes and olive skin thrown into perfect relief by the brilliant white of his open-necked shirt, has a sensitive face and a shy smile. But there are no words of farewell, and from the bare information on the headstone the onlooker can only guess at the history behind the portrait. To Billy, the reticence seems to speak of a grief that lies too deep for words.

Having inspected the graves, he decides to take a look at the church. It's a small building, with traditional blue dome and whitewashed walls, which unfortunately is locked. But this is not a great disappointment, since a peek through the window suggests that it's merely neat, well-kept and plain. No, the main problem now is the sun, which is still high and beating down on this hillside with ferocity. He removes his hat, fans himself and pulls an old rag from his pocket to mop his brow. Looking around for shade, he spots a bench in the corner of the yard beneath a leafy, wide-spreading eucalyptus. This turns out to be not just a welcome refuge, but also, he quickly realises, an ideal place to sit and draw. The drawing – he sees it in his mind's eye – will feature one or two headstones, and the church will form the background. Feeling faint stirrings of inspiration, he pulls his sketchbook and pencils from his bag, and after a tentative move or two marks out the boundaries of the scene with a few bold strokes.

Matt wakes, lifts his head from the pillow and looks around, coming slowly to consciousness. The shuttered room is pierced by chinks of dusty sunlight. He glances at his watch. Just after three. He's been sleeping for almost two hours. Not something he usually does at this time of day. But then, drinking wine at lunchtime is not a regular habit either. Still, he's not at all fuzzy-headed. On the contrary, he feels bright and refreshed. The climate and pace of life here is already beginning to change him. Much more of this and he'll be incapable of surviving the frantic jostle of London. Permanently alienated from the clock-bound tyranny of city life, he'll be unfit to return to work. He shakes his head. Oh no! Return to work! The very thought is hateful. Leaping from the bed, he yanks open the door and strolls out onto the terrace, where the blazing sun strikes his chest and dazzles him, forcing him to shut his eyes. He bathes his face in the warmth and stretches his arms wide.

But now, how to spend the next three hours? He and Billy have agreed to meet at Yannis's at six. He considers a number of options and decides to write. Yes, that's the thing; stretch the creative muscles. For the past week he's scarcely set pen to paper. The climate here is wonderful, but the mind is becoming flabby. Yes, write until five, when the sun will be lower, and then take a short stroll. But *where* to write? He looks around. Well, why not here? Wouldn't here be best? But no, he needs a change of scene. In which case, what about the quayside? No, not a good idea; he needs to be undisturbed. Eventually, after weighing up all the possibilities, he decides to take the footpath that winds up the steep hill behind the town. Good, he thinks: an end to dithering. And feeling pleased with his decision, he packs his bag and snaps on his sunhat. But just before setting out he tears a sprig of grapes from the fat bunch luxuriating on the table.

The path, which is well worn, begins with a short flight of steps built roughly out of loose stones and rocks. Matt strides out vigorously at first, exhilarated by a fine view of the bay that seems to expand with every step. But the steep climb and fierce heat quickly exhaust him, and soon he becomes anxious to find shelter. He casts an eye over the barren landscape. What are the chances of finding a shaded spot to sit and write up here? There's not a tree or bush in sight. What madness made him take this route? Perhaps he should turn back now, before falling victim to sunstroke.

But wait. What's that ahead, half-hidden by the bend in the path? He presses on a bit further. Yes, the very thing! Salvation! Standing just a few yards away, on the far side of a ditch, there's a ruined shed. He leaps the ditch and goes to explore. It's a mere heap of wood, stones and corrugated iron, parts of the structure having collapsed, but the missing front wall gives a view out to sea and inside there's a bench made from a flat slab of rock. It's a godsend. He sits down gladly and gazes at the scene before him, relieved to have found this kindly hovel, this haven of coolness. Below, the land slopes down to the ragged coastline. Ahead, the humps of islands stretch away over the expanse of wrinkled sea. The beauty here seems inseparable from the silence, the sense of eerie desolation. Apart from a few birds of prey, there's not much sign of life, although a few hundred yards to the right, a group of goats are huddled together under an overhanging rock. They make a dark smudge on the dry scrubby hillside.

After absorbing the view for a while, he unzips his bag and draws out a notebook. It's a collection of jottings: bits of prose, fragments of fiction, and a number of poems at various stages of composition. He flicks through it, stopping to reread a passage here and there; and although there are places where the writing makes him wince, from time to time his eye lights on a phrase that brings a tingle of pleasure to his scalp or a faint smile to his lips. But what to work on? It *all* needs working on. He hesitates between a poem that he started recently and a story that he's been tinkering with for years. Yet he knows already that the poem, despite the apparent remoteness of its content, has the more urgent claim. It's a dramatic monologue – a form he has never before attempted – and the speaker, a Hamlet-like figure who ruminates on experience with a sceptical turn of mind, seems, at first sight, quite unlike himself. Nevertheless, something in the poem is clamouring for expression. But will it ever achieve it? He's doubtful. This bundle of words has the shape-changing capacity of a cloud or bubble, a rolling plasticity that he finds frustratingly difficult to handle. The thing is unmanageable; it simply won't keep still. A squeeze in one place creates a bulge in another. It would help, he thinks, if he knew what the poem was about. Is it about too much, perhaps? About everything? Is it overloaded with life, love and loss?

He shrugs helplessly, picks up a pencil and bends to the task, deleting a phrase here, polishing a line there. Indeed, he becomes so completely absorbed in the work that after a while he ceases to ponder these questions; they slide to the edge and drop over the rim. He'll come back to them later, when the poem is written.

Billy holds his sketch at a distance and surveys the finished effect. He's pleased with it. He's used artistic licence to play with the elements of the scene, and the spareness, lack of clutter, makes for a nicely-balanced composition. The sketch is dominated by three centrally-placed headstones, grouped in a close formation, though the eye is guided by lines of perspective to the church standing high in the background. The headstone nearest the viewer, its inscription faithfully reproduced, is that of Alexis Ninou. Billy pencils in his signature, adds the date and blows on the page to remove any dust.

A glance at his watch shows that it's ten to six. Time to head back. Though still quite hot, the sun is lower now and the light is changing, its colour becoming earthier and warmer. Shadows are beginning to appear on the hills. Suddenly a tall-masted ship, its bright sails buckling like the wings of a great bird, rounds the headland and ploughs through the deep waters of the channel, making for the head of the bay. Billy pays his last respects to Alexis, and for a few final moments stands drinking in the scene. Then he swings his bag over his shoulder and moves off. But as he closes the gate behind him, his ears catch the sound of tinkling bells. He looks up. A long line of goats, scampering down a hillside path, are heading homeward for supper, looking, in their determined hurry and anxious jostling, like a column of refugees in flight from some disaster.

At Yannis's the custom is hotting up, as always at this hour. In the main the people who come here are locals who know each other well, but at most times of the year there's a scattering of tourists, for whom this is a regular haunt too. Towards sundown these visitors, representing an assortment of nationalities, drift in from all points of the island. They hale each other on arrival, and lounge around in pairs and small groups, exchanging news in whatever *lingua franca* comes to hand. It's this air of fleeting familiarity that gives the place its appeal. Matt, who arrived ten minutes ago, is sitting alone at a table, his notebook on his knee, making minor adjustments to the poem he's been working on for the past few hours. There's a small cup of black coffee in front of him and a glass of water, and from time to time he lifts a forkful of sticky cake to his lips. He keeps the notebook half-hidden, as if his writing is a secret vice that he lives in dread of being discovered, and when a Danish couple that he's met before enter and greet him he snaps the book closed and smiles shyly at them, like a schoolboy caught smoking behind the shed.

From this brief disruption his attention switches to a tall sailing ship lowering anchor out in the harbour: the same vessel that drew Billy's admiration some minutes ago. The crew on deck are busily furling the sails, and he watches for a while, shielding his eyes from the glare of the evening sun. Then, casting his eye over the wide sweep of the bay, he lights on a small figure strolling casually along the quay. A figure still some way off, still somewhat indistinct, yet instantly recognisable from his shambling gait, his air of rapt self-absorption. A figure so tiny, so perfect, so fragile, that Matt's heart flies out. These moments, he thinks, these killing moments, when the beauty of life seems unbearable – so tender, so bravely delicate, their impression no stronger than a flower. That first night, that meeting in St Pancras, that moment of reunion in Norfield – he recalls them all in a flash. They flare briefly, they fade like sparks. As Billy draws nearer, a sunburnt glow suffusing his freckled cheeks, his mouth breaking into a warm smile, Matt feels his heart swell fit to burst, and on sudden impulse he leaps up in greeting, knocking the table with his knee and almost spilling his coffee. He reaches out eagerly, blinded by sunlight, his eyes glinting; and his grip, when they embrace, is so strong that the intensity takes Billy by surprise.

Yiorgos turns up to take their order the moment Billy is settled. This is impressive, given the pressure he's under from the sudden influx of customers. Moreover, he seems bright and cheerful, quite different from the way he looked this morning. Matt, indicating the rear of the café with his thumb, raises an eyebrow discreetly, as if to say, how *are* things?

Yiorgos nods and smiles. 'Is better,' he says, speaking in a low voice. 'My mother and father, I talk with them.'

'And they see now?' says Billy. 'They understand?'

Yiorgos hesitates, looks thoughtful, nods. 'They try.'

'So you'll go to Athens?'

‘Yes.’ A cautious smile. ‘But not tomorrow. Next year, perhaps.’

‘That’s great,’ says Matt.

He and Billy beam and grasp his hand in quiet congratulation.

‘But Yiorgos,’ says Billy, turning serious, ‘you won’t stay for ever, will you? I mean, this is home, isn’t it? You *must* come back. Promise.’

Yiorgos laughs. ‘Yes, my friend, I promise.’ He bows deeply, then wags a finger. ‘But *you* – you must come back too. Promise.’ They all laugh. ‘And now, to please excuse me. We talk later, yes?’

‘Of course,’ says Matt, shooing him away. ‘Don’t let us hold you up.’

He and Billy settle back with a look of pleasure on their faces. Yiorgos’s news, his relief over the prospect of a satisfactory outcome to his problem, is already beginning to set its seal on the day. So now they turn inward, to each other, giving accounts of where they have been, what they have done. Matt begins, and after a while, with shy hesitation, reaches into his bag and pulls out his notebook. He shows Billy the poem he has been working on, modestly excusing it on the grounds that it’s not yet finished. Billy, who has only rarely seen any of Matt’s writing, reads the poem with slow care. He’s not a practised reader of poetry, and this poem, worlds away from the poetry he knows, makes him work hard. In fact, he’s not at all sure that he understands it. But although he’s unable to say anything meaningful about the poem, much less judge it, the words move him. He feels the power in them, the emotion, the struggle to say something, and a lump comes to his throat, silencing him completely. The best he can do is to turn to Matt with a quiet nod of approval. Matt, secretly pleased, nods in return, again insisting that it’s not yet finished. Billy looks away briefly, feeling on the brink of tears, and to cover his emotion, regain control, he pulls out his sketchbook. But this is an unwise move, for his drawing, which Matt views with a nod of admiration, brings him still closer to the edge. Matt studies the inscription on the grave of Alexis Ninou, then glances up. He spots something in the corner of Billy's eye and, leaning forward, brushes it away with the cushion of his thumb.

Billy turns and gazes out at the bay. The people on the tall ship are now scampering round the deck. They leap from the side with shouts of glee and flail about in the water. Closer to shore two small boys are messing about in a dinghy and an old man in a ragged panama is trying to fire his outboard motor. Billy regards the whole dazzling spectacle with a strange complexity of feelings, a kind of swimming wonder. If I die tomorrow, he thinks, I'll have known this love, this happiness.

They stay for the sunset, as always. It begins unpromisingly, behind some strips of cloud. But then, as the fiery disc slips lower, as sea and sky blush crimson and trails of cirro-stratus are set aflame, the scene burgeons into a lush spectacle of Claude-like splendour. In the dying moments, an eager young man, clutching a fancy camera, leaps to the front of the café. He crouches and experiments with different positions, making a showy display of his expertise. Seconds later the disc slips over the rim and a thin ripple of applause passes through the watching crowd. Matt leans back with a warm sigh, as if to acknowledge that the curtain has fallen, the day is done. He reaches for Billy's hand across the table and squeezes it. They glance briefly at each other with quiet smiles. Billy notes the stubble on Matt's chin. You need a shave, he thinks; and a haircut wouldn't go amiss. But immediately he changes his mind. Matt is surely looking better than ever – tanned, relaxed, splendidly straggly. The new unruly look can stay. Matt's thoughts, on the other hand, are unwavering. He notices again the finer points of Billy's face, the distinctive features that he loves so well. The small cleft in the chin, the sharply-etched mouth, the keen, appraising eyes. You're looking good, he thinks. In fact, better than ever. And the word *ever*, echoing in their heads, hangs in the air, a ripe fruit just out of reach. They say nothing to each other, though, and after a few reflective moments their eyes turn again to the horizon.

Off in the distance, beyond the headland, a large ferry, its lights ablaze, is trailing a plume of smoke as it speeds towards some unknown destination. The sky, though fading, is still pink, and the islands now appear as dark humps, thrown into relief by a vast afterglow. The twinkling lights of the houses round the bay gird the water's edge like a necklace; the same threadbare moon hangs above. They gaze in silence, listening intently to the restless sea. Its constant stirring is all around them: a low breathing – half-comforting, half-menacing – that's just perceptible beneath the quiet chatter of the café; a deep, undying murmur that stretches to the far edges, the last glimmers of land and sky.

Acknowledgements

I am grateful to Phil Bales, Max Fincher, Elizabeth McKellar and Rebecca Nesbit for reading drafts of this novel and offering their thoughts; to members of Cambridge Writers for perceptive and practical comments on parts of the script; to Thure Etzold, David Franks, Richard Gould and Hannah Hooton for help in preparing it for publication; and to friends at Four Guineas for words of encouragement.

Readers may pick up echoes of *La Traviata* in the novel, and indeed I did conceive it as a modern reworking of Verdi's opera, which is itself an adaptation of *La Dame aux Camélias*, the play by Alexandre Dumas, *fils*, based on his novel of the same name. The four parts of my novel correspond very loosely to the four scenes of the opera, but I have played freely with the elements of the story, following it only in broad outline and avoiding its tragic closure by leaving the end open.

Lightning Source UK Ltd.
Milton Keynes UK
UKOW03f0000110314

227894UK00001B/5/P

9 781784 073381